a second
chance

a second chance

ASHER FREND

a second chance

ISBN Paperback: 979-8-9942559-0-2
ISBN eBook: 979-8-9942559-1-9

Book Designed by Mark Karis
Developmental editing by Sally Apokedak
Developmental editing by Brittany Yost
Line editing by Savannah Breedlove
Manuscript evaluation, Editing & Proofreading by Olive Press Publishing, LLC

First printing edition 2026.

www.asherfrend.com

Dedicated to my guardian angel—L.Y.L.A.S. always

"If there is a prophet among you, I, the Lord, make Myself known to him in a vision, and I speak to him in a dream."

(NUM. 12:6).

1

mikaila

I sat on the cold leather seat of the school bus, shivering as freezing rain pounded against the windows. Chara, my best friend since I was five, climbed on a moment later and slid in beside me. My sister, Kaitlyn, breezed past us without a word, heading straight for the back to sit with Tara, like always.

Chara tore her toasted buttered bagel in half and handed me the warmer piece. Heat seeped into my numb fingers. "Thanks," I said. "I didn't have time to eat breakfast."

She smiled. "I figured. Nan said you overslept. Studying late?"

Chara met me at my house every morning, so she always knew exactly how chaotic my mornings were.

I groaned. "Not studying. Mom decided to pick a fight with Pop."

Chara paused mid-chew, lifting an eyebrow as the bus lurched to a stop for the next group of kids. She lowered her voice. "Started an argument about what?"

I rolled my eyes. "Apparently, she's not following the doctor's orders. That's how Nan put it, anyway."

Chara nodded like she'd been expecting that answer. "If you need to do homework at my house tonight, or need to sleep over Saturday night, just let me know."

I smiled, warmth creeping back in my chest. "Thanks. I might take you up on that. We've got track practice, and Elliott's coming over for dinner Saturday."

Elliott is my boyfriend. We'd met in English class freshman year, partnered together to enact *Romeo and Juliet*. Acting out a tragic love story with my crush in front of the entire class should've been mortifying, but Elliott refused to let it be anything but hilarious. He insisted on playing Juliet—pulled his older sister's skirt on over his jeans, pitched his voice high, and fluttered his eyelashes like he'd rehearsed. Then he drew a ridiculous mustache on *me* with a marker and loaned me his flannel so I could be the most unconvincing Romeo imaginable.

The class (and even the teacher) roared with laughter. We got an "A," though I'm still convinced it was mostly for entertainment value. Afterwards, Elliott took me out for chicken sandwiches and milkshakes to celebrate. That was our first official date. We've been together ever since.

Chara brushed the crumbs from her hands. "I'll be at my dad's until after dinner. So, if things get out of control after Elliott leaves, just call me at my dad's house."

I nodded, finishing the last bite of my bagel. "I will."

The bus groaned to a stop in front of the Oak Haven High School, brakes hissing as the doors folded open. Kids shuffled into the aisle. As the guy who lived four houses down slid past our seat, he glanced over his shoulder at me. "Mikaila," he said, smirking, "I saw your mom talking to herself again last night as she walked home from Food Tide. You gonna lose your mind like her?"

My eyes narrowed, but before I could get a word out, Chara shot to her feet and smacked him across the side of the head with her bookbag. "She hasn't," she snapped, "but I might. Keep talking and find out."

He was nearly six feet tall—lanky, all elbows and attitude. Chara barely hit five-three on a good day, but she dipped into a low, ready stance like she was trained for this. What she lacked in height, she more than made up for in fire.

I reached out and rested my hand on her arm. Before anything else could escalate, the bus driver stood up with a sigh. "Chara, you alright?"

She turned to him with the sweetest smile imaginable. "Just fine, thank you."

The driver shot a hard look at the boy, who was still holding the side of his head, jaw hanging open. "If he's starting trouble this early, you let me know. I'll send him straight to the principal's office for another suspension."

Chara gave the guy a slow, satisfied smirk. "I think he just needed a little sense knocked into him," she said. "He should be good now."

He grumbled under his breath as he shuffled off the bus. The driver eased back into his seat and shook his head. "Alright. Have a great day, girls."

I gave him a small smile and a quick wave. Something about the way he handled things reminded me of Pop. I jogged to catch up with Chara as we headed into the building. Her light pink bookbag stood out in a hallway full of black messenger bags and dark hoodies.

"You didn't have to do that," I said.

Her eyebrows drew together. "Yes, I did. He shouldn't have said any of that, and you don't need the whole bus running their mouths about your mom. And I'm sure you'd do the same for me."

I planted a hand on my hip. "Guess it's lucky for both of us we don't have to find out what I'd do. But I *will* pray for him at Bible Club."

Chara snorted, smirking. "Yeah, let me know when you pray his asshole-ness away."

The bell shrieked overhead, and I said, "See you in gym class!"

Elliott jogged up beside me, reaching for my hand. He laced his fingers with mine, and we walked together until the hallway split, and we had to peel off for homeroom.

I bent down to touch my toes as our gym teacher barked orders for us to stretch. We stood in our assigned spots on the basketball court, the glossy floor echoing with squeaks from shifting sneakers. Above the bleachers, Oak Haven's championship banners hung like reminders that *some* people enjoyed physical activity.

The teacher blew her whistle and started dividing us into

teams for handball. Beside me, Chara let out a long, dramatic sigh.

"Why are they torturing us?" She muttered.

The teacher pointed directly at her. "Chara, you're defending the goal for red." She tossed her a red mesh pinnie. Chara glared at it as if it had personally offended her.

The teacher handed me one. "Mikaila, midfielder for red."

I smiled at Chara as she begrudgingly made her way to the goal. "You've got this!" I called.

She rolled her eyes but cracked a tiny smile.

The whistle shrieked, and the game exploded into motion. A girl from the basketball team snagged the ball and fired it to her teammate, but I sprinted forward and intercepted mid-stride. I took my three steps and snapped a pass to one of our midfielders. She caught it cleanly and fed it to our shooter, who launched a perfect attempt...only for their goalie to block it with a loud smack.

Possession swung back to the opposing team. Their goalie scanned the court and tossed the ball out, but I cut across the lane and intercepted again. Three steps—one, two, three—and I sent it to another red-shirted teammate. She pivoted, took her two steps, and hurled it to our forward, who whipped the ball past their keeper and straight into the net.

Score.

Their goalie wasted no time. She threw to their midfielder, who barreled down the court toward our side. Our defenders boxed her in, but she managed two steps, a quick dribble, and a sharp pass to their forward. The girl blew through our last defender and launched the ball toward the net.

Chara jumped, fingers stretching as far as they could reach, but the shot sailed past her hand and smacked into the goal.

I jogged back toward our side of the court, breath steadying, already positioning myself to intercept the next play. "You've got this, Chara," I called.

She curled her lip, grimacing as she scooped up the ball. With a sharp exhale, she hurled it to our forward, but the opposing defender darted in and stole it clean. Within seconds, the ball was back near the red team's goal. Their forward whipped it toward the right side of the net.

Chara leapt, arms stretched wide, and this time she caught it. She landed with a grunt and fired the ball back to our defense as the teacher blew her whistle.

"Bring it in!"

I peeled off my red mesh pinnie and tossed it into the basket she held, then followed Chara into the locker room. "See? That wasn't so bad."

She shook her head. "You're one of those people who could get tortured and still have good things to say about the person torturing them."

I burst out laughing as we grabbed our clothes. We changed quickly, metal locker doors clanging around us. I pulled my long khaki cargo skirt on over my gym shorts.

"That isn't true," I said, smoothing the skirt. "But the Bible *does* say a cheerful heart is good medicine."

I slung my bookbag over my shoulder and waved as Chara headed one way, and I headed the other. She, Elliott, and Kait were all juniors; I was the lone sophomore orbiting their schedules. Chara and I shared lunch, gym, and geometry, but the rest of my day was spent with the other tenth-graders.

I felt a tap on my shoulder blades. Elliott had caught up to me and slipped his hand into mine.

"Hey," he said, a little breathless from weaving through the crowd.

I smiled and squeezed his fingers. "Hey."

He was about five-nine, with wavy brown hair that always fell into his eyes and a smile that made my stomach flip every single time. He practically lived in blue-and-black plaid shirts, and today was no exception.

He wiggled his eyebrows. "Knock, knock."

"Who's there?"

"Lettuce."

"Lettuce who?"

He smirked. "Lettuce thank God it's almost lunchtime."

I laughed. "That's terrible."

He smiled, squeezing my hand. "But so true. I'll see you soon."

Kait glanced at me as she walked past in the hall but didn't say a word—didn't even acknowledge I existed. Typical.

I slipped into history class as the bell rang and sank into my seat, but I couldn't focus on the lecture. My mind kept circling back to Nan's warning about Mom not following her doctor's orders, and the neighbor's comment about seeing her talking to herself on the walk home from the store last night. Maybe he made it up, but…maybe he hadn't.

2

mikaila

APRIL 12, 2003

My heart hammered as I crouched at the starting line, silently praying for my team and for myself. I drew in the crisp spring air, and then the starter's gun cracked through the morning calm.

I exploded forward, legs pumping in perfect rhythm, body weightless, eyes locked on the track ahead. *It's only practice*, I told myself.

Kaitlyn's blonde ponytail bounced ahead, just within reach. Our team captain was a few strides in front, and I gritted my teeth, inching closer with every step.

Pushing harder, I felt determination surge through my limbs. The final stretch loomed, and a grin split across my face. With one last burst, I overtook Kaitlyn and drew level with the captain. Heart in my throat, I edged past her.

Victory.

My legs burned, heavy as though weights were tied to my ankles, but I managed a quick celebratory jump before bending over to gulp in air. I had outrun Kaitlyn—*me*, the little sister—something I'd never done before.

Incredible.

We made our way over to the bleachers to rest until the next practice relay race.

"Good hustle today, taking on your sister *and* the captain. How you feeling, champ?" One of my teammates asked from the row behind.

I smiled over my shoulder, "Great, but tired. Keeping up with Kait is hard work." *And I can't wait to do it again.*

"Get some rest tonight. You earned it. You'll need your strength to help us defeat the next team," The teammate said, tapping my shoulder with a grin before walking off.

"You're gonna need your strength to defeat me next time, too," Kaitlyn teased with a smirk.

I had grown used to watching Kaitlyn excel at everything. Ever since Kaitlyn entered high school, it was as if I had become invisible to her. I seemed to live in her shadows, but today was different. Today, I gained Kaitlyn's respect by proving I was on the track team to win, not to follow my big sister around.

Soon, Kait and I were called to the track to practice a relay. As we got into position, the baton was in my hand in a matter of seconds. My sneakers slammed the gravel track with as much force as I could muster. *I can do all things through Christ who gives me strength.* I thrust the baton into the next runner's hand as she took off, while the coach waved for me to take a seat.

"Good hustle today, Miki," Coach said.

I smiled as I made my way over to the bleachers. Kait followed behind.

Cameron, the hurdler, called out, "You did really well out there today, Kait!" Kait looked like she could melt. Her doe blue eyes lit up as she smiled widely.

"Thanks," she said softly.

After the hurdlers finished, practice was over, and we made our way to the school parking lot, where Aunt Lana was waiting to drive us home. "I beat Kait and the team captain during the 800m!" I said, sliding into the back seat, while my lips spread into a mischievous grin. I watched Kait's expression change from indifference to amusement as she took her place in the passenger seat.

"Really?" Aunt Lana glanced over her shoulder with her eyebrow arched in disbelief. Her brown hair was pulled back into a low ponytail, which made her look younger.

"Really?" Aunt Lana glanced over her shoulder with her eyebrow arched in disbelief. Her brown hair was pulled back into a low ponytail, which made her look younger.

"She did. But it's the last time she'll beat me," Kait smirked as she clipped her seat belt.

"We'll see about that," I said.

The drive home took longer than normal. The salt grass swayed against the backdrop of the clear blue sky, but dark clouds loomed in the distance, over the marshes. *It looks like a storm is coming.* The vehicle slowly decreased in speed; other sedans and vehicles surrounded them, crawling at a snail's pace.

"Oh, no," Aunt Lana said, leaning forward. "It looks like there's a fender bender up ahead. Oh well. You know, I've been meaning to tell you two...your dad's been wanting to talk with you. And Pop told your mom not to interfere with his calls."

My heart skipped a beat. I hadn't spoken to my dad since he had custody of me two years ago and dropped me off at his mother's house in Virginia.

"We don't want to talk to him," Kait said with an edge to her voice.

Aunt Lana turned the radio down. "Girls, he's still your father, and he probably feels bad for how things ended. You know we need to forgive others, as Jesus forgave us."

"He didn't leave Jesus in Virginia with his mother after fighting for custody and pissing off Mom," Kait replied with her jaw clenched.

"Kait!" Aunt Lana exclaimed, shaking her head in disappointment. I twirled strands of my auburn hair and tried to focus on the oldies softly playing on the radio while we crept through orange cones that lined the road. Police officers waved us through as we passed by an ambulance being loaded.

"Miki, why don't you give him a few minutes and see if he apologizes? You're not the same person you were when you were thirteen. I'm sure he's changed in the past three years." Aunt Lana insisted, glancing at me from the rearview mirror.

"Won't that upset mom?" I asked. Mom's mood fluctuated rapidly within the day, and without notice or warning. Last week, she threw the trash can out the bathroom window because Kait forgot to empty it. We avoid setting her off, but Dad's calls would be an immediate trigger for her mood swings.

Aunt Lana drummed the steering wheel and craned her neck to see me in the rearview mirror. "Nan said that while you all live in her house, you need to respect their rules, which is family first. *All* family, not just the ones you choose."

"I bet she took that well," Kait remarked sarcastically.

The car slowly accelerated to normal speed, and traffic began to thin out. Shortly, we arrived back at our 1960s colonial house with a white clapboard exterior, black shutters lining its tall windows, and a simple portico above the centered front door. The Oak trees that lined the sidewalks had started to bloom, leaving strands of yellow and green flowers on the ground.

Aunt Lana pulled up to the curb, and Kait and I got out, waving goodbye as we walked toward the house. We opened the front door, which led to our living room. The smell of Nan's hot chamomile tea and secret snickerdoodle recipe awaited us from the adjacent kitchen. Kait grabbed a cookie from the serving plate on our wooden, weathered kitchen table.

Nan, wearing her grey and white striped housecoat over her long pink dress, was finishing up washing the dishes. "How was your day, girls?" She asked.

Kait, answering with a mouth full of cookies. "Good." And then she dashed up the stairs to her bedroom.

"How was practice, Miki?" Nan asked as she moved from the sink to the kitchen table, where her knitting supplies were.

"Great! I beat Kait and the team captain during the 800m!"

"Great job, sweetie. You're getting faster every day. You know, it must be the cookies," Nan winked.

"Of course, which means I should take an extra so that I can beat Kait again."

Nan chuckled, sweeping her shoulder-length gray hair out of her eyes before returning to her knitting supplies sprawled out on the table.

I grabbed the second cookie off the countertop. "Don't forget that Elliott will be here for dinner. I'll come down to help you prep."

"About time you helped out," Mom said, stepping into the kitchen. At five-eleven, she was impossible to miss, her frizzy auburn hair loosely pulled into a messy ponytail, strands escaping around her face. She carried an air of quiet authority that made the kitchen feel smaller the moment she entered.

Nan sighed. "Sandra, Miki is my daily helper."

"It's okay, Nan." *I'm not gonna let her mood dampen my win.*

I trudged up the stairs and knocked on Kait's door.

"What?" Kait called out.

I cautiously opened it. "You know, James, who lives four houses away, said that Mom was talking to herself last night when she walked home from the store?"

Kait sighed and played with her wristwatch. "Nan said she wasn't doing what she was supposed to do. She probably was talking to herself."

My chest hurt thinking Mom wasn't doing well. "You don't have to worry about James talking about her anymore. Chara hit him with her bookbag, and the bus driver almost sent him to the office this morning because he thought he was causing us trouble."

Kait chuckled. "Chara didn't have to do that."

I fiddled with the ring Nan had given me, worn on my right ring finger—a simple silver band with a small black oval agate set in the center.

"I told her that," I said, "but she didn't want him spreading it to the whole bus."

"Or the whole neighborhood."

I sighed. "Hopefully, Mom listens to her doctors, and we don't have to worry about it."

"Maybe she will. Either way, you can shower first tonight."

I smiled, nodding. "Okay. Thanks."

I trudged down the hall to my room, diagonally across from Kait's. Every inch of wall was plastered with posters—a timeline of my interests: dragons with iridescent scales, fairies that seemed to dance in the sunlight, and a few reminders of my musical obsessions, from the Backstreet Boys to MercyMe.

I grabbed my shower gear and headed to the shared bathroom. The warm water soothed my aching muscles, but my mind refused to follow. One parent had abandoned me, the other couldn't stand me. *Who even needed parents, anyway?*

Afterwards, I dressed and collapsed onto my bed, eyes fixed on the glow-in-the-dark stars scattered across the ceiling. Slowly, the tension in my body ebbed, my thoughts growing hazy. My eyelids drooped, and I finally let myself drift into sleep.

* * *

I opened my eyes to find myself standing in a massive white room surrounded by walls so high the ceiling couldn't be seen. Under my feet was white, misty air which felt a tad bouncy as if I were walking on clouds. It was silent, except for a conversation I could hear in the distance.

To my left was a long hallway with picture frames lining the wall, as if I were in someone's home. The frames weren't empty. Instead, they held what looked like computer screens.

One frame held what looked like a mirror, so I approached it. I realized this was the source of the sound. The mirror disappeared, and I watched Chara slip into the passenger seat of her father's Mitsubishi Montero. He didn't put his seat belt on, and as always, neither did Chara. I couldn't recall how many times I yelled at her for this.

"Put your seatbelt on!" I screamed, as if she could hear me.

I could somehow hear Chara's thought, and her usual response, "I could put my seatbelt on, but we'll be back soon, and God won't let anything happen to us."

I shook my head in rapid succession as I watched Chara's father lose control of the SUV, spinning out on the road. His vehicle jumped over the guardrail and skidded down the embankment, hurtling toward the tree line.

My heart raced as I clutched my temples and shouted, "NO!"

Their SUV flipped over multiple times, and their bodies were expelled as if they were made of plastic and not human flesh. Chara was lying on the ground, not moving. A world without Chara in it was unfathomable. *This can't be happening.* I grasped the frame hard on both sides, inches away from the screen, and in less than a second, I was standing over her, looking down. Chara's eyes flickered open. "I don't know what's happening, but you need to get up!" I screamed helplessly.

In an instant, I was back in the great white room. The screen before me shimmered, its image rippling until it returned to that mirror-like surface.

I turned, and there he was. My Maker.

The breath left my lungs. I dropped to my knees in reverence, head bowed. The light surrounding him was so brilliant that it blurred everything else. I couldn't tell where his robe ended, and the glowing air began; it all blended into one radiant, fog-white halo that seemed to pulse with life itself.

His voice sounded like a cannon launching, startling me. "That's the frame of the present. When you touch the frame of the present or the frame of the dreams, it allows you to interact with the individuals. The other frames are memories. They can't be altered by anyone but Me. I'll change her memories so that you're removed from them."

I don't understand.

"When it's time, you'll understand all."

The foggy white air surrounded me, and I pleaded, "Let her be alright. Save my best friend. Please."

Hearing the anguish in my heart, He spoke, His voice both gentle and powerful. "I have already prepared a place for you in My Kingdom."

Slowly, He extended His arms and lifted me to my feet, the warmth of His presence filling me with a peace I hadn't known I could feel.

"I'll trade places, then." *I'll do whatever I need to do, just save her.*

His voice boomed like a megaphone, but the kindness in it calmed me. His touch on my forearm was firm yet comforting. "You know your days are determined."

I stole a glance, but his face glowed too brightly for me to attempt eye contact.

I focused on the swirly white air as I said, "I do know, and only you know the plans you have made for us. But I am willing to do whatever it takes to save Chara." *Even switching places.*

"You saw for yourself. She tested me."

"Yes, I know your Word says we shouldn't, but I can help

change her heart. I can get her to see You are the truth and the light. Just give us more time!" I begged.

There was a short pause before He spoke. "You have been a faithful servant. I will grant your heart's desire if you get her to believe in Me, without mockery. She must confess her sins and repent."

I nodded eagerly, "I can do that."

"The task set for you won't be easy. You're both young and impetuous. Continue to study the Bible. Keep Chara close to you and demonstrate my love throughout your life. You have twenty-two months. We will reconvene then."

I trembled with relief. "Thank you," I said quietly, almost inaudible.

Before I could say more, consciousness pulled at me, and I found myself awake, lying back in my bed, staring up at the ceiling. I blinked away the grogginess. *What kind of dream was that?* I tried to remember all the details, but I could only recall my conversation with Him. I had two years to save Chara, or else I'd lose her forever.

Did I just give up my life?

I brushed the thought aside.

Two years. Can I do this? God, if that dream was real, please send me a sign.

Pop knocks on my door before he enters. He's only an inch taller than Nan, and he has a ruddy complexion, with tattoos on his right arm, a reminder of his time in the Navy during the Second World War. "Your dad's on the phone downstairs, and Nan wants to remind you Elliott's coming over for dinner, so please set his silverware at the table."

I nodded. Pop smiled and closed the bedroom door behind

him, leaving me alone with my racing thoughts. My stomach twisted in knots, and a cold unease settled over me. I couldn't shake the feeling that something bad was coming.

3

chara

Chara blinked her eyes open. Soft, billowy clouds scattered across the sky. The sun peeked through the clouds; a faint rainbow shimmered in the distance, and the ground beneath her was still damp from the rain. For a moment, she thought she might be sunbathing in her backyard, but she hated bugs and nature. She would never choose to lie on the ground, especially with the scent of wet grass. Her long-sleeved shirt had ridden up, exposing her stomach, something else she always avoided.

Tugging at her shirt with her left arm, she tried to make sense of where she was.

When she attempted to roll over, she couldn't move. Panic rose in her chest as she lay there, seemingly glued to the earth. She mentally scanned her body: right arm immobile, legs heavy but with feeling, fingers and toes still wiggling. The side of her face felt strange; her vision was partially blocked on the right side. She picked caked dirt from her face with her left hand, then froze. Beneath it, a patch of skin was missing. Her head began to pound.

A hazy image of being in a vehicle brushed the edge of her memory. *I had school yesterday, so today must be Saturday, but what am I doing? And why am I doing it here?* She thought. Hoping it was all a dream, she closed her eyes, only to be awakened by a woman in plain clothes peering over her. The woman's lips moved, but she couldn't hear any sounds. *Why can't I hear you? She thought.* Her jaw hurt from clenching it. The woman walked away, and again she was alone. *If today is Saturday, I should be with my dad. Where is my dad?* Chara attempted to sit up, but the effort proved too much; the dizziness set in, and darkness claimed her again.

When she awoke, she was in a hospital room: white walls bordered with a teal stripe and circus animals above it and a smell of bleach. Her right arm still ached and was now in a cast. With her left arm, she felt the bandage on her face where the piece of skin was missing.

The steady beeping of the monitors filled the room. A nurse smiled as she realized Chara was awake and brought her a cup of ice water. A choked, grateful murmur of "Thanks" barely escaped her ravaged throat. The bright fluorescent lights burned against her aching eyes until she looked away. It was bone-chilling cold, the thin sheet offering no refuge against the creeping numbness that threatened to consume her.

Chara sipped the cold water as the hospital door opened. She was relieved to see her mom slip in. The nurse scrambled after her with a frown on her face. She asked Chara, "Do you know this woman?

When she was three, a receptionist at a doctor's office asked Astrid if she had adopted. Chara routinely replies to the stares now with "Yes, she is my mother, and no, I'm not adopted!"

She sighed, rolling her eyes, and said, "This is my mom."

The nurse nodded as she checked the monitor and slipped out of the room. Astrid was tall—about five feet eleven—with thin features, blonde hair, and fair skin. Chara resembled her dad's physical stature: short and round. Her skin complexion was a mix of the two, a light caramel complexion with thick, curly black hair.

Astrid gave Chara a light hug and settled into the chair beside Chara's bed. "How are you feeling?"

"Like I've been hit by a truck."

Astrid pulled her cross-stitch out of the purse and began to thread the needle through the canvas. "Can't imagine why," attempting to make a joke.

Chara took a few more sips of water before the nurse came back in to adjust the IV and told them that the doctors would be in the next day to run tests.

Astrid looked up from her canvas. "If you can remember, can you tell me what happened?"

Chara gazed at the ceiling. *I wish I had all the pieces, she thought.* "I remembered a voice in my head telling me to put on my seatbelt, but I didn't. So, we didn't have them on." She turned toward her mother.

"Ty didn't make you wear a seatbelt?"

"He doesn't ever wear his, and he didn't make me wear mine."

"Is that so?"

Chara's stomach churned with guilt as she remembered daring God to keep them safe, so she didn't have to put on her seatbelt. *What if the accident was my fault? She thought.*

"I woke up, and the guardrail was right there, and I remember screaming, 'Daddy!' but he didn't answer. His eyes were wide and glassy. Then we hit, and his chest slammed into the steering wheel." Chara recalled, swallowing hard. "I'll never forget the look in his eyes, Mom."

Astrid scooted closer. "That's a horrific accident to remember, Chara."

Chara blinked and touched her face with her good arm. "I must have gotten scratched up when we were thrown from the SUV, but I don't know how we ended up outside the vehicle or how it happened or what even caused it. It was such a beautiful day."

"The weather report said we'd get a brief torrential downpour. Looks like it hit while you were asleep, and you woke up right in the middle of it."

"Maybe."

Her mom smoothed Chara's dark curls from her face. "You may feel scared for a while the next time you're in a vehicle. It happens after events like this."

"Yeah, I don't know if I want to be in an SUV anytime soon. Have you checked on Dad? How is he doing?"

Astrid nodded. "He's still in surgery with a brain injury in the adult wing. They'll call me with updates." Astrid and Ty had been divorced for ten years, yet Ty still listed Astrid as his emergency contact. After the divorce, Chara and Astrid moved into a rented house in Astrid's childhood neighborhood—just down the street from Mikaila and Kaitlyn.

Chara grabbed the remote and flipped through the channels. "Looks like *Golden Girls* reruns it is."

Astrid continued to work on her needlepoint project. "Do you need me to call Mikaila and Kait for you? And let them know you're here?"

Chara tore her eyes from the TV and shot her a look. "Yeah, right, because I'm *sure* I won't be going to school on Monday."

"I'll do it first thing in the morning before church. I don't want to interrupt them this evening."

The nurse came in and sighed. "Visiting hours are over, but you can come back first thing in the morning."

Chara rubbed her head. "My head hurts. Can't she stay a few minutes longer?"

The nurse tilted her head. "You have a concussion, so yeah, it's gonna hurt even though you have some Tylenol in your system. And unfortunately, she can't stay longer. You need your rest."

Astrid nodded and gathered her things before giving Chara a side hug. "I'll see you in the morning."

"Great. Just me and the *Golden Girls*."

★ ★ ★

The next morning, Astrid came back. "Good morning. How'd you sleep?"

Chara sat up and winced. "My head hurts a little, and my arm still aches."

"Have the doctors been in?"

"Not yet."

Astrid sat down in the chair and whipped out her needle-point. "Your dad is out of surgery and is stable."

Chara's eyebrows went up. "When can we go see him?"

Astrid shook her head. "They won't let you onto another floor until they discharge you. And we need to see how he does. It was a major surgery."

Chara wiped a tear away. "Fine."

After lunch, they heard a sound down the hallway. "Knock, knock!"

Chara smiled as Mikaila, Kait, and their mutual friend, Kristin, walked in. Kristin was in four of Mikaila's classes but also had a Spanish class with Chara. *La Tortura* is how Chara described it.

Mikaila, wearing her Adidas sneakers with her floor-length khaki cargo skirt, froze at the sight of the bandages and cast, taking a cautious step back. Kait, however, sauntered in without a second thought. She wore her Abercrombie jeans and Tommy Hilfiger running sweater, her usual attire. Kristin, in her favorite "I don't do mornings people" sweatshirt, noticed Mikaila's hesitation and guided her closer.

Astrid set her needlework aside and pulled each girl into a hug. "She's doing alright, girls."

The three of them settled into chairs stolen from the empty side of the room, forming a small circle at the end of the bed.

Kait fiddled with her Casio G-Shock, tapping buttons to set a timer. "Aunt Lana dropped us off, and she'll be back in an hour. Timer's set. So…is this your elaborate plan to meet the Backstreet Boys?"

Chara pointed dramatically at her mom. "I think almost dying qualifies me for backstage passes with my best friends. Mom, notify their tour manager."

Astrid chuckled without missing a stitch. "I'll get right on that."

The room filled with laughter, warm and unrestrained, echoed off the walls and lingered in the space.

What happened?" Mikaila asked, still slightly stiff.

Chara gave her the quick version. "I fell asleep after visiting my aunt and woke up on the ground. Concussion, wrecked arm, missing skin on my face…you know. Dad's worse, though…he's recovering from major surgery."

Mikaila wiped her eyes with the back of her arm. "Sounds like you were both given a second chance."

Kait shivered at the memory. "Yeah…that sounds about right. We drove past the scene yesterday on our way home from practice. I saw an SUV mangled in the trees, but I didn't realize it was yours."

Chara jabbed a finger at her mom. "Use that when you try to get my concert tickets."

Mikaila rolled her eyes, smirking. "Real funny. Seriously, though, I'll put him on the prayer list at church."

Kristin leaned forward. "Is there anything you need us to bring you, Chara?"

She pinched the fabric of her gown. "Can you bring me a new outfit? These hospital gowns are not fashionable."

"I'll bring some clothes with me tomorrow," Astrid chimed in.

"Oh, and I need my CD Walkman and some batteries. There's only so many reruns of the *Golden Girls* I can watch in a week," Chara declared.

Astrid laughed.

"We can bring your homework," Mikaila offered.

Kait crossed her arms and frowned. "Speaking of dads, ours wants us to visit this summer."

"Are you going too?" Chara asked.

Mikaila shook her head and pressed her fingers to her brow, trying to ease the tension. "Not if we can help it."

"Good, because we have plans for people watching on the boardwalk and lying on the beach when I'm out of here, which are the activities I can do with one arm." Chara smiled, lifting her cast.

Kristin grinned, wagging her finger, "No beach volleyball for you." She was referring to last summer when a random group of boys visited Ocean City, Maryland, and invited them to a game. They were all smitten with Kait, but she tried to pass them off to the others.

"Maybe it will be healed by then," Chara said, a note of excitement in her voice.

Astrid tilted her head towards Chara, "Or maybe you'll be the score keeper while you recover."

Chara rolled her eyes and turned her head towards Mikaila and Kait. "Seriously. Did your dad forget that he abandoned you?"

"He apologized to both of us on the phone last night." Kait crossed her arms, twisting her hair tight around her finger. Her jaw tightened, and her gaze stayed fixed downward. Chara could tell she was holding everything in but chose not to push.

"I can forgive him for leaving me, but I can't forget it," Mikaila played with the ring on her right hand as she looked lost in her thoughts. Chara assumed there was more Mikaila wasn't saying.

Kristin tucked her brown hair behind her ear. "Forgiveness is a good start."

Kait's lips tightened. "Pop did always remind us that there was more to the story than we knew, but knowing the whole story would certainly help me forgive him."

Kristin sat up taller. "I'm sure Pop has his reasons for keeping it to himself."

Looking up again from her canvas, Astrid asked, "How's Sandra doing?"

"You know, one minute she's good, and the next everything is a catastrophe," Mikaila waved her arms around to emphasize her point.

Chara played with the blankets on her bed and then turned to Kait. "Have you set the kitchen on fire again?" She was referring to the time Kait had set a paper towel on fire while trying to make macaroni and cheese.

Kait groaned. "That happened once."

Chara turned to Mikaila, "Have you flushed any live animals down the toilet lately?"

Kristin giggled, and Kait looked at her, eyebrows glued together, "What? Is that why we had to call the plumber last month?"

Chara and Mikaila laughed, remembering how she had tried to flush a live frog down the toilet, though Mikaila admitted she had really thought it was dead.

"Uh, no."

Chara smiled, "Then not everything has been a catastrophe."

"When the plumbers pulled the frog out, was he still alive?" Kristin asked, which sent Mikaila, Kristin, and Chara into a fit of laughter.

Astrid smiled. "Enough about flushing innocent frogs. How's Nan and Pop?"

"Nan's good. Napping when we left and Pop's playing chess with the neighbor," Kait said.

The timer on Kristin's watch rang. "Looks like our hour's up," Kristin frowned, looking up from her watch. After each girl hugged Astrid, they gave Chara a light, careful hug to avoid causing her any pain.

Astrid stayed with Chara until after the tests were done. When the doctors mentioned the results wouldn't be available until tomorrow, she lingered a moment longer before saying, "I'll see you tomorrow. I'm off to dinner with Howard."

"Of course," Chara muttered under her breath as she turned on the TV. "Your only child is in the hospital. Why wouldn't you have a date?"

Astrid snapped her needlework into her bag. "You're sixteen now, Chara. I get to have a life too. It's not my fault you're here. Maybe talk to Ty about that when he wakes up. *If* he wakes up...I'm sorry. Of course, he'll wake up."

"Enjoy your date," Chara said with a clenched jaw, her eyes glued to the TV.

Astrid put on her coat and then threw her purse on her shoulder. "You know I love you. You should get your rest."

"Love you too," Chara said in a monotone voice. Once Astrid closed the door and could no longer be seen, she raised her middle finger in silent frustration. Then Chara grabbed the remote and flipped the channel to MTV. *Hope the nurses like my rendition of the Backstreet Boys, "Larger than Life," She thought.*

4

a s a

Asa pushed the lawn mower through the thick, green grass, Blink-182 blasting through his headphones. *Online Songs*—his favorite—was playing.

Rounding the corner of the front yard, he spotted Mark Emery pulling up in his minivan. Lacy and Lexy clambered out and. Lacy waved; Lexy raced toward the door.

Mark walked over with a smile. Asa paused the music, pulled off his headphones, and shut off the mower.

He rested a hand on Asa's shoulder. "Thanks for helping me out, son. Lacy's got a full weekend of cheer competitions, and we've got company coming tonight."

Asa grinned. "No problem. Happy to help."

"I talked with my other girls this week," Mark added. "Mikaila might even visit this summer."

Asa's heart skipped a beat. He raised an eyebrow. "Really? That'd be cool."

"Would be great to have all my girls here. Not sure Kait can make it. Anyway, I'll let you get back to it. Here's your payment," Mark said, slipping Asa a fifty-dollar bill.

"That's too much. I couldn't possibly," Asa said with a smile.

"Nonsense. I'd pay double if it meant avoiding a lecture from the wife." Mark patted Asa on the shoulder and walked inside.

Asa hit play, revved the mower back to life, and hummed along as blades of grass whipped behind him.

He first met Mikaila through Lacy, who was also a senior at Chestnut Hill High School in Chestnut Hill, Connecticut. Back in middle school, he'd had a hardcore crush on Lexy, who was a year older. He'd known he never stood a chance—too nerdy, too scrawny—but instead he'd befriended Lacy in algebra class and helped her study for finals.

A few weeks later, she'd invited him to mini golf and dinner with her family. That's when he met Mikaila, and his crush on Lexy vanished instantly. He couldn't believe Mikaila wanted to stay in touch. Those marathon phone calls felt like minutes, and her laugh always made his stomach flip in that familiar, impossible way.

So much so that he could barely form words when he saw her last summer during that brief weekend, he and his brother had driven down to Ocean City, Maryland. She was two years younger than him, but still hotter than any girl in his grade.

The thought of Mikaila in a bathing suit made heat crawl across his body. He pushed open the backyard gate and continued mowing, trying to shake the feeling. Then he remembered her boyfriend, and the warmth in his stomach twisted into something tighter.

His thoughts were interrupted by Lorainne waving from the deck. He caught her lips moving, but couldn't hear a word until he dropped his headphones around his neck and shut off the mower. He unclenched his teeth, a jolt of pain radiating across his jaw.

"Couldn't hear you, Mrs. E. Is that a new haircut? Makes you look like Lexy's sister instead of her mother," Asa called out. *Her older, greyer sister.*

She smiled and wiped a strand of hair out of her face. "Oh, I was just saying thank you. Aren't you the sweetest? I put some sodas out here on the table for you."

"Sounds good. I'll come back tomorrow and do the edging."

"You'll have to come for dinner this week," Lorainne said.

"Oh, I couldn't possibly…" he said, waving his hands and shaking his head.

"I insist, and you'll hurt my feelings if you say no. How's Wednesday night? We're having prime beef."

Asa walked over to the metal table and grabbed a cold Diet Pepsi. "How could I turn that down? I'll even bring the sparkling cider."

She waved her hand and chuckled. "We'll see you at 6 then," before closing the sliding door.

He sipped his Diet Pepsi, the fizziness slid down his throat, and the caffeine warmed him from the inside out. He finished the rest of the yard within an hour, then rode his bike the two blocks back home. The wind whipped through the blooming chestnut trees as he pedaled. Bursting through the front door, he headed straight for the phone and called Mikaila—no answer. He checked instant messenger; she wasn't online.

With a sigh, he pushed back from his computer desk, spinning once in his chair before running his hands through his long, thin, messy brown hair. He licked his lips as he gazed over the photo he had from last summer on his desk: him and Mikaila in the photo booth on the boardwalk.

He searched Myspace for Elliott's page. No luck. *Who doesn't have Myspace? Only those who didn't have friends. He thought.* Mikaila's page only had a few photos—some of her, but mostly her and Elliott being the main ones. Asa ground his teeth, seething, staring at the happy expression on his own face in the photo. *Do you really make her happy? He thought.*

Later that evening, Mikaila called back. Asa deepened his voice as soon as he answered.

"Sorry I missed your call," she said.

"It's okay," he replied, running a hand through his hair as he sank into his computer chair, eyes drifting to the wall covered in framed Star Wars posters.

"How are you?" he asked, leaning closer to the phone so he could catch every word.

"Great. Elliott and I just went for a run around the neighborhood. He's helping me improve my time."

Great, Asa thought, flicking his brown hair out of his eyes. "If you get any faster, they'll make you team captain."

"Yeah, no way."

"When's the next time you're visiting your dad?"

"Ugh…he wants us to come this summer," Mikaila groaned.

Asa stroked his arm with his free hand, holding the house phone between his ear and shoulder. "We could see a movie… and I could show you the new indoor skating rink…if you want to…"

Skating rink? Why am I talking like I'm twelve? He thought.

"If I visit this summer, I'll let you know," Mikaila replied.

"Will Elliott come too?"

"No, he'll be working with his dad."

Good. Asa exhaled, feeling his shoulders relax. "I'll make sure you have a good time, regardless of how things go with your dad."

She let out a quick, anxious breath. "Thanks. So…my best friend Chara was in a car accident. Her arm's messed up pretty bad, and her dad's had multiple surgeries. The Montero ended up in a tree, and they were expelled while it was still moving. I feel so bad…we drove past the scene on the way from practice and had no idea."

"Wow. That's traumatic. I'm glad she's alright. It sounds serious."

"Thanks. Yeah, she and her dad are on my prayer list."

"I wouldn't expect anything less."

He couldn't wipe the dopey grin off his face as he slouched in his chair, soaking in every word. There was something about her—the way she could make even the most mundane story feel gripping, how she'd snort-laugh at his terrible jokes. He'd come a long way from the awkward kid everyone had written off—the one who knew too much about Star Wars and not enough about being cool. But Mikaila? She actually liked that about him. His brothers friends used him as a punching bag for it until they graduated last year.

The religion stuff should've been a deal-breaker. His folks were front-row-pew Sunday morning types, while he'd rather sleep in and contemplate the universe from his bed. When Mikaila talked about her faith, it was different, like she was sharing pieces of herself rather than preaching, which captivated him.

"Talk to you in a couple of days," she said, as his heart did that stupid little dance it always did for her. After hanging up, noises coming from the hallway drew his attention. Asa turned his chair towards the open door. Hayden had come home to visit and was making kissy faces at him.

Asa frowned. "Shouldn't you be at school?"

Hayden held up his overly stuffed laundry bag that had a dirty sock smell emanating from it. "Assa-whole! What's up? Mom asked me to bring my laundry home."

Asa flicked his hair and tapped his fingers against his knee as he sat in his chair. "Sure, she did. Because you're the golden child who can't do anything yourself."

Hayden shrugged. "She said it saves them money on laundry fees."

"Whatever. Just stay out of my way."

"Just trying to help you get the girl finally," Hayden smirked.

Asa rose slowly from his chair. At six foot two, he was only an inch shorter than his brother. "What would you know about getting the girl?"

"I know because I have a date with Sally from my Economics class tonight, and then her sister tomorrow," Hayden grinned, puffed out his chest in a mock show of toughness, and walked away carrying his tote bag full of laundry.

Asa slammed his bedroom door. The golden child didn't do his own laundry, barely held a job during college, and yet he was perfect in his parents' eyes because he could throw a football and get a scholarship for it. *It must be nice. Some of us have to use our intelligence, he thought.*

His brother hadn't always been this arrogant. He used to play video games with him after school and on the weekends but popularity went straight to Hayden's head before high school. In seventh grade, Hayden's friends had stolen his clothes after swim class, leaving Asa to wander the halls of Chestnut Intermediary School wrapped in nothing but a towel. No matter how tightly he clutched his legs, it didn't conceal enough. Hayden had stood there laughing as the bell rang, the hallway filling, while his friends yelled, "Look! Assa Whole!" for years afterward. Hayden later swore it had been a dare from Lexy. Asa's crush at the time. Then his friend group 'jokingly' gave him punches to the ribs in the locker room when they could, but nothing that ever bruised his face so that they could get away with it.

High school offered no relief. The teasing and criticism only intensified, and his parents shrugged it off, telling him to 'toughen up.' He got a doctor's note to skip swim class, but it didn't stop footballs from being thrown at his backside for Hayden and his friends' entertainment.

Now, years later, Asa grabbed a dumbbell and started curling it. *At least I'll look good when Mikaila gets here*, he thought.

5

mikaila

APRIL 19, 2003

I zippered my jacket as the blustery wind blew through the old, thick oak trees at the park. The coach's whistle cut through the air, signaling the start of our two-mile run. I zeroed in on my pace—one foot in front of the other—blocking out the sounds of kids squealing on the playground, the cars zooming on the highway, and the sound of my teammates' steady breathing all around me.

I pushed away thoughts of the school day and enjoyed

the scenery: the duck pond and the blooming yellow tulips interspersed throughout the trees. Nearing the end of the run, I spotted Kait ahead of me. I didn't slow my tempo, nor quickened it. I liked beating her in practice the other day, but she reveled in the attention of being the bigger sister, the better sister, and now, the faster sister. I had no problem with coming in second and letting her take her spotlight back.

The whistle blew, clocking our times. "Good pace today, Miki!" The coach beamed. "Solid as always, Kait! We're going to take this meet on Saturday! Randy—pace yourself! Light, quick steps!"

Kait and I were too winded to answer, but we couldn't stop smiling as we wiped the sweat from our foreheads. Aunt Lana was waiting in the parking lot with her faithful grey Honda Civic, ready to drive us home.

"Girls, how was practice?" She asked as we climbed in.

I paused to take a breath, my hand on my abdomen, still breathless from the run. "Practice was good. Coach liked our timing."

Aunt Lana smiled. "Wonderful. Oh, I put Chara on the prayer list. How's she doing, by the way?"

I twisted my ring. "Did Nan or Mom tell you about her injuries?"

"Yes, what a shame. I'm sure she'll recover quickly. I put her dad on the prayer list, too. It's wild that we drove by their accident on the way home the other day. It's a miracle that their injuries aren't worse."

My breath quickened as I thought about saving Chara. *The accident had to have been a sign that my dream was real.*

"So true. I want to help her and Astrid because I know her

broken arm is going to take a while to recover. Is there anything I can do besides having them on the prayer list?"

"We can bring Chara's homework and help Astrid with some chores," Kait suggested.

"Great idea, Kait. Did Cameron speak to you today?" Aunt Lana asked.

Kait shrugged. "Not more than usual."

Aunt Lana quickly glanced at her. "Did he ask you for your number yet?"

Kait looked out the window. "No."

If I weren't in the car, I'm sure she would have spilled how he meets her at her locker every day and how she loves it, because she's crushing hard on him. She doesn't think I notice these things, but then again, she barely acknowledged my existence at school.

After Aunt Lana dropped us off, we headed straight to the kitchen for a snack before dinner. Mom and Nan were seated at the kitchen table, knitting together while Pop prepared Nan's herbal tea. The teapot squealed, signaling that the water was ready. The aroma of Nan's meatloaf filled the air, and my stomach growled in response.

"Hey, girls," Mom said.

Kait and I looked at each other and then quickly gave her a smile. "Hey, Mom," we said in unison. We knew to take advantage of her good mood while we could.

"Coach was impressed with Kait's timing today." I gestured to Kait.

Kait turned her head to me and played with her watch. "And yours."

"Those practices with Elliott are really helping," Nan

remarked as her wrinkled fingers worked just as quickly as Mom's.

Mom looked up from her knitting. "Glad you found something you both excel in."

I glanced at Kait, raising an eyebrow. "Why don't you shower first, Kait?"

Both of us lost our appetites, unsure if Mom's good mood was genuine or the calm before the storm. Kait bit her fingernails as we made our way up the stairs. At the top of the landing, I leaned toward her and whispered, "She's in a good mood today."

Kait leaned closer, whispering back, "I heard Pop tell her to take her medicines consistently…maybe she actually listened this time."

I looked down at the ring on my right hand, twisting it between my fingers. Her moods were so unpredictable that it was exhausting to keep up. "I guess we'll find out soon enough."

After showering and eating dinner, Mom offered to watch *7th Heaven* with us. I saved the seat next to me on the couch, and Kait settled into the recliner on the left side of the room.

During commercial breaks, I looked over to Mom on the couch, and she looked half asleep: eyes unfocused, arms crossed, and body completely relaxed. I glanced at Kait, and she shrugged. *Maybe she's not feeling well.*

"How is your new medicine working for you?" I asked, swiveling my head from the TV to Mom.

"I don't need to take it every day because I'm feeling better," she said in a monotone voice, her eyes never meeting mine.

Pop walked into the living room and handed us a bowl of popcorn.

Mom quickly got up from the couch without a word and went upstairs to her bedroom. Kait and I exchanged a puzzled expression before I said, "What was that about?"

"She's not taking her medication like she's supposed to, and I told her that she's required to do it for her own health, but also so that she can be around for you two. She didn't take it well."

I got up from the floor and patted Pop on the back. *I know how it felt to be the target of her fury.* Pop was only a few inches taller than me—about the same height as Kait: five foot eight.

His lips spread into a deep smile, and he pressed a kiss to the top of my head. "Nan's resting now, and I'm going to bed too, but let me know if you girls need anything."

I grabbed handfuls of buttery popcorn and got lost in the episode while Kait finished her homework lying next to me.

* * *

In the middle of the night, I woke to a high-pitched, nightmarish scream. I opened my eyes to the faint glow of stars on my ceiling, then quickly shut them, hoping to drift back to sleep. The sound happened again, and this time it was continuous. *Kait!*

I shot out of bed, not bothering to tiptoe; my feet sounded like weights dropping on the hardwood floor of the hallway. Kait's door was ajar, but the room beyond was pitch black. I flipped the light.

Kait lay curled in a fetal position on her twin bed, shrieking, while Mom held a carving knife to her abdomen. As soon as the light flicked on, Kait's eyes lit with recognition. She screamed, "What are you doing?!"

"I'm going to make sure you don't do that again! I'll teach

you! I'll teach you a lesson!" Mom screamed.

"Do *what* again?"

"Stop it! Stop it!" I chanted and then flung myself onto mom's back. She had been hunched over but tried to straighten and shake me off. I could hear footsteps racing up the stairs and into the room. Mom was still trying to get close to Kait, who had edged herself into the corner of her bed, pressing against the wall, and trying to make herself as small as possible.

"What is going on in here?" Pop bellowed.

Mom turned around with the knife and pointed it directly at him. "You! You are *always* against me!" She yelled toward Pop.

"Mikaila and Kait, leave the room now," Pop ordered through clenched teeth.

I let Mom go and pushed her away from the bed and Pop. The knife fell to the floor, and I kicked it toward him. Kait crawled out of her bed, and we made our way downstairs. Nan was already there, brewing chamomile tea.

Kait had pillow lines across her face with dark bags under her eyes, and I was sure my hair looked like a bird's nest. We both kept yawning, though the events of the night had me too wired to feel tired. *If she could come after Kait, what would she do to me?*

Nan looked at us and put an arm around each of us, and led us to the table. "I've called the police and asked for an ambulance to take her to the hospital. This is a medical emergency. Are you two alright?"

I heard something hit the wall and Pop yelling. I flinched.

Kait stood frozen. Nan guided her to a chair and motioned for me to sit across from her. She settled beside Kait and rested a hand on her shoulder.

Gently, Nan asked, "Are you alright?"

Kait looked up and nodded, then leaned her head against Nan's shoulder, softly crying. Nan wrapped her arms around her in a comforting hug.

The sharp whistle of the tea kettle made Kait lift her head.

Nan smiled and raised her hand. "Would you both like some tea?"

We nodded, and Nan quickly brought us warm, soothing tea.

Kait tapped her feet nervously, clutching her cup as Nan picked up her knitting and resumed her work. I sipped my tea quickly, fingers drumming along to *Perfect* by Simple Plan.

Then flashing lights illuminated the windows—an ambulance outside. Nan ushered the EMTs inside, and we all watched as they carefully strapped Mom to a gurney and carried her away. Pop draped an arm around me, and Nan wrapped one around Kait, holding us both close as the sirens faded.

"Sorry you had to see all that. She didn't mean it, Kait. She just hasn't been on her meds," Pop said. Kait stared straight ahead while she finished sipping her tea.

"Girls, Lana will be here in the morning. Why don't you go on up and see if you can get more sleep?" Nan suggested.

Kait and I padded up the stairs. Nan followed, tucking us in like she used to when we were little. The alarm clock read 1:35 a.m. I closed my eyes, thinking of ways to save Chara, anything to keep my mind off what had just happened. *Maybe I could get her to come to Bible Club with me.* Focusing on a plan helped me drift back to sleep.

The extra hour of sleep we gained from Aunt Lana dropping us off did nothing to keep me from yawning through Geometry. Usually, Chara was in the class, giving the teacher an attitude whenever she got called on. Without her, the class wasn't nearly as entertaining.

When the bell finally rang, I headed to the cafeteria and strode to the table where Elliott and Kristin sat. My eyes spotted Elliott in his blue flannel shirt and black pants, and he shifted his gaze to me, and grinned. I couldn't help but smile. Kristin looked up and waved, and I waved back as I maneuvered the other students getting to their seats. I put my bag down and he gave me a quick side hug, so we didn't get in trouble with the teachers' PDA rule. I did a double take at Kristin's shirt that reads, "I'm the captain. To save time, let's assume I'm always right."

I laughed as I sat down across from her. "That's great. Your sweater covered it up earlier. Is that for a specific class?"

She grinned, and her eyes had a mischievous twinkle to them. "We're doing a group project in Intro to Web Design, and the two jocks that I was told to work with nominated me as head of the group and then didn't listen to anything I had to say yesterday."

I dunked my apple in peanut butter. I raised my eyebrow. "And if they don't listen today?"

She leaned in. "I'm going to make them read my shirt and tell them that unless they want to fail, they'll listen to their captain."

Elliott took a sip of his Snapple and held it up as a cheers. "Not listening to the captain's orders is a great way to drown fast."

She nodded and did a cheers back. I chortled. "I wouldn't want to mess with someone who has your technical expertise. They could find themselves with their inner secrets or worst photos of their life on a webpage for the world to see."

Kristin popped a Now and Later into her mouth as she

zipped up her lunch bag. She raised her eyebrows and smirked. "And the detention would be worth it."

A shiver ran through me, not from the cold. I leaned in, lowering my voice so only they could hear. "I have a secret... and I'd like it to stay that way."

They both nodded, and Elliott's eyebrows furrowed in confusion.

The raucous laughter from the football team's table carried across the cafeteria. Elliott held my hand with his left while eating his roast beef sandwich with his right.

"My mom won't be around for a bit." I filled them in on how the night had started peacefully but ended in chaos.

"I don't know how long she'll be gone," I concluded, twisting the ring on my right hand. It reminded me of Nan, and a comforting warmth spread through me.

Kristin's mouth dropped open.

"I'll ride my bike over to your house tonight," Elliott said. I squeezed his hand and tucked my leg over his under the table.

Kristin set her banana down. "I can ask my mom to drop me off for a little while if you want."

"I don't think Nan and Pop want a big crowd tonight, but this weekend we should visit Chara, she'll be home from the hospital."

Kristin waved her hands excitedly. "I'll bring balloons and beads so we can make matching bracelets!"

Elliott wiggled his eyebrows and said, "I'll make a pink one," as he looked at me and grinned.

I tilted my head back and laughed at the thought of him wearing a small, pink beaded bracelet.

"I think purple's more your color," Kristin said with a

bemused smile.

Elliott chuckled, taking a bite of his sandwich, "Purple it is. Color of royalty."

I nudged him with my right shoulder; he nudged me back with his left. I ran my hands through his thick, wavy brown hair. "We need to get you a crown to match your bracelet."

He threw a French fry at me, and I laughed. Kristin shook her head, chuckling, as the bell rang. I gathered my bag and strolled with Elliott, fingers entwined, to our next class.

6

mikaila

I ran down the stairs to greet Elliott.

"Don't fall. You'll ruin your track career," Pop warned as he sat down in the recliner to watch the Baltimore Orioles play.

I grabbed Elliott's hands, and he pulled me into a light, sweet kiss. Kristin arrived with the balloons and jewelry kit, and I let her in next.

"Kait, we're ready!" I yelled from the living room. *You can stop fixing your hair now.*

She wandered down the stairs in her tracksuit. "Ready to go."

Nan stepped into the living room. "Have fun."

We meandered down the sidewalk under the swaying oak trees. The clouds played peek a boo with the sun as we walked to Chara's house, a block away. She lived in a blue one-story, three-bedroom house with a 1950s vibe, from the siding to the wallpaper in the kitchen and bathroom.

Elliott skipped, just to get us to laugh, and it worked. "Are you that excited for your bracelet?" I asked while skipping next to him.

He grinned, "I'm excited that mine will be better than all of yours."

Kristin gave him a tiny push on the shoulder. "Tough chance. What do you think, Kait?"

Kait smiled. "I think he's just trying to make himself feel better because he knows we'll be better at it than him."

We were still laughing by the time we reached Chara's front door. Astrid greeted us with a wide, relieved smile and ushered us inside.

Chara sat curled on the couch, wrapped in a white, fluffy throw blanket. For a moment, her face looked tight with pain, but when she realized it was us, her expression softened into a slow, genuine smile. My chest tightened at the sight of her casted arm and the bruise still blooming along her cheek.

We took turns giving her careful hugs—gentle, mindful of every wince. Astrid handed us a Sharpie so we could sign her cast, and Elliott tied the cluster of balloons to one of the kitchen chairs, making them bob and sway like they were trying to cheer her up themselves.

"I can tie the balloons around the cast with you if you want, and you can bring the party with you wherever you go," Elliott joked, as he signed a big E on her cast.

"That'll make Geometry class better," Chara smirked.

I bit back my grin and dropped her assignments on the coffee table.

"I brought your English homework," Kait said, giving it a little wave before setting the packet on the coffee table.

"Looks like I won't be watching much TV these next two weeks," Chara sighed.

"I brought beads and *Spiderman*," Kristin said.

I sank down onto the floor while Kristin and Kait claimed the couch. Elliott popped the DVD in and pressed play before taking his spot next to me. Astrid made popcorn for us, and Chara picked out the beads she wanted while Kristin measured our wrists and cut the strings.

"I'm making us bracelets...not you, Elliott," Chara pointed to him. He looked at me with his lip puffed out in a fake pout.

I patted his back, like Nan would have done for me. "Aww."

Chara grinned at us. "Mine will say 'best,' and the rest of you get 'friends.'"

Elliott looked at her with raised eyebrows and his fake pout. "And we're not best friends?"

I put my hand on his shoulder. "Yours will say best boy-friend, and that's the only one you're getting today."

I turned to Kristin. "Is yours going to say, 'Captain?'"

She grinned and said, "Absolutely. And because they listened to their captain, I'll make Dan and Ron 'First Mates.'"

Elliott chuckled. "Better off with scare tactics. Give them ones that say 'Overboard.'"

Chara tilted her head. "Do I even want to know?"

Kait stopped beading. "I know those two. They're in my gym class and sit with the rugby team at lunch."

Kristin continued to make her 'Captain' bracelet and explained to Chara and Kait the dynamics of her group project and how she had to rein in her 'first mates.'

Astrid looked over. "I can't believe they still make you do group projects. You're in high school now." She popped more popcorn into her mouth and turned back to the movie.

Kait finished her pink and black bracelet to match her watch. Then we made bracelets for Nan while Elliott and Astrid were glued to the screen, watching Toby Maguire save the day and crunching on popcorn.

Chara looked up from stringing beads. "Are you guys moving?"

Kait's lips pressed into a thin line. She looked at me, shook her head, and said, "No. Why would you think that?"

"I had a dream there was a for sale sign in front of your house." Chara's shoulders sagged.

"You hit your head pretty hard, huh?" Kait asked, placing her hand on the back of Chara's head.

Chara chuckled and shrugged.

"How's your dad doing?" Kait continued.

"He's still in a coma, but according to the nurses, he's recovering well," Chara said.

"I added him to the prayer list," I offered. Chara was super close to Ty, and I knew how much being apart from him hurt her.

"Thanks. How's Nan and your mom?" Chara asked.

I groaned loudly at the question. Chara tilted her head in confusion.

Kait said flatly, "She's in the hospital again."

Astrid glanced over, rubbing her hands on her pant leg. "Is everything alright?"

Kait again replied with a blank expression that Nan was alright, and everything was good.

"Why did she go to the hospital?" Chara asked.

I suddenly felt lightheaded and chilled, so I grabbed my sweater and wrapped it around my torso. Elliott sat down next to me on the floor and draped his arm around me for warmth and comfort.

I sighed. "She came after Kait in the middle of the night with a knife."

Astrid paused the movie, and Kait's bead slipped from her fingers.

"That doesn't sound like everything is fine, Kait," Astrid said.

Kait bent over to pick up her fallen beads. Meekly, she replied, "We'll know more in a couple of days."

"Did anyone get hurt? What happened exactly?" Chara asked.

"No, we're fine," Kait said.

Astrid pushed a strand of blond hair out of her face. "Are you sure you don't need to talk about it with someone?"

Chara pursed her lips and glared at Astrid, huffed. "Mom, please put the movie back on." Chara was trying to get her to leave us alone. Astrid took the hint but wasn't watching it as intently as she was before.

Chara put a bead on her bracelet. "That sounds scary. Are you sure you're alright?"

I leaned into Elliott for comfort. "Yeah, it was awful to walk into."

I took a quick breath, glanced at Kait, who focused on her beads. "I'm alright."

Astrid turned around in the chair. "If you need anything, just let me know."

I gave her a smile. "We will. Thanks, Astrid."

Elliott sighed. "There's nothing in the Bible that speaks about mental health."

Chara looked up. "Well, if you can't pull a verse for this situation, then that means it must not be there."

Kristin twisted her lips. "I actually agree with him. I don't know of any either."

I nudged Elliott. I need her to embrace the Word, not reject it because it doesn't relate to all scenarios. "The Bible talks about sickness, and God is a healer."

Elliott nodded. "Didn't your mom believe?"

I tilted my head and looked at Kait. She nodded to confirm. "Yeah. I mean, she used to go to church and owns her own Bible. Why?"

He tucked a strand of my hair behind my ear. "She's not healed, and there aren't clear instructions for the sick to get better."

Kristin threw a bead at him. "The Bible doesn't talk about cancer, and sometimes people are healed, and sometimes they're not. All that happens is in His plan and at His timing. Now enough talking, and more watching."

He threw up his arms. "I'm just trying…"

Kristin cleared her throat to change the subject. "How long will you be in the cast, Chara?"

"Until next month. Then I'll have a brace and physical therapy to go to," Chara said, giving a thumbs-down motion with her hand.

"That's a long time," Kristin remarked while eyeing the movie.

"Yeah, I'll have to type my assignments with one hand, since I can't write left-handed," Chara said. Her right hand clenched shut and loosened as she dropped a bead, and Kait leaned over to hand it back to her.

I leaned forward to look at her. "If Geometry is handwritten, and you can't write with one hand, how will you do your Geometry homework?"

Chara's mouth widened into a grin. "I guess I can't."

"Nice try," Astrid said.

Chara sighed and continued to string the beads. When she finished, she held up the bracelet for Kristin to cut and tie. Then she tossed the first one to Kait.

"If you want, we can do the homework together. You'll have to tell me what your answers are, and I'll write them down for you," I offered. In some ways, Chara's body had it easier than Kait's and mine. Bruises fade, bones mend, and physical therapy restores function, but what tests or strategies existed for the wounds on the inside?

I shook the thought from my head. This wasn't the time for that. "I can help with dinner," I offered instead.

She placed her hand over her heart, tilted her head, and said, "Thank you for the offer, but we'll figure it out. You just take care of Nan and Pop."

By the end of the movie, Elliott was stuffed with popcorn and had successfully scattered it all over Chara's living room after starting a popcorn war. I grabbed the vacuum out of the closet, but Astrid stopped me.

Instead, she took the vacuum cleaner. "You don't need to do that. Let me."

Kristin caught on and gently nudged Kait and Elliott to

help straighten up so Astrid wouldn't have to. When we'd finished, we said our goodbyes and walked back toward my house. Kristin's mom pulled into the driveway a minute later, and after a round of hugs, Kristin headed home. Elliott wrapped me in a warm embrace, pressed a quick kiss to my cheek, and then rode off on his bike, glancing back once before turning the corner.

Inside, the smell of pizza hit me like a cozy blanket. Nan and Pop had ordered delivery, which almost never happened. We settled around the kitchen table and dug into the steaming, stringy slices. Pop reached for Nan's hand across the table. His fingers trembled slightly as she folded her smaller, soft hand around his stubby, wrinkled ones. For a moment, everything felt still and safe.

"How's Chara doing?" Pop asked.

"She's doing well," I said in between bites of pizza.

Nan smiled. "That's great to hear. I'm sure she enjoyed your visit."

Kait smiled. "I think she did."

We finished our slices and wiped our hands on the napkins in front of us.

"Girls, your mom's treatment plan involves an assisted living facility for adults with mental health issues," Pop began.

Nan's lips pressed together and quivered. She sniffed and added, "We know it's been rocky the last few years with her mood changes and inconsistent treatment. But Aunt Lana is selling her house and moving in with us to help out."

Pop continued, "We want what's best for you, so we've filed for custody. But if you'd prefer to live with your dad..."

"Absolutely not!" Kait slammed her hand on the table.

Pop gently grabbed it and said, "Your home is here for

however long you want."

Nan smiled and put her arm around me. "For as long as you need."

That night, I couldn't sleep. I stared at the ceiling, the stars casting a muted glow. Seeing Chara today made me realize how much lighter I felt when she was around. My need to save her grew even stronger.

7

chara

By the end of May, Chara's dad had regained enough memory
and independence to come home. It was a big deal—his first
week out of the hospital and Chara's first visit since the accident.
Things were different now: he couldn't drive, and the SUV he
had once prided himself on was gone.

Chara's mom dropped her off at his house, promising to
pick her up later. He lived on the outskirts of Oak Haven, further inland from the coast, in a two-bedroom condo in a small

development. Chara stepped onto the front step and saw her dad waiting in the doorway. She took the next steps unsteadily. At the doorway, he pulled her into a hug, tighter than she expected. She nearly collapsed into him, her mouth dry, her body limp as if she were a deflated balloon.

"I missed you," she blurted, almost surprised by how much she meant it.

He gave her a tight squeeze. "I missed you, too."

They sat together at the small table on the front porch, sunlight slanting through the trees. Chara kept sneaking glances at him, noticing the changes—the way he moved a little slower, his stooped posture, and the rasp of his voice, hoarse and thin since one of his vocal cords was still paralyzed. It wasn't the same as before, but he was here. They were here, together, and that was what mattered.

"Do you remember anything about the accident?" He asked.

Chara cleared her throat. It suddenly felt scratchy. "I couldn't remember it before, but now everything has come back. What can you remember?"

"I remember visiting Aunt Leah, and that's it. They think I had a stroke. They've treated me as if I did, and I've gotten better. I'm sorry you can remember all that," he said, placing his hand over hers.

She smiled. "It's ok, Dad. I'm just glad you're back. It's like your second chance at life."

"Good thing, because I have to see my baby girl graduate from high school and then college. What have I missed in your life?"

"Mom's dating a new guy named Howard."

"She's allowed to see new people. We've been divorced a long time."

"Yeah, but I can't do any after-school activities because she doesn't want to drive me and doesn't trust anyone else to. She just wants to spend her time with men," Chara said drily.

"Once I have a car again, I'll pick you up and bring you home. Just tell me which days. You need some activities for your college applications. Where are you thinking of applying?"

"I want to be warm more than a few months out of the year, so definitely a college in the south."

"Warm is good! How's your arm healing, by the way?"

"Still sore. I wear the brace every day and still have physical therapy, but they said it may be a while before the achiness goes away," Chara said, lifting her right arm to show the brace, then gingerly lowering it to her side.

The rest of the day, they lounged around his house until it was time for Chara to go home. He asked questions about her interests, events at school, and her future educational plans. None of the questions her mom ever asked. Even though her arm ached, Chara felt lighter than she had in a long time.

Astrid arrived a little while later to pick her up. She barely stepped through the doorway before saying, "Wait for me in the car."

Chara did as she was told—at least at first. She walked down the steps and across the porch, but instead of heading straight to the car, she paused. When she saw her mom disappear inside, she quietly crept back toward the house. The front door hadn't fully latched and sat slightly ajar, enough that voices slipped through.

She leaned closer.

Astrid's tone was raised, clipped, the kind of voice Chara had learned to brace herself for.

"I have to interrupt my life, because you, the adult, decided it wasn't necessary for our child to wear her seatbelt. You've cost me time off from work and time away from my friends and hobbies because you haven't been around for visitation, and now I have to chauffeur her to *you*. So, thank you once again, Ty, for your selfishness and childishness!" Astrid yelled.

"I'm sorry that we were in the accident, and I'm sorry that raising our child is an inconvenience for *you*."

"*No*, raising our child isn't inconvenient. You being unavailable to do your part because you're irresponsible and refuse to wear a seatbelt has been inconvenient."

"Is this about not having time to parade around with Howard?"

Her voice rose more, "What I do in my spare time is my business! If you could have acted like an adult, we would still be together!"

"Right, everything is my fault, that much I do remember," Ty said back sarcastically.

Astrid exhaled sharply. "Well, someone has to be the adult. She's a child. And she probably has a permanently damaged arm for the rest of her life because you don't feel the need to enforce rules or laws. Laws that exist to keep her safe."

"At least I act like she exists."

"What is that supposed to mean?" Astrid asked as she opened the front door.

Chara could see her dad shaking his head from where she stood. "You don't know the first thing about her because you're too busy trying to have a life that doesn't involve her. I messed up, and I'm sorry. I apologized to her. Have you?" Ty said, raising his hands, and disappearing out of view.

Chara tiptoed back to the car and acted like she'd sat in it the whole time. She fumbled with the dial on the radio stations, pretending that she was focused on finding a good song. "Ready?" Chara asked when Astrid slid into the driver's seat.

"Yes—Yes, I think I am," Astrid said as she backed out of the parking lot. She flipped the dial to the eighties station, cranked up *Hall and Oates' "Maneater,"* and belted out the lyrics.

Chara rested her head against the window. *I can't wait to see Mikaila tomorrow. At least I have one home where I know I belong, she thought.*

Chara spotted Mikaila as she completed her second lap around the block. She waved goodbye to Astrid and jogged slowly to the corner, waiting for Mikaila to round it again. When she did, Chara waved, and they jogged together for Mikaila's final lap. Her arm ached as it jostled against her side, but the warm sun and the brisk air lifted her spirits.

Chara breathed heavily. "I don't know how you do this all the time."

Mikaila grinned. "It's easier the more that you do it."

Chara's eyebrows bunched together. "Says who?"

Mikaila smirked. "Race you to the house." And then she was off.

"Not fair!" Chara panted.

After they stopped at Mikaila's house, Chara gave her a side hug.

"What's that for?" Mikaila asked.

"I just missed you," Chara said. "I had a rough visit with my dad yesterday."

They walked into the kitchen. While Mikaila filled two glasses with water, Chara recapped everything—the hospital visit, the argument, the tension that followed her home like a shadow.

Mikaila sat across from her and took a sip, tilting her head thoughtfully. "I'm really glad your dad's doing better. When I told Elliott how I felt about my dad leaving me in Virginia, he showed me *Psalm 27:10—'Though my father and mother forsake me, the Lord will receive me.'*"

She tapped her fingers on the glass. "Both your parents love you. Your mom just...doesn't know how to show it. And your dad avoids the hard stuff, like making you wear your seatbelt in the first place. But God doesn't avoid the hard things. He always wants you around, and He gives rules to protect you. You should come to Bible Club with us."

Chara huffed a small laugh. "Elliott really is good for you. But you know how my mom feels about religion. And my dad doesn't even have a car right now."

Mikaila ran a hand through her hair, then scratched her chin thoughtfully. "You know you could just catch a ride with us."

Chara took a sip of water, made a small choking sound, and shot her a look. "And be the third wheel? Yeah, no thanks."

Mikaila threw her head back and laughed. "It's Bible Club, not date night."

Chara leaned back from the table. "No, thanks." Mikaila toyed with the ring on her right hand. "My mom will be living in an assisted living facility indefinitely."

Chara drummed her fingers on the table. "I'm really sorry. How's Kait handling it?"

"She's okay. Aunt Lana's selling her house, and she's going to move into Mom's room."

Chara let out a long breath. "See? My dream is coming true. Thank God you and Kait aren't moving, though."

Mikaila straightened a little, lifting her chin. "How weird is that?"

"Right? The last dream I had that came true…my grand-mother passed away," Chara said quietly.

Mikaila tugged at the sleeve of her shirt. "Well, just…let me know if you have any more dreams about my life, okay?"

After watching an episode of MTV's *Cribs* and discussing a posh lifestyle that Chara wished for, she made her way back home. Astrid was out on another date, and once again she entered an empty house. Her shoulders slumped as she sank onto the couch and watched a movie alone.

Laughter drifted from outside, and she turned to the window. In the streetlights' glimmer, she watched her neighbor, Todd, stroll down the sidewalk with Tara hand in hand. For a moment, Chara tried to picture what it would feel like—someone waiting, someone choosing her first. All she could see was the shadowy living room, the faint trace of Astrid's perfume clinging to the air.

Turning from the window, Chara let the weight settle back onto her shoulders. She ran her hand along the faded brown leather couch and wondered if the world would ever pause long enough for her to catch up, or if she was destined to always be one breath behind, searching for proof that she belonged.

8

asa

The cafeteria smelled like stale pizza and tension. The hum of the vending machines, the restless drum of pencils, and the sharp clack of captured chess pieces filled the air. Hunched teenagers squared off across sixty-four squares at Chestnut Hill High School.

Against the cinderblock walls, coaches hovered close, hands jammed in pockets, eyes fixed on clocks. Asa took steady breaths as his opponent finally nudged a pawn to the center of the board.

He kept his gaze locked on the pieces; his knees bounced under the table. Biting his lip, he pushed his black pawn forward one square. *Let's see your move.*

By the last round, exhaustion clung to everyone's face, but when Asa captured the queen, the Chestnut Hill staff applauded in an uproar. He managed a tired smile, exchanged a final hand-shake, and stepped into the humming hallway. For a moment, beneath the fluorescent glare, he felt seen.

Lacy walked up to him as students streamed out for dis-missal. She tapped his shoulder, "Secure the championship title?"

Asa jumped slightly, pulled from his thoughts, and they fell into step together, weaving through the brown-and-teal halls. "Chestnut Hill High School is undefeated for the third year in a row," he grinned.

"Alright, chess team captain!" Lacy said, giving him a high five.

"You need a ride home?" Asa asked.

Lacy shrugged. "Sure. Why not?"

They walked over to his parents' beat-up pea-green sedan from the mid-nineties. Asa turned the key in the ignition, and the engine sprang to life, sounding like a metal can full of rocks. He turned the music up to drown out the noise of the engine. He glanced at her quickly. "So, I heard Mikaila might be visiting this summer?"

Lacy turned her gaze from the trees outside her window back to him. "Maybe. Haven't talked to her in a while. Only heard from Dad what he thinks may happen."

He ran his hand through his hair while one was on the steering wheel. "That would be cool."

"Yeah, it would be good to spend some time with her before

I leave for Stony Brook U."

Asa pulled into Lacy's driveway. Mark and Lorainne were still at work, their cars missing from the garage.

"Thanks for the ride. I'll let you know if I hear anything else," she said, unbuckling her seatbelt.

Asa smiled. "Sounds good. Thanks."

When she shut the door, Asa turned up Maroon 5 to cover the sound of the engine. A few blocks later, he parked in front of his house. His mom was home when he arrived, because she was off on Fridays.

He wandered into the dining room, carrying his hard-earned trophy, where she was reading. "Hey, Mom." As usual, she waved her acknowledgment. *You can do the golden child's laundry still, but you can't even bother to say hello to me.* He walked out of the room.

"I'll need the car next Friday to bring Hayden home from school," she yelled from the dining room.

"No problem," Asa yelled back from the kitchen. He walked back into the dining room where she was reading her Bible, on the Italian Molteni dining room table that was a wedding gift from her parents back in the 80s.

"Where's he working this summer?" Asa asked.

Eleanor Finn chuckled, looking up from her Bible. "You know your brother can't work with his rigorous football schedule."

"Of course not. Why would I think such a thing?" Asa remarked, forcing a smile.

"What do you have there?" she asked.

"Oh, this?" Asa held up a trophy. "Just won the state championship chess tournament for the third year in a row."

"Oh, how nice. Why don't you put it on the mantel in the living room next to your others—on the shelf next to your brother's *state championship* trophies?"

"Sure," he said, pursing his lips into a fine line as he sulked out of the living room. Nothing he ever did seemed to measure up to his brother in their eyes. Why had he even thought a trophy would make a difference?

He crossed into the next room and set the trophy on the shelf. *At least it can be seen from the couch,* he told himself. The couch, a sagging relic passed down from his grandparents, looked like it had been teleported straight from the seventies.

In the adjacent kitchen, he grabbed a can of Mountain Dew from the fridge, the metal hissing as he cracked it open. Then he headed upstairs, taking the steps two at a time. He powered on his desktop and signed into Instant Messenger.

As he took a long sip of the fizzy soda, a message from Mikaila popped up.

Mikaila: Hey, you!

Asa: Hey, what's up?

Mikaila: Not much. Aunt Lana's house has been sold, and she'll be moving next month.

Asa: Where will she stay?

Mikaila: Here…My mom isn't living here anymore.

Asa: I'm sorry

Mikaila: It's ok. She wouldn't take her medicine like she should, and maybe now she'll get the help she needs.

Asa: Cool that Aunt Lana's moving in. I'm always here to talk if you ever need me. I care about you so much, and I just know everything will work out.

Mikaila: I know. And even better is that Chara is feeling

better, and her dad's home.

Asa: Awesome. I'm sure that helps to have her home.

Mikaila: Yes, it's been boring in Geometry without her!

Asa: Cool. Send me her username.

Mikaila: CharaISFiner

Asa: Bold name.

Mikaila: Chara's middle name is Isabelle, and her last name is Finer. It's kinda clever. I should know, I came up with it!

Asa: Then it's the cleverest name I've ever read!

Mikaila: Gotta Run! Date night with Elliott!

He added Chara to his friend list, then rubbed his temples as a dull ache settled behind his eyes. Mikaila's last message lingered on the screen, and his stomach twisted at the thought of Elliott putting his hands on her. His chessboard sat in the corner of the room, half-forgotten; he moved a piece almost absentmindedly. With her mom out of the picture, she'd be more likely to repair her relationship with her dad, which meant visiting Connecticut and being away from her boyfriend.

He grabbed his dumbbells and started doing rows, alternating arms, feeling the familiar pinch between his shoulder blades. *I'll get jacked...and show her I'm smarter and stronger than Elliott,* Asa thought.

A soft creak from the computer alerted him that someone was online. He set the dumbbells down and stepped back to the desk. Chara had signed on.

Asa: Hey, this is Asa, Mikaila's friend.

Chara: Hey, I remember her mentioning you.

Asa: All good things, I hope.

Chara: Of course, it's Mikaila.

Asa: What are you up to?

Chara: Just seeing if I could catch Miki.

Asa: You actually just missed her.

Chara: Rats! What are you up to? It's a Friday night, and you're a senior in high school. So parties?

Asa: Senior in high school, yes, but parties no.

Chara: Bummer.

Asa: Not really the party type.

Chara: Me either. I'm the movies, mall, and bike riding type.

Asa: Same

Chara: You have a girlfriend?

Asa: No, you?

Chara: Single

Asa: And ready to mingle?

Chara: Maybe

Asa: Why just maybe?

Chara: I don't know what Mikaila's told you about Oak Haven High School, but we've been in the school system with the same kids for about 10 years at least, and the majority of the ones in my grade level rotate sleeping with each other. So yeah...maybe?

Asa: Isn't it like that everywhere?

Chara: I haven't been anywhere else. Did everyone else start sleeping together in 7th grade, or is it just an Oak Haven thing?

Asa: 7th grade?

Chara: Yes. Oak Haven, where everyone knows your name and what you did last night.

Asa: Yeah, that might be an Oak Haven thing.

Chara: Lucky us.

Asa: So, is it your grade or all of the grade levels that are like that?

Chara: Definitely my grade level. Some of the others, but not as much.

Asa: So, Mikaila's grade level isn't like that?

Chara: Not as much. But the Bible Club members do not have their tally marks written in the bathroom stalls of the girls' bathroom.

Asa: Good to know. Why do they have tally marks?

Chara: Well, now, how else would they keep count?

Asa: Haha, good question.

Chara: You got a picture of yourself?

Asa: No.

Chara: You didn't get senior photos done?

Asa: Okay, here it is.

He shared a photo of himself in a button-down polo shirt and jeans standing by a tree for his senior portrait.

Chara: Cute.

Asa: Thanks. You got a photo?

Chara: You can check out Myspace

He quietly scrolled through her Myspace page, the one he'd opened earlier. A photo caught his eye—Chara and Mikaila laughing together at the boardwalk, sunlight glinting off the water behind them.

Asa: Cute.

Chara: I'm not but thanks

Asa: What do you mean you're not? Yes, you are.

Chara: Thanks, but you're just being nice.

Asa: No, I mean it.

Chara: Yeah…okay…

Asa: You are. You're just being humble.

Chara: Ok, sure. This has been fun. I have to go, my mom

is making me get off. Let's talk again soon.

Asa: We absolutely will.

Asa logged off Messenger and ran his fingers through his hair. *If I can't have Mikaila, I'll just become friends with her friends. Maybe if I can get her friends to like me, then Mikaila will get jealous and want me all to herself, Asa thought.*

9

mikaila

Aunt Lana took my makeup brush and gently dusted blush across my cheeks. "I can't wait to see Elliott's face when he sees you."

I smiled. "Thanks." I tried to keep still in my computer chair while she leaned over me, applying the last of my mascara.

She leaned back against the dresser and smiled. "Perfect."

My dress—a hand-me-down from her friend's daughter—didn't bother me in the slightest. Cherry red satin, A-line cut, a black velvet bow around the waist, like a princess.

Before Elliott showed up, I walked over to Chara's house so she could see my dress. "Perfect color on you," Astrid said, smiling.

Chara gave me a thumbs up. "You look like a princess. Make sure Elliott treats you like one."

"Of course! I'm sorry you can't make it."

Chara gestured to her face. "There will be others, and I'd rather have photos of those when my face isn't torn up. As soon as this brace is off, I'll be dancing in no time. I can't Macarena right now, anyway."

"It does require both arms like the YMCA song."

Chara laughed. "Please show Elliot your killer YMCA moves."

I gave her a hug and stepped out of her house. As I walked home, I fiddled with the beaded bracelet on my wrist, the one that said *Friends*. My legs felt heavier than usual. I knew the brace and the scars exacerbated her low self-esteem. She felt subconscious, sure, but she was beautiful regardless. Something I needed to make her believe. My stomach felt like it was in knots. I wasn't anywhere close to saving her. Still, tonight, I wanted to focus on fun.

Elliott's parents pulled up in my driveway right on time. They insisted on taking a few photos in my living room before we left.

So, Aunt Lana played photographer with a disposable camera. "Move this way...Now smile."

Then Kait came downstairs, and Cameron showed up. And Aunt Lana took photos of them. Kait wore a short black sleeveless dress with sequins and black pumps. The black contrasted with her long blonde hair. She looked like a model in my eyes.

Aunt Lana then tapped me on the shoulder. "You and Kait together." So, we posed in front of our couch together.

Nan put her hand on her heart. "The babies are all grown up."

Nan wrapped me in the biggest hug. She clung to Kait next, refusing to let go until Pop pried her away. "Let the kids have fun so we can have fun!"

* * *

During the drive to school, Elliott's parents took turns asking about school. His dad turned from the passenger seat. "How's track season going?"

Elliott held my hand in the back seat, and I leaned into him. "Going well. Running with Elliott has really helped me improve my time."

His mom glanced at me through the rearview mirror. "That's great to hear. And how's your mom doing?"

Elliott sighed and rolled his eyes. I nudged him and smiled. "Pop says she's doing alright."

Elliott tapped his dad. "What's with the twenty questions tonight?"

His mom paused at the stop sign and looked back at us. "Just making conversation." Then they turned on the radio, and Christian music filled the car—*I Can Only Imagine* playing softly as we drove.

We arrived at school a few minutes later and walked hand in hand toward the gym. The moment I stepped inside, the crepe paper streamers transported me back to middle school—all those afternoons spent in detention. I could still picture the pink, crinkled paper from Valentine's Day, the sting of embarrassment after refusing to read aloud in class, and the punishments that followed: taking down decorations, or worse, scraping gum off cafeteria tables.

I'd been assigned cafeteria duty once for throwing my science textbook at a boy who had hit me with a spitball. I scrunched my nose at the memory—the sticky gum under the tables, the plasticware scraping against it. Repulsive. My mom had been furious, calling my "behavior embarrassing." I refrained from laughing as I recalled how Chara had tripped the boy in the hallway later that week and loudly told him to watch where he was going.

When Nan heard the whole story, she handed me a Bible and told Aunt Lana to start taking me to church. I've been trying to make her proud ever since.

Elliott's friends spotted us and waved us over to the left corner of the gym. We joined them, half-listening as the DJ cycled through his usual mix of pop and R&B hits—mostly songs from the eighties. The school insisted on sticking with tracks they considered "safe," steering clear of anything too current or edgy. The music didn't quite match the energy in the room, but it gave us something to talk about as we sipped our iced tea and traded stories.

Kaitlyn mostly hung out with her date, Cameron, and his group of friends. When the DJ started up the "Electric Slide," she was one of the first on the dance floor. I joined her, laughing as we stepped four to the right, four to the left, took it back with three steps, then tapped our feet in unison. Elliott stood in the corner with his friends and smiled from afar.

Out of the corner of my eye, I noticed Cameron wasn't

watching Kait at all. I hoped she didn't notice either.

When the song was over, "Unchained Melody" began to play, and Elliott made his way over to me. I watched Kait with Cameron from a short distance as I swayed to the music with Elliott.

I whispered, "Kaitlyn's trying so hard to impress Cameron tonight. I think she wants him to be her boyfriend."

Elliot replied, "She should know that if she has to work to impress a guy, then he doesn't deserve her."

Another reason I liked dating Elliott: his heart of gold. The cute dimples didn't hurt either. Before I could say more, Kristin stormed over; her face flushed. "David from History just patted me on the head like I'm some kind of pet!"

The same David who'd told our ninth-grade English teacher that my reading of *Shakespeare* was "overrated," and with such conviction that half the class had nodded along and whispered and stared. *Shakespeare* might have been overrated, but my performance wasn't. I was still annoyed with him, years later.

I played with the ring on my right finger. "Why would he do that?"

She played with a strand of brown hair. "I don't know. I grabbed a Sprite and said 'hello' to him and his date, Sarah Chen, because she's in my Intro to Web Design class, and instead of greeting me, he patted me on the head."

Without thinking, I handed her my iced tea, marched across the dance floor, weaving between swaying couples and groups of chattering students. David stood near the punch bowl, talking to his friends and his date, who looked about as thrilled as someone waiting for a root canal.

Getting his attention wasn't easy. I barely cleared his

shoulders. The bass from the speakers thrummed through my bones as I tapped him on his back, stretching to my tiptoes to reach. At 5'5", the height difference felt huge when he turned around: all 6'3" of him looming down with that irritating grin—the one that made me want to knock his perfectly straight teeth in. His cologne was overwhelming, like he'd doused himself in half a bottle of expensive cologne. "Ahem!" I said, tapping him again. He glanced back, smirked, patted my head as if I were a child, and turned away.

Perfect. He was exactly where I wanted him, back turned to most of the chaperones. I *hated* seeing my friends upset. So, he needed to learn a lesson. If he *wouldn't* talk, then actions would have to do.

I tapped him again, and he turned around to face me. My foot shot out, my worn red Converse connecting solidly with his shin. The impact sent a satisfying shock up my leg. David yelped, and his mouth fell open, and he blinked slowly. His friends stood in shock. Sarah didn't even try to hide her smirk.

"You don't like being kicked?" My voice was sugar-sweet, the kind of sweetness that could rot teeth. I tilted my head, mimicking his usual condescending pose. "Then don't pat anyone on the head. We're not golden retrievers, and you're not a dog show judge."

I could hear his friends laughing as I spun on my heel and walked away before he could respond, heart hammering but my steps steady. The squeak of my sneakers kept time with the music as I crossed the gym. Behind me, David sputtered, his voice hitting that high pitch it always did when his ego took a punch. A few scattered laughs rippled through the crowd. Apparently, I wasn't the only one who'd been waiting to see someone take him down a peg.

When I reached my friends, Kristin's hand shot up for a high five, her earlier annoyance replaced by fierce joy. The sharp crack of our palms connecting felt like victory.

"That," Kristin declared, pulling me into a hug that smelled of floral shampoo and vanilla body spray, "was amazing."

Our friend group, Jessica, Jeremy, and Brian from Bible Club, erupted in replaying the moment with laughter and exaggerated reenactments. Even shy Jessica mimicked David's expression at the exact moment of impact. Kristin slipped me my drink. I craned my neck and kept watch for the chaperones, but they were oblivious to anything other than their own conversations.

Jeremy nodded slightly while grinning. "I think he's learned his lesson today."

Brian mimicked my kicking motion. "The next time he says anything condescending in class, I want to make sure I have the form down correctly."

Jessica chuckled. "I'll hold your drink for you, Brian."

Jeremy pointed to her. "That's the key to getting the kick just right."

I smiled and turned my head to Elliott. He gave me half a smile and then changed the topic to the next meeting.

From across the gym, I caught David's eye. He was still rubbing his shin, his face a fascinating shade of red. I raised one eyebrow and patted the air above my own head to mock him. His date, Sarah, burst out laughing, which only made his face burn hotter. Sometimes the smallest victories were the sweetest.

Elliott pulled me onto the dance floor for another dance. Softly into my ear he said, "David was acting arrogant and chauvinistic, but I wouldn't have kicked him. I would have asked him to apologize."

"And you think he would have done it? I tapped him on the shoulder *twice,* and then he patted *me* on the head."

"No, but do unto others as you would have done unto you. That's how you spread the Word."

"Let each of you look not only to his own interests but also to the interests of others. I was looking out for Kristin's interests!" *And every other girl he's belittled.*

He twirled me and brought me back into his arms. "True, but your approach needs work. You can't kick everyone into submission. Seems like Chara's rubbed off on you, but you should have a calmer approach and rub off on her."

With my hand on his chest, staring into his eyes, I laughed, "And maybe we need to help you with your approach!"

When the lights came on and the music stopped, I grabbed Elliott's hand. We said goodbye to our friends before Elliott's parents arrived. They were less chatty on the way home, enjoying the radio and their coffees.

Elliott walked me to the door, leaned in, and softly kissed me, his lips firm against mine. The front door opened, and he shook Pop's hand.

I stepped inside the living room and stood next to Pop. The table lamps gave the room dim lighting. Lana sat on the couch, sniffling with a tissue, dabbing her eyes. She hadn't fully moved in yet, but she was spending the weekends moving her stuff slowly. There were scattered boxes around the room.

He ran his fingers over his bald head. "Come in and have a seat, dear."

I sat down next to her. "What's going on?" She sniffed in return, and I glimpsed Pop's expression as he paced the floor, staring out the window behind us. His eyes weren't dry either.

We saw the reflection of headlights from Cameron's Oldsmobile pull into the driveway. Pop waited until Kait reached the door, then put an arm around her and guided her to the couch next to me.

Kait tucked a strand of hair behind her ear. "What's happening?"

Aunt Lana leaned over to us and said, "I went to say good-night to Nan, and check on her, as I usually do, and she passed away. Nan's gone."

I couldn't focus on Aunt Lana. I blinked rapidly and was at an utter loss for words. I stood up. *This can't be real. She was just here a few hours ago.* "She was fine just a couple of hours ago. What happened?"

Pop shifted his weight from one foot to the other and looked out the window, as if he could see her out there. "The EMTs think she had an aneurysm. She didn't suffer, and you know she wouldn't want you to be sad.

I buried my face in my hands, letting the tears fall. Kait was already crying. I closed the distance between us, wrapping my arms around her and letting my tears soak into her shoulder. She held me until I pulled away, long enough to catch my breath. Pop placed his hand on Kait's shoulder, and Aunt Lana had her hand on mine.

Pop cleared his throat. "Everything's gonna be okay."

"We'll get through this together, okay, girls?"

We both nodded.

"Did you tell mom?" Kait asked in between sobs.

Pop shifted his feet but kept his hand on her shoulder. "We're going tomorrow to tell her in person. We'll leave it up to you if you would like to join us."

I walked over to Pop and hugged him. My chest ached, and my knees were weak. Pop squeezed me back. The house still carried the warm scent of her snickerdoodles, and her photos of violets, her favorite flower, still adorned the living room walls. A subtle reminder of her presence.

I pulled myself from his arms. "I should take off my gown before I get makeup all over it."

He kissed the top of my head. "Why don't you two go to bed?

I passed my mirror and caught my reflection: mascara running down my face, puffy eyes, splotchy skin. I remembered how I had looked right after my makeup was done, and Nan's last embrace.

I slipped into my pajamas and climbed into bed, turning the ring she'd given me over and over on my right hand. *How am I supposed to go on without you?*

I grabbed the Bible Nan had given me years ago, running my finger along the worn spine. It fell open to John 16:22: *"And ye now therefore have sorrow: but I will see you again, and your heart shall rejoice, and your joy no man taketh from you."* My body felt weightless, like it was floating on the bed and my limbs tingled. I drew deep breaths, clasped my hands together, and prayed—for solace, for myself, and for my family.

The next morning, the smell of banana pancakes and bacon woke me. I could hear noises coming from the kitchen and immediately thought it was Nan, but a slow ache crept from my stomach to my chest when I realized it wasn't. *Everything about this house* reminds *me of her.*

I made my way downstairs to find Kait, Pop, and Aunt Lana

already up and gathered for breakfast. I plopped into the chair across from Kait. Dark circles under her eyes, and her mascara was smeared like mine. Normally, I would have made a joke that together we looked like raccoons, but this wasn't the time.

Aunt Lana set the food on the table. "Good morning. How'd you sleep?"

Kait groaned and sipped her coffee mug. "Not great."

I picked up my fork and grabbed a pancake. My throat was scratchy when I replied, "Not the best."

Pop put the newspaper down he was reading and glanced at both of us. "Take it easy this week. You don't need to overdo it at track or school."

Aunt Lana sat down next to me.

She grabbed her fork. "Dig in, everyone." After a couple of bites, she added, "Have you thought about whether you want to come with us to break the news to your mom?"

I shook my head. "I don't think that's a good idea for me to go."

"I'll go," Kait offered.

Aunt Lana took a sip from her mug of hot coffee. "Great, we'll leave after breakfast. Miki, you can catch a ride to church with Elliott or Kristin if you want, or you can stay here."

My heart lifted at the thought of calling Elliott and Chara. "I'll stay here, and I'll let Astrid and Chara know."

Aunt Lana put her fork down on her plate and folded her hands. "We'll talk about services later. But I want the two of you to think about what kind of photos to display, and the memories you want to share."

I twisted my ring. "You think Mom will come to the services?"

Pop put down his paper. "Yes, she will."

Aunt Lana gave a quick smile. "I'll bring her to the service myself, and then she can't miss it."

When the house was empty, I walked into Nan's room, expecting to find her napping. I picked up her pillow and buried my face in it. It still smelled like her: lavender and vanilla. *I don't want to be in the house without you, Nan.*

Walking to the kitchen, I picked up the phone and dialed Chara. "Hello?"

I tried to keep the sadness out of my voice, but she could hear it.

"Hey." I sniffled, and my voice was raspy.

"What's wrong?" Chara asked.

I sobbed. *What isn't wrong, I thought.* "Nan's passed away," I cried.

"What? I'll be right there!" She said before the line went dead.

I trudged from my room to the couch and curled into a fetal position until I heard a knock on the door. I opened the door, and she squeezed me hard with one arm until I pulled away.

"You didn't have to come," I said.

She put her one arm on her hip. "Of course I did!"

We meandered through the kitchen, out the back door to the bench under the willow tree to sit.

She put her hand on my shoulder. "It's gonna be okay. Tell me what happened."

I spun my ring and looked down. Tears splashed onto my long skirt. "She clung to Kait and me right before the dance. She was acting fine. Then, when we came home, Pop and Aunt Lana told us she'd passed, and the EMTs thought aneurysm."

She tapped her foot on the ground. "I'm so sorry. How's

Pop and Aunt Lana holding up?"

"They're upset. They're telling my mom right now with Kait."

"How's Kait holding up?"

I wiped my eyes. "She didn't sleep well last night either."

Chara sighed.

"I don't think I can stay here this summer," I confessed.

"What do you mean?"

"It reminds me too much of Nan," I sobbed.

"Where are you going to go?"

"To visit my dad." *The thought had been nagging at the back of my mind since I woke up this morning. But now, saying it out loud, it felt resolute, decided. Mom's gone, Nan's gone. I need to get away from here, too.*

10

chara

Chara sat in her computer chair after school, waiting for Astrid to get home. The fan hummed at full blast, doing little to cut through the sticky mid-June heat. Her Backstreet Boys posters fluttered gently in the breeze. She pulled up LimeWire, singing along to *I'm Real* as she scrolled through the downloads.

She logged onto Instant Messenger, and almost immediately, Asa's name popped up. Over the past month, he'd been messaging her more frequently, and her stomach gave a little flip at the sight of it.

Asa: What are you doing tonight, beautiful?

Chara: You think I'm beautiful?

Asa: Yes. You know you are.

Chara: Thanks. Nothing much. Waiting for my mom to get home because she promised to take me out to dinner. You?

Asa: Nothing tonight but work the rest of the weekend.

Chara: A senior in high school, and no graduation parties?

Asa: Plenty of party invitations. Too many to choose from, so I'm not going to any.

Chara: Right.

Asa: Seriously, I can't be in multiple places at once, so I'm not going to any of them.

Chara: Good plan.

Asa: I thought so. And why would I want to miss the chance to talk to such a beautiful girl?

Chara: That's true, and if my mom were here, I wouldn't be wasting away from hunger talking to a hot guy. We're very lucky.

Asa: So you think I'm hot?

Chara: Yes

Asa: I knew talking to you would be better than any party invitation.

Chara: Unfortunately for you, my mom just got home, so I have to run.

Asa: Have fun

Chara: You too

Chara logged off Instant Messenger as she heard the front door click shut. Despite her hunger, her pulse quickened, flirting with Asa always did that. He was the first guy to call her beautiful, and she had to admit, he was really cute.

Astrid's voice pulled her back to reality. She was dressed in black pants and a floral button-down blouse. "You ready?"

"Yeah!" Chara called from her room, slipping on her shoes. She hurried to the living room, where Astrid was waiting.

The two of them drove through Ocean City, the seventies station blaring as they navigated the heavy influx of traffic.

Astrid turned the radio off slightly. "How are Kait and Mikaila holding up?"

Chara turned from the window to glance at her mom. "Mikaila's focused on her trip to Connecticut, and Kait's busy with her part-time job at the bookstore."

"And how are *you* doing?"

Chara tilted her head. "Fine. I'll miss Nan. She was the neighborhood grandma."

Astrid tapped her fingers on the steering wheel. "I'll miss her, too."

"Nan did her best to make every person in their house feel welcome. She played the role of mom to Kait and Mikaila when Sandra couldn't. Aunt Lana's moved in, but it won't be the same." Chara's stomach ached for what that must feel like for them. She stared out the passenger window as they passed the different stores.

When they were at a red light, Astrid glanced at her again. "I'm sure Lana and Pop will do their best."

Chara turned the radio off, signaling she was done talking about the topic.

Astrid pulled into the parking lot of Aloha Bites. The sweet scent of pineapple drifted through the air as they stepped inside. The restaurant was moderately busy, tables filled with families, couples, and groups of friends enjoying their meals. Soft afternoon sunlight filtered through bamboo window shades, illuminating one wall lined with colorful surfboards, while the others displayed vintage Hawaiian postcards and ukuleles. Tables were draped in cerulean blue linens, mimicking the ocean.

Their neighbor, Tara, greeted them. "Hey guys! Thanks for coming in tonight. Would you like some virgin piña coladas and water to start?"

Chara smiled. "Yes, please. Thank you, Tara."

Tara returned moments later with the drinks. "On the house. Thanks for supporting my family's restaurant."

Chara took a slow sip of the creamy coconut-and-pineapple beverage while Astrid decided on her order. She tapped her fingers lightly to the soft, instrumental guitar music playing in the background, letting the tropical vibe ease her mind.

"Look who it is," Astrid said, glancing toward the door. Aunt Lana walked in with Kait and Mikaila, weaving through the restaurant's scattered tables.

Chara's eyebrows shot up in surprise. Astrid smiled and waved them over. Tara returned moments later to take drink orders, greeting Kait and Mikaila with bright smiles. The girls slid into their seats beside Chara and Astrid, the table now complete with familiar faces and easy conversation waiting to start.

"Fancy meeting you here," Astrid smiled at Aunt Lana.

Aunt Lana flipped her menu over. "You should know, girls, that we've been planning this surprise dinner for a few weeks, but all of our schedules never seemed to align."

"Surprise...happy early birthday!" Kait exclaimed, handing Chara a card.

"That's from all of us," Mikaila added, with a smile.

Chara leaned over, hugging Kait first, then Mikaila, before

opening the card. Inside were gift cards to her favorite stores, and a genuine smile spread across her face.

"You didn't need to get me anything," Chara smiled and passed the card to Astrid.

"I know, but I'll miss your birthday at the end of this month, and I know that you'll remind me of it the *whole* summer. Just like when you turned fifteen, and I couldn't make your party because I was called into my job at the movie theater," Mikaila said.

Chara smirked. "If you hadn't answered the phone, they wouldn't have been able to call you in."

Mikaila shook her head, but a smile was tugging on her lips.

Kait raised her eyebrow. "You should have just changed your party to the movie theater, and then you could have been there together."

Chara took the paper from her straw wrapper, rolled it into a ball, and threw it at Kait's head. Kait cocked her head in surprise, while Mikaila giggled.

"Why didn't you come up with that plan back then?" Chara asked.

After Tara took their orders, Kait nonchalantly asked Chara about her plans for the rest of the weekend.

Chara sipped her drink. "Other than visiting my dad on Sunday, nada."

Mikaila sipped her virgin pina colada. "Kristin happens to be sleeping over tonight. Why don't you join us?"

Chara looked at Astrid and Aunt Lana, who both were smiling. "Can I?"

"Of course!" Aunt Lana said.

Astrid smiled. "Sure."

Chara grinned. "Awesome! Thank you!"

Astrid smiled at Kait. "What are your summer plans?"

Kait played with her watch. "I'll be working at the bookstore here. Just a couple of stores down."

Chara's eyebrows rose. "Can we visit and get free drinks all summer?"

Kait smiled. "Maybe."

Astrid laced her fingers together on the table. "What about you, Mikaila?" She glanced at Aunt Lana and played with her ring.

"I haven't decided yet."

Tara arrived with their food. The sweet and smoky scent of teriyaki chicken and rice with vegetables made Chara's mouth water. After Kait and Mikaila finished their coconut shrimp, they nodded to Tara, who stood at the hostess stand.

Chara tilted her head. "Where's she going?"

Mikaila shrugged. "Maybe a break?"

Aunt Lana smiled. "Which store do you think you'll go to first with your gift cards?"

Chara smiled. "Macy's. I love the sale they have right before summer."

Tara slid a pineapple upside-down cake with a single candle in front of Chara. Her eyebrows shot up in surprise.

The table erupted in "Happy Birthday," and soon other tables joined in. Chara felt her cheeks flush. *This is so embarrassing,* she thought, trying to hide her grin.

* * *

After the celebration, they left the restaurant. Once Chara got home to grab an overnight bag, she headed over to Mikaila's house. Kait was the one who let her in.

"When Kristin arrives, we can walk to DVD Den and pick out a movie," Kait told her.

Chara shifted her bag from one shoulder to the other. "Sounds good. Nothing too scary, but definitely a hottie has to be in it."

Kait smiled. "Like Freddie Prinze Junior?"

Chara bunched her eyebrows. "Hotter. Like Will Smith, please."

The two shared a laugh as Chara went up the stairs to Mikaila's room and knocked on the door. Mikaila let her in, and Chara dropped her bag on her floor.

"So, Asa's been talking to me through Instant Messenger. You didn't tell me how cute he is." Chara smiled.

Mikaila ran a brush through her shoulder-length auburn hair. "Asa? Really?"

"Yeah, you should bring him here at the end of summer so we can hang out," Chara winked.

Mikaila shook her head and laughed, but her cheeks flushed. Chara thought Mikaila's pinched expression was from the heat, not from discussing Asa.

"Kristin's here!" Kait yelled from the living room.

"Up here, Kristin!" Mikaila yelled back.

Soon, Kristin walked into Mikaila's bedroom and dropped her bag onto the pink carpet.

Mikaila set her brush down. "Now that everyone's here! Ready to go?"

Chara and Kristin followed her to Aunt Lana's room. "We're going to DVD Den. We'll be back soon." Mikaila told her.

Aunt Lana looked up from her desktop. "Thanks for letting me know."

The four of them walked the half mile to the store. Chara pushed open the door and was greeted by a blast of cool air conditioning. The mingling scents of buttery popcorn and carpet cleaner filled the aisles as they roamed past new releases— dramas, kids' movies, horror flicks. Signs at the checkout reminded them to "Be kind, rewind," even though DVDs no longer required it.

Kait wanted a horror movie, but the others voted for a rom-com. They finally agreed on *Two Weeks' Notice* and *Legally Blonde*. The girls made the trek back through the humid, windy evening, laughing at small jokes along the way. Once home, they set up blankets and pillows on the living room floor, while Aunt Lana made a fresh batch of popcorn. Pop shuffled into the living room in his bathrobe, pajama pants, and slippers. "Hey, girls. I'm going to head to bed. Have a great time, and happy birthday, Chara."

Chara smiled. "Thanks, Pop."

Kait popped *Legally Blonde* into the player and curled up next to Chara.

Chara lay on her stomach, turning her head to Kait. "So, tell us about your boyfriend."

"I don't have a boyfriend."

"So, Cameron picks you up for dates, but you're not a couple?"

"We haven't put a label on it," Kait said, nibbling popcorn between words.

"Have you kissed?" Chara asked, leaning closer.

Kait tossed a piece of popcorn at her head. "Of course we have!"

Mikaila, lying on the other side of Chara, turned her head, with her mouth open, "You have?"

Kait threw a piece of popcorn at Mikaila's head next.

"Then he's your boyfriend," Chara declared, flicking a piece of popcorn at Kait's head.

Kristin glanced at Kait. "Sorry, I have to agree with Chara this time."

Mikaila pointed at Kait. "You have a boyfriend. *And* you're in love."

When the second movie finished, Kait's cell phone rang.

Mikaila popped the DVD into the container. "Boyfriend?"

Kait sighed. "Cameron. After this, I'm going to bed. Night, everyone!" She called over her shoulder, padding up the stairs to her room.

Meanwhile, Mikaila and Chara "introduced" Kristin to Asa via Instant Messenger.

Mikaila toyed with her ring. "You know, Asa and Chara have a thing."

Chara's mouth dropped open, and she smacked Mikaila with a throw pillow. "He's cute, and I like talking to him!"

Kristin laughed. "I don't want to get in the way of true love."

Chara rolled her eyes. "You're making fun of me too? Really?"

The three of them finally crashed around two in the morning. The living room floor was a chaotic mix of sheets, blankets, pillows, and scattered popcorn, dotted with sleeping bodies.

* * *

The next morning, as Chara packed her blankets into her bag, ready to leave, she pulled Mikaila into a tight embrace. "This will be our only sleepover this summer. I'll miss you."

"I'll miss you too, but I'll be back."

"You'd better. And you better send me messages and call me."

"Absolutely. I'll miss you too, Kristin," Mikaila said.

Kristin put her bag down. "I'll miss you too. You'd better call and email." Kristin hugged Mikaila and pointed toward Chara. "You can call and email too. Maybe we can go to the beach."

Chara smiled. "I'd love that."

Just then, Kristin's mom pulled up in the white minivan to take her home.

Chara hoisted her bag and walked back toward her house. Her feet felt heavy, and her chest ached. Three months without her best friend. Almost as hard as the time she went to live with her dad. *I can't believe she's forgiven him, she thought.*

11

mikaila

We'd had Nan's funeral two days ago. A small service with just us, and a few of Pop's cousins who'd flown in from Nebraska. Her ashes were buried beneath the willow tree in our backyard, exactly where she wanted to rest. I twisted the ring on my finger as I stood in line at the airport, waiting to board my flight to Chestnut Hill, Connecticut.

Dad had happily paid for the trip and even offered to cover Kait's, but she'd declined. Work, she'd said. But I knew better.

Since Nan passed, Kait had softened toward our father, but she still kept him at arm's length. And honestly, I couldn't blame her.

I settled into my window seat and slid my bookbag under the seat in front of me. With a sigh, I powered off the new cellphone Aunt Lana and Pop had given me. *"So you can always call home,"* Pop had said, pressing it into my hand the morning after the funeral.

I tucked my earbuds in and queued up the playlist I'd made just for the trip. As the seatbelt sign dinged on and the flight attendants began their safety spiel, I let the music fill the brittle quiet in my chest. The seat beside me stayed empty, though a woman in a pink sweater with pearl buttons and a hairstyle straight out of the late eighties had taken the aisle seat. She smiled politely as she buckled in, and I nodded back before turning toward the window, letting the runway blur as the plane prepared for takeoff.

Red Jumpsuit Apparatus, "Your Guardian Angel," flooded my ears. The lyrics reminded me of how I needed to save Chara. I had a sinking feeling in my stomach that had nothing to do with the plane taking off and everything to do with my internal conflict about whether I had made the right choice. *She would have done the same for me. She was the only one to keep in touch when I was left in Virginia, stood up for me against my mom when no one else would, and was always around when I needed her. I don't want to live without her. And what do I have left here? Besides Elliott, Kait, and Aunt Lana?*

I looked out at the fluffy clouds, the plane ascending into the atmosphere. *I bet they'd be bouncy to walk on.* Parts of my dream with God came back to me, mostly fuzzy, but I remembered cloud-like material as I spoke with him. I pinched my bottom lip. *I couldn't get her to join Bible Club this year, but next school year, for sure.*

The song ended, and "Blue and Yellow" by The Used floated through my headphones. I smiled as I remembered Elliott singing it to me when we walked to the DVD Den to rent a movie for date night before I'd left. Our goodbye was bittersweet. He came over last night, and we danced to "Unchained Melody" in the living room. Then he gave me a golden cross necklace, which I told him I'd never take off. I felt the metal piece of jewelry with my fingers, and the ache in my stomach lessened.

The flight was uneventful, and I grabbed my carry-on bag and made my way outside. I could see my dad standing outside a large white van with Lorainne sitting in the passenger seat. He looked older than I remembered. He was wearing white sneakers, khakis, and a blue button-down collared shirt. Lorainne was wearing white heels, a white pleated knee-length skirt, and a button-down pink shirt with a light white sweater over top. Her makeup was perfect, like a Stepford wife. And her chestnut hair had blond highlights, which was pulled into a coiffed bun on the top of her head.

"Miki, I'm so glad you're here," he said. He smiled and gave me a hug.

"Hey, Dad," was all I could manage to say. He grabbed my bags and loaded them into the van. Lorainne wrapped me in a tight hug before I climbed into the backseat.

"Mikaila, the girls will be home this summer. It's the last summer before Lacy goes off to college, and Lexy's on break from college. They're very excited to spend time with you," Lorainne said from the passenger seat.

I gave her a forced smile. I liked my stepsisters, but I still wasn't sure about being around my dad. "Glad I'll get to see them this summer. It's been a while."

He looked at me through the rearview mirror. "Would be nice if Kait came for just a little, and then I'd have all my girls together."

"Yeah." *Good luck with that.*

Lorainne turned around and met my eyes. "I don't know when the best time is to say this, dear, but we are so sorry to hear about Nan."

I swallowed hard, and the familiar ache in my chest returned. I fidgeted with the ring Nan gave me. "Yeah, it's okay, thanks."

"How's Pop doing?" Dad asked.

"He's holding up. He's taking a lot more naps lately and hasn't played chess with his friend in a while, but he's alright."

"He could be depressed or just under the weather. I hope he bounces back soon. He's a good man," Dad said as he glanced at me through the rearview mirror.

I half smiled. "Yeah, he's been better with Mom gone." *He's probably napping more to avoid thinking about how empty the house feels without.* I quickly wiped a tear from my eye. I was not going to break down in front of my dad.

Lorainne turned her head in my direction. "It's been warm this year. We have lots to do around Chestnut Hill."

Dad drummed his fingers on the steering wheel. "Yes! I think you'll have a good time here."

I shrugged. "Okay."

"We have a great mall, there are beaches within driving distance, bowling…is there any activity you think you want to do?" Lorraine continued.

Forget what I've lost. "Nothing that I can think of right now."

We pulled onto their street. Their light-blue, two-story colonial house with black shutters stood among the swaying chestnut trees, the lawn perfectly manicured. My dad handled my bags while Lorainne gave me a quick tour, since it had been years since I'd been there. The front door opened into the living room on the left and the dining room on the right.

The dining room opened into the kitchen, which had a sliding door leading out to the deck and the backyard. Upstairs were the bedrooms. Their master bedroom was at the end of the hall, and she'd let me take the room at the top of the staircase—next to Lacy's and across from Lexy's. The bed was queen-sized, and when I threw myself onto it, I felt swallowed by the light pink quilted bedspread. My twin bed at home had always been the perfect size; on this one, I could stretch out in every direction and still not reach the edges.

Footsteps sounded on the stairs. I sat up as my dad stepped into the room.

He dragged a hand through his hair. "Kiddo, I thought we'd have a quick talk."

"Okay…" I hesitated, twisting my ring.

"I know leaving you with your grandma without notice wasn't the right thing to do," he said, still standing in the doorway.

My pulse quickened, and I spun the ring faster.

"I've not forced you or Kait to reconcile or come out here because I didn't want to set your mom off and make conditions at your house worse."

"What do you know of how things were with mom?"

He sighed. "We were married, you know. A lifetime ago, it

seems, but I remember how things were then. I know that with bipolar disorder, it's important to take your medication and have good communication with your doctor about symptoms and side effects, while she continued to work with her doctors through them."

"So, why did she want us to hide it from you?"

"I'm the one who made her get a diagnosis, for the safety of you girls. I did talk with Nan and Pop at the time, and they agreed to have you stay with them because we all wanted to keep you girls in a stable home. I don't know why your mother would tell you to hide it from me, but she wasn't well."

At the mention of Nan, my gaze dropped to my ring, which I kept spinning and spinning. My stomach lurched into my throat. My pulse hammered. "You knew she wasn't well...things at home were crazy...and you still left me anyway?" I pressed my fists into the bed.

Dad lifted his hands, taking a small step back. For a split second, I wanted to shove him out into the hall and shut the door.

He sighed and dragged both hands down his face. "It wasn't my best parenting moment. I didn't know how to integrate you into our life here. You were...acting out at school, and I didn't want to overwhelm Lorraine. I didn't know how to fix any of it. But I thought my mother, Grandma could."

Nan did fix me. "Nan loved me and wanted me around when you didn't." I jabbed a finger toward his chest.

He took a step closer. "Your grandparents wanted your mom to have custody so that they could have you close. Nan said Sandra was their daughter, and their responsibility to take care of her as well as you kids."

My head started to pound, and the room started to sway.

Why wouldn't they have told us any of this before?

"Nan and Pop always wanted us around. Pop taught us how to ride a bike. Nan cleaned our scraped knees. You were…I don't know where…and then suddenly you were with Lorraine and her family. And we heard from you on holidays, and then that one summer in Ocean City." My voice had risen without my permission, sharp and accusing. I tried to rein it in, but the words kept spilling out, too full to hold.

He glanced down at his feet, then lifted his eyes to mine. "I wasn't around, and not for lack of trying. Nan and Pop told me how my involvement upset your mom, and how that made things harder for you. We all agreed it'd be better for me to stay the holiday parent, so you had a stable, happy home. I did it out of love." He swallowed. "We can call Pop and Lana together if you want to confirm."

"No…I don't want to bother Pop. And I don't want to argue anymore either." I drew in a deep breath and let it out slowly, trying to smooth the crackling under my ribs.

"I forgive you for abandoning me in Virginia. It's taken a while, but Nan taught me to pray and read the Bible. That's how she *fixed* me. She taught me that even when it seemed you and Mom didn't care about me, the Lord will always love me. *Matthew 6:14-15 says if you forgive others when they sin against you, your heavenly Father will also forgive you. But if you do not forgive others their sins, your Father will not forgive your sins.* I forgive you. I'm here this summer because I can't be in my house without being reminded of Nan. But if you abandon me again, we're done," I said. My body was physically shaking, and I had to wipe the wetness from my eyes. After I got that off my chest, I felt lighter.

He leaned back against the dresser, ankles crossed. "Honey, you didn't need fixing. You needed a stable home life, and I didn't know how to give that to you. But I'm never going to abandon you again. I've learned my lesson. Lacy and Lexy have taught me a lot about being a parent. I may be their stepparent, but they feel like mine, too. And Nan was right to take you under her wing. You've grown into a beautiful young woman, and I'm lucky to have this second chance with you."

He stepped closer and opened his arms. I stood and hugged him. The emotions I'd been hoarding finally broke loose—Nan's death, Chara's accident, years of feeling unwanted. My chest shook against him as he patted my back. I took a shuddering breath. Maybe this summer won't be terrible after all. I pulled away, and he cleared his throat.

"I'll get you a tissue box," he said. He returned with it and sat beside me on the bed. I blew my nose as he rubbed my back. "I'll stay with you until you're ready to go downstairs."

After another blow of my nose, I went to wash my face in the hallway bathroom. I grabbed my new cellphone and headed down the stairs. Lorainne sat on the couch beside Dad. The fireplace mantel was lined with happy family photos—none of them including Kait or me. Our latest school pictures hung framed on the wall, just below a decorative photo of a lake.

"Lacy and Lexy are working until dinnertime," Lorainne said. "They're at different stores in the Chestnut Hill Mall. We figured we'd meet them in the food court for dinner. Does that work for you? Any food preferences?"

"I usually eat whatever."

Lorainne smiled. "Great. If you like shopping, I'm sure Lacy and Lexy can drive you over when they're not working."

Dad sat on the couch next to Lorainne and smirked. "More money out of my wallet."

Lorainne hit him with a throw pillow, and a laugh escaped me.

"Sometimes I have to keep him in line," she winked.

I laughed harder.

Dad stood up and jiggled the keys in his pocket. "Maybe we should go over early. I can grab a soda and get us a table at the food court, and you two can go to whatever stores you want before their break."

"Pillow hit some sense into you, huh?" Lorainne smiled, and they both laughed.

I nodded. "Sounds like a plan, I'll grab my purse."

They both stood to gather their things. Lorainne's long chestnut-brown hair, threaded with soft blonde highlights, was pulled into a single French braid. She wore a white linen business suit over a pale pink blouse, paired with white ballet flats. Her nails were perfectly manicured, and her makeup was flawless yet natural. She was beautiful, and, so far, exactly as kind as I remembered from that brief childhood encounter. As I pulled my purse from my bookbag, I couldn't help but wonder how different life might have been if Kait and I had grown up here instead.

When we reached the mall, my jaw dropped. It was enormous—easily three times the size of the Oak Haven Mall, with three full stories. Kait would love it here.

"This place is huge!" I said, still staring.

Dad grinned. "Lorainne, sweetie, why don't you give her a tour? I'll meet you both at the food court. Have fun."

She gave me a warm smile. "The bottom floor has the

stores Lexy likes—Abercrombie, Wet Seal, Express, Aeropostale, Hollister, Charlotte Russe, and Macy's."

I swiveled my head. "You've got everything here!"

"Old Navy and Sears take up most of the bottom part of this floor," she said as we took the escalator to the second floor. Because of the size, the building didn't feel crowded. The second floor had businesses specifically for babysitting. The Tot Spot was a large playroom for kids five and under, and next door was the Kids Corner for kids six to twelve.

As we kept walking, we came across the food court, and my dad sipped a soda. But he wasn't alone. My heart skipped a beat when I recognized who he was with. Dad waved. "Look who I found here!"

"Asa, good to see you," I smiled, giving him a hug. He towered over me as my body relaxed into the hug.

"Are you joining us for dinner?" Lorainne asked Asa.

He raised his hand and smiled. "No, I don't want to intrude."

Lorainne swatted his hand playfully. "You're never an intrusion."

He checked his watch. "I have a shift at the pharmacy starting in about twenty minutes, so I'm sorry I can't tonight, but maybe another time."

Lorainne smiled. "Definitely another time."

"Is the pharmacy in the mall too?" I asked.

Dad draped his arm around Lorainne's shoulder. "Oh yes, on the third floor."

"We hadn't gotten that far yet," I commented.

Asa slurped his soda. "It's easy to figure out once you get the hang of it. Stores on all levels, childcare on the second floor, pharmacy and urgent care on the third floor."

My eyebrows shot up as I leaned forward. "There's an urgent care in the mall? Ours doesn't have one of those."

Dad stood and waved to Lacy and Lexy across the food court, calling them over. "One-stop shopping here in Chestnut Hill."

Asa grabbed his empty cup. "I'm gonna head to work. So good to run into you all."

I gave him a quick side hug. "I have a cellphone now. Put your number in."

He did, quickly, and left as soon as Lexy made it to the table. I gave her a hug, but she was standoffish, though polite. Lacy dodged a few families trying to leave the food court and gave me a tight squeeze and grin as soon as she saw me. Lexy was Kait's height, and Lacy was my height. That's where the similarities ended. Lacy and Lexy had their mom's brown hair, but Lexy wore hers in a short cut while Lacy wore hers in a messy ponytail. Lacy wore a Taking Back Sunday t-shirt and black jeans, and Lexy wore a crisp white polo shirt with ironed black dress slacks.

Lacy took a bite of her chicken wrap and wiped her mouth. "Did I just see Asa leave?"

I played with my ring. "Yeah, he's heading to work."

Lacy raised her eyebrow. "That's interesting. I told him we'd be meeting up with you here. Maybe the timing just worked out with his work schedule." She shrugged and continued, "I'm glad you're here this summer. There's so much we can do."

I smiled. "I'm excited too." I glanced at Lexy. "Are you both working all summer?"

Lexy nodded, continuing to eat her salad while Lacy smiled. "Yes, but we can make time to spend with you." She glanced at Lexy. "Right, Lexy?"

Lexy nodded but avoided looking at me. Lacy seemed genuinely interested in having me stay this summer, while Lexy appeared bored by my presence.

Dad stood up and stretched. "Let me throw away your trash." He collected my tray and Lorainne's.

"I'll help," Lorainne offered, standing up. "Why don't you and I check out the jewelry store while the girls finish talking during their lunch break?"

Dad grimaced. "My wallet's hurting already."

Lorainne gave him a playful shove, and we all laughed. Once they were out of earshot, Lexy leaned in and murmured, "I can't believe you still talk to Asa."

"Why?"

Her mouth pinched, then she shook her head. "Nothing. It's just...he was such a nerd when I was in school. Hard to believe he's changed."

Lacy's jaw clenched. "Not everyone can be in the popular crowd."

Lexy shifted in her chair and then smoothed her shirt out. "And not everyone needs to be around someone strange like him." She stood up, gathering her trash. "Heading back to work. See you around."

Lacy stood up and pushed her chair in next. "I have to get back to work, too. Don't worry about what she said, she's just being a brat."

I laughed. *Lexy may have more in common with Kait than.*

My phone buzzed, and I recognized Elliott's number. I sent it to voicemail, promising myself I'd call him later. I lost my appetite, thinking about how I might enjoy time with my family here, without him. If only I could merge these two worlds.

12

asa

JUNE 23, 2003

Asa's lips curved into a smile as he spotted Mikaila making her way into the food court. Lacy had mentioned at graduation that she planned to visit for the summer, and he couldn't wait for his pharmacy shift to be over.

He nearly bumped into a customer, lost in thoughts of all the places he wanted to take Mikaila. The woman had auburn hair like Mikaila, was of average height, and petite build. She smiled at him. Her shirt didn't quite meet the top of her jeans, revealing a strip of her stomach.

"Sorry about that," he said, returning her smile.

"No problem. You're the guy who won the state chess championship for Chestnut Hill High, aren't you?"

His smile broadened as he ran his hands through his hair. "Yes, that was me. Do you go to Chestnut Hill High?"

She put her hands in her pockets and leaned forward. "Yeah, I was in 10th grade this year, and I'll be in 11th next year. Congratulations, by the way. My brother Ryan was on your team, and he talks so highly of you."

Asa's chest felt light. "You must be his sister, Rachel. Ryan was a great teammate, and I'm counting on him to carry the team to victory next year. If you're free tomorrow, I could show you some chess moves, or we could just grab lunch."

She smiled and tilted her head to the side. "Sure. Want to meet tomorrow around noon at the Pizza Pagoda?"

He nodded eagerly. "Yes, I'll be there. I love pizza."

"Me too. See you then, Asa."

He smiled as he walked into the stockroom, doing a silent fist pump. The lifting must be paying off—no one had paid attention to him before, he thought. His stomach sank at the realization that Mikaila was finally here; this was his chance to win her over. Now someone else was showing interest in him.

He smirked. *If she has Elliott, why can't I have Rachel? Mikaila will have to see that if others want me, she should want me too.*

When his shift ended, he texted Mikaila a good-night message: *Done with work for the night. Great running into you.*

He kept glancing at his phone all night while playing *Mythical Mayhem*, a multiplayer online role-playing game on his computer, but she didn't respond. He tapped his foot against the floor. *Probably too busy talking to Elliott. But by the end of summer, you'll be asking, "Elliott who?"*

* * *

The next day, Asa wore khakis and a polo shirt and waited for Rachel outside the Pizza Pagoda. He leaned against the stucco building and checked his watch. When he was a toddler, his parents had told him the place used to be a Chinese buffet, but it hadn't done well. The current owners bought it for a low price, kept the look—even the roof that looked like a pagoda—and served the best pizza in town.

He had arrived fifteen minutes early. Now she was five minutes late. *Should I have offered to pick her up? Should I have gotten her number first?* He shifted from one foot to the other, shaking out his hands. His mouth had gone dry as he checked his watch again. *Maybe she's just fashionably late,* he told himself, noticing the warmth of the sun on his skin.

A beat-up pick-up truck pulled into the parking lot and stopped in front of him. Asa recognized his former chess team-mate, Ryan, at the wheel. He offered a small smile and wave. Rachel said something he couldn't hear, then climbed out of the truck. She smiled as Asa held the restaurant door open for her.

"Sorry, I'm late. I had to wait for Ryan to bring me," Rachel said as Asa led the way inside.

"No worries," he murmured.

The smell of basil and oregano hit him as they made their way to the table. The lighting was dim, and the décor gave off old-Italy vibes: amber glass sconces on the walls, faux plaster finishes, and burgundy vinyl tablecloths. Framed photos of vintage

Italian towns—Amalfi, Venice, Rome—lined both walls. The restaurant wasn't crowded, making it easy to hear Dean Martin crooning softly in the background. They slid into a booth, and a waitress came over to take their drink orders and hand them menus. Asa licked his lips, unsure what to order. *Do I order a pie for us? Or let her decide?* He wondered.

Clearing his throat, Asa asked, "So…what looks good to you?"

Rachel set her menu on the table. "I usually get a salad with a slice of plain pizza."

He put his menu down and grinned. "You took the words right out of my mouth. That's usually what I get too."

The two of them shared a soft laugh before Asa asked. "So… what do you like to do for fun?"

Rachel shrugged. "I like hiking, reading, movies, running, going to the beach, ice skating—really, I'm up for anything. What about you?"

He tapped his leg under the table. "I like reading, movies, chess…and, of course, playing *Mythical Mayhem*."

"Do you play *Mythical Mayhem* with Ryan? He's on all the time."

Asa raised his eyebrow. "Really? I didn't know he played."

"All the time. I like being outside more. I'd rather explore a state park or find a waterfall than gaming."

I'm happier behind the scenes, controlling the outcome, he thought.

The waitress walked up with their food and slid it onto the table. *Just in time.*

Rachel daintily picked up her fork and ate her salad first. Asa followed suit. "Do you have any plans for this summer?" He asked.

She put her fork down, dabbing at her mouth. "I'm going to help my aunt on her farm. She has three horses and a pony. We give rides to the local camps in the area. What about you?"

Not hanging around horse manure.

Asa took a long sip of water. "Helping out your aunt sounds fun. I'll be working at the pharmacy this summer."

"Oh, nice. Well, I've gone to my aunt's farm every summer since I can remember. I love horses. Do you ride?"

Not large animals that could throw me to the ground.

Asa tapped his finger on his glass. "I have to say I haven't. I have gone hiking in the state parks. And I've camped in my Boy Scout days."

She giggled. "You were a Boy Scout?"

He held up two fingers in a small salute. "Scout's honor." She giggled again, which caused Asa to smile. "So…how into chess are you?"

Rachel gave a small smile. "I like that Ryan's good at it, but it's not really my thing."

Asa tilted his head. "Why not?"

She shrugged. "It takes so much time just to move a few pieces. I'd rather be outside, enjoying nature, you know?" She said, taking a sip of her water.

Asa had no idea what that was like. "Chess is all about strategy, outsmarting your opponent, proving you're the best. What could be better than that?"

Her smile faded. "Sunshine, fresh air, exercise. I don't want to sit still that long."

The waitress came over just in time, and before she could ask if they wanted dessert, Rachel said, "Check, please."

Strange, Asa thought.

But he dug his wallet out and paid the tab. "Why don't we walk back to my house, and I'll show you just how great chess really is." Asa grinned.

"Maybe another time." Rachel stood, smoothing out her shirt. "My brother's waiting for me outside."

As she headed for the door, Asa blurted, "Do you want to go to the movies sometime?"

She paused with her hand on the handle. "Uh…I think it's best if we just stay friends, you know? We don't really have much in common."

Then she pushed the door open, walked out, and climbed into her brother's truck before Asa could even respond. *Does she think she's better than me?* His body tensed. His teeth clenched as he trudged the six blocks back to his house—his mom had taken the car that afternoon.

He stomped up the stairs to his empty house and stormed into his room. Logging online, he searched for Ryan's username to add him on Mythical Mayhem. Ryan accepted almost immediately. Asa chuckled to himself. *Your sister thinks she's better than me? I'm going to prove her wrong.*

Timing his attacks perfectly, Asa unleashed chaos in the emerald forest, attacking Ryan at every twist and turn. Ryan tried blinking in and out of visibility, hiding, and every strategy in the game, but to no avail. His health bar dwindled to nothing, As Ryan's health bar dwindled to nothing, Asa took a long, deep breath, expanding his lungs to capacity, and landed the final blow. Asa stood up from his chair and raised his hands. *Who's better now?*

He heard his front door open and saw from his window that his mom had returned with the car. She went into the living room and turned on her favorite soap. Without waiting for her permission, he ran downstairs, grabbed the spare keys from the key ring by the fridge, and drove to Ryan's house. There he saw his old beat-up truck parked on the street. He drove to the next street over, parked, and acted like he was jogging. Opening his keys, he pulled out a switchblade and slashed the metal into the rubber tires on the driver's side. *Your sister forced me to do this.* He smiled, jogged back to his car, and drove to Mikaila's next. He knocked on the front door, losing his train of thought when Mikaila opened it, wearing a pair of shorts and a tank top.

"Uh, sorry for not calling first," he stammered, "but I was wondering if you've ever been to Ocean Beach Park and if you'd like to tag along with me today?"

"Today, like right now?" She blinked.

He ran his hand through his hair, shrugging. "Yeah. Can you come? I really need to get away."

She chuckled softly and stepped back into the living room, inviting him inside. "Why don't you come in? I'll get ready, and then we can go."

Asa trailed in behind her and sank into the couch, waiting as Mikaila got ready. His eyes wandered to the mantel, where photos of Lexy, Lacy, and the family were neatly arranged. To his left, the dining room looked untouched, as if no one ever used it—a white rug, a solid wood table, and a crystal chandelier gleaming.

Soon Makaila came down the stairs. "I'm ready."

Asa pushed up from the couch and stood admiring her. "Do you need to ask Mark or Lorainne before we leave?"

She swung her purse over her shoulder. "They're at the movies. I texted them, and they said no problem."

He smiled. "After you, then." He gestured toward the door only so he could admire her from the back.

* * *

They cruised down the highway, with the windows down, letting the breeze slap them in the face. Asa gestured toward the radio. "Pick whatever you want."

Mikaila smiled, turning it to the station that played today's greatest hits. Asa tried to focus on the road, but he couldn't stop thinking about how unbelievable it was that she was actually here with him. After all those years of wishing she'd be in Connecticut, she finally was.

Mikaila glanced at him. "What made you want to go to the beach all of a sudden?"

Asa drummed his fingers on the steering wheel, shrugging. "Change of scenery. Thought I'd show you somewhere you might not have seen before." His eyes met hers for a brief second, and the two of them shared a soft smile before he took the main highway. From the corner of his eye, he saw her head pressed against the back of the seat, auburn hair blowing in the breeze, and a smile plastered on her face.

He stole a quick glance at her. "I'm sorry about Nan. How are you holding up? How's it been so far at your dad's?"

She met his eyes briefly. "Thanks. I'm good. It's okay here... just getting used to sleeping in a room that's not my own. Lorainne is so nice. My dad's...he's okay. We had a talk, and I'm going to try to put the past behind us."

Asa's shoulders relaxed. If she made up with her dad, maybe she'd stay after the summer. "That's great. Is there anything on your bucket list you want to see or do this summer...something we can cross off together?"

She tapped her finger to her chin, a playful look on her face. "I don't know yet, but Lacy mentioned something about a bonfire and camping. I've never gone camping before."

"Good thing you're sitting next to a Boy Scout. I can help you with that."

"Boy Scout?"

He held up his fingers. "Scout's honor. Camping...that's easy. Anything else?"

"I want to find a church to go to."

"I can ask around. I don't think you want to go to my mom's. The sermons are three hours long, and they don't even have snacks."

She gasped, clutching her chest. "No snacks? That's unholy."

Asa nodded, smiling. "Sacrilegious, really. Yeah, I can help with this list."

They pulled into the mini golf parking lot and made their way around the building to the sand. The beach was packed with people under beach umbrellas. Mikaila picked a spot, pulled out a beach towel, and laid it on the warm sand before plopping down.

She looked up at Asa, shading her eyes from the sun. "You didn't bring a towel?"

"Uh...I guess I didn't really think about it," he said, rubbing the back of his neck. Mikaila let out a laugh. Asa shaded his eyes against the glare of the sun, and Mikaila patted the towel. He joined her, sitting down beside her so close they were shoulder to shoulder.

Mikaila leaned in slightly. "Why come to the beach without a towel? Did you at least bring a swimsuit?"

He chuckled nervously. "No."

She giggled. "What did you think we were going to do then?"

He shrugged. "I usually just come for the arcade. Want to play a few games?" Asa glanced over his shoulder at the boardwalk littered with shops.

They trudged through the warm sand to the sidewalk and over to the arcade. It was mostly filled with teenagers and pre-teens, the air heavy with cheap body spray and pizza. The tiled floor was streaked with sand and the residue of years-old gum. The games ranged from Pac-Man to Dance Dance Revolution.

Asa leaned close and whispered, "We're the oldest ones here."

Mikaila laughed. "Who cares? Let's play anyway." And she tugged his wrist forward.

Asa headed to the basketball game and, thanks to his height, had no trouble sinking several baskets. Tickets spilled out with a satisfying clatter. "I'm going to do this one again. You want to join?"

She shook her head. "That's all you."

Instead, Mikaila exchanged some cash for quarters and suggested, "Let's go to the Skee Ball machine."

"Sure," Asa said, trailing alongside Mikaila.

Mikaila grabbed a ball and launched it up the ramp. "Not bad," Asa commented. "But you're going to have to do better than that if you want to take my title of Skee-Ball champ."

Mikaila smirked, her eyebrows raised in a challenge. "Let's go."

"Oh, you're on."

But Asa missed his first two throws, and Mikaila stood idle, teasing him for it. Soon her ball landed in the thousand-point. Asa ran a hand through his hair, trying to remain focused, and made his next two shots in the four-hundred ring. "Beat that."

Mikaila glanced at him and rolled her next ball into the five-hundred ring, smirking. "You were saying?" She crossed her arms over her chest.

The first round ended, and she had won by over a thousand points. He fed more quarters into the machine, looking at her. "Beginner's luck." He teased. Asa took the next round, but she won the following three.

He leaned back slightly, curious. "Does your school have a Skee-Ball team? Where did you develop that technique?"

Mikaila chuckled. "No, Elliott and I go to the arcade in Ocean City sometimes for date nights. We play Skee Ball the most."

Asa forced a smile. "That's fun." *Of course, this is a place that reminds you of him.* At the mention of Elliott, Asa felt a burning sensation in the pit of his stomach, and his throat became dry. *It should be me you're having a date night with.*

"Let's try Pac-Man. It's clear now." Asa said, tugging on Mikaila's arm. She followed him only for Asa to beat her twice. Mikaila checked her Nokia phone.

"Do you need to get back?" Asa glanced, trying to read her screen, but Mikaila quickly put the phone away.

"Eventually. Lacy promised to drive me to the mall tonight. She's fun to hang out with."

"Let's see what we can get with our tickets." Asa gestured toward the cashier. They walked over to the cashier, who didn't look old enough to drive. "What can we get with these?" Asa asked, placing all the tickets down on the counter.

The cashier counted up the tickets and pointed to the small row of stuffed animals. Asa turned to Mikaila. "I think you need a blue bear with a Connecticut T-shirt. Pretty sure you don't have one of those yet."

Mikaila laughed. "Somehow I don't."

The cashier scooped the tickets up and walked over to collect the blue bear sporting a Connecticut t-shirt. He handed it over to Asa, who passed it to Mikaila.

"A little reminder of today. Let's walk the boardwalk a bit before we head back."

Mikaila clutched the bear to her chest, smiling. "Sounds good." The two of them walked out of the arcade and along the boardwalk, Asa's eyes continued to wander from the storefronts to Mikaila and back. "Not as fancy as the Ocean City boardwalk, but we have great pizza and ice cream."

Mikaila smiled, taking it all in. "It's nice to have just food and chair rentals. Who needs to go shopping at the beach?"

"Don't tell the owner in Ocean City that." Asa nudged her with his elbow.

She giggled. "Our secret."

They passed families with soft-serve cones and beachgoers searching for the perfect spot. Otherwise, the boardwalk was mostly quiet mid-day.

Mikaila's phone buzzed again.

And Asa glanced at her pocket. "You can get that. We can turn back if you want."

She pulled it out and started texting as they walked toward the exit of the boardwalk. "It's Lacy. I'll just let her know we'll be back soon."

Asa smiled. "Lacy's cool. I'm sure you'll have a good time with her. If you want, I'll do some digging and send you some options for different churches."

"Sure. Just text me when you find something."

Asa's stomach fluttered. "I can do that," he said as they climbed into his car and made the trip back to her house. He turned up the radio as "Hanging by a Moment" came on, and he hummed along. Mikaila joined in, and he glanced at her when the chorus came on before belting out the lyrics off-key, making her laugh as she sang along.

Asa rolled the windows down, and they had their own little karaoke session in the car. When they got back to her house, he walked her to the door as she clutched her new plush bear. He leaned in for a hug, and she returned a slow, side hug. He walked back to his car, whistling and smiling as he drove back home.

Once home, he moved a pawn on his chessboard and logged into *Mythical Mayhem*. Ryan had messaged him while he was out: *My tires were slashed a couple hours ago.*

Asa laughed. *That sucks. Beaten in here and your wheels take a beating...sounds like a rough day.*

13

chara

JUNE 24, 2003

Chara helped her dad count his repetitions of arm raises during his physical therapy session. He wore a white T-shirt and black gym shorts, blending in with the other patients working on their rehab. The exercise room had a tiled floor, handrails screwed into the white walls for safety, and the faint scent of lemon cleaner lingering in the air. Free weights were lined up against the opposite wall next to a treadmill and recumbent bike, while behind them sat five padded treatment tables.

"That makes twenty," Chara said.

The physical therapist came over and gave him an approving nod. "Time for ice," she said.

Ty grinned. "My favorite part."

Chara stood next to the table and looked at him. "Is the treatment working?"

"I can put my shirt on by myself now. And I've been doing speech therapy. I think I sound a little better."

Chara placed a hand on his shoulder. "You are sounding clearer. I just thought you put the beer down."

"Never. How else would I keep my sanity through all this?" Ty winked.

He felt her right arm, and she subtly shifted her weight so he wouldn't notice the slight discomfort it caused.

"Are you still keeping up with your exercises?"

Chara had been discharged from physical therapy a few weeks ago, but still had some strengthening to do. "Yeah, but it still bothers me now and then."

He grimaced, biting his lip. "Hopefully, the pain will go away completely."

Chara knew he felt guilty about her lingering discomfort from the accident, but she couldn't bring herself to admit the guilt that ate at her, or tell him she thought she'd caused it. When the timer signaled the end of his session, she busied herself by handing the ice pack to the technician and calling a cab for them.

* * *

At his condo, they ordered Chinese takeout and settled on the couch to watch *The Pelican Brief.* Chara loved the book, and

Ty enjoyed discussing the legal aspects of the story.

Chara cracked open her fortune cookie. "No fortune," she gasped. "We should get our money back."

Ty took a bite of his fried rice. "Good luck with that. Tell me again why you love this movie so much?"

Chara raised her eyebrows. "How could you not? It's fictional, but the themes—freedom of speech, making sure the press isn't influenced by politicians, ethics, preventing abuse of executive power, and political corruption—ensuring politicians and the justice system aren't bought are always relevant."

Ty pursed his lips. "I'm glad you have a high moral standard, but that doesn't always translate to a high bank balance."

Chara rolled her eyes. "I'm not going into law. I can't, because I can't defend people or companies who intentionally harm others."

"So be the judge." He smiled.

Chara tilted her head. "And then I have to go with either the jury, which could be wrong or bought, or whatever the defendants plead. Either way, justice still isn't served."

Chara had a point. After the movie ended, her dad checked his watch. "You should catch the next bus. I don't want you out too late."

She pushed off the couch. "Alright." Chara groaned. She hugged her father goodbye and walked to the bus stop around the corner from his condo. The sun had set behind the trees, lighting the treetops a warm orange. She stepped onto the bus, claimed an empty seat by the window, and popped in her headphones. *Stuck* by Stacie Orrico filled her ears with its breathy, soulful tones and infectious melody.

Chara walked into her empty house, kicked off her shoes,

and flopped onto her bed with the remote. She stared blankly at the TV, watching *The Bourne Identity*. Her mom was out on a date with someone else—not Howard. James. Jim? It was hard to keep them straight anymore. With nothing else to do, she ate popcorn alone and signed onto Messenger.

Asa: Hey beautiful

Chara: Hey there, handsome.

Asa: What are you doing tonight?

Chara: I'm in PJs, eating popcorn, watching *Bourne Identity*.

Asa: Good movie.

Chara: It is. I love a good mystery.

Asa: I have a mystery for you

Chara: You do? What is it?

Asa: If I tell you, it won't be a mystery anymore...

Chara: OH, I see what you did there-clever!

Asa: Not even a lol? I'm slipping.

Chara: It is kind of funny, so here it is...lol.

Asa: I don't want pity laughs.

Chara: Ok, then no lol for you. What are you up to tonight?

Asa: Nothing much.

Chara: No friends to hang out with

Asa: The one I have is working.

Chara: You only have one friend?

Asa: Well, it sounds bad when you say it like that

Chara: I find that hard to believe.

Asa: I'm a chess champion, not really in the popular crowd

Chara: I'm not in the popular crowd, and I have more than one friend.

Asa: It's because I'm nerdy

Chara: No, you're not.

Asa: lol thank you.

Asa: How's your arm?

Chara: Still hurts at times, and the skin tone isn't the same as the rest of the body. Plus the scars from the surgeries…I'm wearing long-sleeve shirts from now until forever. Thanks for asking.

Asa: You're still sexy, regardless.

Chara: Me? Really?

Asa: Yes.

Chara: Thanks, handsome. I'm gonna go now, though.

Asa: Talk to you soon, I hope.

Chara quickly signed off. She wondered if he was serious. Her heartbeat quickened, and a lightheaded flutter ran through her. She lay down to sleep, unaware her mom had returned.

The next morning, she heard her mom making coffee in the kitchen. She found Astrid by the coffee pot, wearing her green satin pajama set. Chara rubbed her eyes and yawned.

Astrid smiled, pouring a cup of hot coffee for herself. "Have a good visit with your dad?"

"Yeah. Therapy's helping him get better." Chara said, rubbing at her arm. Sometimes in the morning, after tossing and turning in the night, she had some minor aches.

Astrid's eyes trailed down to her arm, noting the discomfort written on Chara's face. "Maybe you should do more exercises, take the ache away."

Chara squinted. "It's fine, Mom."

"You know, the more you do the exercises, the sooner you'll heal."

"Yeah," Chara mumbled, grabbing a bowl from the cabinet. Astrid sat at the kitchen table with her cup of coffee as Chara made herself a bowl of cereal. "Going out today?"

Astrid yawned into her coffee mug. "I'm heading to the mall in a few hours. Want to come?"

"No thanks. I was going to see if Kristin wants to go to the boardwalk."

Astrid took another sip of her coffee. "Sounds like a good plan."

* * *

Chara had finished her breakfast and then showered and gotten ready for the day before she dialed Kristin's number. "Hey, Chara," Kristin answered.

"Hey. Wanna go to the boardwalk later?"

"Sure. Let me ask my mom if she can give us a ride. One sec..." A short pause, then Kristin came back. "We'll pick you up in an hour."

From the living room, Astrid called, "Heading out now!"

Chara yelled from her doorway, "Sounds good, Mom!" Then Chara heard the front door shut.

She rifled through her closet and settled on a denim skort with a slightly torn and frayed side pocket—rock-and-roll enough for her taste—paired with a black T-shirt and her favorite Skechers.

By the time Kristin's mom pulled up in their minivan, air conditioning blasting and Christian radio playing, Chara was ready.

Kristin hopped out and gave her a quick hug. "I'll sit back here with you." Her light blue T-shirt read, *If you think I'm short, you should see my patience.* Which made Chara snicker. They climbed into the back and buckled their seatbelts. "Mom, can you turn down the radio a little, please?" Kristin asked.

Her mom lowered the volume. "Sorry about that."

"Great T-shirt," Chara commented, pointing at the shirt with a grin.

Kristin glanced down, grinning. "Thanks. I like your outfit too."

Mrs. McGill cleared her throat. "Matches her mood."

Chara chuckled. "I'm sure my mom would say I need one of these, too."

Mrs. McGill pulled over and dropped them off on 11th Street. "Kristin, call me when you're ready for me to come back. I'm going to get a pedicure."

"Thanks, Mrs. McGill." Chara smiled.

"No problem."

Chara and Kristin made their way from the street onto the boardwalk. It was a mildly warm summer day with a light ocean breeze. The smells of cotton candy, funnel cake, and pizza hit their noses, while the screams of kids on the rollercoaster filled their ears.

Passing the soft-serve ice cream stand, Kristin turned to her. "Have you talked to Mikaila lately?"

Chara massaged her right wrist, wincing at the soreness before meeting Kristin's gaze. "No, you?"

Kristin's eyes were shaded by her sunglasses, but her mouth was a tight line. "No. I thought I would have by now."

Chara pursed her lips, frowning. "I hope no news is good news, because Astrid wouldn't let me take a bus there alone to back her up if I had to."

Kristin tucked her hair behind her ear. "My mom wouldn't either."

Chara stared out at the ocean as they strolled along. "I just hope Mikaila's alright."

Kristin slowed to admire a pair of sunglasses for sale. "How's your summer going so far?"

"Alright, I guess. I started working part-time at Food Tide as a cashier."

Kristin turned to her, new sunglasses perched on her nose. "Earning money is always good. You can buy more things. Like these sunglasses. What do you think of these? Do they look good on me?"

Boys around their age zipped past on rollerblades, blasting Simple Plan loud enough to be heard through their headphones. One boy in a black shirt, long hair, and ripped jeans shouted back to Kristin, "Hey! Great shirt!"

Chara laughed, turning back to Kristin. "I think the glasses look fine, but the shirt is an obvious keeper."

Kristin returned them to the display with a sigh. She didn't have the money to purchase them. They walked to the end of the boardwalk, turned, and headed back. The afternoon sun blazed overhead, the temperature climbed, and the breeze had all but died.

Passing an artist drawing caricatures, Kristin pointed. "That's what our moms need. A caricature of us."

Chara smiled. "Yes, framed front and center in our living rooms. What are your plans for the rest of the summer?"

"My parents signed me up for Intro to Networking at Oak Haven Community College."

Chara tilted her head. "That sounds advanced…and very techie."

"It's way better than what our school offers. The other

students actually care about being there, so I'm learning from them and the professor."

Chara raised an eyebrow. "Any cute guys?" She asked, nudging Kristin's arm with her elbow.

Kristin's eyebrows lifted, and she lowered her voice. "There's one that reminds me of Orlando Bloom. His name's Dylan Caldwell, and he's showing me how to track IP addresses."

Chara whispered back, looping their arms as they continued down the boardwalk, "Is that against the rules?"

Kristin smiled. "Technically, yes, an invasion of privacy. But…there's a way to not get caught, and he's teaching me how. I want to become a web server administrator, and this knowledge will impress my future interviewers."

Chara smirked. "I'm guessing in this class you don't have to wear your Captain T-shirt?"

Kristin grinned. "No, but if I get stuck with dimwits in my classes next year at Oak Haven High, it'll make a comeback."

Chara chuckled. "Speaking of shirts, I shouldn't have worn black today. I'm dying."

Kristin nodded. "Let's walk back fast. My shirt's sticking to me, too. I'll call my mom to pick us up."

They hurried back to Kristin's mom's van parked on Fifteenth Street, the sun sapping their energy until they finally sank into the cool air conditioning. Mrs. McGill smiled as they climbed in. "How was the boardwalk today?"

Chara grinned. "Fun. Kristin's shirt even got a shout-out from some boy."

Kristin's cheeks flushed pink.

Mrs. McGill raised her eyebrows. "I'm assuming he didn't stick around for a chat?"

Kristin scoffed. "No, he didn't, Mom."

She fiddled with the radio dial. "I'm just kidding, dear."

Chara heard the station shift from pop to country before settling on the oldies station, playing the Beach Boys. "How was your pedicure?"

Mrs. McGill tapped the steering wheel in time to the music. "It was relaxing. They have a great selection of colors at the Ocean Breeze Spa."

Kristin's mom pulled up at Chara's driveway. Chara smiled. "Thanks for the ride."

Mrs. McGill looked at her through the rearview mirror. "No problem, Chara."

She leaned over and hugged Kristin. "Thanks for a fun afternoon."

Kristin hugged her back, sweeping her brown hair from her eyes. "Thanks for getting me out of the house."

Chara walked inside and saw a note on the table: he was visiting a friend—a female friend this time—and wouldn't be home for dinner.

Alone again, she ordered from Bamboo Garden, her favorite Chinese restaurant. She ate her chicken pad Thai, queued up her LimeWire playlist on her computer, and let the sounds of Alicia Keys fill the room. Then she signed into Messenger. Asa messaged her immediately, and she smiled.

14

asa

JUNE 28, 2003

The rain poured, forcing the windshield wipers to work twice as hard. Eighties music blared, nearly drowning out the engine. Asa's shift at the pharmacy was over, and he looked forward to talking to Chara again soon.

He pulled into the driveway beside his dad's Cadillac DeVille and stepped inside. In the living room, he was surprised to see his dad on the couch.

Asa raised his eyebrows. "Not working this weekend?"

His dad turned. "Hey, Asa. The flight was canceled today because of the weather, so we rescheduled the client. Besides, now I get to have a date night with my best girl."

Asa nodded. His dad sold technology to companies along the East Coast and was often out of town.

"Please take your wet shoes off before tracking mud all over my house."

Asa's lips pressed into a fine line. "Sure, Mom."

Asa slipped off his shoes by the door. His dad turned and smiled. "Thanks, son. Don't want you making more work for your mother. You know how I am about a clean house."

He nodded and headed upstairs. His dad might not be home much, but his mother spent countless hours making sure everything was the way he liked it.

Asa could vaguely remember his dad yelling at her in the kitchen when he was six. She'd been promoted at her office job and didn't have dinner ready when he got home.

"I don't work all day for you to make coffee and chit-chat with other men at the office!" His dad had shouted.

Her face had flushed red, arms waving. "We can't afford this house on just your salary alone! Do you want me not to work?"

His dad's face had turned red, and he had crept closer, gripping her shoulders. "You do what I tell you to do if you want to stay here with us. I'll figure out the bills. You figure out dinner." After that, Asa remembered his dad traveling more and his mom working less, but doing more cleaning around the house.

He slipped into his bedroom and closed the door. Changing out of his wet clothes, he pulled on a pair of khakis and a button-down shirt. Then he texted Mikaila: *Looking forward to bowling tomorrow.*

He moved a pawn on his chessboard in the corner, then set his cellphone on his desk, logged into Messenger, and messaged Chara.

Asa: Hey. I missed you.

Chara: Hey. Missed you too.

Asa: How are you doing today?

Chara: Good. You? You have any more mysteries today?

Asa: Good. I do have mysteries. But I'm not sharing them today because I can't get a laugh.

Chara: HAHA

Asa: I'm not taking pity laughs.

Chara: Well then, I'm not sure I have anything for you.

Asa: Good thing you're sexy, or I might stop talking to you.

Chara: Good thing you're hot or I'd stop talking to YOU

Asa: You think I'm hot?

Chara: Yep.

Asa: Why don't we chat with our webcams turned on?

Chara: Ok.

Asa: Ok good.

Chara turned on her webcam, and Asa flashed her a smile. She wore a tight tank top and a pair of blue shorts. Her hair was pulled into a messy ponytail, untamed curls framed her face.

Asa: What is a beautiful girl like you doing alone on a Saturday night?

Chara: My mom is out with a friend, and I just got home from work. Why are you home on a Saturday night?

Asa: I just got home from work.

Chara: What are your plans after this summer?

Asa: Chestnut Hill Community College. You?

Chara: Senior year of Oak Haven High School.

Asa: One more year to go. I could look at you all night long.

Chara: One more year. I could look at YOU all night long.

Asa: Really? Do you know that just looking at you turns me on?

Chara smiled, and her cheeks flushed beet red. Asa grinned, running his fingers through his hair. He enjoyed watching her get a little anxious around him.

Chara: My mom came home and is calling me to do something. Talk to you soon.

Then she shut her camera off and logged out of Messenger. He tapped his feet on the carpet. Getting her to break down her walls would be a challenge. Asa smirked and moved a knight on his chessboard. Chess required patience and the ability to play the long game—skills he excelled at. He'd crack Chara's wall down soon enough.

* * *

The next afternoon, he pulled into Mikaila's driveway. Before opening the car door, he checked himself in the mirror. His white polo and black pants were spotless, and his hair was tamer than usual. He ran a hand through it one last time and walked up to the door, ringing the doorbell.

Lorainne opened it with a smile. Even on the weekend, she was dressed to the nines—pressed white pants, a pink blouse, and matching pink pumps. "Asa, come on in! Lacy, Mikaila... Asa's here!"

Asa smiled. "Thanks, Mrs. E. Having a good weekend?"

"We are," She smiled as she led him to the living room and gestured for him to sit. "And how about yourself?"

Asa grinned, plopping back on the couch. "Great. Working

and getting to hang out with Mikaila and Lacy now. Couldn't ask for more."

Mikaila came down the stairs first, wearing light blue jeans and a pale green t-shirt from Old Navy. His stomach flip-flopped as she brushed her auburn hair out of her face and smiled at him.

He smiled, trying not to make it obvious he was checking her out. "Hey. Lacy ready yet?"

She looked behind her. "Lacy, you ready?"

He heard a few footsteps, and then Lacy emerged at the top of the staircase. "Hey Asa, I'll be right down."

"Sure. Take your time."

"Don't tell her that or we'll never leave," Mikaila whispered teasingly.

Lorainne, seated in the living room, laughed. "You found out Lacy's secret, huh? She takes forever to get ready and makes it look like she just threw herself together. Lexy, on the other hand...she could be runway ready in ten minutes."

"That's a skill," Mikaila commented.

Lacy plopped down the last stair. "That's because Lexy doesn't care what people think about her."

Lorainne raised her eyebrow. "And you do?"

Lacy put her hands on her hips. "It takes effort to look like this, okay?" She gestured to her ripped jeans, a black AC/DC t-shirt. The neckline was cut off and sliced, while her belt displayed metallic spikes.

"I think everyone looks great. And you'll look even better when you're smiling at my victory." Asa teased from the couch.

The room filled with laughter. "Have fun, kids. Shame Lexy doesn't want to go." Lorainne sighed.

Lacy's eyebrows drew together. "Lexy, have fun? When was the last time that happened?"

"Ready?" Mikaila said to Asa. Asa led them out the door to his mom's car and opened the door for both of them. "I'll let you ladies fight over shotgun."

"I'll sit in the back with Miki," Lacy said.

Mikaila chuckled. "Yeah, we don't need to sit next to *you*."

Asa put a hand to his chest, feigning sadness. "Fine."

When they arrived, he opened the door to the Bowling and Billiards Alley. The scent of pizza and fries drifted out, and Michael Jackson's *Remember the Time* could barely be heard over the chatter of kids arguing over bowling balls. Through the door on the left, the billiards area was crowded—teens monopolizing the tables during the day, adults taking over at night.

Asa headed to the cashier, but before he could pay, Mikaila nudged him aside, and Lacy blocked his way. At first, he was confused, but then he realized what they'd done. "You didn't have to pay for me."

Mikaila smiled, making his stomach flip. "We didn't. Mark and Lorainne did."

"I'll pay them back. I can't ask them to do that."

Lacy shrugged. "I'm sure they don't mind."

Mikaila tugged Asa forward, and he fell in step behind her. Mikaila and Lacy picked the lightest ball each. "I think that's for the kids." Asa teased them.

Lacy placed a hand on her hips. "I think you're just afraid of losing."

Asa smirked. "I'm not going easy on you now. That's for sure."

Mikaila laughed as she typed their names into the system.

"I'll go first!" She volunteered for tribute. She grabbed the pink ball, pulled her arm back, and released. The ball dropped behind her, startling the couple at the next lane. She covered her mouth in embarrassment.

Lacy nearly fell out of her chair laughing, and Asa, sitting across from her, bit his cheeks to keep from laughing. He got up and grabbed a ball. "Here...let me help you. The pins are over there, Miki."

"I know that." She scuffed, though she couldn't help but smile.

"These arrows point to the pins. For the first round, aim for the middle. Pull your arm back like this," Asa instructed. "Follow through and then release."

He stepped back toward the chairs to give her space. She did as he said, pulling back, following through, and releasing, but the ball slid straight into the gutter. She spun around, pouting, and gave a thumbs-down.

Asa chuckled at the sight of her and gave her a thumbs-up. "It went in the right direction this time."

Lacy laughed, covering her mouth, while Mikaila's second throw barely knocked down the last pin on the left.

Mikaila walked back to the chairs, shoulders slumped. "Lacy, I hope you can do better."

Lacy wiggled her eyebrows. "We'll wipe the floor with him, don't you worry." She lined up, pulled her arm back, and sent the ball down the lane with a satisfying smack. All but two pins on opposite sides fell. She turned around, smirking at Asa.

Pulling out the next ball, she sent it straight down the middle—missing entirely. She smacked her leg and whined, "I'm just warming up, Asa!"

"Sure, you are." Asa laughed.

"She was. You'll see." Mikaila nudged his arm with her elbow. Soon it was Asa's turn. He stood, grabbed his ball, and sauntered to the lane. Pulling back and releasing, he knocked down seven of the ten pins. Turning around, he said, "That was my warm-up, too."

The girls sneered. "Sure, it was."

He grabbed his second ball and sent it soaring down the lane and knocked over the last three on the left side. He turned around with a smile. "You were saying?"

Mikaila got up from her seat. "I was just saying that was practice earlier." She grabbed her ball, closed her eyes, pulled back, and released. The ball glided toward the pins, knocking down six—the center and right side. She turned, grinning. Asa clapped for her, and Lacy fist pumped.

Mikaila picked up her second ball, lined up with the arrow on the lane, closed her eyes, whispered a quick prayer, and released. Three of the remaining four pins fell. "Score!" She raised her hands and ran over to high-five Lacy.

Midway through the game, the waitress came over to take their orders. Asa and Lacy each got a Diet Pepsi, and Mikaila chose a strawberry lemonade. Asa was leading with 42 points, Lacy with 36, and Mikaila trailed behind with 29.

The bowling alley had grown busier, kids in the middle lanes celebrating a birthday. Their squeals were barely drowned out by the faint strains of Hanson's "Mmmbop" over the radio.

Mikaila's turn came, and Asa watched her stride down the lane and deliver a strike with far more confidence than when she'd started. He grinned, clapping as he cheered her on.

The waitress arrived with their drinks, and Mikaila sipped

her fruity beverage as Lacy knocked down eight pins and walked back for another ball. "Did Lexy stay home because of me? Or because she doesn't like bowling?" Mikaila asked Lacy.

Lacy tilted her head, looking at Asa. "She hasn't hung out with us in years. I can't really remember when it started. But that's just Lexy for you. Whatever it is, it has nothing to do with you."

Asa tapped his foot and set his soda down. "It's no secret I used to have a crush on her, and that probably made her uncomfortable when I asked her out. I assumed that's why she didn't hang out with us. I agree, nothing to do with you, Miki."

Lacy nodded while Mikaila toyed with the ring on her finger.

"Doesn't hurt my feelings. I'm here if she wants to be friends. If not, I get to torture Lacy and you with my awesome bowling skills." Asa joked.

Lacy and Mikaila chuckled. Then it was Lacy's turn. When she returned, Asa said, "Looks like I'll be undefeated once again today."

Lacy playfully punched his arm as she passed. "How could anyone not want to be friends with such a humble guy?"

Mikaila laughed, and Asa pulled his eyebrows together. "How offensive."

At the end of the game, Asa had won with 105 points to Lacy's 75 and Mikaila's 60. On the ride back, Queen's *We Are the Champions* came on the radio, and Asa played it loudly just to tease them more over his win. He pulled into their driveway, turned off the car, and the three of them stepped out.

Lacy rolled her eyes. "If this is how you are after winning a bowling game, I can only imagine how you react when you win a chess tournament."

Mikaila giggled.

"I have no idea what you're talking about." Asa turned to Mikaila. "Hope you had fun today."

Lacy linked her arm with Mikaila and grabbed the door handle. "She had a great day, right?"

Mikaila smiled widely. "It was fun. I'll talk to you later, Asa." Her cell phone buzzed in her pocket, and before the door closed, he heard her answer, "Hey Elliott."

Asa arrived back at his empty house and spotted a note on the table: his parents had gone out and wouldn't be back until after dinner. He headed to his room, closed the door, and signed onto Messenger.

Asa: Hey, Beautiful

Chara: Hey, Handsome

Asa: I liked our conversation yesterday.

Chara: Me too

Asa: Can you turn your camera on again?

Chara: I'm just lounging around, so I'm a hot mess, but sure.

Asa: Hot you are!

Chara: Camera on.

Chara turned her camera on, and she was wearing a black spandex tank top with thin straps and a pair of denim shorts.

Asa: I like your tank top

Chara: Thanks

Asa: Can you lower it a little?

Chara: Umm. I don't think that's a good idea.

She tucked a stray curl behind her ear.

Asa: Just a little. Is someone home with you?

Chara: No...

Asa: It's just you and me. Our secret. ...so why not?

Chara leaned forward, dipping her tank top a little, but making it not obvious.

Asa's pulse quickened as he smiled.

Asa: I'm going to be thinking about you all night long now.

Chara: Really? Maybe you should lower your top

Asa stripped his shirt off on camera, displaying his washboard abs to Chara, who was grinning from ear to ear.

Chara: Wow. Now I'll be thinking about you all night long.

Asa: Really?

Chara: Absolutely. You could be the Sexiest Man of the Year.

Asa: Haha, no, I couldn't.

Chara: You're selling yourself short.

Asa: I have to go run an errand, but we'll talk soon.

Chara: Enjoy your dreams tonight.

Asa: You too.

Asa logged off Messenger and smirked at his reflection in the mirror. He pushed back from his computer chair and moved a rook on his chessboard.

15

chara

Chara trudged home from Food Tide, peeled off her uniform, and collapsed onto her bed. She opened her journal, her mind still lingering on the last conversation with Asa.

He's so hot, I can't believe Mikaila doesn't see it. I can't tell her about what he asked me to do, because she'll probably throw a Bible verse at me.

The house phone rang. Her mom was still out with friends, so Chara snatched it up. "Hello?"

"Hey."

Chara closed her journal, as if Mikaila could read her words over the phone. "Hey. It's been a while. How are things?"

"They're good. I just wanted to say hi."

Chara sat up and tossed the journal to the end of the bed. "Things going well with your dad? Or do I need to rescue you?"

Mikaila laughed. "No rescue needed. Things are actually good. Lorraine's been great. My dad and I talked when I first got here, and...he's making an actual effort. I've been hanging out with Lacy, too. Lexy hasn't really been around, or if she is, she's avoiding us."

"I miss you so much. Kristin and I went to the boardwalk, but it wasn't the same without you."

"Did you know there's a boardwalk here? Doesn't have the stores ours does, but it's almost like home."

"Really? Did Lacy take you?"

"Oh, no, I went with Asa."

Both of Chara's eyebrows shot up, a sharp jolt tightening her stomach. "He's so hot, Miki. You need to bring him here at the end of the summer. But wait...how does Elliott feel about this?"

"I've barely gotten to talk to Elliott because of his work schedule, so when I did, it just didn't come up. But we went bowling with Lacy, so it's not like I'm just hanging out with him alone all the time."

Chara let out a sigh of relief. "Good. You don't want Elliott to get jealous over nothing."

"And Asa's going to help me find a church here to attend. You know Elliott won't be jealous over that."

Chara's stomach began to burn again. "Right. Of course not."

"I have to go now. Miss you. See you soon!"

And the line went dead. Chara put the phone back on the receiver and went to bed, missing her best friend but also wishing they could swap places.

The next afternoon at Food Tide, the rush of customers finally eased after a steady few hours. She wiped down her conveyor belt, humming along to *Smooth* by Santana and Rob Thomas drifting through the speakers. At the next register, Bree did the same, while Sierra, the bagger at the end of the lane, restocked the candy bars in each aisle.

Bree stopped wiping and looked over at Chara. "Sierra and I are having a party tonight at our apartment in Ocean City. You should come."

Sierra straightened up from the candy display. "Yeah, it's going to be a great time. Some friends from school are coming."

Bree nodded, still leaning on her rag. "I checked the schedule. We're all off tomorrow, so we can sleep in."

Chara paused mid-wipe. "Sure." They attended the University of Virginia and chose a resort town for their summer jobs and housing.

Bree scribbled the address on a blank receipt slip, which Chara folded and tucked into her pants pocket. The customer flow picked up again, cutting short any more conversation. Her shift ended before theirs, so she gave them a small wave as she stepped outside into the heavy, humid air and began the walk home.

Her mom was in the living room when she arrived home, half-watching a cooking show while working on her cross-stitch. Chara smiled and dropped onto the couch beside her.

"Just the person I wanted to see," Chara said. "Bree and

Sierra...the cashier and bagger I told you about invited me to a sleepover tonight at their apartment in Ocean City. None of us work tomorrow. Can I go?"

Her mom looked up from the pattern and gave a small, warm smile. "Sure. But I can't take you. I have to meet Joanne from work for our boss's dinner."

Chara leaned forward, her grin widening. "Thanks. No problem. I'll call a cab. Now that I've got a paycheck, I actually have spending money."

She hurried to her room to pick out an outfit for the night. For her first college party, she didn't want to look too young. After rifling through her drawers twice, she settled on a denim skort and a plain black T-shirt—casual, but older-looking.

Her mom called down the hall that she was heading out.

Chara popped her head out of her bedroom door. "See you tomorrow, Mom!"

Back in her room, Chara turned on her TV to a channel playing music videos and applied her makeup, humming along to the pop songs. She packed an overnight bag, checked herself in the bathroom mirror more times than necessary, and finally called for a cab.

The ride was short, the orange sun dipping into the horizon and painting the clouds soft reds and purples. Chara stepped onto the sidewalk with her bag and stared up at the beach condo in awe—she couldn't believe two summer job cashiers could afford a place like this.

She climbed the stairs to the second floor and knocked. The door swung open to reveal a guy with dark brown hair, a soccer jersey, and a cigarette tucked behind his left ear. He couldn't have been more than five-foot-five.

Chara shifted her weight, suddenly unsure. "Bree and Sierra invited me."

He stepped aside and jerked his thumb toward the living room. "Bree and Sierra, you have a visitor!"

They came out of the bedroom, smiling. "You made it! We're about to get started. You can put your bag in our room."

The door opened into a narrow kitchen that fed into the living room, and just off to the left were two small bedrooms. Chara was led into one of them—two twin beds, mismatched comforters, a fan humming in the corner. She set her bag down on the floor.

"If you share a room, who's in the other one?" Chara asked.

Bree grinned. "That's Josh's and Max's room. We all work and split rent. Like college, but without classes."

Sierra appeared in the doorway. "What can I get you to drink, Chara?"

Chara smoothed her T-shirt down, trying to look casual. "Diet Coke is fine."

She followed Sierra back to the kitchen as another knock sounded at the door. Bree opened it, and suddenly three girls and three guys crowded into the apartment, making the already small space feel like it had shrunk in half.

Sierra handed Chara her drink. Chara took a sip and almost choked.

"Too much rum?" Sierra giggled.

Chara's stomach flipped. *Yes.* "No, just right," she lied with a quick smile.

Sierra turned to greet the new arrivals and introduced them one by one. They all went to University of Virginia together. Chara nodded politely, but the names slipped right through her mind. Standing there with her too-strong drink, she felt the outsider more than ever.

Several of them went out on the balcony to smoke cigarettes. But Bree stayed, sitting down next to Chara on the couch. "Your drink tastes okay?"

Chara smiled, nodding. "Yeah. Just taking it all in."

"In a few minutes, they're gonna start playing drinking games. The last time the guys came over and did that, they broke into a house two blocks over, thinking it was this one."

Chara's eyebrows rose. "Did they get in trouble?"

Bree laughed. "Sierra and I found them in time. We convinced the owners that they were trying to visit our elderly grandmother, and she gave us the wrong street, but the right house number. So, they didn't call the police."

Sierra walked back in from the deck. "Yeah, I know to be on my toes when those guys come."

A male walked in with his shirt off and was about to take off his shorts before he stopped to ask, "Who's up for edibles and swimming?" He pointed to Chara, hoping she'd say yes. But she shook her head no. Bree and Sierra laughed beside her.

Another guy came in. This one wearing a *College* t-shirt. "Forget bathing suits, who wants to go skinny dipping?" He winked at Sierra, who blushed.

I don't like where this night is headed.

A girl in a bright blue bikini top and black shorts came in from the deck next. "Shots anyone?"

Chara got up from the couch. "I'll get the next round. Gotta check in on a friend real quick."

Bree's eyebrows furrowed together. "You sure?"

Chara smiled. "Absolutely." She walked into the bedroom

and waited for everyone to go outside. Hearing no one, she snuck out to the kitchen with her bag to call a cab.

She hung up and took the stairs two at a time to get out of there. *This isn't the place for me.*

The door was locked when she tried to get into her house. She walked around to Astrid's bedroom window and knocked on it. Astrid came to the door with wild, wispy hair, bags under her eyes, smeared mascara, and pillow marks on her face.

"I'm sorry, Mom."

"What happened?"

Chara filled her mother in on her night but skipped telling her about the guys who lived there.

Chara sank further into the couch. "There were these guys and girls that showed up from their university, and they were about to play drinking games and take edibles. I didn't know anyone besides Bree and Sierra, so I left."

Astrid placed her hand on Chara's shoulder. "This is why I know I can trust you to make good choices."

"Yes. Now I'd like to go to sleep."

"Good call."

They both stood from the couch and walked down the hall to their bedrooms. Chara lay back on her bed, staring up at the ceiling. *Would she still trust me if she knew the choice I made the other night with Asa?*

* * *

The next morning, after her mom went to work, she signed into Messenger. She saw that Asa was online and quickly sent him a message.

Chara: Hey handsome

Asa: Hi.

Chara: What are you up to?

Asa: Playing Mythical Mayhem, you?

Chara: Day off!

Asa: That's cool. Any plans?

Chara: None. Mom's at work and Mikaila's away. As you know.

Asa: Yeah.

Chara: She told me you guys were hanging out.

Chara waited a few minutes for his reply, tapping her fingers on the desk in impatience.

Asa: I've seen her around.

Chara: Did you tell her that you think I'm cute?

Asa responded almost immediately.

Asa: No. Did you tell her that I said that?

Chara: No. I only told her I thought you were hot.

Asa: Ok. Everything else between us is just for us. Our little secret.

The hair on the back of Chara's neck prickled.

Chara: Right.

Asa: What are you wearing right now?

Chara rolled her eyes.

Chara: Clothes. You?

Asa: Same.

Asa: I'm going to call you.

Chara logged off from Messenger and almost jumped when the phone rang. "Hey."

"Hey. I thought I'd give you a call because I'm about to head to work."

Chara smiled. "Awesome. Are you talking and driving?"

Asa chuckled. "Not yet. I'm changing into my work clothes right now."

"Miki said you were going to help her find a church."

Asa sighed. "Do you girls talk about everything?"

"Pretty much."

"And I bet you go to the bathroom together when you're out, too?"

Chara giggled. "That's a myth. We only go to the bathroom together when we're talking about someone."

He whistled. "You just broke the girl code by telling me that!"

"I guess I'll be kicked out of the girls' club."

He laughed. "Membership revoked! I'm heading to work now, so I'll let you go. We'll talk soon, though."

"Sounds good."

Chara hung up the phone and grabbed her journal, eager to write about the college party the night before and her conversations with Asa. She turned on the TV for background noise, and the news was on. An update flashed across the screen: arrests had been made on the boardwalk late last night.

The mayor appeared, face flushed, speaking sternly about property damage and disturbances of the peace. Starting immediately, the town would impose a strict ten p.m. curfew for anyone under eighteen without adult supervision.

Chara's stomach churned. *What if the damage was caused by rowdy college kids over eighteen?* She shivered at the thought. Good thing she left when she did—who knew what those kids had gotten up to last night?

16

mikaila

JULY 4, 2003

I wandered into the kitchen, the scent of onion and butter drawing me in. Lorainne greeted me with a cup of coffee and began explaining her family's summer salad recipe. *Too early for cooking lessons.* She wore a khaki knee-length skirt, a blue tank top, ruby earrings, and a necklace with a ruby set in gold.

A car door slammed outside, and muffled voices grew louder as they neared the front door. The door creaked open, and Dad stepped in, grinning. He wore blue shorts, a red tank top, and white flip-flops. "There she is! Our summer renter!"

Behind him, Aunt Lana peeked in. "Hope you don't mind some company! We brought reinforcements." She wore a red cotton dress with white flip-flops and a blue pendant necklace, slipping into the kitchen behind him.

She hugged me so tightly I had to set my coffee mug down on the counter to avoid spilling it.

Cameron followed, wearing a white T-shirt, long denim shorts, and sunglasses, hauling a cooler with the lazy bravado Kait seemed to adore. Kait hugged me and handed Lorainne a salad she insisted was "internet famous."

Lorainne placed the salad in the refrigerator and rested her arm on Kait's shoulder. "Thanks so much. I can't wait to try it. How was the drive?"

Kait took a deep breath and glanced at Cameron, who was perched on the cooler in the middle of the kitchen. "It was fine, until someone insisted on a shortcut that ended up taking twice as long." She shook her blonde hair, pulled it into a ponytail, and smoothed her light blue dress with a red belt. White flip-flops completed the outfit.

Cameron shrugged. "My parents recommended it."

Last through the door was Pop, shuffling in his bedroom slippers, dressed in a white linen shirt and shorts. He moved slower than last year but still managed a playful wink. He walked over and gave me the biggest hug he could muster.

Finally, Elliott followed close behind, wearing a blue-and-black checkered shirt left open over a white T-shirt, long denim shorts, and brown flip-flops. He carried a tray of cupcakes with careful, awkward balance. Once Lorainne took the tray, I lunged toward him, almost knocking him over.

He hugged me, leaning against the doorframe. "I've missed you too, but please don't wrinkle my shirt. I'm perfectly patriotic right now." He winked, and the whole kitchen erupted in laughter.

"Look at this crowd," Dad said, glancing at me for some kind of reassurance. I gave him an exaggerated eye roll that had him laughing as well.

Lorainne lined up the ingredients on the kitchen counter, ready to continue prepping for the festivities. She turned to me with a bright smile. "We have lots to do. Where do you want to start?"

"How about we make Nan's apple pie recipe?" Aunt Lana suggested, resting a hand on my shoulder.

I fiddled with the ring on my finger. "Sounds perfect."

Dad clapped his hands together. "Men, let's head to the grill. Pop can supervise while we play with fire. Cameron, grab the cooler." Cameron hopped up, carried it outside, and followed Dad, Elliott, and Pop.

Aunt Lana pulled Nan's well-worn pie dish from one of her bags and handed it to me. Making apple pies had always been a holiday tradition, and as I lined up the apples and sprinkled cinnamon from the cupboard, it already felt like home again. Lorainne busied herself rearranging items in the refrigerator so everything would be within reach while we worked.

She sniffed. "Smells delicious, and it hasn't even gone in the oven yet. I can't wait to taste it."

Pop shuffled in the kitchen. "Kait, dear, I think you need to supervise Cameron and Elliott. They're seeing how many marshmallows they can roast on the grill."

Lorainne raised her eyebrows. "Kait, I think we're needed outside."

I did the finishing touches using a fork to make the crust and popped it in the oven.

Aunt Lana and I meandered to the porch where the rest of the family congregated.

Pop looked like he was napping in his chair at the table with his arms crossed. Elliott and Cameron and Elliott were seeing how long they could hold their breath while Kait timed them. Lorainne and Mark were having a private conversation by the grill, his arm draped around her shoulders as they giggled like children. I sat down at the table next to Kait. Lacy and Lexy emerged from the sliding door.

I smiled. "Hey, let me introduce you. You both know Kait, but I'm not sure if you remember Pop and Aunt Lana." Pop snorted at the mention of his name.

Aunt Lana beamed at them. "It's been so long since I've seen you. You're so tall now."

They smiled back, and Kait added, "Lexy, I have that same Tommy Hilfiger bag." Lexy grinned and sat across from Kait, and they dove into a conversation about name brands I couldn't keep up with.

Lacy came over and sat next to me, and I introduced her to Cameron and Elliott. When the timer on my watch went off, I looked at Aunt Lana. "I'll check the pie." I slipped through the sliding door and took it out to cool, idly playing with the ring on my finger. The scent was exactly like Nan's had been.

I saw Elliott get up from the table and come into the kitchen. Alone with me, he leaned in and gave me a quick kiss, then handed me a cupcake, his lopsided smile lighting up his face. "Something sweet for my sweetheart."

I I smiled, letting his knuckles brush mine, and stole a glance at him. He returned the smile and rested his head against mine, pulling me close to his shirt. With one hand, I placed the cupcake on the counter and stepped back.

"We've barely had a chance to connect this summer," I said. "I'm sorry. It's been busy, catching up with Lacy and my dad. I've tried, but you've been working so much."

He nodded but held onto my hands. "I'll make more of an effort. I thought you wanted some space from everything at home."

My mouth hung open. "I didn't want space from you. I needed space from my house because it reminds me of Nan."

He pulled me into his chest for another hug. With his head on top of mine, he said, "Let's try to talk more before I leave."

I stepped back and rested my finger under his chin, pressing a quick kiss to his lips. "Will do."

We left the kitchen as Dad set out grilled chicken and fish for lunch, and Lorainne brought out the salad Kait had made. After eating, Dad brought out his chess set.

Lacy and Lexy exchanged groans. "We need to wash our hair," they said in unison.

Lorainne placed a hand on her hip and shook her head. "Girls…"

Aunt Lana stood up. "They can play chess inside, and I'll grab the Uno decks so the rest of us can play too."

Lorainne smiled, lips pressed together. "I'm going to clean up the kitchen first, but please, Lexy and Lacy, join them. You can deal me in. I'll be right back." She grabbed plates and walked into the house. Aunt Lana followed but returned with an UNO deck in hand.

Elliott started as dealer.

Cameron eyed his cards. "Stacking the deck there?"

When it was my turn, I slammed down a Draw 2 on Kait, who immediately countered with her own Draw 2. That meant Elliott had to pick up four cards.

I laughed. "Still think he's stacking the deck?"

The sliding door opened, and Asa stepped out. "Hey," he said, giving a quick smile that faded as he smoothed back his hair and glanced down.

"Hey," I replied.

Lacy waved and smiled, while Lexy shifted in her chair, her previous grin gone.

Lorainne peeked out from behind him. "Why don't you sit next to Aunt Lana and take my cards?" She handed him her deck. The chatter at the table fell silent.

I stood up. "Asa, this is Aunt Lana, and this is my boyfriend Elliott, and Kait's boyfriend Cameron. You know everyone else."

He smiled at Aunt Lana and slid into the seat next to her. I sat back down and studied my cards. "So…whose turn is it?"

"Cameron's," Kait said.

He drew a card and then slammed a *Draw Four* down on me. I gave him a sharp side-eye.

The game continued until Kait emerged victorious.

Lexy leaned across the table to Kait. "Great job. I'll see if Mom needs help in the kitchen."

Lacy stood up. "I should check on her too. Fun game."

Asa rose from the table. "Fun game. I'm going to see how Pop and Mark's game is going." Aunt Lana gathered her cards. "I'll help Lorainne and check on Pop."

Meanwhile, Kait, Elliott, Cameron, and I kept playing Uno until it was time for dinner.

Elliott leaned over my shoulder, mock anger on his face. "No cheating, cheater!"

Kait laughed, and Cameron grinned as he made her draw four. I laughed at her reaction. Within a few rounds, I was out, since Cameron and Elliott spent most of their turns trying to reverse and foil each other.

The sliding door opened, and Aunt Lana called out, "Come on in, kids! Dinner's ready!"

Dinner sprawled across the table, with Nan's pie glowing like a halo at the center of the seldom-used dining room. Pop sat at the head of the table, Aunt Lana to his left. Dad took the other end, flanked by Lorainne on one side and Lexy on the other. Kait plopped between Lexy and Lacy, across from Cameron, leaving me next to Elliott and across from Asa.

Pop's chess strategy dominated the conversation. Wiping barbecue sauce from his mouth, he said, "The trick is to make deliberate moves. Sometimes striking quickly, sometimes slowly. Your mind has to stay agile. The board changes every play, so you can't commit to any one move."

Asa tapped his finger against his water glass. "Why do you prefer pawns over knights?"

Pop leaned back, crossing his arms. "Knights alone can't win the game. Pawns are meant to fall, but if you use them right, they help your knights succeed."

Dad took a sip of water. "Chess is fascinating. I wish I had the focus to play like you two."

Lorainne smiled. "I'm glad our old board is getting some use, and this room too. I can't remember the last time we ate in here."

Lacy leaned over. "When we got back from Ocean City, we had to eat in here because a leaky pipe flooded the kitchen. We ate in here for a week."

Aunt Lana gasped, "Oh, no."

Lorainne and Mark looked at each other and chuckled. "That was quite the surprise to come home to."

Kait leaned into the table and gazed at Cameron. "That was the trip we have in our photo album. We went to the Raging Rapids Waterpark, and Asa and Mikaila capsized and lost their tube on Racing Tides. The little kids behind me and Lexy were pointing and laughing at them."

I could barely breathe through my giggles, and Asa, across from me, grinned wide, eyes on my face the whole time, nodding along.

Elliott offered a polite laugh, but he kept staring at Asa, glancing at me and then back. His arm settled around my chair, tighter than usual.

I stood up from my chair. "I'm gonna get more lemonade."

Asa stood up from his chair next. "I could use some Diet Coke."

Asa glided into the kitchen after me, away from the noise, leaning on the counter close enough to bridge the gap. He quietly observed, "You seem happier this summer. I can't figure out if it's the barbecue or just being back here."

I felt a jolt of electricity being so close to him. "I guess it's just everyone being together." I sipped my lemonade and slipped out of the kitchen.

Back at the table, I noticed Elliott's thumb tracing circles on my palm. Is he affectionate, or anxious, or both?

"Young man, why don't we sit down for a game?" Pop asked Asa.

Asa smiled and met my gaze, and I smiled back. *Glad to*

*see him come out of his shell and give Pop some real competition.
He'll enjoy that.*

Elliott turned to Lorainne. "Miki and I will clean up,
Lorainne. You don't need to lift a finger after going to the
trouble of preparing our meal."

She grinned. "Thanks, Elliott. I wouldn't mind the help."

While loading the dishwasher, he asked me quietly, "You
and Asa have known each other a while, then?"

I rinsed a plate and handed it to him to load. "Yeah, we met
years ago when I was little and have kept in touch ever since."

"You didn't think to mention him to me in, I don't know,
the year we've been together?"

I looked around to make sure no one was watching us and
lowered my voice. "We're just friends. Are you jealous?"

Elliott shook his head. "No, but he's more into you than
you realize."

If I were honest with myself, I knew there was a familiarity,
a connection you could pretend was an old friendship, or you
could see for what it might become, if you let it. I shook my
head, finished loading the dishwasher, and gave Elliott a kiss.

"Let's just enjoy the time we have together this summer,
please," I pleaded.

He held my forearms tightly and pressed his forehead against
mine. Kait walked into the kitchen, eyebrows raised. "Sorry. I
was trying to catch Miki."

Elliott gave her a smile. "I'll let you two catch up."

Once he was out of earshot, Kait pulled me further into the
kitchen and whispered, "Dad tried to talk to me this morning.
He tried to pull me aside once I arrived."

I played with the ring on my finger. "What did you tell him?"

She fiddled with her watch. "I don't want to talk or rehash anything."

Her lips pressed into a fine line. I placed a hand on her shoulder. "He's trying. Nan and Pop told him years ago that when Mom was diagnosed with bipolar disorder, they wanted to raise us. He said he wanted to respect their wishes and not aggravate Mom further."

Kait's expression softened. "You think he's telling the truth?"

I met her gaze steadily. "Pop told me I should spend more time with him. So yes, I think he's telling the truth."

"I can forgive him," she said, "but I wouldn't come up here for longer than a weekend. He had our whole childhood to make it up to us. I'm not dropping my job, school, or time with Cameron just to get to know him now."

I nodded. "I don't think he'll push it. We should probably get back to them."

While Pop and Asa set up their game in the living room, Lorainne waved us over to the table. "Let's all play charades."

Lexy grabbed her stomach. "I'm not feeling well...It'll be fine. I can play through it."

Dad pushed back from the table. "I'd like to watch Pop and Asa play. See if I can learn a thing or two."

Aunt Lana put her finger to her mouth. "I'll take Miki, Kait, and Cameron on my team."

The three of us moved to the seats next to her.

Elliott grabbed my elbow and made a sad face, clearly unhappy to be on the opposite team.

Lorainne sat down where Dad had been. "Alright team, let's see what we've got." She handed a card to Lacy. Lacy frowned.

Kait glanced at her watch. "I'll start the timer for sixty

seconds. Go!"

Lacy began waving her arms wildly. Lexy shouted, "A bird! A plane! Superman!"

Lacy put her hands on her hips and shook her head. She started gesturing again, this time with a graceful, flowing motion like a princess wave. Elliott tilted his head. "Princess Diana?" Lacy smiled and nodded.

Kait yelled, "Time!" Lacy turned to Lexy. "Superman, really?"

It was my turn next. I grabbed the card and sighed. Squatting slightly, I stomped one leg, then the other, moving my arms in a rhythmic, exaggerated fashion. Aunt Lana grinned. "Gorilla!" I shook my head and pretended to slam something to the ground.

Kait furrowed her eyebrows. "A superhero?" I nodded and made a dramatic motion, slamming an imaginary object down with force.

Kait screamed, "Batman!"

I shook my head. Then I tucked myself into a ball, sprang up, and smashed down.

Aunt Lana yelled, "Hulk!" I nodded and held up two fingers, trying to mimic wrestling moves, but the timer buzzed.

I dipped my head. "Hulk Hogan."

Kait and Aunt Lana raised their eyebrows and simultaneously said, "Ooh."

Lorainne smiled. "Good try. Elliott, why don't you go next?"

He grabbed his card and smirked. Turning around, he picked up a glass and pretended to sing into it, pointing at me. I giggled.

Lacy pinched her lips together. "A singer?"

He nodded, then turned his back to us, spun around, and

began lip-syncing while doing a little jig.

Lexy tilted her head, leaning toward Lacy and Lorainne. "A dancing singer?"

Elliott pointed to himself and jigged. Lorainne squinted, trying to read his lips. "I...dance. With you? Anybody?" He nodded, motioning her to continue.

"With somebody? Oh! Whitney Houston!" she guessed as the timer buzzed.

We continued playing for a few more rounds until Lorainne's team was announced the winners. Darkness hummed through the windows when Dad walked into the dining room. "Why don't we head to the park for the fireworks?" he said, rubbing his stomach. "Need an excuse to work off that delicious pie." Everyone groaned but followed.

We grabbed camping chairs from the garage, and Lorainne handed out towels to sit on. I held Elliott's hand as he steadied Pop. Asa walked right next to me. "Perfect night for fireworks."

I nodded. "Not as hot as before." I didn't understand why my stomach fluttered—not like it did with Elliott. With him, it was different; comfortable. This feeling with Asa...I wasn't sure.

We passed neighbors' houses decked out in American flags, barbecues sending smoky aromas into the night air.

Out on the field, kids ran wild with sparklers, laughter carrying across the grass. Dad glanced at me—a look that meant more than "I love you." It was almost as if he was glad I was here, and maybe a little unsure how to process that feeling.

Pop lingered behind, so I slowed to match his pace under the first flare of color in the sky. Aunt Lana brought a camp chair and set it up for him. I waited until Elliott had spread his towel and sat down, then plopped into his lap, letting my body relax against his. The fireworks lit the night, painting the sky in bursts of red, blue, and gold.

Cameron pointed upward. "Look, Elliott! A zero—a goose egg—just like your Uno score."

Kait, sitting in Cameron's lap, playfully punched him. Asa and Lacy snorted with laughter, and Elliott's face turned bright red.

"Look, Cameron, a star, which is what you wish you were."

Everyone chuckled except Cameron, of course.

I whispered in Elliott's ear, "I had fun this summer, but I missed this." He kissed me in return.

A twig snapped against my head. I looked up and saw Lacy laughing. "Get a room, you two." But then she smiled at us.

Asa looked pale, tapping his leg on his blanket next to Lacy. Lexy nudged her. "Finale."

When the final bursts of color faded from the sky, the crowd at the park clapped. We gathered our towels and made our way back to the house.

Elliott helped Pop out of his chair, supporting him as they walked.

Dad strolled up beside me. "You're braver than I was, staying here all summer with your old man," he said quietly. "But I'm glad. Life feels better with you in it."

I smiled. "Same."

Dad moved to the other side of Pop, and I made my way over to Asa.

I smiled. "Hey. How's the chess game going?"

He slowed his pace. "I didn't realize he was a master."

"I'm glad you're playing with him. That really makes him happy. I can tell."

"That's what I'm here for."

When we got back to the house, Pop put a wrinkly hand on Asa's shoulder. "Son, stop by tomorrow morning, and we can finish our game. It's past my bedtime tonight."

Asa smiled. "See you tomorrow, Pop."

I walked him to the door with Elliott close behind me. "See you tomorrow."

Pop sat on the living room couch. "Miki, dear, come here so we can have a little chat." I looked at Elliott, and he nodded, walking towards the deck where Kait and Cameron were. I took a seat next to Pop.

"I've missed you," he said, putting his hand on mine.

I patted his hand with my left. "I've missed you, too."

"I think you need to spend more time with your dad. Maybe some holidays coming up. We've had many good years and memories made, and I don't want him to miss out on anymore."

"I don't want to miss out on holidays with you, either." *Can I split myself in half?*

"Your Nan and I thought that if we kept you at our house, we could keep you safe. It may not have been the right choice, but it was the best choice we thought we had at the time. I'm sorry we interfered with your relationship with your dad. But now it's time to rebuild it."

I couldn't speak any words. I simply rubbed his hand and nodded.

"I'm not as young as I once was and my health isn't doing well. If something happens to me, you know you don't have to feel bad about moving up here. Lana won't be mad, and your sister will eventually be in college. It's ok to get closer to your dad again."

I can't lose you, too. I swallowed hard. "I'm sure you'll have many years of chess left."

I hugged him. Aunt Lana walked into the living room. "Hey, Pop, you ready for bed?"

Smiling, he replied, "Help me up, will you?" I grabbed one arm and Aunt Lana the other. Together, we helped him up the stairs and turned out the light. "Good night, girls."

Before heading down to find Elliott, I leaned my head against the hallway wall and took a deep breath. My stomach felt tight, my head dizzy. I hoped I wouldn't have to think about life without Pop—or leaving Oak Haven permanently—for a while. That would only make things more complicated with Elliott.

17

asa

AUGUST 29, 2003

Asa and Mikaila lay side by side on a blanket in Asa's backyard, a thermos between them. Fireflies blinked in the grass. Mikaila glanced over. "I can't believe I'm leaving tomorrow. The second I got used to being here, it's over."

"Yeah. It feels like you just got here. I was starting to think your dad was gonna adopt me or something." Asa laughed.

She looked up at the sky, then back at him. "He still talks about how you beat Pop in chess. You realize you're the only guy I know who's ever done that, right?"

"That's because I'm the only smart guy he's met. Had to set the bar high for all the others. What can I say? I'm sophisticated." Asa grinned, nudging her.

Mikaila shook her head. "He's met Elliott and Cameron. I see your point about being smarter than Cameron, but you're on the same level as Elliott."

A small burn tightened in Asa's stomach, and he knotted his eyebrows. "When did Elliott learn how to beat a master in chess?"

"He didn't. But you don't have to be good at chess to be smart."

"Fair enough. You don't play chess, and you're the most intelligent woman I know."

Mikaila grinned. "At least you don't call Dad 'sir' or 'boss' or anything like that. That would be weird."

"That was my backup plan if the chess game failed. See that one over there? That's Cassiopeia. Looks like a 'W.'" He pointed to the formation of stars to his left.

Mikaila followed his gesture. "I see it. Wait...are you sure it's not just a bunch of random stars?"

Asa chuckled. "It's all a bunch of random stars. But someone a million years ago connected the dots, and now we get to pretend it means something."

"Reminds me of *Psalms 147:4—'He counts the number of the stars; He calls them all by name.'*"

"Huh. That's kind of nice."

"This is kind of nice," Mikaila smiled, but a yawn escaped her. She checked her watch. "10:30! I have to be up at 6:30 tomorrow. I should go."

Asa climbed to his feet and helped her up. "I'll drive you back to your dad's."

He drove with one hand on the wheel, the other drumming absentmindedly on the console. Mikaila stared out the window, watching the houses slip past. "Your playlist is still tragic, huh?"

Asa laughed and turned down the dial. "You mean you don't enjoy the punk version of 'Time After Time'? It's a classic."

Mikaila shook her head, laughing. "No way, Finn! The original is a classic, not this version!" Asa smiled as he pulled into the driveway, and Mikaila reached across the console, hugging him.

"I'm still walking you to the door. I'm classy, remember?"

"Of course you are! How could I have forgotten?"

They got out of the car, walking to her front door. Asa wrapped his arms around her again on her doorstep. And this time, he didn't want to let her go.

Asa's cell phone rang, and he stepped into the backyard so his brother couldn't overhear him talking to Mikaila. She had left the week before, but her voice brought back memories of their last night together.

"Hey."

"Hey. How are you?" Asa asked, dragging a chair out to the yard and settling into it so he'd be far from the house and free from interruptions.

"Good. Elliott and I went to Ground Zero on our last date. He's been volunteering at our church and starting collections for victims' families. He's...amazing."

The early morning rain hadn't done a thing to cool the air. The sun glared down, making an uncomfortable topic even more unbearable in the August heat. *I found you a church to go to and got your dad's family to embrace you. Why aren't you calling me amazing?*

Asa clenched his jaw and spoke through gritted teeth, forcing himself to stay calm. "That's great. Did you do anything else in the city?"

When she had arrived in the summer, she barely took Elliott's calls. He hadn't emailed her, hadn't sent a letter—nothing—before he arrived. But during the thirty-six hours he was there, he'd come across as overbearing, possessive, and obnoxious in Asa's eyes. And since Independence Day, she couldn't be separated from him. She was glued to her phone, waiting for his calls. He needed a play-by-play of church and every little activity she did. The more Asa tried to arrange for them to do, the more Elliott called.

"We walked around the Museum of Biblical Art and then had lunch with our youth group."

Asa scratched the back of his neck, jaw aching from clenching it shut. *I need to get her back here...away from him.* "How's Pop doing? Has he had any strong chess competitors?"

"He's tired a lot but no change. He complains because no one he plays is as good as you."

Asa chuckled. "You should come back here soon so he and I can play again."

"I'll let him know you invited him. He'll love that."

"Do you get a fall break in October?"

"Not till Thanksgiving, but we had all planned to go to Annapolis this year to spend the holiday with Elliott's grandparents. Well, not Kait and Aunt Lana, they'll be at Chara's."

Asa balled his fists and then relaxed them. *If you don't want me, I know someone who will.* "Sounds like fun. I need to pick up something at the store for my mom but let's talk again soon."

"Talk soon. Bye."

Asa hung up the phone and trudged through the grass toward the back door, his legs heavy, sweat clinging to his shirt. In the kitchen, he brushed past Hayden, who was rummaging through the fridge.

"Secret lover on the phone?" Hayden taunted, eyebrows raised.

Asa rolled his eyes. "Yes, the one you were with last night."

Hayden scowled, balled his fists, and lunged forward, but their mom stepped into the kitchen.

"Asa, Hayden's dropping me off at my women's Bible group tonight and taking the car. You'll have to take the bus to work."

Asa's stomach dropped. "Why do I have to take the bus when he's the one without a job?"

His mother's lips pinched. "We share this house, Asa. If you don't like it, you're welcome to live somewhere else."

"Yeah, Asa, why don't you live somewhere else?" Hayden added with a satisfied smirk.

"Why don't *you*?" Asa shot back as he stomped out of the kitchen.

He went into the bathroom, slammed the door, and took a quick shower. Memories of cold, boring football games he'd been forced to attend because of Hayden flitted through his mind—the taunts from his mother during the games: *Don't you want to play football like your brother? Don't you want to be popular like him?* Once again, the golden child could do no wrong.

After his shower, he sat down at his computer, logged on to Instant Messenger, and sent a message to Chara.

Asa: Been thinking about you.

Chara: Really?

Asa: Yes. What are you up to?

Chara: Just finished walking the boardwalk with Kait.

Asa: Fun. What are you wearing?

Chara: Blue Tank top and denim shorts. It's hot.

Asa: Show me.

Chara: See? Nothing Special.

She turned on her webcam.

Asa: You're incredibly special.

Chara: Thanks.

Asa: You're welcome. But you should lower your top.

Chara leaned forward, and the tank top dipped.

Asa: More.

Chara slipped the tank top lower.

Chara: If I show you what's under my clothes, you have to show me what's under yours.

Asa: Deal.

He took off his shirt completely and smiled.

Asa: Your turn.

Asa's body warmed all over as Chara removed her top, and he could see her exposed breasts as she thrust them towards the camera.

Chara: What do you think?

Asa: That I'm going to be thinking about you while I'm at work tonight, and all night long.

Chara: Really?

Asa: Yes. See what you do to me? What do you think of me?

Asa slipped his boxers off and rolled his chair back so that the camera showed how turned on he was.

Chara: You already know I think you're hot. But now I'm

not going to get any sleep tonight because I'll be thinking about you.

Asa: Do you tell anyone that we talk like this?

Chara: No. I tried telling Mikaila how hot you were and to bring you here when she came back at the end of the summer, but she clearly didn't listen.

Asa: Haha, she didn't listen, and she didn't tell me that. What did you want to do with me if she brought me there?

Chara: I want to kiss you.

Asa: I want to kiss you too.

Taking deep breaths to slow his racing heart, he said, "I'm going to go clean up and get ready for work now, but I'll be thinking of you."

She smiled and blew him a kiss. "Same."

He hung up, logged out of Messenger, and turned off his webcam. Moving to his chessboard, he captured a rook and grinned. Another quick shower later, he got ready for work, teeth gritted at the thought of taking the bus thanks to the golden child.

The ride to work gave him time to plan his next move. He leaned his head against the window, watching the buildings blur past. *Messaging Chara is a good move…why didn't I think of it sooner? She obviously tells Mikaila about me, so that should make her jealous. But what if it doesn't? What if multiple friends are into me? Then Mikaila will have to see for herself that I'm better for her than Elliott,* he thought.

18

chara

SEPTEMBER 12, 2003

The howling wind whipped through the trees, and rain poured from the sky, battering the windows of her bedroom. She sat on her bed, listening to Yellowcard's *Ocean Avenue* CD and flipping through college pamphlets: Coastal Carolina University, University of Virginia, and East Carolina University. The start of her senior year had begun with a hurricane—and a day off from school—leaving her time to think about her future. She was tired of the cold, bitter winters in Maryland but didn't want to stray too far from the beach. Who really knows what they want to do with the rest of their life at seventeen?

Chara signed onto Instant Messenger to check if Kait was online, but she wasn't. Her heart skipped a beat when Asa's name popped up.

Asa: Skipping school?

Chara: Hurricane. They're afraid we'll float away.

Asa: Are you all safe?

Chara: Of course. Just a lot of rain. I haven't lost power yet.

Asa: Good.

Chara: You don't have classes?

Asa: Not until later. So right now, I have time for fun. Do you?

Chara: With you, I just might.

Asa: You look more beautiful than ever. Your arm brace and all.

Chara: Thank you. You look hotter than ever.

Asa: Thank you. I wish you were here so I could explore your body in person.

Chara: Same.

Asa: Have you ever talked dirty to anyone?

Chara: No.

Asa: I haven't really either. But I'm going to call you, and I'm going to try. Just listen. Keep your camera on.

"Remove your top?" Asa said.

Chara did, and Asa smirked. "Beautiful."

"You're so hot, Asa."

"You want to see what you do to me?"

Chara rubbed her legs to calm the butterflies in her stomach. "Yes."

He removed his pants, showing her how turned on he was. "What do you think?"

"Incredibly hot."

"Thank you. Slide off your jeans now...Yes...Now slide off the panties."

Asà told Chara how to pose for him. He told her all the explicit things he learned from R-rated videos. After he finished, he said, "I have to clean up. This was fun. We should do this again."

After Chara's shower, Mikaila called. "Hey. You want to come over for a movie?"

"Yeah, Mom's still at work. You know how the hospital never closes." Chara left a note on the table, grabbed an umbrella, and ran through the downpour. By the time she reached their house, she was soaked.

"Why didn't you use an umbrella?" Kait asked.

"Now, why didn't I think of that?" Chara said, shaking it out. She winced as her right arm throbbed in the cold, wet weather.

Kait stepped back from the door. "Oh...it's that bad."

"It's torrential. I was looking for you on Messenger earlier. How do you even know what program you want to do in college?"

Kait shrugged. "I'll figure it out when I get there."

Mikaila scurried into the living room carrying a plate of snickerdoodles. "Hey." She set the cookies down on the coffee table and waved her over. Aunt Lana followed, holding a bowl of buttery popcorn. "I'll grab you a towel to sit on until you dry off."

Chara sniffed the air, catching the scents of cinnamon and popcorn. "The cookies remind me of Nan."

Aunt Lana lifted a hand to her chest and nodded. She

disappeared for a moment and returned with a towel for Chara to sit on.

Kait lightly touched Chara's shoulder before walking over to grab some popcorn herself.

Chara shrugged off her coat and hung it on the rack, grabbed a cookie, and plopped onto the couch. "So…what are we watching?"

Just as she asked, the power went out. They all froze, waiting to see if it would come back on. Darkness held the room, the wind howled, and rain battered the house.

"I'll check on Pop and call the electric company." Aunt Lana hurried out of the room. Mikaila passed out the flashlights. Chara grabbed another cookie for good measure.

A few minutes later, Aunt Lana returned with an old battery-powered AM/FM radio, some candles, and matches. Kait helped light the candles and set them around the room. Aunt Lana turned the dial until she caught the news: most of the surrounding towns were also without power, and the worst of the storm hadn't hit yet. She switched the radio off. "This is going to be a while. Do you want to play card games?"

Mikaila grabbed the photo albums from the bookshelf. "Why don't we go through some photos of Nan?" She spread them out on the coffee table, and they huddled around, flashlights in hand.

Aunt Lana pointed. "How about Thanksgiving when Mikaila was five and tried to help Nan with the turkey? While she was setting the table, she used all her stickers and sprinkled glitter on the turkey before it even went in the oven! That picture has to be in an album somewhere." Lana chuckled.

Kait laughed. "That was the prettiest turkey we ever had."

"Hey, I was five! I didn't know what she meant by 'getting the turkey ready!'" Mikaila couldn't help but smile. "Good thing we had a spare chicken, or I would have ruined dinner!"

"I think that photo is probably next to the one of me baking Christmas cookies with Nan for the first time," Kait said.

Mikaila couldn't hold back her laughter. "The flour was everywhere! It was like a snowstorm on steroids!"

Kait pressed her lips together in a thin line. "At least they were somewhat edible."

Aunt Lana covered her mouth to stifle a laugh. "Half the ingredients were all over the kitchen!"

"Still edible!" Kait interjected. "Here's where we went roller skating for the first time!"

"Why am I on the ground in most of these photos?" Mikaila asked.

"No one's perfect the first time," Kait winked. "Here's a shot of us with Dad, Lorraine, Lexy, and Lacy at the beach in Ocean City."

Mikaila put her finger on the photo. "Mom probably didn't enjoy them coming to the beach with us, but Nan made her deal with it! I remember her telling Mom that we should get to know our stepsisters, and she would take us with or without her."

"Nan stood her ground, and that day was fun. Look, here's where Pop helped you ride your bike," Kait said, her eyes lighting up with the memory.

"Will she ever live on her own again?" Mikaila asked.

"I don't think so. She hasn't been well for a long time, and it'll take a while to correct that," Aunt Lana said.

The room had an eerie glow as Kait and Mikaila flipped through the memories of their childhood, while Chara watched and smiled. A clap of thunder made them all jump. Aunt Lana went to check on Pop, and Mikaila put the albums back and grabbed another.

She opened a page and started laughing, tapping the photo. "Look, it's us as the Spice Girls—except there were only four of us, including Tara."

Chara smiled. "We predicted there would only be four left… just didn't predict which one would leave."

Just then, Kait's cell rang, and she sprang up to answer it. Chara and Mikaila called after her, "Tell Cameron we said hi!"

Mikaila flipped through the pages until she reached Chara and Kait's eighth-grade graduation photos. Chara groaned. "Why didn't either of you talk me out of bangs?"

Mikaila giggled. "They weren't that bad."

"How's Pop doing? And how are things with your dad now?"

Mikaila sighed, her hands trembling slightly as she turned the next page. "Pop's tired a lot, and he said his health isn't doing so great. Things with my dad are better now than they were at the start of summer."

"Sorry to hear about Pop," Chara said quietly.

"There are so many things to do in Chestnut Hill. Asa and I went camping with Lacy, and there's this mall with three stories…"

Chara's eyebrows drew together, and her stomach warmed. "You went camping with Asa? How did Elliott feel about that?"

Mikaila took a deep breath and spoke quickly. "He and I couldn't connect at the beginning of summer. We kept missing calls, and we didn't even realize we could email each other until after he came up for Independence Day. So I didn't get a chance to tell him, but—"

"He still doesn't know?"

Mikaila groaned, raising her voice. "It's not like anything happened! I was in a tent with Lacy, and Asa had his own tent. Lacy asked me why my faith was important, and I explained that Christians believe Jesus died on the cross to save us from sin, and that whoever believes in Him has everlasting life. I told her how my faith has helped me through everything in my life so far. She said she wanted to come with me to a youth group and try it out. Asa was just there. And Elliott's jealous of me spending *any* time with Asa, so I avoided telling him about the beginning of summer. I focused on my conversation with Lacy. Elliott and I have talked almost every day since the Fourth of July."

She exhaled slowly.

Chara tilted her head, pursing her lips. "I've never had a boyfriend, but that doesn't sound healthy."

Mikaila flipped her hair. "Well, maybe you should get a boyfriend."

Chara's stomach rolled, her fists balling. *Maybe if you brought Asa down here, I would have a boyfriend, and Elliott would get over it,* she thought.

"You can tell Elliott that Asa and I have been seeing each other, so he doesn't need to be jealous," Chara added.

Mikaila's head popped up from the photo album. "What?"

"I told you I thought he was hot. We've been flirting all summer. I told you to bring him here. Maybe if you had, Elliott wouldn't be jealous."

Mikaila started tapping her finger on her leg. "When did he start flirting with you?"

"Beginning of summer, but more intensely after Independence Day."

Mikaila closed the album. "I'm going to check on Aunt Lana and Pop. Do you need anything?"

"Uh, no thanks."

Weird how she can't be happy for me, but I'm always here to listen to her about Elliott. Maybe Pop's health is affecting her more than she's letting on, and she's missing Nan more than she admits, Chara thought.

When Mikaila returned, Chara had her coat on and her umbrella ready. "I'm heading home for a nap; it looks like movie day's a washout." She trudged back to her dark house. No power there either. She tore the note off the table and tossed it in the trash; her mom was still at work. The weather had drained her.

She lay down on her bed. When she opened her eyes, she was on a street she didn't recognize, walking with Mikaila. The trees weren't maples, but Mikaila carried herself with confidence, as if she knew this suburban neighborhood well. She turned to Chara and said, "I'm moving here."

Chara's stomach twisted into knots, and a cold pain ran through her body from head to toe.

"I don't think that's a good idea," Chara said.

The look on Mikaila's face said it all—she had made up her mind, and nothing Chara said would change it.

"Whose neighborhood is this?" Chara asked, her voice tight.

They approached a mailbox at the end of a driveway. Mikaila pointed to the white box with letters printed on it. The name read: *Finn.*

Chara's eyes snapped open. She sat up in bed, her stomach twisting with nausea. She grabbed her journal and scribbled down the dream from memory, but the sense of impending dread lingered, weighing on her body like a heavy fog.

19

mikaila

I gripped the dense metal golf club, clumsy in my hands, and widened my feet like Elliott had shown me. I swung, and the ball cut through the air, landing almost directly in front of the windmill—only three inches short of a hole in one. My fingers tingled as I smiled at Chara and Kristin, who high-fived me.

Kristin tucked a brown strand of hair behind her ear. "Did you practice a lot in Connecticut?"

"Not really. This is all Elliott's training."

The hurricane a few weeks ago had brought mild, temperate fall weather—nice enough for mini golf, but too breezy and cool for the beach. The Ocean City boardwalk wasn't as busy this time of year, but the vendors didn't waste any chances to entice tourists with the smells of crab fries, pizza, and monkey bread. As soon as we approached Manic Mini Golf, Chara declared her need for monkey bread.

Her ball knocked mine in. "Thanks," I said.

Kristin swung—no hole in one. "How were your summers?"

"Working part-time at Food Tide drained my soul. I'm ready for school. I'm not built for customer service," Chara said.

"It couldn't have been *that* bad."

Chara put her hands on her hips. "The friends I made invited me to a rage party. I snuck out and later found out two of their friends were arrested for damaging property and being under the influence. They thought I ratted them out, so the rest of the summer with them was rough."

I shifted my weight from one foot to the other. "That's crazy. My summer was pretty good...I guess in comparison. Connecticut has a boardwalk similar to ours, but also different. No shopping. The mall had three stories and was the central place where people hung out. It was fun when Kait, Cameron, Elliott, Aunt Lana, and Pop came up to visit. Pop said his health wasn't doing well and to hang out with my dad more. So I don't know how I feel about that."

I didn't want to dwell on his comment about staying with my dad more. I can't think about losing Pop. I took my club and swung—the ball splashed straight into the water, much to their amusement. I groaned. "Kristin, how was your summer?"

"Great! I was a camp counselor at a Christian camp in

Baltimore for inner-city youth for a few weeks. We had weekly field trips to the Inner Harbor Aquarium. I also took a computer course and learned all kinds of things. It was a really fun time."

"That's great," I exclaimed. "We need to get this one into Bible Club this year." I nudged my elbow into Chara's side.

"You need to work on Astrid not being anti-religion," Chara remarked.

"What made her anti-religion?" Kristin asked.

"She didn't get along with my grandmother, who was Catholic, very conservative, and strict. My grandfather got along with my dad, but my grandmother thought my mother had only picked a Black man to spite her. She used to tell her that God wouldn't approve of her working, and that women were made to live in the kitchen."

I shook my head. "What about religion does she not like?"

Chara swung her club, hitting her ball even with Kristin's. "She doesn't like it when people interpret the Bible to manipulate others. And she says it happens more than we realize, at levels higher than most think."

I lined up my ball and took a swing. It sailed past theirs, almost straight into the hole.

Kristin clapped with glee. "Great swing! I don't think the three of us can convince Astrid that not all churches and people are like that. But Bible Club isn't like that."

"I think if you keep sharing what you learn with me, then I'll feel like I was there," Chara said with a sly grin.

I grinned back, leaning my arm on her shoulder. "I'm gonna do exactly that…because I need to get back to saving you."

"Last hole!" Kristin yelled. Chara lined up her shot, but the ball barely moved. I swung next. The ball sailed through the air and landed—*plunk!*—right in the hole. I pumped my fist in triumph. "Hole in one!"

Chara and Kristin clapped, jumping up and down.

"Elliott's not going to believe this," I commented. *He'll probably want to see it for himself…and then I won't be able to do it again.*

We made our way to turn in our clubs and stopped at the stand next door for some monkey bread. We shared a single plate of gooey, cinnamon-scented dough.

"How's your mom?" Kristin asked me.

I nearly choked on my bite. "We hear she's fine. She's being monitored for her bipolar disorder and living in an apartment with other women with similar diagnoses," I said, my appetite fading as I spoke.

"That's tough. When do they expect her to come home?" Kristin asked.

I shrugged. "It doesn't matter if she does, because Kait will be off to college next year, and the year after, I'll be somewhere, working or in school, or both."

Kristin leaned over the table, resting her arm on my forearm. "I'm sorry. I didn't know how that all played out. Let me know if you need anything."

I smiled, feeling my shoulders relax. "Thanks. I appreciate the offer." Not many people at school would be cool knowing my mom wasn't mentally stable and thought it wouldn't rub off on me.

Chara draped her arm around my shoulder. "Don't worry, you'll always have us. I don't plan on letting you go too far. Who else will let me eat their portion of monkey bread?"

Kristin laughed, and I felt a smile tug at the corner of my

mouth. But a gnawing sensation returned to the pit of my stomach, and it wasn't hunger. *I was close to losing you once. I can't lose you again.*

"I've been focusing more on church and Bible Club because that's what Nan told me to do when things with Mom were rocky. And since she's gone…" My voice trembled, and Chara leaned in closer, her arm still around my shoulder.

"Since she's been gone, I've been making more of an effort to do a daily verse, or a verse of the day."

"I like that," Kristin commented. "Maybe we can do a verse of the week at Bible Club, instead of just one each month."

"What should the week's focus be?" I asked.

Chara dropped her arm and tapped the table. "Strength. I'm not there, so I don't know what you cover, but look at what you've gone through and how you're still standing. Start with strength."

My insides warmed at her suggestion. "How do we get people to remember the verses when they need strength?"

"What if we made notecards to give members, something they can put in their planners and turn to when they need it?" Chara suggested.

A thrill ran through me, thinking this could be the first step in my plan to save her. "I'll call Aunt Lana," I said, dialing her number. "Hey, can you give us a ride back to the house? We've got a project to work on." She picked us up on 25th Street, and we slid into the car, eager to get started.

"Hey girls, whatever you need help with, just let me know."

I filled Aunt Lana in on our project and watched the delight wash over her face. "I can't wait to see how it turns out."

Once back at the house, Kait was in the living room watching VH1.

"Hey, we'll be in the kitchen working on a project."

"No problem. Just hanging out here."

I called Elliott next and invited him over. Kristin and Chara didn't mind, and if I were being honest, I also wanted to brag about my mini golf skills.

He arrived wearing a blue-and-black checkered T-shirt. We shared a brief hug and kiss. Once we pulled apart, Chara asked, "Do you own any other shirts?"

Sheepishly, he replied, "Doesn't everyone have a favorite shirt?"

He glanced at the kitchen table and raised his eyebrows. We were knee-deep in scissors, scrapbook paper, glitter, and stickers.

"Never fear, ladies—your former Bible Club President is here," he said, removing his Oak Haven Baseball cap.

Kristin and Chara laughed at his antics. I shook my head and explained what we wanted to accomplish. "Together, can we come up with a verse for this week?"

Elliott flipped through his Bible, stopping at Isaiah *40:29: He gives strength to the weary and increases the power of the weak.*

After we'd made enough notecards, Chara turned to Elliott. "How was your summer, Elliott?"

He smiled. "Great but visiting Miki in Connecticut was the highlight." He leaned over and kissed my forehead.

"I asked Mikaila to bring Asa back here at the end of summer for me, but she didn't," Chara faked a pout.

Elliott stiffened against me, and my chest tightened. "Why would she bring him here?"

Chara put her hands on her hips, cocked her head, and said, "For me. Do you have a problem with that, Elliott?"

"Uh…no. But what do you see in him?"

I rested my hand on his back, stomach twisting into knots. "Don't even get her started."

"He's hot, he's funny, he's smart, he's charming…do I need to go on?" Chara pressed.

Elliott bristled as she listed Asa's positive traits; his smile had long faded. "I think you can do better, but that's your choice. Not mine."

Chara shot me a pointed look. "Why don't we talk about having a verse of the week and not my love life?"

* * *

A few hours later, after Kristin and Elliott had gone home, I turned to Chara. "Why'd you bring up Asa?"

"I told you, if he knew I wanted him, he'd be less jealous. Makes things easier for you, right?"

My stomach twisted. *I don't think this makes things easier.* "But I asked you to leave it alone, and you didn't."

"Sorry…I thought I was helping."

"I think you need to leave. I really need some time to myself."

She grabbed her coat, stormed out, and slammed the door behind her. I stormed upstairs to my bedroom and dialed Elliott on my cell.

"Hey, how do you think today went?" I dared to ask.

"Today was…interesting."

"How so?"

"Chara is into Asa? What is that about?"

I rolled my eyes. *I knew this wasn't over.* "According to her, they're into each other."

He scoffed. "Did you tell her he was glued to your side this whole summer and can't seem to leave you alone?"

"He's just a friend, and nothing has happened between us. Maybe he's just being nice to me because he wants to be with her."

"I don't get a good vibe from this guy."

"I can't tell her who to date, and neither can you!" I shouted.

"You can always choose to tell the truth," he said before the line went dead.

I can't believe he hung up on me. Maybe Pop is right. Maybe I do need to move back to Connecticut.

20

asa

Asa glanced across the table at Veronica, tapping her pencil with a pinched expression. She had soft brown eyes, light brown hair, and a great figure—none of which he'd noticed when he'd slipped into class late on Thursday morning, nearly oversleeping and forced to take one of the last seats in the lecture hall. Only when she muttered in frustration after class that she ought to drop physics had he realized how pretty she was. He'd offered to help, and she had agreed immediately.

Now they sat in the mostly deserted campus library on a Friday night. A few students clicked quietly at computer terminals, but Veronica's pencil was the loudest sound in the room.

"Force equals mass times acceleration," he said, pointing at the diagram in her book. "If you increase the force but keep the mass constant, the acceleration increases."

She lifted her head. "Like a car?"

He smiled. "Exactly."

She let out a sigh. "You're a natural at this. I can't believe you're a first year and you understand all this."

"The forces of nature fascinate me. Like how some objects are pulled together by magnetism." Asa paused, lips curling. "I think people can be drawn together the same way."

Veronica smiled as she began gathering her things, and his pulse picked up. "If you can help me study for the quiz, I might be able to pull up my grade and stay in the class."

"Do you want to meet here on Sunday afternoon?"

She flipped open her planner, frowning. "I work all weekend. But…" Veronica looked up at him through her thick lashes. "If you're free, we could keep studying at my apartment in about an hour?"

"I'll be there," he said. Veronica wrote down the address, a lightness blooming in Asa's chest as he tucked it away. He stopped at a convenience store to kill some time, then made the short drive to her apartment.

Veronica opened the door. "Come on in, Asa."

Asa stepped inside, taking in the soft white carpet, the cream curtains, the tidy kitchenette. A few framed photos hung on the wall—Veronica smiling with friends. "This is a great place. I've never been in this development before. It's nice."

Veronica gestured toward the couch and sank into the gray leather cushions. Asa sat beside her, setting his physics book on the ottoman, but his body betrayed him—heat surged through him, his stomach fluttering, and suddenly the words she was asking about blurred into a haze he couldn't focus on.

She turned her face toward him, waiting for an answer, and before he even processed the movement, he leaned in to kiss her. Their lips brushed (barely), and he leaned further, laying a hand on her leg.

Veronica jolted to her feet, a scowl across her face. "What are you doing?" Her voice was sharp, wounded. She crossed her arms, pointed to the door. "You need to leave. And never speak to me or look at me again. What is wrong with you?"

Asa's mind fuzzed. Lightheaded. Embarrassed. He stood, stumbling for the exit. "Sorry...I thought that's why you invited me in."

She followed, yanked the door open. As he stepped through, she snapped, "Creep!" and slammed it behind him.

Heat spread through his body—humiliation curdling into anger. *You're the one who sent mixed messages,* he thought. *Let's see you pass the class without my help now.*

Asa got into his car and sped home, ignoring the speed limit, jaw tight, teeth grinding the whole way.

When he walked inside, the house was surprisingly quiet except for the familiar soundtrack of a James Bond movie—his mom's guilty pleasure. His parents were on the couch: his dad, long-legged, blond, and unbothered, stretching his six-foot-four frame across the coffee table; his mom perched beside him, tiny at five-foot-two, feet barely grazing the floor.

"Class get out late?" His dad asked.

"No, I was just helping a girl from class study for our physics quiz. At her apartment."

His dad smiled with approval. "Studying at her apartment? Very nice, son. I like the sound of that." He pointed vaguely toward the driveway. "You know, you'll need the car more often. You can take the one out there. I'll get something for your mom to use."

His mom paused the movie and tapped his dad's arm, but his dad just grinned. "He's studying at apartments with girls now, dear. He'll need the car more often," he said with a wink.

Asa had never once seen his mom contradict his dad, and she didn't start then. She nodded, frowned, and pressed play. *Don't let me interrupt your romantic evening with James Bond,* he thought bitterly.

"I'm going to finish my homework. I have to work all weekend," Asa said.

His dad winked again, the same stupid wink, and told him to "make sure he's safe" next time he was studying at someone's apartment.

None of my accomplishments mean anything to you, Asa thought as he walked toward the stairs. *But the second you think I'm acting like the golden child, suddenly I'm worthy of the car.*

He went up to his room, shut the door with more force than he intended, and signed onto Instant Messenger. His fingers hovered over the keyboard for a moment before he typed a message to Chara.

Asa: Hey there. How are you?

Chara: Missing you. How are you?

Asa: Missing you too. You want to see how much I miss you?

Chara: Of course.

Asa turned on his webcam and got completely undressed.

Asa: Your turn.

Chara turned on her webcam and smiled at him. She was wearing a light pink dress.

Asa: Who you looking cute for?

Chara's cheeks flushed.

Chara: You.

Asa: You look so great in that dress, but I'd love to see you take it off.

Chara: Really?

Asa: Can't you tell how much I missed you?

Chara slipped the dress over her head and then removed her bra and panties.

Asa's pulse quickened at the sight of Chara clad for him.

Asa: Definitely prefer you like this

Chara giggled and blew him a kiss through the webcam. The sound hit him like a spark—light, foolish, easy. There was something intoxicating about the secrecy, about knowing he could tug at Mikaila through the person closest to her. A back door into her life. A pressure point.

Riding the high—and the humiliation he still hadn't shaken—he pushed it further. He queued an X-rated video and played it for Chara, telling her this was what he wanted to do to her. She froze, uneasy, clearly not liking it, but she didn't call him a creep. She didn't reject him. And that was enough. He kept going, letting the leftover frustration from Veronica's apartment pour out in crude, escalating messages.

When he finally logged off the call, he leaned back and moved a rook across his chessboard. *One step closer to the queen.*

The room felt too quiet. Too still. So, he opened another

chat window and messaged Mikaila's friend—Kristin.

Asa: Hey, how are you?

Kristin: Good, you?

Asa: Good. How was your summer?

Kristin: Great. Yours?

Asa: Great.

Kristin: Glad to hear that.

Asa: I hear you're a fellow techie

Kristin: I dabble

Asa: How so?

Kristin: Making webpages primarily for my parents businesses. Sometimes for their friends.

Asa: That's cool. Do you do any coding?

Kristin: Not a whole lot yet. That's next year.

Asa: If you need any help at all, I'm pretty good with it.

Kristin: Thanks. I'll let you know if I run into any problems.
Have to go now.

Kristin signed off, and the silence of his room pressed in
again. Asa exhaled sharply and opened a new window, signing
into the *Mythical Mayhem* group chatroom. Dozens of user-
names blinked online. He filtered through the list, searching for
female players around Mikaila's age. One profile photo caught
his attention—auburn hair, the same shade Mikaila had worn
in late summer. Close enough.

He invited her to a session. She joined immediately. He
played well enough to keep it interesting, then let her win.
People liked you more when they won.

"I liked talking to you," he typed once their match ended.
"This was fun. You can find me on Messenger by my name,
AsaFinder."

Her reply popped up fast. "I liked talking to you too! My name is **WarriorKelly**. We can talk again soon."

He smiled and added her to his friends list. Another piece on the board.

The next morning, before he had to leave for work, he logged in. Her username glowed there—**online**.

Asa: I liked your use of your power crystals to take on my warding charm.

Kelly: Thanks. I liked your use of firepower to take down my health. I might have to steal that tactic sometime.

Asa: Do you play this game with your boyfriend?

Kelly: I don't have a boyfriend.

Asa: What qualities are you looking for in a boyfriend?

Kelly: Thoughtful, good communicator, and a little bit funny.

Asa: Sounds like you're describing me.

Kelly: Why don't we exchange photos?

They exchanged photos, and though she wasn't Mikaila, her hair was the same, and that's all that mattered.

Asa: You're cute.

Kelly: Thanks, handsome. You're attractive too.

Asa: Me attractive?

Kelly: Very attracted, but you're in a different state, so how do I know you really look like that?

Asa: You're a smart girl for asking. I have a webcam that I can turn on and prove to you right now.

Kelly: You're definitely him.

Asa: Now your turn.

Kelly: What do you think?

Asa: You're more beautiful than you are in your picture.

Your hair brings out your eyes.

Kelly smiled at him, and Asa's body warmed as her shoulders relaxed.

Kelly: You're cuter than you are in your photo, too.

Asa: Thanks. You have such a nice smile. I have to get ready for work. Can't wait to talk to you again.

His muscles tightened as the memory of Veronica's expression flashed through his mind—the shock, the accusation, the insult. *Creep.* The word echoed. He refused to let it sit unanswered.

He opened his laptop again, jaw ticking. In a few quick keystrokes, he created a new email account using the name of a student from their physics class—*Brad W.* Perfect. Generic. Unremarkable. Believable.

He drafted the message to the professor carefully, each sentence crafted to sound apologetic rather than malicious:

He explained that he had stepped away from his table at the student union after leaving his homework out, and when he returned, he *thought* he saw Veronica leaning over it. He wasn't certain—he didn't want to get her in trouble. But he also didn't want to be accused of sharing answers. "I just thought you should know, in case anything seems off," he wrote. "I don't want to break any rules."

He reread it once, smirked, and hit send.

What else could he do? She'd made a fool of him. Actions had consequences.

Shutting down his computer, he leaned back in his chair. *You'll need me to corroborate your whereabouts today,* he thought with a curl of satisfaction. *You can't get out of this without me, Veronica.*

As he stood, his gaze slid to the mirror across the room. For a fleeting second, he caught the expression on his own face—the slight upward twist of his mouth, the cold gleam in his eyes. He saw himself as someone else might: a boy playing a game only he understood, shifting the pieces exactly where he wanted them.

At the chessboard on his dresser, he reached out and nudged the knight forward.

Almost to checkmate.

21

mikaila

The air was damp and chilly, the sky a blanket of grey clouds that matched the heaviness in my chest. Every time my foot struck the sidewalk, it felt like I knocked loose another piece of the disappointment clinging to me—disappointment in Asa, in Chara, maybe even in myself. When I wasn't running, or drowning myself in homework or church, my last conversation with her replayed in my mind like a song I couldn't turn off.

Two days after she'd told Elliott she was into Asa, I went

to her house without calling first. I shouldn't have. She wasn't expecting me, and I definitely hadn't expected to walk in on her talking to Asa on webcam. And when she told me what else they'd been doing on webcam, my stomach churned.

"I told you we'd been flirting," Chara said, arms flung wide as if *I* were being unreasonable. "Why are you upset?"

"This is the type of relationship the Bible warns us against, to protect us…" I tried to remember the verse, but she cut me off.

"You're using the Bible to shame me? Maybe I should become antireligion like my mom."

My fingers twisted anxiously around my ring. "No, I'm—"

"You're judgmental," she snapped, crossing her arms. "And you need to leave. Now."

I picked up my pace as I rounded the bend into the track park, the familiar loop where the team practiced. On days like this, I usually relish the escape—breathing, running, *moving.* But today the memory followed me, uninvited.

"Why are you crying?" Chara had asked, her voice sharp, suspicious.

"I don't know…" I'd tried to breathe, but it felt like my insides were collapsing in on themselves.

Her eyes widened. "You have a thing for Asa too. You're dating Elliott, but you want Asa. And you've been hiding it from me this whole time."

My stomach rolled. *I'm supposed to be in love with Elliott. So how can I want to be with Asa too?*

I didn't have an answer. So I did the only thing I could…I ran home.

Up in my room, door closed, still panting from the run, the memory, and everything in between, as I dialed Elliott.

"Hey."

I sighed. "You're not going to believe this. Chara and Asa have been stripping on webcam for each other and... ugh." I balled my fists, anger and disgust twisting together.

Elliott exhaled heavily. "She said she had a thing for him. Why is this a problem, other than her immoral behavior?"

I paced the length of my room. "I'm trying to get her to live by Christian values, get her to come to Bible Club, show her that faith could help her with her self-esteem issues, her anxiety, her relationship with her dad..."

"Did you tell her the Bible condones that behavior?"

"Do you really think that's going to stop her? She told me she didn't want me judging her. I can't throw scripture at her to prove my point. I don't know what to do."

I'm supposed to save her. I'm supposed to guide her. I'm supposed to bring her closer to God. But now she's pushing the Bible away entirely because of me. I don't know if I can save her anymore. I don't know if I ever could.

Elliott didn't speak for several long, suffocating minutes. I could hear him breathing, steady at first, then uneven. Finally, he said, "You're upset because they're together, not because of her actions. I don't think I can be with someone who's into another guy." Then he hung up.

We haven't spoken since.

The oak trees around me swayed as the wind picked up, their branches creaking like they were tired too. Kids on the nearby playground shrieked with joy, oblivious to how heavy the world felt on my shoulders. My joints ached, my legs throbbed, but I kept running until my lungs burned and the trail ended beneath my feet.

The past two weeks of school had been torture—dodging Elliott in the hallway and at Bible Club, dodging Chara everywhere else. That was harder. Kristin was caught painfully in the middle: me versus Chara, then me versus Elliott. Bible Club felt like walking into a storm every time.

I walked the rest of the way home, breath still uneven. After a long, hot shower, Kait knocked on my door. "You look like you need some hot chocolate. Java Joint?"

My ears perked. Nan used to make hot chocolate for us whenever we came in from playing in the snow or on especially cold days. I nodded and grabbed my purse.

Kait's used 1998 Toyota Camry—courtesy of Aunt Lana—meant she'd been chauffeuring us around a lot more. She blasted *"First Date" by Blink-182*, one of the many mixed CDs Cameron had made for her, as we drove toward Ocean City.

When we crossed the bridge, Kait turned the music down. "Have you heard from Dad lately?"

I fiddled with the ring on my finger. "We talked last week. Lacy emailed me to say hi."

Kait smiled. "Lacy and Lexy are nice. I'm glad we got closer to them this summer."

I stared out the window as the ocean came into view, the horizon a soft blur. "Yeah. Lexy acted like I bored her, but maybe she already has a younger sister and didn't want another one. I don't know."

Kait tapped her steering wheel. "I didn't notice. She seemed cool to me."

"She actually talked to you and opened up. That didn't happen before you got there."

We pulled over on the street outside Java Joint. As we

stepped inside, the aroma of freshly ground coffee hit me, mingling with the light jazz playing over the speakers. The fall décor—pumpkins, orange and yellow leaves—reminded me that Thanksgiving was around the corner.

Kait and I stood in line, scanning the shop. Couples huddled together, some on dates, others grabbing a quick caffeine fix. One couple caught my eye. The guy's blue and black plaid shirt, the way he ran his hand through his hair, the way he nodded and laughed—it all mirrored Elliott. My chest tightened.

It was him. Holding hands with another girl.

I tapped Kait's shoulder and pointed. She shot me a determined look, then without a word, turned and strode over. I followed, trailing a step behind.

She tapped him on the back. "Hey, Elliott, what are you doing here?"

He spun around, surprised, mouth dropping open before he forced a nervous smile. "Guys…what are you doing here?"

Elliott glanced at the girl he was clearly on a date with. "Can I call you later?" she asked, and he nodded. Then she scurried away.

"You guys want to sit down and talk?"

Kait dropped her bag on the table and took the seat across from him, crossing her arms. I lingered next to her, unwilling to sit.

Elliott folded his hands in front of him. "I just met her for hot chocolate. She's in my Intro to Law class and mentioned she was interested in attending church tomorrow."

Kait leaned forward, whispering, "So…you needed to hold her hand to get her to church?"

He furrowed his brow. "No, it just…sort of happened."

"How exactly did it happen? Did she fall into your hands?"

Elliott sighed and glanced at me. "Can't we talk about this somewhere else?"

"We don't talk at school, and you haven't called me since you dumped me over the phone, so why don't you start now?"

He nodded toward the chair next to Kait. I sat, fingers tracing the cross necklace he'd given me, still faithfully worn.

"I've known her for years," he began. "We've been friends. She told me she was interested in me last June, but I was in a committed relationship and in love with Mikaila. That was true. But after Independence Day, it became clear I'd have to compete for your attention...with Asa."

I shook my head, unable to speak.

"Then things seemed better when you were back here, but then you became livid with Chara and Asa for being together. Which makes it clear you have feelings for him."

I shook my head. "I'm upset with Chara for how she acted with Asa, and then for telling me I used religion to shame her, when all I'm trying to do is help her accept the Lord and walk the path like us."

He looked at me, eyes soft and forlorn. "I can't compete for your heart. You know...our lives are pre-written in some way. If you have feelings for him, maybe that means you're not supposed to be with me." Lowering his chin, he glanced at Kait and said quietly, "I love your family. I'm sorry it didn't work out." Elliott rose from the chair with his hot chocolate, and he was gone.

Kait grabbed my hand, and we walked to her car. I silently sobbed the whole way back. She ran into a Quik-Mart at a nearby gas station and came back with a package of hot cocoa.

I gave her a small, grateful smile. Back home, she made us

both steaming mugs, topped with tiny marshmallows, just like Nan used to do.

She placed mine carefully on the table. "Do you want to talk about anything that happened with Elliott, Chara...or Asa?"

I shook my head, fingering my cross necklace. "No, but thanks." I picked up the mug and trudged upstairs, legs heavy from my earlier run.

I sank into bed, careful not to spill the cocoa, and thought about the last time Nan had made us hot chocolate. I couldn't remember which year it was, but the memory came flooding back: Kait and I building snowmen, tracking snow through the house, Mom yelling about the puddles by the back door, Pop putting down towels, shooing her away, and Nan handing us all cocoa. Mom eventually relaxed as we sipped and laughed at Kait's marshmallow mustache. Nan had a way of making everything feel right.

This house didn't feel like home without her.

I finished my cocoa and set the mug on my dresser. I still had a photo of Elliott and me tucked into my mirror. I slid it into the top drawer. My fingers lingered over the necklace he had given me. I couldn't believe I never took it off, and he hadn't even noticed or cared. Slowly, I unhooked it and placed it in the jewelry box, closing it with a sigh. I thought it might ease the ache, but it only made me feel emptier.

Pop is right. I need to go back to Connecticut.

22

mikaila

DECEMBER 6, 2003

Kait knocked softly on my door.

I pushed myself upright. "Come in."

She stepped inside and sat on the edge of my bed, hands folded in her lap. "It's another Sunday where you've skipped church. And while I'm okay with whatever you decide, that's not usually like you. Kristin mentioned to Aunt Lana that she missed you, so I called her to see what was going on since you wouldn't talk to me." Her eyes searched my face. "You need to talk to Chara."

A chill ran through me. It felt like an entire lifetime since we'd last spoken. "I'm not sure I can."

"You've been friends with her for years. Are you really going to let this erase all that?"

You're sounding like Nan these days. If I turn my back on Chara, I can't save her. Sixteen months to go, and I'm not even back at square one. I've made negative progress. My stomach hurt thinking of life without her permanently. "We can try to talk it out, I guess."

Kait grabbed her cell and dialed Chara. "Hey! Can you come over? Like…now? Great! See you soon!" She left my room, and a few minutes later, Chara appeared in the doorway, Kait right behind her. I was still stretched out on the bed, staring at the ceiling.

Kait gave Chara a look so sharp it could have cut glass. "Talk it out." She patted Chara's shoulder, closed the door, and disappeared down the stairs.

I grabbed a tissue and scrubbed at my face, forcing in a steady breath. "Elliott's seeing someone else."

Chara's mouth dropped. "Who?"

"I don't know," I said, wiping my eyes. "He said a friend of the family, but I've never met her."

Chara handed me another tissue. "You want me to throw her into a locker?"

A laugh slipped out of me as I dabbed my eyes. "No."

"You want me to throw him into a locker? Or the ocean?"

I laughed again. "No. He'll think I put you up to it."

We sat there in silence for a long moment, looking at each other. Then something shifted—Chara's expression dimmed, her shoulders sagging. "Things are over with Asa."

Relief flickered through me before I could stop it. *Why do I feel relieved? Because you're making better decisions, or because he's done with you?*

"As you know," she continued, eyes dropping to her hands, "it started out innocently. Just flirting. Checking in…"

I nodded, urging her on.

"Then we started stripping for each other," she said quietly. "It was slow at first. Just a glimpse. Then he asked for the top. Then he told me how to pose…" Her eyes drifted unfocused as she rubbed her hand along her thigh, a small, grounding motion.

"Then what happened?"

"Then he started playing…x-rated videos and making me watch, which was not what I wanted."

I gulped. *What? That's not the Asa I know.*

"The past couple of weeks, he'd been more distant. When I asked him about it, he told me he didn't need to tell me anything because we were 'just friends.'"

"Didn't need to tell you anything…like what?" I asked.

"I asked him if he was seeing other girls, and he said yes, but that he didn't need to tell me anything about it because we're just friends. I asked if he was seeing them online or in person, and he said both. That he liked to keep his possibilities open, and that you were the love of his life, but if you weren't available, he needed to keep busy."

I remembered our camping trip, how our hands brushed while setting up the tents, and how close he had stood to me on Independence Day. *If I'm the love of your life, why are you getting involved with my friends?* I wanted to scream.

Chara took a deep breath before continuing. "Last week, Kristin and I talked about everything that happened between

Asa and me, and why you and I weren't talking. She told me Asa started coming onto her, too. We both blocked him. I'm done with Asa Finn."

I gasped. "Why didn't you tell me sooner?"

"Because I knew you wouldn't approve," Chara explained, "because it violates your religious code."

"I'm still your best friend even when you make bad choices."

Chara exhaled, her shoulders slumping. "The only bad choice I made was seeing Asa. However you feel about him, he is bad news."

Heat flared in my chest. I'd spent so long trying to save Chara—telling myself her heart had changed, that she'd lost her way somehow—but this wasn't that. She hadn't drifted. She'd been pulled. Caught up in something reckless and wrong with Asa Finn. Asa, who should have known better. Asa, who I'd believed had changed.

"Your bad choice was taking your clothes off. That's sinful."

"My entire high school class is sleeping with one another. How is what I did any worse?" Chara shot back.

"Just because you can't beat them doesn't mean you join them."

Chara's voice rose. She pointed at me, her hand shaking. "What he did was manipulative. It made me feel violated and confused." Her eyes burned. "And all you want to do is throw the Bible at me and tell me this is *my* fault."

"I'm just trying to show you that living a faith-based life would prevent this from happening, if you have a guy who's also living a faith-based life."

"You went to church with him! He said he was a Christian. He told me what we had was a secret! He wanted to keep it secret because he knew it was wrong. When he finally admitted it, he was out trying to date other girls. And then, when I learned from Kristin what he was trying, I realized he didn't like me. He liked the control he had over me."

Dizziness washed over me at Chara's words. I needed to call him. My stomach twisted, my ears ringing, my thoughts skidding uselessly. I didn't know what else to say. "Thanks for telling me what happened."

Chara nodded, relief softening her face. "I feel better now." She managed a small smile. "Forget Elliott. We'll find you someone better. But...I should probably go." She slipped out of my room, pulling the door closed behind her.

The moment she was gone, I slammed my fists into my pillow. Then I grabbed my phone. My fingers trembled as I dialed. Asa answered on the second ring, his voice light. "Hey! How are you?"

The sound that came out of me was closer to a growl than a greeting. "What happened between you and Chara?"

"What are you talking about?"

"Did you come onto Chara," I said, tapping my foot hard against the floor, "lead her on, and then turn around and come onto Kristin?"

"No...Chara came onto me, and I thought it was just something for fun."

"That's not what she said at all. Don't lie to me." My chest tightened. That could be true, but why would she lie? Why make this up?

"I wouldn't ever lie to you."

"Then why didn't you tell Chara you weren't interested?"

"I didn't want to hurt her feelings. She seemed down about

her arm, and I wanted to boost her self-esteem. You know me, I'd never do harm intentionally."

I wanted to believe him. If he's right, if this is a misunderstanding, maybe I could finally step out of the grief I'd waded through for so long.

"Then how do you explain Kristin saying you also came onto her?"

"Did she tell you that, or did Chara make it up to make her story believable? Kristin's a nice girl, but why would I come onto her? I offered to help her with coding; that's not a come-on. Sounds like Chara's trying to make me out to be the bad guy because she's embarrassed. She took her clothes off and seduced me, and Kristin's a loyal friend, so she's just backing Chara's version."

"She seduced you?"

"Yeah. You knew she had a crush on me. I didn't encourage her, but she instigated taking things further. I told her any guy would be lucky to have her, but she's not my type," he said quickly.

That didn't sound like Chara, but I didn't know. She had kept saying he was cute.

I fiddled with my ring. "When did she do that?"

"Uh...I don't really remember."

"How many times did it happen?"

"Quite a few times she tried," he admitted.

I exhaled sharply. "You expect me to believe she took her clothes off several times after you told her she's not your type?"

"She's persistent," he said.

She is, but this doesn't sound like her.

"And the times she did this, you told her she wasn't your

type, and you didn't instigate this whatsoever?"

"You've been here with me. Do I act like that?"

He does have a point. I've only seen him obsessed with Lexy. He did consistently ask her out, but he never tried anything like this. At least I think so. It doesn't fit.

"And what about playing X-rated videos and making her watch them?"

"Why would I do that?"

My face burned, jaw locked tight. "I don't know, but she said you did, and that's not something she'd make up on her own." *I've never caught her in a lie; why would she say it if it weren't true?*

"She asked me what I was into, and I showed her. She wanted to know. She asked for it."

"Even if she asked for it, why would you show her that?"

"I didn't think she had anyone else to talk to about this stuff, so I thought I'd help her out."

I paced the floor of my bedroom. "I don't want to see my friends get hurt," I warned.

"I didn't do anything to them, I swear. *1 Thessalonians 5:21—test them all, hold onto what is good.*"

"Testing it out right now," I muttered, and hung up. My jaw ached from clenching, chest still tight. Something nagged at the back of my mind, but I shoved it down.

Instead, I dialed Kristin. "Hey. You have a minute?"

"Yeah."

I paced the floor again. "This might sound crazy, but…did Asa come onto you?"

"Yes."

My head pounded. "Really?"

"Yes."

I stopped walking. "Why didn't you tell me before?"

"You never asked. I blocked him. He's not my type. What's this about?"

I sank onto the end of my bed. "Nothing. Thanks. I gotta go." I hung up the phone and threw it next to my pillow.

Who am I supposed to believe? Asa has always been friendly to everyone I know, and he's been committed to going to church. Why would he do that to Chara and Kristin? Would Chara try to seduce him? Would she ask to see what he was into and then lie about it?

23

chara

DECEMBER 6, 2003

Chara walked from Mikaila's house to the neighborhood gym,
pulling her winter coat tight around her. Since she'd stopped
chatting with Asa, she'd been using exercise to work through
her anger. The gym was nearly empty on a Sunday afternoon,
and the sharp scent of disinfectant filled the air. She stored her
coat in the locker room and hopped onto the elliptical, playing
"Fighter" by Christina Aguilera on her MP3 player. Each stride
brought a memory.

She thought of the late-night chats with Asa—how, at first, he'd been charming, making her feel special. He hadn't cared that her arm was healing; he had seen her. But slowly, the charm faded, and she realized she'd become nothing more than a pawn on his chessboard. She pushed harder on the machine, wincing as the pain in her right arm flared with each stride. *I'm no one's pawn. I'm the queen,* she thought.

The resistance increased, as if she were climbing a mountain. Her conversation with Mikaila earlier came to mind, and a dull ache throbbed in her head. *You gave me a blank stare as I described how the man who claims to love you systematically used me for his pleasure, and you didn't defend me. If it had been any other guy, you wouldn't throw Bible verses at me—you'd be there, helping me kick his ass.* She lowered the machine's intensity slightly, barely able to breathe—not from the workout, but from the betrayal she felt. *My own best friend is blaming me for being seduced by the guy she introduced me to, and now she has nothing to say about it.*

Chara fought the primal urge to hit or destroy something, pumping the elliptical faster and pulling harder on the handles. She switched her MP3 to Destiny's Child's *"Survivor"* and kept going—pushing until her muscles burned, until the fight inside her had been exercised out. Finally, exhausted, she shut off the machine, wiped it down, and walked home.

After a shower, her mom knocked on her door. "We need to go see your dad. He's had a stroke, and the hospital discharged him to a rehabilitation facility."

They rode in silence to the facility that Astrid had called. Upbeat holiday music flowed from the radio, though it didn't feel like the holidays. When they arrived, garland adorned the front desk, a Christmas tree stood in the lobby, and a Menorah was set up on the counter.

Astrid nervously tapped her foot, waiting for the front desk staff to look up Ty's room. Instrumental holiday music played softly over the speakers as they passed rooms filled with older people in various stages of recovery.

When they finally reached his room, Chara's heart sank. Half of his face drooped from the stroke, and when he greeted them, his words slurred. She gave him an awkward hug. Astrid gestured toward the door. "I'll wait for you in the car." She said before slipping out.

Chara sank into the chair beside his bed. He gave her a half-smile. "Small stroke. No need to worry."

Easy for you to say. She grasped his hand. "Do you need water or anything?"

He shook his head. "Did you send in your college applications?"

Chara tapped her toes on the tile floor to the Trans-Siberian Orchestra music drifting in from the hallway. "Nah, I decided to be a permanent dog sitter."

He shook his head slightly. "Hilarious."

Chara paused mid-tap. "Could be lucrative."

"You're smarter than me and your mother combined. Where are you applying?"

She folded her hands on her lap. "I applied to East Carolina University and Coastal Carolina University in South Carolina."

"They have the majors you want?"

"They have the beach and warm weather I want."

He tilted his head as best he could.

"Yes, after helping you with your physical and occupational

therapy sessions, I think I want to explore that field. Both schools offer it."

His eyes lit up, and he tried to smile with the side of his face that wasn't affected. "You would be wonderful at that."

"Not as good as a dog sitter, but I'll do my best," Chara said with a smirk.

A nurse with long brown hair entered the room. "I'm the nurse practitioner on duty today. Looks like you have physical therapy in a couple of hours."

Chara sat up straighter. "What caused the stroke?"

The nurse glanced at his chart at the end of the bed. "Mini stroke. Could be complications from the head injury during the vehicle accident he was in. I'm sure he'll be back to normal by the end of the week."

Chara's stomach churned at the thought that he was still suffering from the accident. She texted her mom that she was ready to leave. Standing, she leaned down for a gentle hug. "I have homework to work on. I'll check on you soon." Then she walked out to her mom's waiting sedan.

"Mini stroke. Possibly from residual trauma from the car accident. They think he should be good by the end of the week," Chara repeated quietly.

Astrid offered a small smile. "Good news that he'll recover soon."

* * *

The next day, Chara awoke sweaty, nauseous, with a tingling sensation in her chest. She trudged into the kitchen, where her mom was pouring a cup of coffee in her robe.

"I don't feel good," she groaned. "My stomach hurts, and I

woke up sweaty and…disgusting."

"You may have picked up something from the rehab center. You should go back to bed. I'll call you out of school."

Chara walked back to her bedroom, rolled back into bed, and tried to rest. But the longer she lay there, the more her last conversation with Mikaila replayed in her mind, and with it, her nausea worsened. She blasted Christina Aguilera's *"Walk Away"* on repeat, hoping the music would take some edge off the sickness.

Did I do something to make him pick me? Is it because I thought he was cute? Is it because I'm too much? Why me, Asa? What did I do to deserve this, Asa?

Her mind drifted to the dream she had of Mikaila moving to Connecticut, being closer to Asa, and the nausea returned with a vengeance. *How can I tell her about the dream without making it seem like I have a personal vendetta against him?*

She sat at her computer, trying to string together her thoughts to tell Mikaila how she felt. She typed a few lines, erased them, then started again. She didn't know where to start. *How do you tell the person who's supposed to always have your back that she's failed you?*

Her mind wandered back to the day she had been a wreck because her crush had humiliated her on the bus during a school trip.

Miki,

Remember when we said we'd always have each other's backs? I need you to have mine now.

You can also talk to Kristin about her experience with Asa or her friend's experience with him. It's not just limited to us. And why do you think that is? He enjoys playing games with our friends, as if we're chess pieces on his board. I'm not a pawn. I'm a queen, and I refuse to let him play with me or anyone else I care about.

I miss the days before him and before Elliott. They weren't so complicated. Well…our lives have always been complicated, but never like this. Everything else can fall apart, but our friendship is supposed to remain. And I don't know if it can survive this.

L.Y.L.A.S. Always,

Chara

24

mikaila

DECEMBER 23, 2003

I lay on my side in my twin bed, flipping through my Bible—
the pages earmarked, the spine worn. Yellowcard's *"View of
Heaven"* played on repeat as I thought of Nan and the advice
she would have given me. My stomach churned thinking of Asa
using Chara for his own pleasure. *Did he? But why would she
exaggerate any of that?*

My mind drifted back to seventh grade, to the third time
I got detention for kicking Brantley Ford. He had smacked

my butt as I walked up to turn in my quiz, and, of course, the teacher and principal didn't believe me. No one in class would back me up—Brantley's parents were both lawyers, on the PTA, and part of the Board of Education. I hadn't known that at the time. And now…was I really sure Chara hadn't made something up? I buried my face in my hands.

When the guidance counselor called my mom to say I was dangerously close to suspension, she lost it when I got home.

"He smacked my butt, and the teacher's going to let him get away with it!" Kait glanced at Mom and retreated to her room. Nan did the same, not wanting to make Mom angrier. Later, she told me she'd spoken to Pop not to intervene and promised to help me afterward.

My mother leaned in, pointing. "You're making up lies about one of the nicest families in this town just to save your own skin. You're no good, just like your father."

He may have been from a nice family, but that doesn't make him nice.

"Maybe I should live with him, then," I said, my voice rising, fists clenched.

Her face reddened as she yelled, "You're ungrateful for everything I do for you, so I don't care if you go live with him! Go ahead! See if I care!"

That's when I ran away to Chara's house. She sat with me on her living room floor while I sobbed. She let me call my dad and ask him to come get me. It had rained that day, and I was soaked from head to toe. Astrid gave me dry clothes and dried my wet ones for me.

Chara had been there for me through everything—she wrote me letters when I was stranded in Virginia. When I got back, we made a pact: no matter where we were, we'd always have each other's backs. She would trade her life for mine. I traded mine for hers. But if she doesn't stop acting sinfully, I'll lose her forever. And if I believe her over Asa...I'll lose her forever, too. This situation is impossible. I don't even know what to think about Asa anymore.

Kait knocked on my door, interrupting my thoughts.

"What?" I asked through sobs, curled up in the fetal position.

She sat in my computer chair, facing me. "You want to talk about it?"

"Not really," I whispered.

She moved to the edge of my bed. "Chara might be your best friend, but you don't have to tell her everything."

"It's not just that. Elliott was my boyfriend, but I didn't know how I felt about Asa, and what he and Chara did...it bothered me," I said, sobbing.

"I have a boyfriend, but I still think other boys are cute or nice sometimes. They don't stop being attractive just because I'm with Cameron."

I wiped my face with the back of my hand. "Asa and I hung out while I was at Dad's. He was completely different from how Chara makes him out to be." I filled Kait in on everything Chara had said. "She even claimed he tried hitting on Kristin."

Kait raised her eyebrows. "Yeah...that makes me think he's not a good person to be hanging out with. Why do you think Chara would make any of it up?"

I sighed. "I don't know. Maybe to make me not like him. If she can't have him because he doesn't like her, then I shouldn't either."

"Hmm...have you ever known Chara to be like that?"

I shook my head. "Never."

"Lexy only introduced you to him because he was obsessed with her. Now he's obsessed with you. Would he lie just because what he did makes him look bad?"

I sat up and tucked my hair behind my ears. "It's not the Asa I know."

"Chara's been your friend for so long, I find it hard to believe she would lie, exaggerate, or be so obsessed that she's delusional," Kait said.

My head ached, and I rubbed my temples. "Well…he didn't exactly call her delusional."

"He's basically saying it's all in her mind, that it didn't happen the way she said. But I've never heard you say she gets upset over things that aren't real."

"To my knowledge, she hasn't…"

Kait cleared her throat. "I've known her a long time too. She practically lives here. She's not delusional. Which means…"

I sighed, my body tense. "Which means he did what she said."

Kait pressed her lips into a thin line. "It's fine to like whoever you want. But I wouldn't waste my time on someone who can hurt you or your friends like that."

I took a tissue and wiped my eyes. "What should I do now?"

"If it were me, I'd call Asa and tell him exactly where he can stick his webcam for messing with my friends," Kait said.

I laughed a little but still felt the weight of the conversation I knew I had to have with him. "I don't know why I don't want to believe he did it."

"Because you believe the best in people. It's what everyone loves about you," Kait said.

"Thanks," I said through sniffles. "You're getting to Nan's level on giving advice."

Kait gave me a half-smile. "Pretty sure she wouldn't tell you to get physical, but Pop might."

I sat quietly long after Kait left my room. Nan would pray. *God, I pray for wisdom to use the right words when I speak with Asa. I pray for Chara because, regardless of what happened with Asa, she's hurting. Please comfort her and bring her peace. If Asa is as lost as it sounds, please change his heart and show him the dangers of leading others astray.*

Please give me clarity as I try to figure out how to navigate this situation and show me how to guide Chara back to You. I've been trying, and I feel like I'm failing miserably. She's done a complete 360—she's different now, harder to reach, harder to recognize.

I paused and grabbed another tissue, my fingers trembling. *This feels impossible, and I need help. Please tell Nan I said hi. Amen.*

The room felt too small, too quiet. Even after praying, a stone-heavy feeling settled in my stomach—an awful, sinking certainty that if I didn't somehow reach Chara, if I couldn't help her turn things around, something terrible was waiting for her. Something permanent. Something I didn't know how to stop.

And I had absolutely no idea where to begin.

25

a s a

Asa walked up the steps to his bedroom, tossed his bookbag onto the bed, and queued Duran Duran's *"Love Voodoo"* on his Napster account. He smirked, remembering that afternoon's tutoring session with Veronica. *I knew you'd come back.*

After he emailed the professor, she had found him in the parking lot before their next class—shoulders hunched, sobbing, begging him to tell the professor she hadn't cheated. His body tingled at the memory. *She only has herself to blame for leading me on like that.*

Asa scratched his head, leaning against his car door. "I don't understand. If I'm so creepy, if I have such bad intentions…why would I help you now?"

"I can't get kicked out of college! I'll pay you to tutor me. I'll pay you to go to the professor and tell the truth. But I can't get kicked out!" she had sobbed.

He relished the way her tears made her hair cling to her face, mascara streaked around her eyes, making her look as pitiful as she felt. His whole body warmed when she agreed to his terms: he'd continue tutoring her, and she'd pay a low rate of $2.00 an hour to cover his gas. *I'm not a monster.*

They would meet at the library, but he insisted that he be introduced to a friend of his choosing. She agreed without hesitation, and he cleared everything up with the professor. He smirked, pleased at how easily she had played right into his hands.

Neither she nor the professor knew the email had come from him. The classmate he had pretended it came from told the professor he must have been hacked. The professor, not very tech-savvy, bought it. Asa warned her that if she didn't keep her promise, she would regret it. She swore to uphold her end of the deal and stay silent. Satisfied, he agreed to tutor her biweekly until finals so she could pass.

Asa's smile widened as he answered his cell phone, delighted to see Mikaila's name on the screen. But the smile vanished quickly.

"You'd better tell me the truth once and for all, Asa Finn!" She yelled.

His heartbeat quickened. "What do you mean?" he asked, feigning innocence.

"You know what you did!"

"Hey, hey, I'm not sure what you're talking about. Can you start from the beginning?" He said in a tone carefully measured to sound concerned. He caught his reflection in the mirror and smirked as she continued to yell, savoring the control he still held over the conversation.

"You came onto Chara, acted like you were interested, then hit on our friend Kristin. And then you made Chara watch things you shouldn't have shown her," she accused.

"I haven't led on anyone, and I didn't make anyone do anything they didn't want to do," he said. His voice stayed level, careful, controlled.

"Why are you lying!?"

Asa's head began to throb, but his tone didn't budge. "I already told you...she came onto *me*. And I only showed her what she asked to see."

"I call bull," she said, breath catching.

"I can't believe you'd think I'd do that, Miki." He let his voice sound wounded.

"I can't believe you'd be so creepy either! So why were you?" Mikaila shot back.

"Is that what Chara told you? She told me all kinds of things about you that I'm not repeating." He smirked at his reflection in the mirror.

"What are you talking about?"

"I didn't want to hurt your feelings, so I kept quiet. But she... embellishes things to make herself feel better."

"Tell me," she demanded.

"She said you were more like your mother than you think. Irrational. Quick to judge. Like dating Elliott." He lowered his voice. "I'm the one who told her that wasn't true."

Mikaila gasped. "Why would she say that? She defended me when someone on my bus talked about my mom...she could've gotten suspended. Why would she say those things?" Her voice rose, cracked.

He smiled, but his tone stayed flat. "Because she wants me. Is that really so hard to believe? If she paints you in a negative light, *she* looks better."

"Why are you lying about her?"

Asa's fingers tightened around the phone, and he let out a short, irritated snort. *I'm not losing control.*

"That's just the most recent thing she said. She used to call you a little puppy dog, following Elliott around like he had you on a leash." *She didn't say it, but I've seen it with my own eyes.* "Can you handle the truth?"

"She would never say things like that," Mikaila said, but there was a tremor at the end.

"I'm not lying. I just don't think you really know who Chara is. And if you can't trust her not to say cruel things about you..." He let the sentence dangle.

"She's never said anything bad about me," she shouted, but her voice faltered.

He took a soft, intentional breath loud enough for her to hear. "I don't know if you ever knew who she really is. Did you ever think she'd get naked and throw herself at me?"

"Well...no, but—"

"She was resentful you left her this summer. Her feelings were hurt. She couldn't handle being alone," he murmured. He had to fight the smirk threatening his mouth.

"So, she made up lies about me to get to you?"

His tone turned reflective, almost thoughtful. "Hmm. It kind of seems like that. And when it didn't work, she threw herself at me even more."

"And Kristin's lying too? That you hit on her?"

"Chara's convinced her I'm a horrific human being. Kristin thinks she's helping you. Isn't she a techie? Isn't it possible she hacked herself and blamed me to help Chara prove her point?"

A stretch, but he let confidence carry it.

He took a slow breath. "Why are you coming after *me* when you should be asking Chara why she's making things up about you and me to serve her own purpose?"

Silence. A long beat of hesitation.

"Her and Kristin's version don't match yours at all," she finally said.

"After all the time we spent together this summer, and all the years we've known each other, how could you think I'd lie to you like that?" His voice was barely above a whisper.

She exhaled shakily. "I've known her almost my entire life and she's never said anything about me behind my back."

"Maybe she hid it. Maybe she couldn't keep it inside anymore after you left her this summer. She was beat up in that car accident. Maybe she thought you'd be around to take care of her…and she's angry that you weren't."

"I don't think that's it…"

"How can you be sure?"

"I'm not sure of anything right now other than someone isn't telling me the whole truth," she said with a sharpness.

"She's jealous I've always had feelings for you. She can throw herself at me and make up all the stories she wants, but that will never change how I feel for you. I don't know how I can still have feelings for someone who thinks so low of me?"

She groaned. "I've never known her to be like that, Asa."

"I only know her as the girl who's desperate for attention and willing to make terrible accusations against me to accomplish her goal."

"And how do you describe Kristin?"

"Loyal. To Chara. She's a techie and a hacker. Who are you going to trust?"

"Whatever. I need time to think about this."

Warmth spread through his chest as he ended the call, a slow satisfaction unfurling in his limbs. He stepped toward the mirror, smoothing a hand through his hair, admiring the calm in his own reflection. Another move made. Another piece nudged exactly where he wanted it.

He crossed the room to the chessboard on his dresser and slid a pawn forward with deliberate precision.

"She'll come back to me," he murmured, the corner of his mouth lifting. "They always do."

He paused, savoring the quiet click of the wooden piece settling into its new square.

"And if they don't..." His grin sharpened. "I'll make them."

26

mikaila

APRIL10, 2004

The crisp evening air made me shiver in my strapless, floor-length black satin gown with white satin piping. I waved goodbye to Aunt Lana as she dropped me off at my junior-year prom, held in a hotel ballroom off the Ocean City boardwalk. The sidewalk was lined with Oak Haven's eleventh-and-twelfth-grade students and their dates, parents scrambling for last-minute photos. The ocean waves rumbled in the background, and the smell of funnel cake wafted through the air. I watched

Kait and Cameron saunter ahead and tried to catch up.

The theme was "A Night of a Thousand Lights." The ballroom was dark, save for cream columns swirled with white lights, trees with illuminated branches, and chandeliers suspended from the ceiling. Candles dotted the tables, but the dim glow made it hard to see. I needed to check every table to find Kait.

My stomach dropped as I passed Elliott's table. His arm was draped over his new girlfriend, whose dress seemed deliberately revealing. *Don't make me throw up.* I'd avoided them at Bible Club and sat on the opposite side at church but seeing them close up cemented our breakup.

I moved past tables of girls in glittering gowns and guys in uncomfortable tuxes, laughing and complaining about shoes. The DJ played Eric Clapton softly as students mingled, took photos, and found seats for dinner. I finally spotted Kait and Cameron and slid into a seat at their table, giving Kait a quick smile. She looked like a princess in her hot pink, floor-length gown, hair swept into an updo with curls framing a tiara.

Kait turned to Cameron. "Take our photo?"

We stood, posing with the table in the background. I felt plain next to her and forced a smile.

At a table to my left, I saw Kristin laughing with a guy I didn't recognize. My heart sank. *I guess we won't be catching up tonight.*

The waiter came to take our orders, and I fought to keep my thoughts from drifting to last year's prom—me in Elliott's arms. I shook my head slightly. *I will not waste tonight mourning what could have been.*

A teammate at our table leaned over. "Who do you think will be team captain next year?"

I swirled my straw in my water glass. "Not sure. Jamie killed it in the 800m, but he can't beat my 1600m time."

A shiver ran through me as I remembered Asa telling me I'd be captain eventually. *I don't want to think about Asa or Chara, or the clock ticking for her, or Elliott, or anything else that's fallen apart this year.*

Dinner came and went, and the DJ started playing songs for dancing. Kait grabbed my hand and pulled me to the dance floor.

I rose from my chair, following her as she bounced to the rhythm. She went over to her friends, Tara and Todd, and I stopped cold when I saw they were with Chara.

Her dress made her look regal—strapless, floor-length aqua blue with ornate beading and a petticoat that gave it a soft volume. She lingered on the edge of Kait's group. Her jaw trembled slightly, but there was a gleam of resolve in her eyes. When she turned, our eyes met, and for a moment, it was a silent face-off only we knew was happening. The DJ played on, and prom-goers danced to the infectious beat of *"Hey Ya."*

For a few beats, neither of us moved. *We're going to have to talk it out. If you don't come to me, I'll go to you.* I weaved through the dancers, narrowly avoiding elbows, and stopped beside her. She barely moved, barely dancing.

"Hey," I said.

"Hey," she replied.

We said nothing as the music throbbed around us, the twinkling lights overhead a reminder that this was her last prom. *It's her last night. We shouldn't waste it not speaking.*

I leaned closely so she could hear me over the music. "It's your last prom night. We shouldn't waste it. Can we go to a table and talk?"

She nodded, and we padded to a quieter table near the exit, away from the DJ's speakers.

For a few moments, neither of us knew where to begin. My stomach quivered as I replayed my last conversation with Asa in my mind.

I cleared my throat. "I've missed you. I remembered last year's prom. We were in such a different place."

She nodded, her chin trembling. "Last year...it really was a different time."

"I think I underestimated the long-term effects the car accident had on you and your dad," I said carefully.

"He's recovered from the stroke they said was a byproduct of the accident," she explained. "But they can't be sure there won't be more."

We sank into the chairs, Britney Spears playing faintly in the background.

"I chose to go to my dad's this summer because it didn't feel like home anymore after my mom moved out and Nan passed," I admitted.

Chara nodded. "I understand. I missed you a lot, but I didn't hold it against you."

I groaned, stomach twisting. *This is the part of the conversation I didn't want to have.* "I didn't realize...I was jealous of you talking to Asa."

She cracked her knuckles, and her tone deepened. "He's not worth being jealous over."

I opened my mouth, but nothing came out. My thoughts were scattered. "He hasn't ever acted like that around me. We spent a whole month hanging out before Elliott came to visit, and he didn't try anything."

Chara leaned forward slightly. "You know I'd never pursue someone I knew you liked."

I nodded. "I did know that. I didn't think I did at first. I didn't really know how I felt about him because I liked Elliott. I never thought about Asa that way before this summer. I denied it because I felt like it meant I was cheating on Elliott."

"I understand how we were acting didn't fit with your Christian values, so I didn't tell you. I'm sorry if you felt like I hid something."

"I was hurt because you didn't tell me everything up front," I admitted. "We don't have secrets, not to mention I'm trying to save your life, and it feels like we've taken so many steps backward."

"No more secrets."

"Promise?" I asked, though in my heart I wasn't sure I could keep it.

"Pinky swear," she said.

I debated how much to tell her about what Asa said to me last—wanting to warn her without stirring more drama. I settled on a hint. "I know Asa's always had feelings for me. He admitted it. Elliott was right about that."

"Forget Elliott," she said.

I half-smiled. "I just don't get what he would gain by not coming clean about being attracted to you, or what he did with you and Kristin. What was his angle?"

Chara shrugged. "He's a chess player. Playing a long game that I quit a while ago. I refuse to be manipulated by him—or anyone—ever again. I'll do whatever it takes to protect my friends from people like him."

"How would lying to me and thinking he wouldn't get

caught ever end well?" I couldn't see a clear answer. I should've paid more attention when Pop tried to teach me chess.

Chara shook her head. "He's not worth thinking about, not one more minute. But we did say no more secrets."

"Yeah..." My stomach sank. What else could there be?

She paled. "I didn't know the best time to tell you, but I had a dream that you moved, and when you showed me whose house we were near...it was his. I had the worst nausea in the dream. And when I woke, it didn't go away. Every time I think about it or talk about it, the nausea returns."

I relaxed my shoulders and smiled. "I'm staying right here. No need to worry about that."

"How did you and Elliott break up anyway?"

I sighed. "Over Asa. I was in denial about our feelings for each other, and Elliott didn't want to be caught in the middle."

Chara's eyes narrowed playfully. "You need me to go trip him?"

I shook my head, laughing. It felt so good to laugh again. "No, it's my fault."

She shook her head, scanning the dance floor. "No, it's his fault for not sticking around. Come on! I bet if I act like it's a mosh pit, I won't get kicked out for punching him."

I laughed harder but rested a hand on her shoulder. "It's fine. Really."

The DJ switched from a slow dance to the *Cha Cha Slide*. I grabbed her hand and pulled her onto the dance floor, where Kait and Cameron were still going strong. Lucky for Elliott, he wasn't near them.

Kait grinned. "Finally, you two made it over here."

I couldn't have said it better myself.

27

chara

It was warming up—summer flirting with spring—but Chara wore a light pink long-sleeve shirt to school anyway, covering her arm. She and Mikaila strolled through the hall, chatting about Chara's acceptance to Coastal Carolina University and the scholarship money she'd been offered compared to her other choice.

As they turned the corner toward Chara's locker, the usual hallway chatter stopped. Girls whispered, eyes wide; guys snickered and nodded. Chara glanced at Mikaila, silently asking if she knew what was happening.

"Chara, you can take your top off for me anytime, baby," called out some guy she barely knew, but who'd been in school with her for years.

Laughter erupted around her. Chara put her hands on her hips and shot back, "Thanks for the offer, but I prefer someone who didn't have to repeat kindergarten."

Another guy stepped closer, inches from her, and said, "With my G.P.A., I'm used to being on top, but for you, I'd be on the bottom."

Chara edged closer, looked him up and down, and replied, "I prefer them larger."

The girls around her burst into laughter. Chara slammed her locker shut, and she and Mikaila moved toward Mikaila's locker. It wasn't much better—stares and whispers—but at least there was no catcalling.

"The hell is happening?" Chara asked, her voice sharp.

Mikaila shrugged. "No idea. But thanks for not starting a fight at 8:00 a.m."

Chara sighed as the bell rang. "I don't have enough caffeine in my system for this."

In homeroom, Jack Elmer turned around. "I didn't expect to see you in my emails last night."

Chara leaned back. "What are you talking about?"

He slid over handouts of private conversations between her and Asa, doctored to make it look like she asked to strip for him and watch X-rated videos. Heat flooded her body. Without hesitation, she ripped the pages in half, balled her fists, grabbed her book bag, and stomped toward the front of the room. She threw the papers in the trash and asked to go to the nurse, but before she could leave, a page summoned her to the principal's office.

A page the whole school could hear. Asa, I will get you for this, she thought.

Before rounding the bend, a hand grabbed her arm. She looked up to see Kristin.

"I heard them page you. I wanted to catch you before you went into the office. I think it's because of the emails between you and Asa that he leaked," Kristin whispered.

Chara's chin trembled. "And changed," she said through gritted teeth.

She crossed her arms. "Yeah. He came on to me too. I'm going to log into the school server and trace the IP. I have my friend Dylan on speed dial. He's willing to help. Call me after school."

Kristin nodded, and Chara slipped into the bathroom as the hall monitor approached. Then she traipsed to the office, tapped her foot nervously, and waited until the principal was ready for her.

After about fifteen minutes, her mom walked into the office, lips pressed tight. Chara was finally allowed into the principal's office, her head pounding. She rubbed her leg to keep herself calm.

"Young lady, can you explain the emails that were pushed to the entire school?" the principal asked.

Chara took a deep breath. "I can't...but I didn't do it. I didn't say those words."

"So, you were hacked?"

"That's possible," she said.

"That may be so, but this lewd conduct violates our code of

conduct. The Board wants this discussion as an intervention. They're concerned things aren't right at home."

"Is this going on my high school record? Will the university I'm attending next year see it?"

He shook his head. "No. This is to make sure you're alright."

"I didn't do anything. What about all the guys making comments in the hallways?"

"Immature, for sure. Maybe take a sick day, come back tomorrow. Teenage boys...this will blow over by tomorrow."

Astrid ground her teeth. "Thank you," she said, and stood. She grabbed Chara's elbow, and they walked to the parking lot.

Once inside the car, Astrid's voice rose. "What were you thinking, Chara?"

Chara let out all her pent-up frustration in a primal yell.

Her eyebrows knit, face red. "Don't take that tone with me! Spill it, or we'll sit here all day. They said I can't be in the building, not that I can't be out here." She pointed to the parking lot.

Chara's composure crumbled. She sobbed, struggling to find the words. Where do I start? I was chatting with an older guy out of state, but it's safe because Mikaila knows him...I was stupid...but never again.

Between sobs, she said, "I told you I didn't do this. This is my screen name, but these aren't my words. It's a guy who's pissed because I told Mikaila he came onto me and Kristin while he kept saying he wanted to be with her."

Astrid's voice trembled. "Elliott did this?"

Chara shook her head. "No...another guy, someone who doesn't even go to this school, trying to get back at me." *Not a lie.*

Astrid started the car. "Should I call his mother?"

Chara shook her head. "No. We leave it alone. I still have to go here until I graduate. I don't want more issues."

Astrid nodded, driving the rest of the way home in silence.

Once home, Chara dropped her bag, waved her mom off, and let out another primal scream. She fantasized about catching a bus or train to Connecticut and confronting Asa in person. No screen. No chessboard. Just truth.

She dialed his number.

"Chara, long time, how are you? You seem upset," Asa said evenly.

She paced her hallway, teeth clenched as she gritted out, "I can't believe you'd stoop this low to twist my words. No matter what you do, Miki will *never* want you. How did doctored versions of our conversations end up emailed to my entire school?"

"And you think I had something to do with that?"

"Don't act like you didn't. You're lucky I'm not confronting you in person."

He laughed. "Wait...are you threatening me? Why would I do this?"

"I'm not repeating myself. I haven't talked to you in months. What is your problem?"

"Gee, Chara...I'm not sure how this happened. You really think I'd do that?"

Her guttural roar shook the hallway. "No one else had access to that information but you!"

"I cared about you. Why would I go out of my way months later just to hurt you?"

"That is exactly what I am calling to find out, jackass! Now answer the question!"

He sounded wounded, but Chara felt no sympathy. "You're calling me names now. I'm offended. I can tell you're just looking for someone to blame. I didn't do it."

She snapped, her voice sharp and rapid. "You did it. And you're a liar." Then she hung up.

She burned it out at the gym. Christina Aguilera's *"Fighter"* thundered in her ears as she pounded the treadmill, breath harsh, muscles screaming.

I'm a fighter, she told herself. *You'll see how hard I can fight back.*

Showered and ready, she jogged to Mikaila's house. *We said no secrets. I'm not holding anything back.*

Mikaila opened the door immediately, a confused look on her face.

"What's up?" she asked, letting Chara in.

"I need to talk to you," Chara panted, trying to catch her breath.

They went to Mikaila's room and closed the door. Chara paced, tension coiling in her body. "This has been the worst day of my life. Asa sent out doctored versions of our conversations, and who knows what else. When I confronted him, he pretended he didn't do it."

Mikaila crossed her arms, pursed her lips. "Is it possible he didn't?"

Chara whirled, throwing her hands up. "You think I was hacked?"

Mikaila shook her head. "Not quite...Is it possible the conversation really happened, but not how you remember it?" *Are you taking his side again?*

Chara's mouth fell open. "I can't believe this. You think I

threw myself at him?"

Mikaila's face remained blank.

"You think it's not possible for *him* to like someone like *me*."

Mikaila shook her head. "No! I never said that."

Chara stood, crossing her arms over her chest. "You're not saying anything like last time. If I weren't being an Antichrist, none of this would have happened, right?"

Mikaila gasped.

"You think you're better than me," Chara gritted out, pointing toward Mikaila's chest. "That everyone would be in love with you. You're not better than me."

Mikaila broke down, tears spilling over. Chara spun and bolted from the room, down the stairs, through the front door, and out onto the steps.

I have no one left to turn to. Her chest constricted with frustration and despair.

28

a s a

Mikaila. Just the call I've been waiting for, Asa thought.

In a cheerful tone, Asa asked, "Hey, stranger! Haven't spoken to you in a while. How are you?"

She didn't bother with pleasantries. "Not good. Did you leak your private conversations with Chara?"

He gave a short, practiced gasp. "Leaked how?"

"You know exactly how." Her voice sharpened. "She told me she called you earlier today."

"I just checked my phone. I do have a missed call from her, but we didn't talk earlier."

"You're kidding me."

A slow smirk tugged at his mouth. "I'm dead serious. I don't know what's going on at your school or what she's talking about, because I was in class when she called."

"The whole school had your private conversations emailed to them last night," she snapped. "I had to listen to her get cat-called at eight in the morning. She was shamed by the principal."

Asa clicked his tongue. "That sounds like she's been hacked. Does she even have a firewall?"

"Don't lie to me! How else would the entire school get those messages?" Mikaila paused. "She thinks you doctored them."

Asa ran his hand through his hair, the gesture audible in the soft rustle near the receiver. "Me?" He gasped again, too perfectly. "How would I doctor it?"

"Doctor to change and make it look like she came onto you."

"She did come onto me," he said lightly. "But I didn't leak anything. Come on, Miki. You know me."

Mikaila sighed. "Why would she lie, Asa?"

"I told you she's lied before about me," Asa said, sighing as if the burden were familiar. "And I hate to say it, but…I think she'd do it again."

"What? Why?"

"I think she's been unstable for a while," he murmured. "She made up a conversation today that never happened. She insists I came onto her, when it was the opposite. Now the messages are leaking, and she blamed me the second she saw them. But I didn't do it."

"Why would she lie about something like this?"

Asa's voice dropped into a slow, poisonous whisper. "Who's to say she didn't do this herself? Or have Kristin do it?" He had to cover his mouth to keep the laugh from spilling out.

"You think she'd publicly humiliate and shame herself?"

Asa sighed, heavy and regretful. "I do. Or she had Kristin do it, so she stays technically blameless. Kristin has the know-how. And Chara's been trying to ruin my life ever since I made it clear I didn't want to be with her. I'm honestly concerned for her. This isn't healthy."

"*None* of this has been healthy," Mikaila murmured.

"I agree." His tone softened. "What does Elliott think about these leaked emails? Who does he think is behind them?"

Mikaila paused for a long moment. When she spoke, her voice was flat. "We broke up a while ago. He was jealous over our friendship."

Asa smiled, slow and triumphant, but he masked it instantly, letting his voice fall into gentle concern. "Aw, Mikaila...you should've told me sooner. I had no idea I caused a rift in your relationship."

"It's fine," she said with a tired exhale. "But if I asked Elliott who he'd believe, he'd take Chara and Kristin's side. Chara has always defended me...I don't know who to believe anymore."

Good thing he's out of the picture, Asa thought, a satisfied chord vibrating through him. A steady thrill drummed in his chest. He nudged another pawn across the board.

"Maybe," he said gently, "it's time you stepped back from all of this. They're not acting in your best interests, Miki. Chara and Kristin are working together, turning you against me, and for what? Wasn't Kristin your friend first? And now Chara's talking to her way more than she talks to you. Are you sure

Chara isn't trying to turn Kristin against you?"

"I…never thought about that."

"It sounds like they're dividing things up and pushing you out of their circle. You said your dad wanted you to move, right? Rebuild that relationship? Maybe that's what you need. A clean start. Somewhere away from all this drama."

There was a pause. He could practically hear her thoughts clicking into place.

"It might be time to go," Mikaila whispered. "Nan would know what to do. She'd know exactly what to say, but she's not here."

Asa lifted both arms into a triumphant. This was exactly what he'd been waiting for.

"I know," he said softly. "And losing her guidance is probably weighing you down, too. But you only have a few more weeks of school. This is the perfect time. And Kait will be off at college next year. You could spend your senior year here. Or even just the summer. Give yourself space to heal from everything they've put you through."

"I'll let you know when I'll be there," Mikaila said.

The moment the call disconnected, he pumped both fists into the air. "Yes!" He moved his knight across the board.

Checkmate.

Footsteps thudded on the stairs—unexpected, unwelcome. He froze; he thought he was alone.

Then his father appeared in the doorway, leaning a shoulder into the frame.

"Dad, what are you doing home early?"

"I wanted to change the title of the vehicle over to your name. I tried to drive it to the DMV just now, and that engine sounds awful. Has it always sounded that loud?"

"Ever since I can remember. Mom says Rusty does the maintenance like clockwork and that it's just how that vehicle runs."

His father sighed. "I don't know why she still uses Rusty. She doesn't have to take it to the dealership, but Milestones Auto can fix it up. I'll have them take a look at it."

Asa nodded. "Just let me know when so I can take the bus to class and work."

"I'll do one better for you. I'll drop you off myself."

Asa smiled. "Thanks, Dad."

His dad returned the smile. "No problem, son. Can't have it breaking down while you're at your friend's apartment." He winked and whistled as he plodded down the stairs.

Asa laughed. He knew as long as he acted like the golden child, he could get whatever he wanted.

Asa looked up florists in Mikaila's area and had a bouquet sent to her with a card that said *Sorry for what you're going through.* Then he played *Mythical Mayhem* until early in the morning.

The next afternoon, his cell rang as he moved a chess piece on his board in his room.

"Hey, Miki."

Her voice sounded hoarse. "Hi. Thanks for the flowers."

"I'm glad you liked them, and you got them so soon. I really am sorry for everything you're going through. Sounds like a lot of drama you don't need."

"Yeah."

Asa ran his fingers through his hair. "You know, I can never repay you for listening to me all the times I complained about being bullied when I was younger. Which is why I felt so hurt that you thought I could do something like that to Chara. Why don't we try to make it up to each other this summer?"

"Friends listen to each other, Asa. That's what they do."

He sighed. "Oh, I know, but I wouldn't have gotten through middle school or high school without you. The torture from Hayden and his friends was unbearable."

"I remember. Is Hayden nicer to you now?"

Asa chuckled. "No, but he lives on campus, so I don't have to run into him often."

"That's a relief."

"You're telling me. It's nice to go to the grocery store and not hear *assa-whole* being screamed down the aisle."

"That's a terrible nickname. They're just intimidated because you're smarter than them."

"I am smarter than them, but they were not intimidated by me." *Not then, anyway, but they are now.*

He smiled to himself, remembering the look on Hayden's friend's face when he realized Asa had slipped nighttime cough syrup into his liquor last year. The guy had slept straight through a major football game. Their mom had been busy chauffeuring Hayden around—typical—and Asa had taken the opportunity to finally get back at him for years of torment. They lost that game and almost lost the championship. Totally worth it.

He settled into his computer chair and gave it a slow spin. "So you're planning on finishing the year there and then coming here after?"

"Yeah, that's the plan."

He grinned. "Maybe me, you, and Lacy can go see *Spider-Man 2* when it comes out. Don't girls love Tobey Maguire? Or maybe that's just Lacy."

Mikaila laughed. "Kait likes him, too. But if Lacy goes, I'll go. Don't all boys love Kirsten Dunst?"

Asa chuckled. "You know, I *do* have a thing for redheads."

"I should go. I have to finish a paper."

"Have a good night, Miki." He hung up and drifted back toward his chessboard, a slow smirk pulling at his mouth. The board waited for him—pieces arranged in perfect tension, the queen exposed and ready.

The capture could happen at any moment.

29

mikaila

JUNE 17, 2004

My phone buzzed on the empty dresser, and I answered.
"Hello?"
A deep sigh came through. "Mikaila, are you home?"
I exhaled. "Yes, Elliott. Why?"
"I'm outside."
I hung up and walked down the stairs slowly, wondering what he could want.
His bike was propped against the house, and he sat on the

front step. He stood as soon as he heard the door open.

"Hey, you want to come in?"

He nodded and stepped inside the living room. "I heard from Kristin you're leaving for Connecticut, and I wanted to say goodbye."

I sank into the recliner while he took the couch, his fingers picking at the seams of the cushions. "What is it?"

He avoided my gaze. "Listen, I'm sorry I ended things the way I did."

"Okay."

He ran a hand through his hair. "I wanted to make things work, but I don't think we're evenly matched. I didn't have the guts to tell you. I spoke to our pastor, and he agreed it would be best if I moved on earlier rather than later."

I fiddled with my necklace and held it out to him. "I don't need to keep this then."

"Are you sure?"

"Yes."

He sighed. "What a year this was. If Chara had spoken to me, I probably would have said something about the emails that went around."

A shiver ran down my spine. "And what would you have said to her?"

He paused, his eyes darkening. "That she shouldn't be throwing herself at guys like that. The locker room gossip about her now...it's—" His eyebrows shot up, a mix of disbelief and frustration.

I pressed my lips into a firm line. "Thanks for stopping by. Have a great summer, Elliott. And by the way, that talk is just talk." I walked him to the door, opened it, and waved goodbye.

He walked off, and I slammed the door. *Good riddance.*

Stomping upstairs, I peeled the last picture off my wall. Bare white stared back. Do you feel as stripped as I do? As tired?

The remaining photos of Elliott and me went into a shoebox at the bottom of the closet. Maybe I'd come back for them one day. The photos of Chara and me stayed tucked at the bottom of my suitcase, waiting for when I was ready to hang them at Dad's house.

"The Middle" by Jimmy Eat World blared from Napster, a song I remembered from one of Kait's mixed CDs. I sang at the top of my lungs, knowing Aunt Lana was at work, and Pop rarely left his room except for meals, so he couldn't hear me. Kait was at Cameron's, soaking in the last few days together before summer jobs began.

Footsteps on the stairs froze me mid-verse. I dropped the headphones. "Who's there?" I yelled.

"It's me...Kristin."

I emerged from my room. "How'd you get in? I didn't even hear you knock."

"I let her in. You thought I wouldn't come to say goodbye?" Kait called from behind, stepping up the stairs with Cameron.

"Hey, Mini Kait!" Cameron yelled, giving me a high five once he'd made up to my bedroom door.

My stomach dropped. I wondered how long they could hear my singing.

I invited Kristin into my room. Her eyes were puffy, her posture stooped, her skin splotchy—she didn't look as happy as usual. "What's wrong?" I asked.

"Aunt Lana told us you were leaving, and I came to say goodbye," she cried. "But you don't have to go, Miki."

I wrapped her in my arms, holding her close, silently willing her to feel even a fraction of the comfort I wanted to give. "I'll miss you, Kristin. But I do have to go. It just...doesn't feel like home without Nan."

"Is it just about Nan?"

"It's not just about Nan, no. Things with Chara have gotten complicated, and I can't do it anymore. Plus, Pop's health is declining. I just need to go, Kristin."

"You and Chara can make up," Kristin pleaded, tears streaking her face. "She didn't make any of it up. Asa tried to hit on me, too. I blocked him." The only sound echoing in my head was Asa saying she was loyal to Chara. She wiped the tears from her eyes. "You know you can stay at my house. My mom loves you, and Chara will be away for school next year."

My chest ached. She'll be away, and I'll be gone, not able to save her. No matter how hard I try to model living the Word, the farther she slips away from me.

I hugged Kristin tightly, holding back my tears. *I'll miss you so much,* I thought.

If only we went to different schools, where rumors and confusion couldn't touch us. Then Asa's voice slipped into my thoughts, reminding me: it would be better to leave all this turmoil behind and find peace at my dad's. I just need a calmer environment.

We were shaken from our embrace by the beep of my dad's horn.

"I'll email you. Okay? I'll miss you. I love you and your family. And I wish the circumstances were different. I wish I could stay."

Kristin sniffled. "If things change and you want to come

back, you know where I live."

I smiled and nodded. I walked her out, then went into Pop's room to say goodbye. I had already said my goodbyes to Aunt Lana that morning before she left for work.

Hours later, my dad arrived and helped me load the van with my belongings. As he slid the last box in, he placed a hand on my shoulder. "Take as long as you need. Lorainne and I want to give you space to say goodbye to Pop on your own terms. His health is failing, and I don't want you to have any regrets later. We'll wait for you in the van."

My chest ached thinking of Pop not being here if I returned. I walked into his bedroom and threw myself onto him, his eyes popping open from slumber. Mid-embrace, I whispered, "I love you, Pop, and I'm glad I spent my life growing up with you and Nan."

He patted my arm and spoke softly, "Don't worry about me, dear. I'll be right here. You live your life and get to know your father. I love you more than I could ever tell you. I always have and always will." Pop gave me one last look before closing his eyes.

"I'll always love you too, Pop," I murmured.

I wandered through the empty downstairs and lingered in the kitchen. I didn't know when it happened, but the scent of Nan's snickerdoodles had disappeared from the house. Closing my eyes, I could still see her at the stove, waiting for them to bake, and Mom talking to her from the table. Goodbye memories, fading like a dust cloud dissolving.

Kait came down the stairs. "Ready to go?"

I nodded. She ran to me and squeezed me so hard I gasped. "Um, I can't breathe."

She stopped squeezing but didn't let go. "I'll miss you. You'll always have a home no matter where I am. Understand?"

I nodded. "I'll miss you too."

She finally let me go, and Cameron gave me another high five. "Keep cool," he said.

They walked me out to my dad's waiting car. I gave the Oak Haven house one last glance. I remembered the countless sleepovers with Chara over the years, movie nights with Elliott, and of course, Nan's cookies and her comforting presence. I turned my head, got into my dad's car, and looked out at the road ahead. Onto whatever comes next.

Dad adjusted the air conditioning and glanced at me in the rearview mirror. "Their track team is top-notch. State championship title last year."

I raised an eyebrow. "That's awesome."

"They also have a program where you can take college courses as a senior and earn college credit for free," he said.

"That's helpful," I replied.

I focused on the scenery blurring past. Sometimes we drove through sleepy farm towns, other times through cities bustling with life. I wondered what it would have been like to grow up somewhere other than Oak Haven.

Lorainne turned down the music. "Do you need to stop anywhere or need anything?"

I smiled politely. "Thanks for asking. I'm good." I didn't need anything, just space between me and the past.

Hours after we left Oak Haven, we arrived in Chestnut Hill. The chestnut trees were in bloom, and the grass had been perfectly manicured—no doubt by Asa.

We unpacked my main suitcase, the one with immediate

overnight needs, and Dad said we'd tackle the rest later. Fine by me. He helped me carry it inside, and though I'd spent the summer at this house, nothing felt the same. Lacy peeked into my room. "Hey, glad you're back." And then she disappeared down the hall. I could hear Lacy and Lexy's laughter trickling down the corridor, which would have piqued my interest in previous years, but now, it did nothing.

Later that night, I sat alone in my room with an emptied suitcase and a few scattered boxes my dad had brought up. I couldn't bring myself to unpack them yet. I sat down to compose a letter to Chara. Where do I start?

Dear Chara,

I'm sorry about how things ended between us. I wish I had had the chance to say goodbye. This time, I left because the drama between you and Asa became too much. You said you wouldn't ever lie to me or keep secrets from me, and I'm not sure I can trust you anymore. I needed space away from you.

That's as far as I got. What do I put next? You made things up so I wouldn't end up back here? With the guy you wanted? In the place you didn't want me to be? What was your endgame in all of this?

I opened my laptop and hopped onto instant messenger to see if she was online. My heart sank. She wasn't, but a message popped up immediately from Asa. I didn't respond right away. I let him wait a few minutes while I thought. My body felt suddenly light, my hands trembling with relief at seeing that he had messaged me.

At least he cares enough to ask. Chara could call—she hasn't. She could text, but she doesn't.

Asa: You made it okay?

Mikaila: Yeah, I'm here now.

Asa: Let me know if you need anything.

Mikaila: I will.

30

mikaila

Summer still had its grasp on Chestnut Hill, unwilling to let go and give in to fall. The green leaves on the chestnut trees lay still, the air thick with humidity that offered no breeze against the unrelenting heat. I stepped off the school bus and made my way into the halls of Chestnut Hill High School for the first time. My stomach was tied in knots, nerves twisting at the thought of starting over for my last year of school. Lorraine had offered to drive me on my first day, but I'd told her it wasn't necessary.

The halls resembled my old school and every other high school we'd visited for track meets. The walls were striped in their school colors, brown and teal. The lockers were a faded grey, and students bustled from their lockers to their classes. I looked down at the schedule in my hand, which told me where my homeroom was, and tried to figure out how to get there. The school was larger than my last one, and the hallways definitely weren't in alphabetical order. Why would anyone put E wing next to B wing? And where was C wing? Maybe I should've listened to Lacy when she talked about this place.

The bell rang, and the remaining students scattered like roaches into classrooms. I would have too, if I knew where to go. I turned the corner, and a security guard stopped me.

"Freshman?" he asked.

I cleared my throat. "Senior, but I transferred here, so…first day." I handed him my schedule.

He chuckled. "Nothing worse than being a freshman except being new. Come on, I'll escort you so you don't get detention your first day."

My whole body warmed, and I was certain I was blushing with embarrassment as he found my homeroom for me and quietly told the teacher I was new. I slipped into an empty seat as quickly as I could.

I turned my head to survey the classroom. Students clustered in groups, talking excitedly about their summers. Most of them wore name-brand clothing, and I knew mine didn't stand out, but didn't quite blend in here either. The homeroom teacher approached and told me the guidance counselor wanted to see me. I asked for directions to the guidance office, and when the bell rang, I made my way there.

Just like at my old school, friends circled around each other's lockers, laughing and reminiscing about summer. That would have been me and Kristin this year. I brushed the thought aside, refusing to get nostalgic so early in the day.

When I reached the counselor's office, she sat me down and reviewed my credits. I asked about the credits Oak Haven had given me for Bible Club. She paused.

Clearing her throat, she said, "You're welcome to join our Bible Club, but that doesn't give you credit here. Those credits are non-transferable. You'll need to take another elective course to graduate on time."

I nodded, understanding, and chose an Intro to Social Work course, which sounded like an easy A. The rest of the day blurred, nothing memorable. My classes seemed challenging but not so hard that I couldn't get decent grades. I had thought I needed to graduate with honors to follow Elliott to his choice school, but now I didn't have a solid plan at all.

Thoughts of the future made my heart race because, for once, I had no idea what that even looked like here.

After school finished, I came home to a delivery of a bouquet. I assumed Dad had gotten them for Lorraine, but a card slipped out when I unlocked the door. *Miki, hope your first day goes well. —Asa.*

I smiled, carried them into the empty house, and set them in a vase on the table.

Upstairs, in what was now my room, the boxes were unpacked and my suitcase had already been moved to the attic—Dad's way of telling me I was here for the long haul. I didn't put anything on the walls, but I tucked photos of Kait and me, and of Chara and me, into the mirror of my vanity.

As I held the frame, a flashback hit: the white lights, the room with the floor that looked like clouds, the deal I made to trade my life for hers. My heart sank. I was so far from my goal now that I didn't even know where to begin, and time was running out. And if I did accomplish it, what would that mean for me now? I'd give up my future…but what did my future look like right now anyway?

I sighed and pulled out my first reading assignment for English class along with the discussion questions I needed to complete. I couldn't focus. My mind kept drifting back to Chara and how fractured we'd become. Nan would have told me to pray, so I did. And the answer to those prayers brought me here, so I needed to focus on my schoolwork and make her proud.

Lorraine arrived home first and called up the stairs to let me know. I was grateful for the distraction, from homework and from my thoughts. I walked down to the kitchen.

"Can I help with dinner?"

She gave a smile that felt forced and patted my arm. "You just need to focus on your schoolwork right now and let me handle the rest."

She nudged me gently toward the staircase. "I'll let you know when dinner's ready, and then we'll talk about how your first day went."

I trudged back up the stairs. This past summer I'd felt like a visitor, not a resident here. Still, I smiled to myself thinking about the trips to the lake, the bowling nights, and the youth group outings with Asa. He knew I needed to get out of the house, and Dad and Lorraine seemed relieved I'd made a friend and was out of their hair.

Even Dad still felt stiff around me, as if I could decide at any moment to return to Pop's house and disappear again. Lacy had stayed home over the summer and hung out with Asa and me once, but she never invited me out with her friends. Lexy had taken an internship abroad and didn't come home at all. She sent postcards from London addressed to the whole family.

Lorraine called up to say that dinner was ready. I joined her and Dad at the table, not realizing he'd already come home. "Where did the flowers come from?"

I smiled back. "Asa. For my first day of school. He had them delivered."

Dad and Lorraine both smiled. "How thoughtful."

"How was your first day of school?" Lorraine asked.

I forced a smile. "Good. It's a big school."

"It is a big school. Glad your day went well."

She took a sip of wine. "Did you meet with the track team coach or sign up for any clubs?"

I finished chewing. "I didn't have time to do any of that yet, but I will."

Dad finished his hamburger. "I'm sure you'll get the hang of things quickly."

I took a sip of iced tea. "Yes. The teachers seem nice."

Lorraine smiled and looked at Dad. "Lacy and Lexy always said they had great teachers."

He nodded and clapped his hands together. "I'm gonna get some paperwork done for tomorrow."

I finished my last bite. "I'll help clean up."

Lorraine drained the rest of her wine. "No need. Just rinse your dish and leave it in the sink. I'll get it."

* * *

The next day at school was just as hot, and the air conditioning had broken in half the building—unfortunately, the half I had to be in. By lunch, my auburn hair was untamed and wild. The girls I'd already figured out were popular, took one look at my clothes and my hair, and quietly laughed to themselves as I passed them in the cafeteria. I ate lunch alone, sitting near the door so I could make a quick exit.

The rest of the school day didn't go any better. By the final bell, we were all stuck to the plastic chairs, sweat practically dripping from us.

During the bus ride home, my legs tingled with the need for a long run, even though the weather was far from ideal. When the bus pulled up to Dad's house, I stepped off with fists balled, thinking about the past two days: the looks, the stares, the emptiness of my dad's house, even when people were in it.

After showering and changing, I picked up my cell and called Asa, who answered on the first ring.

"Rough day?" he asked.

How did you know?

I tapped the pen I'd pulled from my book bag against the bed. "Thanks for the flowers. They're beautiful. I'm still lost. It was hot as a furnace. And I don't fit in here. My hair's too curly, especially in the humidity, and I don't wear name brands like everyone else."

"I'm glad you liked them. If I didn't have classes, I'd have delivered them in person. And you'll find your way around the building; it just takes a few days."

I smiled. "I know. But no one's introduced themselves or tried to make friends."

"You're too good for them, anyway. You don't need to make friends with any of them."

"I don't wear name-brand clothes like they do, or listen to the music I hear them talking about."

"You don't need to look like them or act like them. You're perfect just the way you are."

"You should have seen the looks they gave me. I don't think they'd say that."

"That's because they know you look better than them, on the outside *and* the inside. They don't deserve your friendship."

"I'm thinking of running away. I don't know how much longer I can go to school there." I guess I'd become used to Chara fighting my bullies for me.

His voice softened. "Then let me be the one to save you from it."

My shoulders relaxed for the first time all day. "Thanks."

"You're welcome. Don't let them get to you."

I hung up the phone with a smile. He was probably right. He had graduated from there, after all. This is just what starting over feels like—fighting my own battles, finding new friends, figuring out where I belong. He'll help me navigate this.

I'm not alone.

31

asa

Asa waited his turn in line at Milestones Auto, one of several customers eager to pick up their vehicles. He tapped his foot to the eighties music playing on the radio. When it was his turn, he skimmed the mechanic's report and flinched as he scanned the final bill, the total glaring at him from the bottom.

The mechanic looked disheveled. He could barely zip his overalls, smelled faintly of day-old socks, his eyes sunk into his balding head, cheeks puffed as he chewed gum and tried to speak at the same time. His voice alternated between monotone and condescending.

Handing over the key, the mechanic said, "There's an unusual problem with the exhaust that I think is fixed."

Asa scratched his head, glancing at the bill. He didn't think the number justified the work.

"It's imperative the car is serviced every three months. We need to check for ongoing corrosion or rust, just to be certain."

Asa crinkled his nose at the smell. "And coming back every three months will prevent that?"

The mechanic shifted his feet. "The car's old, but in decent condition. We tuned her up so she's quieter and happier. There isn't a hole in the exhaust or corrosion yet, but that's why it's important she's serviced every three months, to keep an eye on her. If the noise suddenly gets worse, bring her in."

Asa dug his hands in his pockets and nodded, forcing a smile. "Sure. I'll see you in a few months, hopefully not sooner." He used his credit card to pay the bill, determined to prove to his dad he could handle it and didn't want to lose his newly earned respect. If that was the cost of a tune-up, he shuddered to think what an actual repair would cost. *No wonder Mom used Rusty all these years,* he thought.

Sliding into the driver's seat, he turned the key in the ignition. For the first time since learning to drive, he didn't have to crank the music to hear it over the engine. For the amount he'd paid, it better be healthy for a while.

His phone dinged. A text from Mikaila. Pulling into his driveway, he smiled at the message: *"A friend loves in all times."And you're falling in love with me,* he thought.

He texted back: *"A sweet friendship refreshes the soul."* She responded with a smiley face. *Keep you right where I want you,* he thought. Without Kristin, Elliott, or Chara swooping in with whispered doubts.

He walked from his car to the house, tossing the milestones report and bill into the trash. Then he headed to the backyard, timing it perfectly for when she'd get off the bus and call. He let a few rings go to make it seem like he was busy.

"Oh, hey."

"Am I interrupting something important?"

"Only biomedical science. I could be curing cancer over here," Asa joked.

Mikaila laughed. "I can let you get back to it then. The world's been waiting a long time for it, and I'd hate to make them wait longer."

"I'm glad you called. I've hit a wall and need a distraction. You're doing the world a favor."

"In that case, do you want to go for a walk around the neighborhood?"

Asa's body warmed all over. "How about the park? I know the perfect trail."

"Sounds good. I can be ready in twenty minutes," she said.

Asa went back inside, changing into khakis, a button-down polo, and a hoodie with the community college logo on the lapel. He climbed into the sedan, started the engine, and kept the radio at a normal volume. The chorus of *Float On* by Modest Mouse played as he drove two blocks to her house. He pulled into the driveway, slipped the keys into his pocket, still humming the tune, and knocked on the door.

It swung open, and she smiled. She looked cute in jeans, an Abercrombie shirt, and a jacket. "Hey. I just told Dad and

Lorraine you were coming to get me."

He grinned. "Good. Ready to go?"

She pulled the door shut. "Yeah. How was your day?"

Asa opened her car door. "Pretty good. The car went to the repair shop and sounds healthier now." He turned the key in the ignition.

Mikaila laughed. "Glad you got some medicine. I can hear myself think now."

Asa drove them to the park a few miles from her dad's house, filling the ride with easy, meandering conversation. Pulling into the parking lot, Mikaila swiveled in her seat, taking it all in before stepping out. "I've never been here before."

He cut the engine off and walked around to her side. "I'll take you to the trail I used to walk in high school."

Asa led her arm in arm toward the path that wound through the chestnut trees. She tilted her head, eyes scanning the canopy above. "They're so tall."

"The mayor's family started this park in 1935. That's why the town's called Chestnut Hill. I can't believe Lacy never brought you here for running or to give you the history."

"I know. This park has great shade. Would have been perfect for summer runs."

Asa led her to a covered bridge, the red paint peeling and cracked.

"This bridge is cool," Mikaila commented.

He pointed to a spot on the interior wall, marked with scratches and indentations. "When I was in high school, couples used to carve their initials and hearts right here."

She smirked and lightly tapped his arm. "So, you brought me to a make-out spot?"

He shifted, tapping his foot nervously. "Probably was a make-out spot. Looks bad, huh?"

She laughed. "I'm kidding."

He cleared his throat; eyes fixed somewhere past her shoulder. "I brought you here because it's quiet. I wanted a place to tell you that I've always felt something deeper for you than friendship. I tried to bury it when you were with Elliott, and again when everything with Chara happened. But I couldn't. My heart keeps leading me to you."

"Do you have any hearts etched in here that I should know about?"

Asa ran his hand through his hair, a sheepish grin tugging at his lips. "What? No."

Mikaila laughed at having caught him off guard, and his laughter joined hers, warm and easy.

Asa took her hand, and they walked out of the bridge, back through the swaying trees. The fall air made her shiver. He gave her a longing look, and she met it, her lower lip pinched. He leaned in and pressed his lips to hers; the aroma of her strawberry shampoo and vanilla body spray sent his heartbeat racing. Mikaila returned the kiss with equal force, and he pulled her closer, their tongues colliding in a dance that felt like sweet victory to him. *Finally, you're mine.* His whole body buzzed with electricity while they remained tangled together. She pulled back first, smiling softly.

He grinned. "See? This is what we were meant for all along."

Mikaila squeezed his hand. "Come on, follow me." She led him back to the covered bridge, reached into his pocket, and retrieved his car keys. Using the tip, she scratched *A+M* inside a heart. She looked at him, grinning.

"Now you do have initials here with someone."

Asa grinned back, held her hand, and lightly kissed it. "I would've waited forever for our initials to be scratched here."

He could have played this game forever, just to get her exactly where he wanted her.

32

mikaila

DECEMBER 22, 2004

The sounds of *"View of Heaven"* by Yellowcard filled my ears as I ran as hard and as fast as I could on the treadmill in Dad's basement. "Early Christmas present," he had said, so I could prep for the track team in the off-season when it was too cold to run outside. Sweat dripped down my face as I focused on my breathing, my stride, and beating yesterday's time. Focusing on a goal kept thoughts of my upcoming trip to Maryland at bay.

My watch beeped, signaling cooldown time. I slowed my

pace and let my heart rate drop. That's when the trip crept back into my thoughts.

Aunt Lana had called in November to tell me that Pop couldn't make the drive up for Thanksgiving. My first without him in years. My chest ached as I talked to him on the phone, but his raspy voice made it hard to understand him. Kait stayed in Oak Haven to spend the holidays with them, and I didn't blame her.

A few days before Thanksgiving, Aunt Lana called again. Pop needed hospice, and it wouldn't be long. I called Kait, and for the first time ever, we cried together on the phone. When I got the next call that he had passed, it was Kait on the line. "We'll do cremation and have the services during winter break from school, so neither of us misses anything. It's what he would have wanted," she said.

I agreed. He had told me to live my life. In a few short days, I'd be on my way back to Oak Haven for another goodbye.

I wiped my face with a towel and took a long sip of water. Stretching my calves, hamstrings, and glutes, I lingered in the newly refinished basement. Dad had worked on this surprise all summer, and I hadn't even noticed. Part of the area was a workout space with a treadmill and free weights, while the other part was a hangout area with new furnishings and a TV. He said I was older now and needed my own space.

Upstairs, I showered and changed, making sure I didn't forget my new promise ring from Asa at the end of October. I slipped it on my finger; the diamond caught the sunlight streaming through the window, and the sparkle still made me smile. Since we kissed, we'd been calling each other every evening, enjoying a date night every weekend, and attending church together on Sunday. My dad asked about him during the week, as if Asa lived here too.

That evening, just as we were settling in for dinner, the doorbell rang. I glanced at Lorraine and Dad, but neither of them looked like they were expecting anyone.

At the door stood Asa, holding a bouquet of roses and a sympathy card.

I stepped back. "Come in."

He tilted his head down, and I rose onto my toes to brush a quick kiss across his lips. Pulling back, I said, "I'll put these in a vase." I trailed into the kitchen, reached for one on top of the refrigerator, and he stood behind me.

Lorraine set down her wine glass. "Those are lovely. Would you like to join us for dinner?"

Asa smiled. "They're not nearly as beautiful as you and Mikaila, but I like how they decorate the table. I'd love to stay. I'm pretty sure I smelled your ziti from my house. My mouth's been watering since."

Lorraine tucked a strand of hair behind her ear, clearly amused. "Such compliments. Please, have as much ziti as you'd like."

I handed him a plate, and we slid in beside each other at the table, the air light with laughter and the comforting scent of garlic and tomato sauce.

Dad wiped his mouth. "How are finals going, young man?"

Asa swallowed. "Best ziti in the entire world! And finals are pretty good, thanks."

Lorraine swirled her red wine. "And you're still working at the pharmacy?"

"Only about ten hours a week. I stock shelves and cashier.

During the holidays, I'll pick up more hours. But for now, I need all the time I can get to study."

Dad nodded, taking a sip of wine. "You're right, son...about the ziti and studying, of course."

"I'm also looking into helping a professor as a teaching assistant one semester. You know, earn some money and help struggling underclassmen."

I smiled. "You'd be good at that."

Dad finished his plate. "Excellent meal. Wonderful company, but I do need to get some paperwork done."

Asa finished his ziti. "I'll help Miki clear the dishes. Would it be alright if we went for a quick drive after?"

I glanced at Dad, who checked his watch. "Just be back before eleven p.m. It's a school night, and six a.m. comes quicker when you're older."

"Absolutely. Sleep is of utmost importance."

We got in Asa's car and drove to a nearby neighborhood. He fumbled with the radio until a holiday classic filled the cabin, turning it up over the engine's hum. I pointed to the dashboard. "Your engine's sounding a little louder. You have to turn the music up over it again."

He waved a dismissive hand. "It's still healthy. Just something this car does."

Asa slowed down and pointed to a house outside my window. "These people go all out every year. Every year is better than the last in lights and decorations." We admired the blinking, colorful displays and the signs for Santa. My stomach fluttered as a memory stirred.

"What is it?" Asa asked.

I smiled. "Reminds me of a house in our Oak Haven

neighborhood that had a bull's-eye in Christmas lights on the roof every year that said, 'Santa, stop here.'"

"Sounds like an elaborate setup."

I whispered, "Yeah," still seeing the house in my mind as we used to drive past it daily on the bus.

He continued through the neighborhood and then pulled into a coffee shop drive-through for hot chocolate. He lifted his cup toward me. "Cheers, for our first holiday activity, and here's to many more."

I smiled, sipping my hot chocolate as he drove us back to my house. At my doorstep, he walked me up, gave me a kiss, and said, "We'll both taste chocolatey," making me laugh.

As I pulled back, he kept his hands on my waist, his gaze locking with mine. "Be good while you're there and call every night." My stomach tightened at his piercing gaze and the way his hands gripped me. If I weren't wearing a winter coat, I'm sure I'd have felt his fingers through my bones. *I'm going for a week, not a lifetime.*

I gave him a lingering kiss, my way of promising to do exactly that. "I promise."

I stepped inside, shivering slightly, my stomach still tight from the memory of his embrace.

* * *

When I arrived back at my house in Oak Haven that Friday, everything seemed smaller than I remembered: the house, the town, the mall, even my room. Kait picked me up from the airport. She looked at the single bag in my hand and gave me a side hug. "You still pack so light."

I laughed. "We still have a washer and dryer, right? I can

do laundry if I need to."

Kait tapped her fingers on the steering wheel to Franz Ferdinand's *"Take Me Out"* playing on the radio. "We do, but I didn't think that's how you wanted to spend your time here."

I shrugged. "Not like we can spend our time on the beach. It's freezing."

After breaking free from the gridlocked cars around the airport, the rest of the ride was smooth. I rested my head against the window as we drove. Shortly after, we pulled into the driveway and walked inside. Aunt Lana was sobbing on the couch.

Kait and I hung our winter coats on the rack before I walked over to the couch and wrapped Aunt Lana in a warm embrace. "It's okay," I tried to reassure her.

She sniffled. "I'm hanging in there. I just had to get a few tears out. How are you, Miki? It's so good to see you."

My gaze darted from Kait, who sank into the recliner, and then back to Aunt Lana. "I'm as good as I can be. I miss Pop. I've missed you guys, too." I wiped a tear that slid down. "Do we know what we want to do about the service?"

Aunt Lana shook her head, unable to answer, her chest heaving from sobs.

Kait stood up, her voice wavered. "Why don't we get you settled in your room?"

We walked up the stairs, and I threw my bag down. Everything felt so different. The twin bed looked tiny compared to the queen I'd been sleeping in.

Kait embraced me, her wall of stoicism finally gone. The tears flowed freely now. Things had certainly changed since I'd been gone. I held her and groaned. "You're going to make me start crying again."

She laughed through her sobs as she pulled away. "I've been strong around Aunt Lana, so she doesn't have to worry about me. I just couldn't hold it in any longer. I'll get it together, though."

I put my hand on her shoulder. "You don't have to be strong for all of us. You're allowed to feel however you want. You're allowed to break down sometimes."

She wiped her wet face with the sleeve of her hoodie. "Very Nan of you."

I smiled. "It would also be very Nan of me to make sure Aunt Lana is okay. Let's go down here and stay with her."

We went down the stairs and into the living room. I sat next to Aunt Lana, hands resting in my lap. Kait sat on the other side of me. "What can we do for the service?"

Aunt Lana wiped her eyes with a tissue. "We need photos to display."

Kait grabbed the albums off the shelf and placed them on the coffee table. I pointed to the one I wanted to select. "Let's start with this one—him and Nan's wedding photo."

"The one with him in his Naval uniform and Nan at his side should be front and center," Kait said.

"We need the one with all of us at our last Christmas together, too," I added.

Aunt Lana took a deep breath. "Your mom wants to be at the service."

"She can come, but she doesn't get a say in any of the arrangements," Kait warned.

Aunt Lana looked weary and reached over, gripping Kait's hand. "She can come, but doesn't get a say. I think that's fair."

"I sold my house to live here, and I've enjoyed it. I wouldn't have done it any differently. Now that Pop's gone, Kait's at school, and you're at your dad's, it's time to sell this house. I don't think I should keep that secret to myself any longer."

I gasped. "This is our home! How can you let it go?"

Kait sighed. "You can't expect Aunt Lana to live here alone."

My eyes bored into Aunt Lana's, pleading. "I understand you don't need the space, but—"

Aunt Lana placed her hand over mine. "Let's talk about this tomorrow. It's not just the space, Miki. It's the cost as well. Maybe now wasn't the right time to bring this up, but I'm upset, and it slipped out."

I played with the ring on my finger. "We can talk later. You're right, it's not a good time to discuss this. Plus, I'm going to call Asa." I pushed off the couch, walked to my room, and dialed his number.

"Hey. I was starting to worry you didn't make it there," He answered.

I toyed with the ring on my finger, sighing. "Well, I've made it. But Aunt Lana's devastated, and I want to help her as much as I can. I just—"

"That makes sense."

"We've got a busy day planning tomorrow's service. How was your day? How is everything there?"

"I'm sorry for your loss. Pop was an amazing chess player and a wonderful man to meet. I wish there was something I could do. Everything is fine here. Work was good. Nothing crazy happened."

"I'll miss him," I sighed. "I'm glad your day went well. I miss you, too."

"I know. I miss you, but I should let you get some rest. It's been a lot for you lately, and I've got work soon."

* * *

After breakfast, we walked into the church I had grown up attending, there to celebrate Pop's life. It felt familiar, yet somehow different. I tapped my leg nervously, silently praying that he and Nan were together again. Mom came up, wrapped me in a warm hug, and then turned to embrace Kait.

The pastor entered and began the service. It was short, as Pop had requested in his will. I read a passage:

> *"John 14:1-3: Don't let your hearts be troubled. Trust in God, and trust also in me. There is more than enough room in my Father's home. If this were not so, would I have told you that I am going to prepare a place for you? When everything is ready, I will come and get you, so that you will always be with me where I am."*

Aunt Lana walked to the pulpit, speech in hand. She wore a black dress and her silver cross necklace, as she smoothed out the crumpled paper in her hand. "My father served in the Navy, where he learned strong work ethics and a sense of right and wrong. He met my mother while on a weekend pass from boot camp and married her a month later before shipping off. It wasn't uncommon in those days, and he always said he wouldn't have done anything differently." She paused, dabbing at her eyes. "He loved his wife, his children, and his grandchildren. Dad taught us the value of hard work, but also the importance of caring for family. In his retirement, he shared his chess skills with neighbors and anyone who wanted to learn. We will miss you, Dad."

Aunt Lana walked back to her seat, and Kait read the cards sent from church members. "Thank you for your kind words. We'd like to invite everyone to join us for food in the community center. You can access it through the door on the left-hand side." She gestured to the door, then walked down from the pulpit with Aunt Lana and me. We set our purses on a table as people began to flow in. Mom came over to Kait and me. "I miss you guys." She said. Kait and I didn't say anything, and Aunt Lana quickly pulled her away.

I turned toward the table with the lunch options, and ten feet away, I saw Chara. She looked slimmer, her posture relaxed, and she wore a natural smile I hadn't seen in a long time. She approached me first, and I froze in place. She wrapped me in a long embrace and whispered, "I'm so sorry Pop's gone, Miki," and my chest heaved with tears I hadn't realized were still there. She pulled back first, placed her arm on my shoulder, and wiped her eyes. "When you get a chance, let's talk." *Where do we start?*

I nodded, still rooted to the white tiles beneath me. Kait came over and guided me to the food line. I grabbed a piece of chicken breast and some salad. Back at the table, she said softly, "I think you should speak with Chara." I ate half my food, barely hungry, and discarded the rest.

I walked over to where Chara was seated with Kristin, laughing. For a moment, it felt almost like high school again, in the cafeteria, before everything had gone crazy. I blinked, and Kristin was guiding me to the table. *I'm so glad these chairs are more comfortable than cafeteria benches.*

Kristin directed me to a seat between her and Chara. "Why

don't you sit with us?"

I nodded and took the seat between them.

Kristin leaned in and gave me a side hug. "The service was great. I'm so sorry for your loss."

I offered a quick smile. "Thanks—Thanks for coming. I've missed you."

"I miss you too. School's not the same without you." Kristin's phone buzzed. She checked it and then looked up with a frown. "My mom's outside to pick me up." We stood, and I gave her a goodbye hug.

She placed a hand on my shoulder. "Keep in touch. Promise?"

I smiled. "Promise."

I sat back down at the table, now alone with Chara, and found myself at a loss for words.

"That's some ring," she said, pointing to the promise ring on my finger.

"Thanks," I glanced down at the ring on display. "It's from Asa. You know we're seeing each other now. Right?"

She stiffened briefly, then relaxed. "Remember my dreams about you moving there?"

I nodded.

"I had a dream last month that you had passed away. I thought I should tell you. My mom said it meant our friendship had changed, and sometimes that happens."

My heart sank. I remembered my own dream and the promise I had made to save her. *No, it can't be,* I thought. I've failed my promise. How could I be the one to go now?

She shook her head. "Think of everything that's happened between us. Our friendship has changed. We haven't spoken in months."

I bit my lip. "I'm sorry."

She shook her head. "I'm sorry too. I didn't realize how easy it is to get swept up in classes and clubs. I'm making up for all the lost time."

"You look happier," I commented.

"I am. I live with my dad in an apartment complex in South Carolina. He gets home nurses, who he loves to flirt with."

I laughed at the mental image.

"I'm going to be a physical therapist, inspired by the physical therapy my dad and I received."

I smiled. "That sounds like a great plan."

She nodded, but her smile faded, brows furrowed. "I still miss you, Miki. But I don't want Asa in my life. I don't think he's a great person. Let's just agree to disagree about him."

I nodded. Some things aren't worth arguing over.

Aunt Lana walked over, placing a hand on the back of my chair. "Our time here is almost over." She said before getting pulled in another direction.

"I rented a car. Let's go talk on the beach," Chara said.

We rose from our seats, and before heading out, I grabbed Aunt Lana's arm. "Going to the beach with Chara. She rented a car, and she'll drive me back," I mumbled in her ear.

"Sounds good. Be safe," Aunt Lana said.

We walked out to the parking lot and got into the blue Chevy Malibu, listening to Yellowcard's *"Ocean Avenue"* on the drive to the beach.

My body pressed into the seat. "I love this CD."

"Same. And so does Kristin."

I looked out the window at the businesses we drove past. "It's weird how everything looks the same but feels smaller."

She nodded. "I feel that way too. Like instead of us getting bigger, everything shrank."

We parked close to the beach, sitting for a moment as the waves roared and crashed beneath the setting sun.

Chara kept her eyes forward, smiling. "Do you miss this?"

I sighed. "I do. The waves crashing over and over but never sweeping us away reminds me God's in control, and I don't need to worry about the small things because, in the end, He'll take care of them."

Chara glanced at me. "I started attending Coastal College's Campus Ministry regularly, and when they asked what led me to join, I told them you."

I sat up, my mouth dropping. "Really? How did I influence you? What did Astrid say about it?"

She chuckled. "I live with my dad, and he used to take me to church. As long as I don't bring it up with Astrid, she's fine. She said there are worse things I could be doing in college. And you influenced me because you're strong in your faith no matter what happens. I understand that now. There's a peace in knowing God's in control even when it feels like the world is ending."

I smiled and rested my hand on her arm. "That's exactly it. And Astrid's not wrong. What does your campus ministry do?"

"We meet weekly, play games, sing songs, and invite other students to accept Christ."

I squeezed her arm, unable to contain my excitement. "Do you know how long I wanted you to do Bible Club with me? That's exactly what we do!"

For a moment, it felt like the months of silence between us had vanished, like nothing had ever come between us. *Thank you, God. Maybe I've partially succeeded in our deal after all.*

Then my throat tightened. *What does that mean for my future? Is Chara's dream a message that we'll be switching places?*

I played with the ring on my finger. The chorus of "View of Heaven" drifted through the speakers. "Can you turn it up? This song reminds me of Nan...and now Pop."

Chara turned the volume up, and we sang at the top of our lungs as the sun slipped behind the ocean.

When the song ended, she glanced at me. "I have an early flight tomorrow, and I have to get back. I'm sorry."

I smiled. "No problem. I'm glad we came out here and talked."

We sang *"Blue and Yellow"* by The Used as she drove me back to Aunt Lana's. She lowered the volume as she parked in front of the house. "We need to keep in touch more often. We can't just go back to not talking."

I sighed. "Yeah. You call me, because I don't want to interrupt your schedule."

"I can do that."

Kait's car was gone, probably with Cameron. I leaned over, hugging her one last time. "I've missed you."

I breathed in the floral scent of her shampoo. "I've missed you more."

I got out of the car, gave her one last wave, and walked inside. I could hear her playing Blink-182's "I Miss You" as she drove away. Inside, the living room lights were off. Kait was gone. Aunt Lana had gone to bed. And all I could wonder was...how could a place that once felt so alive feel so empty now?

I trudged upstairs, got ready for bed, and collapsed onto my mattress. *I'm glad You found Chara, Lord, especially since I didn't know what to do for her from another state.*

But the gnawing sensation in my stomach didn't fade. *Does that mean my time's almost up? Maybe it means that because she believes in You like I do, we'll both be alright.*

I smiled to myself. *That must be it. We'll both be alright now.*

33

mikaila

DECEMBER 23, 2004

The air hovered slightly above freezing, and snow drifted down in small, powdery puffs. The kind that made driving annoying but didn't require shoveling. Asa drove us to Pizza Pagoda, Christmas music softly playing on the radio, on my first night back in Chestnut Hill. He had arrived at my door with a brand-new scarf and glove set, which I was now wearing, the fabric warm against my skin.

We slid into a booth, and before sitting across from me, he

leaned in for a quick, lingering kiss.

"Now that we're not driving behind grandparents with a death wish, please tell me all about your trip back home."

I laughed. "They were just being cautious. And not much else happened. My mom acted like she was happy to see me, which was…different. I'm not sure it wasn't an act." I rolled my eyes, thinking about the mini reunion we'd had before the service. Thankfully, Aunt Lana had stepped in.

Asa tilted his head. "It's possible she's stable enough now to realize she missed out on raising you and Kait and regrets not being able to do it when you were younger."

"I told her I forgave her a while ago, and that I didn't mind talking on holidays."

I still think that's a fair compromise.

He nodded. "That makes sense." He reached across the table and took my hand.

"I don't want to open myself up for more hurt," I said quietly.

"I don't blame you," he replied. "I believe she parented to the best of her ability, but because of her disability, she couldn't connect with you emotionally."

I nodded slowly. "No one's ever said it that way."

"You've never been to therapy?"

I shook my head. "I don't think that was covered under our insurance, but either way, it was never offered."

"I've been in and out of therapy my whole life."

This time, I tilted my head. "Really? Why?"

He let out a short laugh. "You know when you try to cure the world of cancer, they call you crazy."

"I'd think they'd give you an award, not punish you with counseling."

He chuckled. "You'd think that."

The waitress approached with a smile, notepad ready. Asa handed her our menus. "We'll split a cheese pizza. Thanks."

My stomach tightened. *I must be hungrier than I thought.* When she left, I squeezed his hand again. "So why were you in therapy?"

He took a sip of water. "My parents thought I needed counseling because I was introverted, and they didn't understand it. They assumed it was because I'd been bullied when I was younger. They're both extroverted in their own ways, and of course, Hayden, otherwise known as the golden child, was perfect and just like them. How could I not be like one of them?"

I raised my eyebrows. "Did therapy help?"

"Hayden becoming a football star for them to focus on... that helped me. I'm basically invisible to them. It helped me tame my frustrations that I'll never please them until I act like Hayden. Which I'm not doing."

The waitress brought our pizza, and I grabbed a slice. "I don't think you're invisible to them. They just value football over chess."

Asa took a bite, swallowed, and wiped his mouth. "Right. They value chauvinism and masculinity over strategy and intelligence."

I didn't want to dwell on his parents, so I shifted the topic. "Almost forgot to tell you...I had a great conversation with Chara after the service."

His hand went slack, eyebrows knitting together. "How did you almost forget that?"

"It slipped my mind. You know, things with my mom kind of overshadow everything else. Still does."

He narrowed his eyes. "What did you talk about?"

I kept my voice light. "Her dad's progress, and her college major. We agreed to start speaking again. But she doesn't want to talk with you and won't bother you. She's happier now than I've seen her in a while."

He squeezed my fingers. "I'm glad her dad's doing well. That sounded like a horrific ordeal they went through."

He looked like he had more to say, but the waitress walked over.

"Delicious," I mumbled, shoving a piece in my mouth without worrying about being ladylike. Anything to avoid reopening that conversation.

After a few slices each, he wiped his mouth and paid the check. Outside, the earlier snow had melted, leaving the roads wet and slick.

As we neared my dad's, he lowered the radio.

"I think your engine's getting louder."

He shrugged. "Are you sure you can trust Chara?"

"Of course I can trust her."

"I'm just saying…she's been manipulative before. Don't let her get back into your head."

I dropped his hand and raised my voice. "She's back to being normal. And if you hadn't allowed her to 'seduce you,' she never would've been able to manipulate anything."

"She tried to seduce *me* because she was unhinged, and she still could be, for all we know."

"I know she's normal now because I spent time with her. I can see the change in her."

He scratched his head, flicking his hair. "You thought you knew her before."

"She'd just been through a horrific accident. I don't know if that caused her behavior, but she's different now. She's joined her campus ministry."

He put his hands up in surrender and softened his voice. "It's okay. I'm just looking out for you. You know I care."

I nodded. "The other thing I wanted to tell you before you flipped out over Chara...Aunt Lana said she's selling the house."

"Makes sense. Why would she keep a four-bedroom house just for herself?"

I sighed. "I don't *want* her to sell the house. I want to move back. That's my house. Oak Haven is my home. You can pursue whatever kind of engineer you want to be in Maryland."

"How are we supposed to afford to buy a house right now?"

I glared at him. "We could rent it from her while she keeps the mortgage."

"And how do we pay for both school *and* rent?"

"I can get a job, apply for scholarships, or delay school until you're done. You expect us to live with our parents forever?"

He groaned and rubbed his temples. "Not forever...just until I'm done with school."

He leaned toward me. I leaned toward the door, widening the space between us. "You know you're happier here. Think about all the stress you went through before coming back. Why would you want to go back to that? I'm just thinking about you."

My stomach twisted. *Bad pizza or bad company?*

I forced a smile. "I just can't see myself staying here after high school."

"Your dad literally renovated the basement so you could have your own space. And that's how you're going to repay him? By leaving? How do you think that's going to make him feel?"

"I didn't ask him to do that. He did it on his own and didn't tell me until it was already done. And Lacy and Lexy can still use it if they want."

He laughed, dry and humorless. "They aren't going to do that. He thought you'd be different. You're his daughter. His flesh and blood. And you're just going to walk out again?"

I narrowed my eyes, lowering my voice. "He'll understand, Asa."

"He won't," he said, shaking his head. "And you're going to regret not sticking around."

I pressed my lips together. "If you want to be with me, you'll consider moving with me to Oak Haven. Renting my childhood home until we're ready to buy it."

Before he could answer, I opened the car door and stepped out. The cold hit me like a slap. I wrapped my arms around my stomach and walked the rest of the way alone, the slick pavement crunching under my boots.

34

chara

Chara drove her used sedan from the main campus of Coastal Carolina University to her dad's apartment; he bought her the vehicle with the sale of his Maryland condo. The sight of palm trees was a welcome change of scenery from the Oak trees that reminded her of her childhood years. She tuned the radio until a song she recognized came on.

She moved with her dad at the completion of high school, not feeling compelled to stay in a town that reminded her of a tumultuous time of her life. When they first moved, they lived with their cousin for a few months while her dad apartment hunted. He settled on a two bedroom in a complex, with a pool, gym and monthly community events. Centrally located twenty minutes from campus and the beach, it was the perfect location when she started her courses.

She pulled into her designated parking spot in the complex. Her cell rang and she smiled, recognizing the ringtone she specified for Mikaila. She pulled it out of her handbag and brought the phone with her while she unlocked the apartment. Her dad had made friends at a local church, and they had a weekly luncheon that lasted hours. The perfect time to talk to Mikaila uninterrupted.

They had been talking regularly, the same day and time of the week, so that life didn't distract either of them. Chara recently sent her a postcard from Myrtle Beach and on the back, she wrote, L.Y.L.A.S, Always.

South Carolina, which is typically warmer than Connecticut and Maryland, but that year the temperature dropped unseasonably low. *Maybe we should have moved to Florida, where I'd be warm all year long. At least I can be at the beach more days throughout the year than when we're in Maryland, she thought...*

"I got your postcard in the mail yesterday. I don't know if any place can beat Ocean City," Mikaila giggled.

Chara laughed. "I didn't say it was better than Ocean City. It's just warmer here most of the year, except this month, when I'm wearing a winter coat, I thought I wouldn't need unless I visited my mom."

"Speaking of winter coats, Asa took me ice skating for the first time. He got me the rail thing to hold onto."

Chara's stomach twisted at the mention of Asa. "How'd you do? Is it like rollerblading?"

"It's a little different, but it wasn't hard with the railing. He had to hold onto it, too."

Chara raised an eyebrow. "What else is new?"

Mikaila paused. "Not a whole lot. Running outside is harder here with the snow than at home. Bible Club's going well, though."

"That's good."

"And Ty? How's he doing?"

"He's doing well. At his weekly church group luncheon."

"Do you remember when he told you he was picking up nurses at the hospital?" Mikaila asked, laughing.

"Unfortunately, yes. And I'm sure if there are women at this luncheon, that's why he's there, and why he stays for hours."

"If he's well enough to flirt, I guess that's a good sign," Mikaila said. "How's Astrid?"

"She's fine. We talk every other day, and it's better now that we don't live together. It helps that she doesn't talk about her dates anymore."

"That's great. Did you get to campus ministry this week?"

"Yes!" Chara's voice perked up. "They're hosting a mock-tails-and-movies night on Friday. I'm going."

"That sounds fun! I wish I could come."

"Start running now, and you'll be here by then." Chara teased.

"I wish," Mikaila groaned. "Let me tell you about the argument I had with Asa."

Chara's fingers tightened around the phone, and she bit the inside of her cheek at the mention of his name. *Here we go.*

Mikaila exhaled. "We were at dinner, and I tried to tell him about Aunt Lana selling the house and how I didn't want her to. I said it's my home, and he brought up how sad Dad would be if I left. I told him he could go to engineering school wherever, and we could stay at the house."

Chara sank into the couch and stared out the window overlooking the front door. "I'm guessing he didn't take it well?"

"He didn't even want to consider it," Mikaila admitted.

Chara took a deep breath, keeping her voice calm. "Miki... is returning to Oak Haven something *you* want to do? What about college? Does Kait want the house?"

"Kait doesn't care one way or the other. I always thought I'd follow Elliott to Towson, so I never considered what I wanted or where I'd go. I can finish my degree after Asa does. But that house...that's where we grew up. I don't want to lose it."

"It sounds like you know what you want, then. It's okay to have your own plans for the future and not base them on what someone else wants for you."

Mikaila paused. "I didn't expect him to get so upset over it, you know?"

"Yeah, it's weird to be fixated on something like that."

"Exactly. There's just something off about him, and I can't explain it. Even when I left for Pop's funeral, he said something like... 'be good.'"

Chara's pulse quickened. There he was. The guy she remembered, the one people said didn't exist.

"You need to trust your gut. Try journaling your interactions, starting with the first time you had that feeling. When you read over a few entries, you might understand what it is you're feeling."

"I can do that. I just thought if someone loved you, they'd want you to be happy."

"Still single over here," Chara teased. "But you better believe that if I told my future boyfriend I wanted to live in a shack on the beach, he'd better find me the best shack he could afford or build me one."

Mikaila laughed. "Thanks. I feel better about my decision."

"As you should."

But once the call ended, Chara couldn't shake the dread creeping from her stomach to her head. She called Kait, which was rare, and Kait picked up immediately, sensing her urgency.

"Hey. It's been a while."

"Yeah, it has. I just got off the phone with your sister. I'm going to add Kristin to this call. Can you hang on a minute so we can all be on the same page?"

"Yeah. I'm done with classes for the day. Is she alright?" Kait asked.

"For now...hold on," Chara said, adding Kristin to the call.

"We're all here?" Chara asked.

"Hey Kait."

"Hey Kristin."

"I'm going to start from the beginning with Asa, then talk about my conversation with Mikaila just now. Feel free to add your thoughts, but I'm concerned for Miki," Chara said, curling into a fetal position by her window, watching to make sure her dad didn't walk in. She shivered as she rehashed the past.

"Asa swore he had nothing to do with the leaked emails being sent to the school and altered to make it seem like I pursued him. He basically called me delusional for even thinking he'd have anything to do with it. Now he's trying to keep Miki there and told her to 'be good' when she went home. I just have a bad feeling."

Kristin groaned. "I knew parts of that because we talked after the leaks. And he started acting all nonchalant with me, just like you said...innocent compliments at first. Then he tried to come onto me, turned on his webcam when he was naked, and I blocked him. I told Mikaila, but I don't think she believed me either."

"And I've tried to explain to her last year what he's like," Chara said, "but somehow she didn't see it."

Kait made a guttural noise. "I knew something was up with that leaked email fiasco last year. I wanted to ask, but I knew you guys weren't speaking, and I didn't want Mikaila thinking I was picking sides."

"It's okay. I'm okay," Chara said, her voice tight. "But I'm worried. She's feeling the same discomfort that I experienced, and Kristin too, and things could spiral downhill."

Kristin sighed. "He also started messaging my friend Maria, trying the same thing. I didn't know at the time. I only found out weeks ago when she asked about Mikaila. After the email leak, I went to the computer lab and called Dylan from that summer course I took. Together we hacked the school server and traced the IP address where the emails originated."

Kait gasped. "Was it Asa's computer?"

"That's the thing...we don't know who's at the other end. Chara would have to make a police report about being hacked. Then I could give her the info to pass along to the authorities."

Kait groaned. "That sounds...complicated."

"Oak Haven PD wouldn't do anything anyway," Chara said. "And he made it seem like I wanted him. They'd just see me as another angry black woman trying to get a man in trouble for rejecting me. Not happening."

"I don't blame you," Kristin said softly.

Kait groaned again. "If we can't get him through the IP address and can't prove to her what he's like...what do we do? I mean, I know him too, and I've never seen this side, but I believe you."

Chara's shoulders relaxed. "Then we need a plan."

Kristin asked, "Do we want to video chat while we figure one out?"

Kait and Chara said "yes" simultaneously.

Chara moved to her bedroom, closed the door, and stuck a sticky note on the outside: Virtual meeting in progress. Her dad didn't need the details.

They logged onto the video chat, faces in separate squares, but it felt almost like they were in the same room.

Kait's lips pressed into a thin line. "I'm in Maryland, Kristin's in Connecticut, and you're in the South. Not like we can take a joy ride to see her."

Kristin tapped her pencil. "Will any of her family in Connecticut help? Your stepmom?"

Kait let out a dry laugh. "Asa's like their adopted son. I saw it myself. They love him. That's why they don't see an issue with him being so close to Mikaila. He's never given them a reason to distrust him."

Chara lowered her head, rubbing her temples. A familiar nausea crept in. "If we try to enlist their help, we're going to look crazy. Ask me how I know." She stared at Kait.

Kait's lips tightened. "We need to intervene without involving anyone in his inner circle."

Kristin said, "I don't know how we do that when we're in separate states."

Chara lifted her chin, eyes sparkling with determination. "I think I know." She explained her idea excitedly, though they would have to wait until next week to execute it. She signed off her laptop with a small grin. Her nausea eased, and her fingers tingled. *Miki's more likely to believe all of us this time—something Asa won't see coming. When she confronts him, he won't know what hit him.*

A sudden, searing pain hit her between her eyes. *If this doesn't work...he's going to double down. And who knows what chaos he'll cause next.*

35

mikaila

The snow swirled outside the bus, the freezing air seeping in through the windows. I pulled my scarf tighter around my neck and crossed my arms for warmth. The bus seemed to crawl today, as if it knew I just wanted to get home and talk to Chara. Finally, it pulled up to my dad's driveway, and I was free.

Once inside the warm house, I made a cup of chamomile tea. *I still miss you, Nan.* I carried it carefully to my room, mindful of Lorainne's rugs.

I signed onto my laptop and clicked the link for the video chat. Chara's face appeared, and I couldn't help but wonder—why we hadn't done this sooner?

Her shoulders relaxed, and she smiled as we said hello. She wore a long-sleeve shirt with her university's name on it, no winter coat or snow boots needed. Lucky.

"I have a surprise for you," she said.

I sipped my tea. "Um…okay," I dragged out the last vowel.

Suddenly, Kait popped onto the screen. I almost dropped my cup. "Hey, you," I said, smiling and waving.

Then Kristin joined as well, and memories of sleepovers in Oak Haven flooded me.

"I miss you guys," I said with a sigh. "I'm glad you thought of doing this, Kristin. At first, I thought Chara had been getting into tech for school."

The three of them burst out laughing.

"We wanted to surprise you, but we also have something important to talk to you about," Kait commented.

"What is it?"

"Last week, after we spoke," Chara began. "I called Kait and Kristin and explained how concerned I am for you."

My mouth dropped. "You shared my argument with Asa that I told you in confidence?"

Kait's eyebrows furrowed, her mouth tightening. She held her hands up, palms out. "Remember, we talked about Asa before, and after hearing Kristin's side, I think the concern is warranted."

Kristin nodded, giving me a small, sad smile. "I too had interactions with him. He showed himself naked without my permission. That's when I blocked him."

I gasped. "You never told me that! Why didn't you tell me sooner?"

Kristin's voice was soft but firm. "I didn't think you'd believe me. I tried to tell you he came onto me, and it didn't seem to make any difference."

Kait shook her head. "We're not telling you to stop seeing him. We're saying you need to be careful. He's not the guy he's pretending to be."

Chara's mouth tightened. "He's emotionally manipulating you. He used your relationship with your dad as a reason for you to stay there."

I clenched my fists under the laptop so they couldn't see. No way.

"Your relationship with your dad has nothing to do with him. He's deliberately trying to make you feel guilty," Kait said.

Kristin added, "He's trying to control your future by making you stay in Chestnut Hill. As if he can't move here. Why can't he move here?"

Chara nodded. "Because then he couldn't isolate you. When it was just me warning you, he could talk you out of it. But if you're back in Maryland, you have backup, and he loses control."

You've lost control, you mean.

"You're in the South. I'd be in Maryland."

Chara's eyes narrowed. "Does he know I'm down there?"

I paused. "I...don't think so?"

"Exactly!" Kait declared. "He thinks it's like before. He doesn't know Chara's not there. What did he think of you two speaking again?"

"He warned me not to trust her."

Chara's lips pressed together, eyes sharp. "Not to trust me?

Not to trust me…because I tell the truth?"

Kristin put her hands up in a "time-out" motion. "What would he gain from saying that? You'd be less likely to listen to her point of view. Did he tell you not to trust Kait or me?"

I sighed. "You guys didn't come up in that argument, so no."

"Then listen to us," Kait pleaded. "Because it's not just Chara who can see something's off here. I've been with Cameron longer than you've been seeing Asa, and Cameron would never tell me not to leave the state without him."

I nodded, speechless. Kait wouldn't steer me wrong, and Kristin could be loyal to Chara, but Kait's loyalty had always been to me.

"I love him, and I can handle this. Really. He wants to be with me, and he loves me. He's always loved me, so he'll come around."

I glanced at the different boxes on my screen as Chara let out a heavy sigh, Kait's lips pressed together, and Kristin's eyebrows knitted tightly.

"I can handle him. I was just venting, and Chara overreacted. That's all," I added quickly. *Maybe next time, you'll stay out of my relationship.*

Kait crossed her arms. "Let me know if you need me, or us, for anything. You call me if you need anything."

I nodded.

Kristin opened her mouth, closed it, and finally said softly, "I miss you. I hope your senior year is going well."

I smiled. "Thank you."

"You know where to find me if you need me," Chara said before leaving the meeting.

Slowly, Kait and Kristin signed off, and then I left the chat.

With trembling fingers, I dialed Asa's number.

"Your call's earlier than usual today. Have another bad day?"

I could hear a jumble of voices in the background.

"You're busy, we can talk later," I said, trying to sound calm.

The sounds faded slowly, leaving only him on the line. "What's up?"

I took a deep breath. *Here we go.* "I just had a video chat with Kait, Kristin, and Chara. They all agree that my need to move home is validated. I think we need to consider it."

"I told you not to let Chara get into your head. She's manipulative and trying to control your emotions, get in between us."

My entire body felt like it was on fire. "And what about Kait? You think she's manipulating me too? That she's controlling my emotions? Is it Chara who's the manipulative one?"

"Who else would it be? And no, Kait thinks she's being the protective older sister. There's nothing wrong with that."

I paced my bedroom floor, breathing like I was back on the track team. My voice rose. "And what about Kristin? Is she still loyal to Chara? Or bored? You're the one who used my dad as a reason to keep me here in Chestnut Hill."

"Yeah, I think Kristin believes she's being loyal to you," Asa said. "She doesn't know me like you know me. No one knows me like you do. And I didn't use your dad to emotionally control you. I just know he'd be upset if he put in all this effort to make you happy and you left him anyway. Mark and I were close before you moved here full-time."

Kait's voice echoed in my head: You're close because he thinks of you as a son. Because you inserted yourself there.

"Why are you close to him then?" I asked, jaw tight.

"You know my dad worships the ground Hayden walks on,

and I'm invisible in my own house. But not at Mark's. I always had a home there. He's like a father figure to me."

I swallowed hard. "There are other people's dads you could've gotten close to."

He groaned. "Miki, come on, it's me. And I was friends with Lacy. I knew Lexy before I ever met you. You know that's bull. You don't need them telling you what to do. You need me."

My head pounded; my stomach flipped. I felt like I might hurl. "I need to go."

I hung up and powered off my phone. *I can't do this right now. I just need to sleep.*

When I finally walked into the living room, I mumbled, "Sorry...I didn't feel well."

Dad felt my forehead, and the moment he did, I burst into tears. Every emotion from earlier came pouring out. He froze, clueless, so Lorainne pulled me into a hug while he patted my back awkwardly.

"You must miss Nan and Pop. Poor thing," she said gently.
I do. And only Nan would know what to do.

I stepped away, wiping my nose with my sleeve. "I think I'm going to go to bed."

Lorainne nodded.

Dad touched my shoulder. "Take tomorrow off school. You're a senior. It's one day. You'll still walk at graduation. You're allowed to mourn."

I went back upstairs and crawled under my covers. After a short, restless nap, I turned my phone on. Five voicemails from Asa. One from Aunt Lana.

I called Aunt Lana first.

"Girlie, I miss you. How is everything?"

I couldn't answer; the tears came instead.

"What's wrong?" she asked, alarmed.

"I'm not okay, Aunt Lana."

She exhaled heavily. "Kait called me last night. She tried calling you, too, but your phone was off. She's concerned. And, sweetheart…I'm concerned. You just turned eighteen. You're not even done with high school, and you're wearing a promise ring. You have your whole life ahead of you to make major decisions."

Not if the deal I made with God happens. Then I'll be gone. And I want Kait to have the house to remember me.

Quietly, I said, "I don't want you to sell the house. It's the only place that's ever felt like home. It's my reminder of you… and of Nan and Pop."

"I love you," she said softly. "I want you to be happy. Wherever that is and with whoever that is. But I don't want you making major life choices because you're grieving or because you're in an argument."

"I don't want to lose my last connection to Nan and Pop," I whispered.

Aunt Lana sighed. "If I can rent the house to someone, I'll have enough money to get an apartment and live comfortably. Then you can inherit it when you're ready. But only if you promise me you'll hold off on any major decisions for at least six months."

My stomachache eased a little, though my head still throbbed and my chest still felt tight. "What if…what if he proposes?"

"I don't want you rushing into an engagement or a marriage while your feelings are still so raw. If he loves you, he can wait six months."

I swallowed. "I can agree to that."

"Good." Her voice softened. "I love you. We'll talk soon."

"Love you, too."

When I called Asa back, he picked up on the first ring. "I've been so worried about you."

I tried to keep my voice steady. "I had a migraine and turned my cellphone off."

"Yesterday was a lot for you."

"Yes, it was. Kait called Aunt Lana. She agreed to rent out the house for the next six months, as long as I don't make any major life decisions like engagement or marriage."

There was a long silence on the other end of the line. So silent, I thought the call had dropped.

"Hello?"

"I'm here. I just…don't understand why she's renting the house instead of selling it."

"Because she can live in an apartment comfortably if it's rented out. She knows that's where I want to end up. I can't see myself living anywhere else," I said, trying to keep my voice calm.

I could hear long sighs coming from Asa's end. "Fine. I was going to propose after graduation, but we can hold off. It's fine."

I felt tears streaming down my face. "I love you, Asa."

"I love you too," he said, his tone flat. *Are you sure that's love?* His indifference gnawed at me, but I pushed it aside.

"My headache's back. I'm gonna go."

"Maybe I should take your shift tomorrow."

I bit my lip. "No, I'll be fine. I just need some rest."

"Why don't I swing by the house tomorrow to pick you up for work?"

My head throbbed. "That would be great."

"Good. If you want, you can drop me off at my house and take the car for the day. If you're still not well at work, you can leave anytime you want."

"Sounds good."

I hung up and immediately called Chara for our weekly call. *If I talk to Asa and not her, she'll never let me forget it.* I dialed while lying in bed.

"Hey," she answered. "What's wrong?"

"I don't feel so great. I'm curled up in bed. Instead of going out tonight with Asa, I'm just going to rest. My head hurts, my stomach hurts…I don't know where I picked up this bug."

"Your voice sounds raspy, like you have the flu. If it gets unbearable, go to urgent care. They can send you to the ER if needed," Chara said, calm but firm.

"Thanks. I'm sure I'll be fine."

"How's everything else? I'm worried."

"Good. Everything is fine. Asa got me a part-time job at the pharmacy where he works. That's why I need to rest tonight. I have to work tomorrow."

"Make sure you take care of yourself first. Is Asa helping at all?"

"He offered to cover my shift."

"If you end up at urgent care or the ER, send me a text."

I yawned, my body finally settled into the mattress. "Will do. Miss you."

"Miss you too."

36

mikaila

FEBRUARY 19, 2005

The next day, when I woke, it felt like I could sleep for another three days. My mind was hazy and heavy, but I forced myself into my work uniform anyway. Asa pulled up in his sedan a few minutes later.

I must have drifted off again on the short ride, because he nudged me when we pulled into his driveway.

"Are you alright to drive the rest of the way?" Asa asked.

I smiled weakly. "Why wouldn't I be?" I yawned, grabbed

my bag, and walked around to the driver's side. Asa leaned down to kiss me, and I tilted my head up, pressing my lips to his. I pulled away and took the keys from his hand. "Love you."

He smiled. "Love you too, sleepyhead."

I turned the radio to the Christian station and hummed along to "Indescribable" by Chris Tomlin. My head throbbed in rhythm with the music, and nausea twisted in my stomach. *I am not losing a day of work.*

I merged onto the main highway, falling in behind a beat-up minivan. The trees blurred by. My eyelids grew heavier. I told myself to stay awake, but the fatigue rolled through my body like a wave, leaving everything limp.

A moment later, I wasn't steering anymore. I couldn't move my legs. My body was in the car, but my mind wasn't connected to it. I drifted across the grassy median, barreling straight toward an oncoming semi-truck. The driver's horn blared, long and sharp.

And then the sedan collided.

My eyes closed—

—then opened in a white room.

I wasn't driving. I wasn't hurt. I was standing. Before me stretched a never-ending hallway, walls rising higher than I could see. The floor beneath me looked and felt like clouds: soft, weightless.

The dream from years ago surged back in an instant.

But this time, my Maker wasn't waiting in the main room.

I stepped forward gingerly, moving down the long hallway as scenes appeared in picture frames along the right wall.

A happy Christmas. Mom in one of her good moods. Nan making snickerdoodles.

Then the next frame: Chara's accident. Except it wasn't the way I remembered it. This wreckage was far worse. A green sedan crushed beneath the grille of a semi-truck; green shards of metal scattered like confetti.

But Chara's father drove an SUV. This wasn't her accident. *Wait.*

That was Asa's car.

My breath hitched. I bit my bottom lip hard. I had just been driving that car.

When I turned back to the wall, the other videos had disappeared.

Uneasy, I walked to the main room, where the brightness intensified until it enveloped everything. My Maker stood within it.

"My child, I have been waiting for you."

I felt no pain. No fear. No regret. Only peace. I bowed my head, unable to look directly at Him; His light was overwhelming.

He touched my arm—firm, kind. "Walk with Me."

We moved through the hallway again, the light spilling around us.

"Not everyone remains as faithful as you during times of trial," He said. "Look at this. When your mother belittled you, you turned to My Word. Look at the time you and Elliott ended your relationship. You used your hurt to introduce Lacy to Scripture."

The scenes appeared as we walked: me and Chara sitting in her rental car after Pop's funeral, staring out at the ocean.

Then new memories—ones I had never seen. Asa cornering a girl in his class, manipulating her until she nearly got expelled.

The screen faded. Another appeared: Asa altering messages from Chara, changing timestamps and wording, then emailing them to the school.

I didn't feel anger, but I understood that I would have if emotions existed here.

He tugged my arm gently. "Let us continue."

A memory of Asa fiddling with his car appeared, his voice echoing: *She'll realize she will always need me.* Then him handing me the keys, letting me drive off—knowing.

I saw then that he had never loved me the way I believed. But even that realization didn't hurt the way I expected. The scene dissolved into blackness.

The next frame looked like a mirror.

"This is a reality frame," He said. "When it lights, it will show you a loved one in the present. Do not touch the frame. If you do, you may enter their moment. You did this once before, though you do not remember. You visited Chara during her accident. She sensed someone but did not know it was you. I removed the memory from both of you."

I turned toward Him, though the brightness made it impossible to see His face.

"My child," He said, resting a hand on my shoulder, "you asked to switch places, and I told you I had already prepared a room. You said you trusted that my plans for your life were already written."

My eyes drifted to the hem of His white robe, where the fabric seemed to melt into the swirling air beneath us. "I tried," I whispered. "I tried to get Chara to change her heart. I thought if she saw how happy I was by living Your Word, she would eventually want that too."

"My child," He said gently, "the room I prepared was always meant for you. It was only a matter of time. You both received a second chance. Yours, to show her what walking in My Word looks like. Hers, to learn, to grow, so that when her time comes, I may prepare a room for her as well."

He motioned for us to continue.

We walked past familiar memory frames until we reached another section of the hallway, where the frames looked like computer screens displaying drifting clouds.

"These," He said, "are dream frames. Stay here and watch the impact your life has had on others. When it is time, a door will open at the end of the hallway, and you may enter the room I have made for you. If you touch a dream frame, you may enter the dreams of those you love."

"Your holiness…" My voice trembled. "I haven't been able to save her. I thought I could, but I failed."

He turned to me, resting His hand on my shoulder. "Look again, My child. The truth will reveal itself. You were never asked to be perfect. No human is. But your friendship and your devotion shaped her heart. She began to follow Me because of you. You have done what I asked you to do. Your life has touched more than you know."

He led me back to the Reality Frame and swept His arm toward it. The screen flared to life.

Chara appeared, standing in the middle of her campus ministry group, handing out food and supplies with quiet, steady confidence.

"Because of you," He said, "she is now a light to others."

When the image faded, He stepped away. The brightness that had filled the hall dimmed, fading from brilliant to muted.

The memories and scenes from the life I'd left behind dissolved into empty whiteness.

I was alone in the vast, quiet hall, the echo of His words lingering like a warm breath in the stillness.

37

chara

Chara picked out a pink button-down blouse, a black fleece sweater, and black pants from her closet. Once she got dressed, she grabbed the hot coffee her dad had made and poured it into a travel mug.

"Thanks for making coffee, Dad."

Her dad sat on the couch in his blue pajamas, watching the weather. "No problem, sweetie. Have a great day."

She smiled, walked over, and gave him a hug. "You too."

Before she grabbed her keys from the coffee table, she headed for the front door.

"I'm proud of you. Getting a real job is a big deal."

"Thanks. I gotta go before I'm *real* late for my real job."

Ty laughed and turned the TV up as she stepped out the door.

Chara slid into her sedan, turned the radio up, and merged onto the highway. The morning traffic was light, and within minutes, she was pulling into the physical therapy office. She stepped inside, exchanged quick hellos with the therapists, and headed behind the check-in desk. Phones rang, charts waited to be filed, and patients flowed in and out, but Chara didn't mind. This was her starting line, and one day, she'd be more than the receptionist. She'd be right there, assisting the PTs, learning the work that mattered.

★ ★ ★

After her shift, Chara drove home, singing along to the radio, savoring another successful day. She parked, grabbed her purse, and tried calling Mikaila, but it went straight to voicemail.

Maybe she made it to work and turned her phone off, Chara hoped.

Inside, she shrugged off her coat. Her dad lowered the TV volume.

"How was work?"

"Great! Scheduled new clients and got to watch a patient get discharged. She was so happy."

"That's great, sweetie. I'm making barbecue chicken for dinner. It's almost done."

"Sounds good."

She tried calling Mikaila again, but it went to voicemail. She texted, *Everything alright?*

The oven timer dinged in the background.

"Dinner's ready," her dad called as he pulled a sheet pan of barbecue chicken and vegetables from the oven.

Chara took her spot at the table across from her dad. "It's Aunt Charmaine's recipe. Been in the family for years. Can't wait to see what you think." He smiled.

Chara took a bite and then marveled, "It's delicious!"

"I think so too," he said proudly.

The conversation was cut short when Chara's phone rang. "It's Kristin. I'll be right back. Sorry." She padded down the hall, into her room, pushing the door ajar behind her. "Hey, Kristin. What's up? Have you heard from—"

Chara's voice trailed off at the wail coming from Kristin's end. "What's wrong?"

Kristin's voice came out hoarse. "Chara…I don't know how to tell you this."

Chara's stomach dropped, and her lungs felt as though they were deflating. "What? What is it?"

In between sobs, Kristin finally forced the words out. "Aunt Lana called my mom. There's been an accident…and Mikaila didn't make it. Chara, she's dead."

Chara's knees gave out as the room began to spin. Thankfully, the bed caught her fall.

"That can't be right. She told me she wasn't feeling well…she said she was debating going to the emergency room."

Kristin sobbed harder. "She's gone, Chara."

Chara's hands shook so violently she could barely hold the phone. The last few months replayed in flashes she couldn't stop.

A cold shiver ran through her, and her stomach twisted violently. She hung up and broke down, the sound raw and uncontrollable.

Her dad rushed in and wrapped his arms around her. "What happened, Char?"

Her chest heaved. She couldn't wipe the tears fast enough. "Mikaila's gone. She was in an accident, and she's gone, Dad."

He held her tighter, pressing his lips to the top of her head. "It's gonna be alright."

"How?" Chara wailed. "She's gone!"

"I know. I know it feels unbearable right now. But she's in your heart. Your memories. You'll never be without her."

"I need to call Kait."

He kissed the top of her head. "I'll clean up dinner. You rest. I'm right here if you need me."

She nodded and tossed herself back on the bed. The call with Kristin replayed in her mind, but she tried to convince herself it had been a living nightmare. Surely, it wasn't real. Chara dialed Kait's phone. No answer.

Kait's phone was never off.

Chara dialed Mikaila. Each time she called, it went straight to voicemail. This had to be a nightmare. Her body lurched forward, and she ran to the bathroom, throwing up. *I can't do this without you, Miki,* she thought, trembling. She crawled back into bed, exhausted, and eventually fell asleep.

In the morning, the reality of everything she wished had been a nightmare came crashing down again. Her hair was tangled, and she was still in yesterday's clothes. She dragged herself out of bed to brush her teeth. When she stepped out of the bathroom, he didn't say anything, just wrapped her in a hug.

Tears spilled again. Her throat was painfully dry. "I don't

want this to be real, Dad."

"I know, sweetie."

"Will it always feel like this? Like I've lost a part of myself?"

He pulled back, eyes soft. "I wish I could say it'll be gone in a month. But grief doesn't work like that. I still miss my mother. Especially on holidays. She'd know exactly what to tell you right now. I can only do my best."

Chara gave him a small, broken smile. "You're not doing too badly."

He smiled. "How about I make you some chocolate chip pancakes? I can even make them Mickey-shaped if you need me to."

A soft laugh escaped Chara as she wiped her face. "Regular pancakes are fine."

Her phone buzzed in her palm. A text from Kristin: *The funeral will be next week in Oak Haven. I'd call you, but I don't think I can talk right now.*

Chara texted back: *Thank you. I understand. I don't think I have it in me to talk either.*

"The funeral's next week."

He pulled pancake mix from the cabinet. "Then we'll get flights."

She sat on the stool at the bar. "You'll come with me?"

"I'm sure your mom will be there, but I want to support you too. Mikaila meant a lot to you, and I'd like to say my goodbyes. Is that alright?"

She nodded. "Yes. Thank you."

He flipped a pancake. "Good, because I've already started looking up flights."

Her eyebrows rose. "Really?"

He slid the first pancake onto her plate. "Yes. I'll book them after breakfast."

She took a bite and swallowed. "Tastes great. Thank you, Dad."

He added another pancake to her plate. "I haven't called your mom yet. You should call her after you eat."

"I will. I'm done after this one. I can't eat more."

"Alright. I'll make some for myself and refrigerate the rest for tomorrow."

She poked at a melted chocolate chip. "Sounds good."

After finishing, she set her dishes in the sink. "Thanks again. I'll call Mom." She returned to her room, closed the door, and dialed.

After a few rings, her mom answered. "Hello?"

Chara's stomach knotted. "Mom…are you sitting down?"

"Yes. I'm drinking my coffee."

Chara exhaled shakily. "I have to tell you something."

"I'm listening."

Tears ran down her face again. She wiped them away, inhaled, and forced herself to speak. "Kristin told me Mikaila was in a car accident in Connecticut."

"Is she okay?"

Chara sank onto her bed, her voice cracking. "No. She didn't make it, Mom."

"She's…" The unfinished word hung in the air.

Chara pressed her hand to her chest as it tightened painfully. "She's gone, Mom."

"Oh...oh, no…"

"The services are next weekend. Dad's buying our flights now."

She heard her mother begin to sob quietly on the other end. "Okay...I'll send flowers to Lana and to the church."

"Okay."

"Are *you* alright? I know you're not, but if you need to come home sooner—"

Chara sighed, trying to steady herself. "I can't. I have classes. But I'll see you soon."

"I love you," her mom whispered.

"Love you too."

Chara ended the call and stepped back into the living room. Her dad sat at his desktop beside the couch and turned when he heard her. "The tickets are bought. We'll get there Saturday and leave Sunday, so you won't miss any classes."

She nodded, her voice barely above a whisper. "Thank you."

She sank onto the couch, the cushion dipping beneath her as if absorbing her weight and grief. The hollow ache in her chest didn't lighten—it sat with her, heavy and unmoving. She wasn't sure it ever would.

38

chara

FEBRUARY 26, 2005

The Myrtle Beach airport was nearly empty before dawn. The sky was still dark as Chara and her dad boarded their flight to Maryland. They found their seats—her dad at the window, Chara in the middle. She gripped his hand as the plane accelerated, and he smiled.

"You hated flying when you were little."

Chara's legs felt wobbly. "I like my feet on the ground. What can I say?"

He laughed softly. "Put in your headphones, close your eyes, and we'll be there before you know it."

She sighed and did exactly that. Blink-182's *I Miss You* filled her ears, and she closed her eyes, slipping into memories: the rental car after Pop's funeral, sleepovers, the boardwalk, lunches, geometry class, bus rides, inside jokes—Mikaila's laughter cutting through each scene. The images looped endlessly until the wheels touched down. Her dad squeezed her hand. She wiped the wetness from her cheeks with the back of her hand.

They grabbed their carry-ons and headed off the plane. At the rental-car counter, her dad said, "Go ahead outside and wait for me. I'll load the luggage."

She nodded, pulled her coat tighter, and stepped into the freezing morning. The sun was starting to break above the tree line, but the cold was sharp enough that her breath clouded in front of her. A few minutes later, he pulled up in a red Honda Accord. She climbed in and immediately turned the heat to max.

Her dad chuckled. "You got used to the South, didn't you?"

"I love Maryland in the summer and fall. After that? Take me back south."

He shook his head, smiling. "We should be at your mom's in about an hour. I'll drop you off, go to my cousin's, and see you at the service. Alright?"

She nodded.

He put on an R&B station, and "Celebrate" started playing. He turned the volume up as he eased out of the parking lot and merged onto the highway. As warmth slowly filled the car, Chara leaned her head against the window and closed her eyes.

When the song ended, he lowered the volume and glanced over at her.

"Talk to me."Her voice cracked. "I keep thinking about the argument we had last year, and how much time we lost."

Chara's dad reached over and squeezed her hand. "You had no way of knowing this would happen. How could you have known to do anything differently?"

Chara felt a wave a nausea. *You wouldn't believe me if I told you,* she thought. She put her headphones back in, pressed play on her CD Walkman, and closed her eyes until Oak Haven came into view.

She texted her mom: *Almost home.*

Her mom responded immediately: *Thank God.*

"Mom's awake," Chara said.

"Good. Last thing you want is to get arrested for breaking into your own house."

"Very funny, Dad."

"No, really," he said with a grin. "Very few people look good behind bars."

Chara laughed. He smiled, winked, and pulled into her driveway. She reached over and hugged him. "See you soon."

Then she grabbed her bag from the back seat and headed inside. "Honey, I'm home!" She called.

Her mom jumped up from the couch, dressed in black flannel pajamas and a green bathrobe. "Welcome home."

Chara walked straight into her arms, and her mother held her tightly. "We'll get through today, okay?"

Chara nodded and stepped back. "I'll put my things away and get dressed."

Her mom wiped a tear. "I'll make us some coffee."

Chara slipped into her old room. The Backstreet Boys and LFO posters still stared back at her. *How can everything look the same and feel so different?* she wondered.

She changed into a long black dress and her black Adidas sneakers—*like Mikaila would have*—applied her makeup carefully and put on waterproof mascara. With her purse in hand, she followed the smell of coffee into the kitchen.

Her mom sat at the table, tears streaming down her face.

Chara sat beside her. "Are you okay?"

Her mom dabbed at her eyes and tried to smile. "Just remembering how Mikaila would try to help me clean up after dinner or vacuum or do whatever she could after your accident. She was such a good friend to you."

Chara blinked away a tear. "Thank God for waterproof mascara." She hesitated. "You know what's weird? Actually... never mind."

Her mom raised her eyebrows. "What's weird?"

Chara rested her elbow on the table, chin in her hand. "I had dreams about her life. And they came true. I dreamed she'd move. First to her aunt's sale, then to her dad's. I dreamed it wouldn't end well, but I didn't know why. And I dreamed...I dreamed I was at her funeral. You told me it was just because friendships change. But everything came true. And I couldn't stop any of it."

Her mom reached across the table and put a hand on her shoulder. "I was hoping you didn't have dreams like that. Like mine."

Chara's eyes widened. "That would've been helpful to know."

Her mom shook her head. "No. People don't understand. It's not a party trick. You can't just see the future on command. You're shown only what you're meant to see. And if you couldn't stop anything…then you weren't meant to."

Chara's jaw dropped. "Why would I be able to see Miki's funeral if I couldn't stop it?"

"If you weren't meant to change it," her mom said gently, "then there's either a lesson in it or something else you're meant to do with that knowledge. But you might not know what that is for years."

Chara groaned and dropped her head onto the table.

"Let me get you some coffee. Then I'll get ready."

Chara nodded. Her mom poured her a cup and left the room. More memories—movie nights, bus rides, summers—flooded her mind. She forced herself to blink them away. *I can't fall apart yet.*

Chara met her dad in the church parking lot. With her mom in front of her and her dad behind her, she walked toward the entrance. Her stomach twisted as her mom pulled open the silver handles.

Inside, Chara accepted a pamphlet from the basket. Mikaila's senior portrait smiled at her from the front. Her chest ached. The wooden pews, the red fabric, the red carpeting—they were arranged exactly as in her dream.

She scanned the room: Kait. Kait's mom. Kait's dad. Lorraine. Her stepsisters. Former coaches. Teammates. Elliott.

She slid into a pew beside her mom. Kristin and her family were already seated. Her dad sat on her other side.

For the first time in years, both of her parents held her hands as she cried.

The pastor stood at the pulpit and cleared his throat. "Welcome, friends and family. We gather today in the presence of God to remember and celebrate the life of Mikaila Emery.

We come together with grief for the sorrow we feel, and gratitude for the ways Mikaila touched our lives.

As we begin, hear these words of comfort from Psalm 139:16: *'Your eyes saw me when I was formless; all my days were written in your book and planned before a single one of them began.'* Our days have been predetermined, but our path to heaven isn't. We cannot get in with favors, good deeds, or money. There's not enough money in the world to buy your way in. But John 3:16 says, 'For God so loved the world He gave His one and only Son, that whoever believed in Him would have everlasting life.'"

The pastor paused. Chara saw Aunt Lana nod and wipe her eyes.

He smiled softly. "I had the honor of getting to know Mikaila, and if anyone could enter heaven by believing in Him, I know it's her. She believed wholeheartedly, and from everything I've seen and heard, she modeled Jesus' teachings. She touched every life in this room. If you have any memories of Mikaila, I ask that you share them with us now." He stepped aside and sat in a chair on the right side of the sanctuary.

Chara glanced at Kristin, who was dabbing tears. Even Elliott wiped his eyes. The one person missing, just like in her dream, was Asa. Her mom nudged her and whispered, "This is your chance."

Chara shook her head. "I won't make it through," she whispered back.

Her dad rose and walked to the pulpit. His gray hair caught the light, the black flecks almost matching his all-black suit and the black sneakers. Mikaila would have teased him for copying her. Chara smiled through her tears.

He cleared his throat. "Miki was..." His voice cracked; he

paused, wiping his eyes with a handkerchief. "I'm sorry. Miki was a pistol from the time she was little."

Soft laughter rippled through the room.

He took a steadying breath. "From the moment she was born, she had an energy that commanded every room she walked into. She lit up the world. I didn't have enough time with her, but I cherished every minute we had. Miki, we love you. We'll miss you."

He stepped down, eyes red.

Kait stood next. She wore a black dress nearly identical to the one she'd worn at their Pop's funeral—paired with black sneakers, of course. She lowered the microphone. "My sister loved wearing sneakers with skirts and dresses, even her prom dresses." More gentle laughter.

She inhaled shakily. "When our Nan passed, Miki found a song that described exactly how she felt. I'm going to read the lyrics now, because they describe how I feel today."

As she read *Yellowcard's "View of Heaven,"* Chara couldn't contain her grief any longer. She covered her face with tissues, silently mouthing every lyric she and Mikaila used to sing together.

Kait returned to her seat, wiping tears.

Mikaila's former coach approached the pulpit. "I'm so glad you mentioned her energy. We harnessed it on the track to motivate the whole team. She was only a sophomore, but she had more maturity than some of my seniors." A few heads nodded knowingly, followed by scattered chuckles.

"I knew from her file that she was resilient. She gave 110% every practice and meet, always working to better herself and uplift the team. I can't recall a single moment of poor sportsmanship from her. She was a joy to coach. I'm truly sorry she's gone."

She stepped down, squeezing Aunt Lana and her mother's hands before returning to her seat.

A woman with brown hair and green eyes walked up next. "I was Mikaila's history teacher. I didn't know her as well as many of you, but I adored having her in my class. She was polite, always helpful. One day, I'd had a death in the family and assigned desk work so I wouldn't have to speak much. Mikaila noticed, and at the end of class, she asked if she could write a Bible verse on the board. I said 'sure.' She wrote Psalm 55:22: *Cast your burden unto the Lord.*"

The teacher paused, eyes shining. "It was incredibly sweet of her. I know she'd repeat that verse to all of you today. I'm grateful for the time I had with her."

She stepped down. No one else rose.

The pastor returned to the pulpit. "Thank you for sharing your memories so we can celebrate her life together. If anyone would like to be saved, as Mikaila was, I invite you now to bow your heads, close your eyes, and raise your hand."

Chara raised her hand. She'd been saved once as a child, but this felt like the moment Mikaila would want her to recommit.

"You may lift your heads," the pastor said gently. "At this time, please join the family for fellowship in the community center."

Chara wiped her face as people shuffled toward the adjoining room. She followed her dad to a table, set her coat on a chair, and joined the line for food. She grabbed a grilled chicken sandwich and chips while *Here I Am to Worship* played softly from overhead speakers. A line of people formed in front of Kait, each offering their condolences.

Chara carried her plate back to the table and sat beside her dad.

He smiled. "I'm glad I came here today."

Chara picked at the food on her plate. "Me too. I'm glad you came to support me."

"I'm glad there's free food." He winked, and Chara nudged him with her elbow.

She took a few small bites, then noticed Kait standing alone. "I'll be back," she murmured.

She crossed the room and wrapped her arms around Kait, holding her tightly. "I'm so sorry," she whispered into Kait's ear.

For the first time Chara could remember, Kait's composure shattered. Her chest heaved as she sobbed openly, clinging to Chara like she had nothing left to anchor herself. After a few minutes, she pulled back, still holding Chara's hand, and led her toward Kristin, who was seated beside Chara's mom. Then Kait gently tugged Chara and Kristin aside.

Kristin stood and hugged Kait. "I'm so sorry."

Kait wiped her face with her sleeve. In a shaky whisper, she said, "She didn't feel anything. They said she died on impact. But…she was driving Asa's car. And he said someone told him it wasn't a good idea to be here."

Chara's stomach twisted. "Who told him that?"

Kait shook her head. "I talked to Aunt Lana and Lexy. No one in my family said that. I bet he made it up to throw suspicion off himself."

Kristin nodded firmly. "We need to keep an eye on him. See if there's any connection to Mikaila's death. I'll watch his social media. If he posts anything weird, I'll tell you."

Kait pressed her lips together. "I'll have Lexy watch him up in Connecticut. Lacy's too close to him. She'd warn him."

Chara nodded, pain clawing at her ribs. *I can't believe how far Asa would go to keep control. I should have been able to save her. I warned her. I told her my dream. I wish she'd believed me.*

Before she could say anything else, Lorainne approached and touched Kait's arm. Kait excused herself and went with her.

Chara turned to Kristin and hugged her. "I wish this wasn't the reason we were seeing each other."

Kristin squeezed her back. "Me too. It still doesn't feel real."

"I know. I keep thinking I'll wake up, and this will all be a nightmare."

Chara spotted Kristin's parents heading toward them. "I think your parents are leaving."

Kristin nodded. "Then I'd better go. But we'll keep in touch, alright?"

"Yeah. Definitely."

Chara returned to the table where her dad waited. "Ready to go when you are."

Her dad stood, said his goodbyes to the people at the table, and placed a gentle hand on Chara's shoulder as they walked toward the exit.

She slipped into the passenger seat of the rental car, the weight of the day settling into her bones. She felt like a shell of the person she'd been the last time she set foot in Oak Haven, like something vital had been carved out of her and left behind.

This place will never feel like home again without you, Miki.

39

chara

Chara lifted her suitcase into her mom's trunk. She was planning to stay in Oak Haven until school started again in August. Her dad had insisted she needed her mother—and her friends—right now.

I need Mikaila back, she thought. *That's what I need.*

Her mom turned the radio down and gave her a quick side hug as Chara climbed into the passenger seat. "Have a good flight?"

"The plane didn't crash, so…yes?"

Her mom gave her a small laugh as she merged onto the highway. "Yes, I'd say that counts as good."

"I'm gonna head to the beach with Kait when we get back."

"That's fine," her mom said, glancing over. "You can unpack tomorrow."

*　*　*

Chara slipped into the passenger seat of Kait's car. "Hear You Me" by Jimmy Eat World, played softly as they drove toward Java Joint.

"Hey," Chara said.

Kait turned the volume down. "Hey. How was the end of your semester?"

"Busy. Papers, finals. You?"

Kait groaned. "Same. I powered through it, though."

"Nothing else to do with finals except survive them."

They parked on 16th Street, grabbed beach chairs from the trunk, and walked through the warm sand until they settled about twenty feet from the shoreline. The waves rolled in, steady and slow.

Kait stared at the water. "She died without knowing I loved her."

"You know she told me in my dream after the funeral that you knew she'd always be around for you," Chara said, glancing at Kait.

Kait's voice tightened. "Because she loved me. Not because she knew I loved her."

Chara shook her head. "She knew. You tried to intervene with the creeper. She *knew* it was because you loved her."

Kait drew in a shaky breath. "You think?"

"I know." Chara paused. "Look, you can read my journals if you want, because it's all in there. I had dreams about the big stuff before it happened. When your house was going to be sold. When she moved to Connecticut. That she'd get involved with Asa, and I had this horrible feeling about him. And then… that we'd be at her funeral. We talked about all of it. She knew I had those dreams and that they came true. And after she died, she came to me in a dream just to tell me she'd always be with us. That's not nothing."

"You never told me any of this."

Chara let out a breathy laugh. "Because I didn't want to get called irrational again. And when the dreams started coming true, I realized I couldn't stop any of it. I tried to warn her about Asa, but the more I tried, the more he reeled her in."

"I didn't have any proof to give her. Just what I saw. How he treated you, how he treated Kristin. And she swore he'd changed. She said she was happy." Kait's voice cracked. "I just wanted her to be happy."

Chara listened to the waves, nodding slowly. "I did too."

"By the way…the autopsy and toxicology report came back. She had carbon monoxide poisoning. The investigation didn't show any tampering. They said she didn't feel anything. She lost consciousness before the crash. She didn't suffer."

Chara swallowed hard, steadying her voice. "That explains why she kept saying she felt sick before she died. She thought it was the flu."

They sat quietly for a moment. Then, as if on cue, both of them looked up. A shooting star streaked across the sky above the ocean, bright and sudden.

Chills rippled through both of them.

Kait pointed to the sky. "Nan used to say that when we die, we become stars looking down on us. Now I have three stars watching over me."

Chara bit her cheek, swallowing the lump in her throat.

"I'm going to Connecticut for a couple of days to pack up her things. My dad said he didn't know what I'd want to keep or not. Do you want to come with me? We can stay in a different room. I can't sleep where she used to sleep."

"Absolutely."

Kait smiled. "I'm leaving in two days. Does that work for you?"

Chara nodded.

Two days later, Kait picked her up. Chara hugged her mom goodbye.

"Text me when you get there," her mom said softly.

"I will." Chara threw her bag in the trunk, climbed into the passenger seat, and handed Kait a stack of mixed CDs.

"I've got music," Kait said, popping in a mixed CD Cameron had made her.

* * *

Maryland drifted away as the scenery blurred past.

"Do you think Lexy found anything out?" Chara asked.

Kait turned down the music. "I think she did, but she wants to wait until we get there to discuss it. What about Kristin?"

Chara shook her head. "She saved the information from when she hacked the school's server, but unless we can access Asa's computer, we don't have proof tying him to anything."

Kait's lips pursed. "I think we can get Lacy to help."

Chara's eyebrows shot up. "Isn't she his friend? Why would she help us?"

"Mikaila was her stepsister…and her friend. Lexy thinks she can convince her."

Chara stared out at the ocean. "I hope so."

Hours later, they pulled into Kait's dad's driveway. Grabbing their overnight bags, they walked to the door. Kait knocked, and her dad opened it.

"Come on in." He stepped aside and took their bags. "I'll show you where you'll sleep."

They followed him upstairs to the second bedroom. "This is Lacy's room, but she's staying at a friend's house," he said, dropping the bags. The twin bed was covered in a deep purple bedspread, black sheets beneath, and the walls were plastered with band posters. A blow-up mattress was tucked under the bed for Chara. "Lorainne went to the store, and Lexy will be home after work. Can I get you sandwiches?"

Kait and Chara nodded, following him to the kitchen. He handed them lunch meats and cheese from the fridge along with a loaf of bread. They made their sandwiches and sat at the table while he grabbed a beer and sat down.

"How was your drive?" He asked.

Kait took a bite of her sandwich. "Not bad. We made good time."

The front door opened, and Mark helped Lorainne bring in groceries. She smiled. "Hello, girls. Glad you could make it. I wish it were under different circumstances."

"Me too," Kait mumbled, eating her sandwich.

Lorainne unpacked a few bags, putting items in the fridge, as Lexy returned from work.

"Hey, Kait," she said.

Lorainne nodded. "Make yourself a sandwich if you want."

"I ate at the mall. I'm good," Lexy said, sitting down next to Kait and Chara. "How was your drive?"

"Not too bad," Chara said. "We left early and beat traffic."

"You two must be exhausted. Why don't we all catch up later?" Lorainne suggested from the kitchen.

That night, Kait and Chara slept in Lacy's room. The next morning, the smell of coffee, bacon, eggs, and pancakes drew them downstairs. Even early, Lorainne's makeup and hair were perfect.

"Good morning! Eat whatever you'd like," Lorainne said.

Kait and Chara sat down as Lexy came into the kitchen. "Have to run to work. I'll catch you guys later."

"Talk to you later," Kait replied.

Lorainne's tone softened. "We left everything as-is, girls. Take your time. There are boxes in the hallway and trash bags for whatever you don't want. No rush."

They ate quickly, then Chara grabbed a coffee cup and followed Kait upstairs. Kait slowly opened Mikaila's door and sank to the floor, air leaving her lungs as she cried. "It looks exactly as it did when I visited her last."

Chara placed her coffee cup on the dresser next to a blue bear wearing a Connecticut t-shirt. She sank down next to Kait and hugged her as she wiped away her own tears. After a few moments, Kait asked, "Where should we even start?"

Can we start over? And have her back again? Chara thought.

She picked up an ad for a new coffee shop stuck to Mikaila's mirror. "You want to get some coffee?"

Kait glanced at Chara, "Yeah. Let's do this later."

Using Kait's GPS, they arrived at a large, trendy coffee shop with a stage on the left. The smell of ground coffee hit them as they opened the door. Signs advertised open mic nights on Fridays. Behind the massive counter stood a girl who looked startlingly like Kait's sister.

Kait froze, and Chara followed her gaze. Holding up the rest of the line, leaning in for a kiss with a coffee cup in one hand, was Asa Finn.

Chara's pulse raced. Her chest tightened. Her blood boiled. She gasped, slapped a hand over her mouth to stop the noise from escaping. *Three months after she's gone, and you've replaced her, you creepy bastard,* she thought.

Kait's fingernails dug into her arms. Chara wanted to surprise him, and as he turned toward the door, she stepped sideways, blocking his exit.

Her voice trembled, but she leaned closer, hand on her hip, standing in his space. "What is wrong with you? How could you—"

He interrupted smoothly, as if reading her mind. "You don't understand. I miss her…Mikaila. I miss her so much. This is just…comfort. Grief. It's not what you think."

Chara's brain screamed: *You love yourself.*

Kait pointed at his chest. "If we don't understand, help us understand. She drove your car. Wore your promise ring. If she's the love of your life, why couldn't you make it to the funeral? Because you replaced her with a lookalike?"

Asa raised his hands in surrender. "I didn't know anything was wrong with my car. I met her in class this semester and didn't talk to her until finals. I swear, I just miss your sister. I'm not dating her out of malice. You know me. I've always loved her, and she'll always have a special place in my heart."

Kait clenched her jaw, fists tight. Chara placed a hand on her shoulder to give silent support. "You know what? I can't believe anything you say right now." Kait turned on her heel, pulling Chara with her, and stormed out of the shop.

"You alright?" Chara asked as they reached the car.

"I don't know. Are you?"

"I don't know either. We should check in with Lexy and Kristin. I don't trust him." Nausea churned in her stomach at the memory of seeing him.

Back at Kait's house, they stomped up to Mikaila's room. Kait paced the floor. "I can't believe him. He replaced her in three months." She sank onto Mikaila's bed. "Let's keep going through her things and wait for Lexy to get back."

Chara nodded. "I'll go through her school stuff. You do the drawers."

Sorting through notebooks, Chara paused at Mikaila's journal. She handed it to Kait. "This is her journal. Maybe the last entries will tell us what happened before her accident."

Kait flipped to the final entries. "I brought up waiting six months for engagement or life decisions so Aunt Lana wouldn't sell the house. Asa wouldn't consider moving to Oak Haven. When he brought me home, he pulled over and I had to walk the rest of the way."

Kait frowned. "I wasn't feeling well. Asa said I could drive myself to work if I needed to leave early because I wouldn't let him cover my shift." She wiped a tear. "That was the last entry."

Chara tapped the page. "Interesting. Instead of driving her, he had her take the car. If something happened later, why not drive back?"

Kait's eyebrows knit. "Because she couldn't leave immediately?"

Chara shook her head. "If he tampered with the car, he wouldn't want to be in it. That explains her symptoms."

Kait dropped the journal. "It almost makes him seem thoughtful."

Chara's lips pressed together. "That was his plan."

A door creaked open, and Lexy called out, "I'm home!"

Lorainne responded from the living room, "Hey, Lexy. Kait and Chara upstairs."

Kait grabbed the journal. "Get your laptop."

They followed her downstairs to the basement. Lexy followed behind. "I thought you'd be out sightseeing," Lexy commented.

Kait shook her head. "We tried, but there's no time to rehash that."

The basement was spacious, white carpeted, with a treadmill and weights at one end, entertainment system and couch at the other. Kait hooked Chara's laptop to the Ethernet cable.

"We're going to video chat with Kristin, but we'll have to sit on the floor for us all to be seen."

Soon, Kristin's face appeared on camera. Kait sighed in relief as soon as she appeared. "Hey. So…lots to tell you. But to start, Chara and I ran into Asa and his new girl at the local coffee shop. Not only does she look exactly like Mikaila, but she also has the same name." She swiveled to Lexy. "Did you know anything about this?"

Lexy shook her head, just as shocked by the news. "I've been trying to keep tabs through Lacy, but we don't go to the community college here, so we wouldn't have known."

Kristin waved. "Hi, Lexy. We haven't been formally

introduced. I'm the techie, used to be in Bible Club with Miki and had four classes with her last year at Oak Haven."

Lexy smiled awkwardly. Kristin continued, "I've been stalking Asa's social media. There's nothing there. No pictures of him and Miki. If she was the love of his life...where are those is what I keep asking myself."

Kait pursed her lips. "We looked in her room and didn't see any. It's very strange."

Chara shook her head. "Not if he didn't want anyone to know she was still in high school."

Lexy sighed. "She turned eighteen in January. Why would that matter?"

"Appearances," Kristin commented. "But Lexy, if you can access Asa's computer or laptop, I can walk you through tracing his IP address. Then we can see if it matches the person who leaked Chara's messages with him."

Lexy's eyes widened in surprise at the request. "We'll tell you about that later," Kait said to her.

"I'll have Lacy handle it," Lexy said.

"Isn't she his friend? Why would she help us?" Chara asked.

Lexy sighed. "Let's just say I know the type of guy Asa was, and I thought he'd change. Once I explain it to Lacy, she'll do it. Trust me."

Kristin nodded. "Okay. If Lacy's info matches mine, Chara, you'll need to press charges to move forward. That will prove harassment."

Kait frowned. "And murder? How do we prove that?"

Lexy pulled folded pages from her purse. "A friend of mine works at Milestones Auto. Official title: administrative assistant, but she's basically a receptionist. She pulled Asa's file: he had the exhaust system fixed a few months before Mikaila's accident. The notes say he had to return every three months for monitoring or immediately if engine noise worsened." She handed the pages to Kait. "It doesn't prove he tampered with the car."

Kait handed over Mikaila's journal. "This says he wanted her to drive his car to work, under the guise that she could leave whenever she wanted. Didn't have to wait for him."

"Looks thoughtful, but if he had tampered with it beforehand, he wouldn't want to be in it himself," Chara noted.

"Of course!" Kristin exclaimed.

Kait's eyebrows knit. "If he wanted to marry her, why would he try to hurt her?"

"He didn't love her. He loved control. He only loves himself," Chara remarked.

"I agree. Kait, once we get the IP address, you can press charges," Kristin said.

"Why wait?" Lexy asked.

Kristin explained, "If they move too fast, he could wipe evidence before we get the IP. We need it first."

Chara nodded. "Lexy, call Lacy. Let's get this started."

Lexy nodded. "Whatever we need to do for Mikaila."

Kait glanced at Lexy. "You sure you want to go through with this?"

Lexy squeezed Kait's shoulder. "I should have done something sooner. It's time he got what was coming to him. If it brings you peace, Kait, then I owe it to you."

Chara signed off, closed her laptop, and felt dizzy, drained, but resolute. She hadn't been able to save Mikaila when she was here, but now, maybe she could help give her justice. Maybe one day, they'd heal from the Mikaila-sized holes in their hearts.

40

chara

MAY 21, 2005

Chara sat in the police station in Chestnut Hill, the metal chair digging into her back, and handed over the printouts: the doctored email conversation, the IP address where it originated, and confirmation of Asa's IP from his own desktop.

The female officer scanned the pages. "You're here to press formal charges for harassment that occurred May 25, 2004?"

Chara anxiously bounced her leg. "Yes. He needs to think twice before doing this to someone else."

The officer flipped through the documents. "The statute of limitations for harassment is one year. You're just within that timeframe. Why would Mr. Finn do this?"

"He claims he had nothing to do with it. I called things off with him, and this is how he responded."

The officer scribbled something on her notepad. "I see. How did you obtain the IP address from which the emails originated?"

"A friend got it from the computer lab at our high school."

"And the confirmation of Mr. Finn's IP address?"

"My friend's stepsister borrowed his desktop, with his permission, and got it for me."

The officer put the pages down. "Was this the only time he did something like this?"

Chara felt the anger rising. "To me, yes. I know he tried to hit on my friend Kristin, but she blocked him. I don't know about anyone else."

The officer nodded. "Please provide your friend's name and her stepsister's name so we can contact them. We have your info and will be in touch."

Chara stood and extended her hand. "Thank you for your help."

The officer smiled, shook her hand, and walked Chara out.

Chara slid into the backseat of Kait's car. "My part's done."

"How'd it go?" Kait asked, glancing in the rearview mirror.

Chara shrugged. "I was within the statute of limitations by four days."

Lexy shook her head. "I can't believe they only give one year to report."

"Yeah…like the effects just vanish after that," Chara scuffed.

"Our turn." Kait exhaled.

"Good luck, guys," Chara said. Once Kait and Lexy were out of the car, she called Kristin. "Hey. My report's been filed, and they may contact you. I just wanted to give you a heads up."

"Good thing I graduate next month. They can't discipline me for breaking into their weak system," Kristin remarked.

"You might not want to phrase it like that if they ask," Chara chuckled.

"Already told my parents. Their response: Tell them '*I didn't know you shouldn't do that. It's not written in the student handbook.*'"

Chara laughed. "You could probably write their technology policy for them."

"Why do you think Lacy agreed to hack Asa's computer?"

Chara toyed with the beads on her bracelet. "I don't know... whatever she has on him must be big."

"Mikaila said he liked Lexy first. I wonder what she could have."

"They're coming back out. I'll call you later." Lexy and Kait climbed into the car, and Kait started the engine. "Well?"

"Report filed. Evidence given. Now we wait," Lexy said.

"Should we tell Dad or Aunt Lana?" Kait asked.

Lexy shrugged. "Maybe Aunt Lana. But if your dad is close with him, I wouldn't tip him off," Chara suggested.

Kait nodded. "We're lucky Lacy's on our side. Without her, we'd have nothing." Lexy sighed.

They pulled into Lexy's driveway. Kait's dad and stepmom were busy at work.

"Need help with Mikaila's room?" Lexy asked.

Kait shook her head. "Other than her journal, now with the police, and Nan's ring, which I have. I think we're good."

Chara added, "I only saw the other half of my bracelet. I didn't find it, but it helps me believe she's still out there, wearing it somewhere."

"She is," Kait said earnestly.

"So…is our Connecticut trip done?" Chara asked.

Kait checked her watch. "I don't want to keep sleeping in Lacy's room. We made the report. It's time to go home."

"I'm glad we came today," Lexy said.

"Same," Kait sighed.

Inside, Chara focused on packing. Bags loaded, trunk closed. The three of them collapsed in the living room.

"Let's just put on TV until Dad and Lorainne get home," Kait suggested.

"Is that…Punk'd?"

Chara grinned. "One of my favorites."

Lexy smiled. "I think Ashton Kutcher's so cute."

Kait grinned. "I thought we could use a laugh."

The show ended, and "Total Request Live" came on.

Chara sighed. "I forgot to vote today."

"You still vote?" Kait asked, surprised.

"How else are we going to get *Incomplete* to number one?"

Kait and Lexy laughed as Mark and Lorainne walked through the door together.

"Hey, you're all down here," Mark commented.

Kait stood, walked over, and hugged him. "I don't need anything from her room. We went through it, and we're done."

Lorainne entered the living room and set her briefcase on the end table. "Are you sure?"

Kait smiled and hugged her next. "Yes. We're heading home, but we wanted to say goodbye before we left."

"You can stay as long as you need," Mark said with pleading eyes.

Kait placed a hand on his arm. "I know, but we have to get back to work and give Lacy her room back."

"It's a vacation for her to stay with her friends. She doesn't mind," Lorainne insisted.

"Thanks for letting me stay. I appreciate it," Chara said, pushing off the couch.

"Our pleasure," Lorainne and Mark said in unison.

Lexy hugged Kait and Chara. "We'll be in touch. Okay?"

Kait and Chara walked to the car. Chara slipped in one of her mixed CDs. "Sorry, my turn to pick the music."

They belted *Since You've Been Gone* at the top of their lungs as they pulled out of the driveway.

The next morning, Chara's cell buzzed. She was still in bed, exhausted from the Connecticut trip. "Hello?" Her voice came out in a sleepy rasp.

"Ms. Finer?"

"Yes?"

"This is Officer Polani from the Chestnut Hill Police Department."

Chara jolted up. "Yes?"

"We've issued a warrant for the arrest of Mr. Finn based on your report. Officers are on their way to his home now."

"Alright."

"Are you still in Chestnut Hill?"

"No, I left yesterday."

"Alright. I'll call you when he's in custody."

"Thank you."

The line went dead, and Chara immediately called Kait.

"Did Officer Polani call you?"

Kait sounded groggy. "Not yet. Why?"

"She just informed me a warrant was issued for his arrest."

"Wow…that was fast."

"She'll call me when they have him in custody. I'll let you know."

"Thank you."

Chara hung up and exhaled. For the first time in a long while, she felt a sense of relief wash over her.

41

chara

Chara, Kait, and Kristin meandered along the Ocean City boardwalk. The rising sun painted the sky in red and orange, a stark contrast to the deep blue of the ocean. Though they smiled, their hearts were heavy. The boardwalk was eerily quiet, the only sounds the gentle crash of waves against the shore. They sipped their Java Joint coffees as they approached their destination: a white bench with a shiny placard.

Kait's shoulders shook, but Chara and Kristin wrapped their

arms around her.

"This is the perfect spot," Kait said softly. "It overlooks the water, but you can still see parts of the town from here."

Chara read the placard aloud:

"In loving memory of Mikaila Emery, a faithful heart always running toward God's light. Her kindness endures in every life she touched. Rest here and let her spirit remind you to run your race with joy."

Chara played with the beaded bracelets around her wrist and lowered her head. "She'd love this spot. Those words...they describe her perfectly."

Kristin shuffled her feet, shifting her weight. "I'm glad we could see this before the trial starts."

Kait fiddled with the ring that had belonged to Nan, then Mikaila, and now her. "Same. I'm nervous about everything, but this is a visual reminder of why we need to do this."

They all agreed. The police had initially charged Asa with harassment, since Chara and Kristin had been over sixteen when his behavior occurred. Had they been younger, the charges could have been more severe. His bail was set, and his parents had paid it, placing him under house arrest.

Kait trembled, but her voice was steady as she said, "You know he called me while on house arrest. He tried to say I had everything wrong, but he didn't hold it against me because he thought I was doing it out of love."

After all the evidence compiled against him, Chara couldn't believe he'd attempt to talk his way out of this.

"What did you say?" Chara asked.

Kait's lips pressed into a tight line. "I loved my sister. I might not have shown it when she was here, but I'm going to do whatever I need to, to prove I love her even now."

Kristin placed a hand on her shoulder. "He can't con his way out of this trial. He knows it."

They left the boardwalk and climbed into their rented minivan. Soft rock played on the radio as Maryland's scenery faded behind them, and for the first time in a long while, the weight of justice felt within reach.

42

chara

MAY 20,2006

Chara, Kait, and Kristin meandered into the courtroom. Kait took a seat with the state's attorney, while Chara and Kristin sat on the bench behind her. Lexy slipped in beside Chara. Lacy and Mark entered shortly after, nodded to them, and took seats at the back on Kait's side.

Asa Finn sauntered in, hair slicked down, wearing a business suit designed to make him look professional and unassuming.

He should be in cuffs, Chara thought.

He avoided their gaze, whispering to his lawyer until they reached their seats, and the proceedings began.

Chara's toes tapped nervously; Kait twirled her hair, and Kristin tapped her pen against her leg as the prosecutor delivered her opening statement.

"Ladies and gentlemen of the jury," she began, "you will hear the story of a life lost too soon. The defense will claim this was unintended, but the evidence will show the defendant's actions set in motion a chain of events that led to irreversible harm. We are here to examine the facts: the defendant purposely caused his vehicle to become unsafe and, with utter disregard for basic safety, caused the death of another human being. His history of volatile behavior toward the decedent's social circle demonstrates a pattern of aggression and planning. At the conclusion of this trial, you will see that the only just verdict is first-degree manslaughter."

She returned to her seat.

Asa's lawyer rose, hands in his pockets, and approached the jury. His pinstriped gray suit matched his graying hair. He leaned on the jury box, using casual gestures as if addressing old friends.

He painted Chara and Kristin as vengeful exes. "This distraught gentleman has lost the love of his life to a faulty exhaust system he had already repaired," he said, "and now, under the guise of grief, these exes have convinced the decedent's sister that he deliberately planned her death. Please, consider the facts and spare this man more suffering."

The prosecutor stood again, her gray blazer and skirt set pristine, black pumps clicking softly. "Your honor, ladies and gentlemen, I present evidence of the charges brought against Asa

Finn for harassment of Chara Finer. He admitted, as part of a plea bargain, to doctoring a private conversation between them and emailing it to the entire high school. This demonstrates a calculated escalation in his aggression."

The defense lawyer barked, "Objection! Under § 4-5(a), prior acts of harassment are inadmissible when used to suggest the defendant acted in conformity with bad character. Harassment of a friend bears no logical relevance to the defendant's intent toward the victim. This risks prejudice by implying guilt based on unrelated behavior."

The judge cleared his throat, tilting his head. "Under Connecticut law, evidence of prior misconduct is generally inadmissible to show mere character. However, it may be considered for purposes such as motive, intent, or a common scheme. The Court finds that the prior harassment is relevant to the defendant's state of mind and hostility toward the victim and her social circle. Its probative value outweighs the risk of prejudice. This evidence is admitted, with instructions that the jury may consider it only for assessing motive or intent—not as proof of bad character."

The prosecutor nodded. "Your honor, members of the jury, in addition to the police and autopsy reports confirming death by carbon monoxide poisoning which caused the vehicular accident, I present data from the defendant's computer, his search history, and emails all date and time stamped, showing a pattern of escalating volatility, motive, and premeditation."

Chara's jaw tightened. This was it. The culmination of months of fear, grief, and planning. Asa Finn could no longer hide behind lies.

Chara let out a small breath as Kristin squeezed her arm.

"My first witness is Lexy Emery, the decedent's stepsister."

Chara glanced at Asa. His face paled. *Good,* she thought.

Lexy stated her name for the court, and the prosecution began questioning.

"Tell us how you met Asa Finn."

"He went to my school and lived nearby. He started following me in the hallways, then became friends with my sister Lacy. She invited him over for mini golf with my family because she felt bad. He didn't really have friends and was bullied."

"Objection. Hearsay."

The judge glanced at Lexy. "Did you have direct knowledge of him being bullied?"

She nodded. "Yes. I saw it happen. His own brother, Hayden, laughed while stealing his clothes."

The judge pounded the gavel. "Objection overruled."

The prosecutor stepped closer. "After that initial interaction, what was his reaction?"

Lexy shivered, chewing her lip. "He continued following me in the halls, even when we didn't share classes. I ignored him. He became friends with my stepdad Mark and my mom Lorainne, offered to cut the grass, and occasionally played video games with Lacy."

"What about when you ignored him?"

"He didn't act out around my family or at school, but one day I found him in my closet after I got out of the shower... home alone."

Chara's stomach twisted. *Why didn't you tell anyone sooner? And why did you let him hang around Miki?*

"Who did you report this to?" the prosecutor asked.

"No one," Lexy said quietly, "because he had taken photos

with a disposable camera and threatened to use them if I said anything. He said he'd do the same to Lacy or worse if I ever mentioned it to anyone."

Chara's face heated, and beside her, Kristin jabbed her pen into her leg.

"What happened to those photos?"

"I never asked. I just avoided him."

"And what did he say as his reasoning?"

"He said it was because I watched him get bullied after swim class and supposedly had something to do with it. I didn't, but he didn't listen. He said he'd been tormented, forever called 'Assa-hole,' and if I told anyone, I'd feel the same torment."

"Thank you. That's all."

His lawyer stood for cross-examination. Lexy looked pale and ready to faint.

"This incident in your closet. How did he get in?"

"He knew where my stepdad hid the spare key under the doormat, in case Lacy or I forgot ours."

"And afterward, when did you tell your parents to not invite him to family events?"

Lexy's voice cracked. "I tried to warn Mikaila, but I didn't want retaliation. I didn't tell anyone about him until after Mikaila was gone."

"So maybe you wanted it to happen?" the lawyer pressed. "Maybe you enjoyed the cat-and-mouse game with Mr. Finn?"

"No."

"Objection, argumentative," the prosecutor said.

"Sustained," the judge ruled.

The defense attorney lifted his hands. "The defense rests."

The prosecution called Kait next. The defense declined to

cross-examine. Then they called Veronica Stillman. Chara and Kristin exchanged glances, leaning forward, attentive.

"Thank you, Ms. Stillman. Can you tell us how you met the defendant?"

"He sat next to me in physics. I said I was worried about failing, and he offered to tutor me. We met in the library."

"What other interactions did you have?"

"I invited him to my apartment to study. He tried to make a move on me, and I kicked him out. Then, the professor showed me an email claiming I cheated on homework using his answers. I didn't. I had to beg Asa to tell the professor I'd been with him during that time. He made me pay him to tutor me and give him someone else's name so he could manipulate them."

"When were you aware that Asa emailed the professor and orchestrated the cheating scandal?"

Veronica's voice was steady. "When you called me. I didn't know until then."

"Members of the jury, you have been provided a copy of the email the defendant sent, along with proof of origination: his IP address, obtained through a warrant following his arrest on May 25, 2005. We have no further questions."

She returned to her seat.

The defense chose not to cross-examine.

Next, Kristin was called to the stand to read aloud the conversations pulled from the instant messenger platform.

The prosecutor paced in front of her table. "What happened after you told him you weren't interested?"

Kristin exhaled. "He suggested we talk with our webcams on. I agreed, thinking he needed to see my face saying 'no,' but instead, he appeared on camera naked without warning or consent."

Her gaze pierced the defense table. Asa didn't look back; his eyes were fixed on the judge.

"And your interactions with him after that?" the prosecutor asked.

"I blocked him. I haven't spoken to him since."

"Thank you. No further questions."

The defense attorney stood, glanced at Kristin, and shook his head. "No cross-examination."

The judge rapped the gavel. "We will now break for lunch and reconvene in one hour."

43

chara

MAY 20, 2006

Chara and Kristin stood and followed Kait, the prosecutor, and Lexy close behind. They crossed the street to the hotel suite that the prosecutor was using. Sandwiches in hand, the five of them sat around the small table.

The prosecutor took a sip of water. "Ladies, I applaud your courage. Chara, we need to prep for your examination."

Chara nodded, stomach twisting.

The prosecutor smiled. "We can celebrate our small win

with Veronica Ford, huh?"

Chara swallowed her bite. "You found the email to her professor with a subpoena?"

"Yes," the prosecutor said. "It proves a history of controlling behavior. He lost control with Veronica, started a cheating scandal, harassed Kristin…then tried to manipulate you. The pattern of escalating behavior is clear."

She handed Chara a stack of notecards. "Study these."

Chara shoved the rest of her sandwich into her mouth and focused on the cards. Minutes later, it was time. They walked back across the street and filed into the courtroom.

The prosecutor stood. "The state calls Chara Finer."

Chara took a deep breath and approached the stand, her eyes locking on the clock at the back of the room. The questions were already memorized.

"When did the defendant start messaging you?" The prosecutor asked.

"June 2003."

"When did he show interest in you?"

"He was flirty by late June and into July 2003."

The prosecutor nodded. "Let the record show this matches the message dates. When did his flirting intensify?"

"June 2003."

"When did you inform Mikaila about his pursuit?"

"November 2003."

"And when did you call things off?"

"December 2003."

"What contact did you have after that?"

"I didn't. Kristin told me he approached her in November 2003. I blocked him and had no contact until May 2004, when he altered my emails to make it look like I pursued him and sent them to the school."

"What was his response when you confronted him?"

"He denied it, claimed I was hacked. But Kristin tracked the IP address, and in 2005, we confirmed it matched his computer."

"What was his reason for the harassment?"

Chara shifted slightly. "He never said."

The prosecutor paused. "I submit Mikaila Emery's journal, showing she moved in with her father after the email scandal, proving the harassment was part of the defendant's plan. Thank you, Ms. Finer."

The prosecutor sat. The defense lawyer rose. "We'll cross-examine."

Chara clenched her jaw, keeping her gaze fixed on the back of the courtroom. In her mind, she pictured the beach—her safe place—waves crashing, sunlight on the water, a quiet calm to steady her nerves.

"Ms. Finer, why didn't you tell an adult about Mr. Finn's unwanted attention?"

"I didn't realize until it was too late what his endgame was."

"After you believed he distorted the conversations and emailed the school, why didn't you go to the police then?"

"I was afraid he would retaliate. I just wanted to be left alone."

"Ms. Finer, isn't it true that at times you came onto him?"

"I wasn't aware of his endgame at that point."

"Isn't it true you wanted to date him and told Ms. Emery that?"

"I wasn't aware of his true nature or his intentions then."

The attorney circled the courtroom like a predator, then returned to the stand. Chara kept her eyes on the clock at the back of the room, biting the inside of her lip. *Your intimidation tactics aren't working. Get on with it,* she thought.

"Ms. Finer, can you read the statement here, pulled from the instant messenger platform?"

Chara shifted in the chair, forcing herself to look down at the page. These were her private words, now exposed to the courtroom. She read the date and time aloud. He raised his eyebrows but said nothing.

She swallowed and began. "Before I knew these words would be distorted and used against me, I said, 'I wish you were here, so we could do all of this in person.'"

"Thank you, Ms. Finer. Can we strike the beginning statement from the record?"

"Objection. It's relevant to establishing the timeline."

The judge nodded. "Sustained. The jury will note these words were said before the alleged harassment incident occurred."

Chara's shoulders relaxed slightly. She stopped biting her lip, but her face remained blank. She stared at the clock, willing the time to move faster.

The defense attorney exhaled sharply. "The defense rests."

Chara stepped down from the stand. The judge banged his gavel. "The first day of trial is complete."

Back in their hotel room, Kait hugged Lexy tightly. "Thank you for coming forward."

"I thought you'd hate me after I knew what he was capable of and didn't say anything when he pursued Mikaila," Lexy whispered.

Chara shook her head gently. "She wouldn't want us to blame you. She'd want us to forgive you…and tell you to forgive yourself."

Kait and Kristin nodded. "Tomorrow's going to be harder. Not for us, but for the prosecutor to prove vehicular homicide."

"Let's pray," Kristin said softly. They joined hands, bowing their heads. She led a prayer for justice, clarity, and the truth, each word a quiet vow to honor Mikaila's memory.

44

chara

Chara set the pen to paper, her hands trembling slightly. "Mikaila was more than a sister, more than a friend. She had a heart that reached everyone she met. She laughed with abandon, loved freely, and trusted too easily. She deserved to live her life without fear, without someone plotting against her."

Kristin leaned in. "Add that she was always looking out for others, even when she was hurting herself. That's the part of her that should never be forgotten."

Lexy nodded. "Include that her spirit inspired all of us. Even now, she teaches us how to stand up for what's right, even when it's hard."

Kait swallowed hard and read aloud what they had so far. Her voice cracked slightly. "Mikaila Emery's life was taken from her too soon. She deserved love, safety, and the chance to chase her dreams. The defendant's actions stole that from her and left a hole in our hearts that can never be filled. We ask that the court take into consideration the magnitude of the pain and loss he has caused, and that justice be served in a way that reflects the gravity of his actions."

Chara added quickly, "Include that this isn't just about punishment. It's about accountability, about making sure no one else is subjected to the harm he caused."

Kristin nodded and wrote in the margin. "And that even though we will always grieve her, we will honor her by speaking the truth and protecting others from this same fate."

Kait folded the paper carefully. "Thank you, all of you. I couldn't have done this alone. She would be proud."

The prosecutor smiled, gently taking the paper. "This will carry weight. I'll make sure it's read aloud in court during sentencing. Let's get you all back to your hotel rooms so you can rest. The sentencing will start shortly."

Chara, Kristin, Lexy, and Kait walked back across the street, quiet and somber, the weight of the moment pressing on them. None of them spoke much, but their shared glances said everything. They were carrying Mikaila with them, her memory, a shield and a guide.

Back in her hotel room, Chara sank into the chair by the window, staring at the Atlantic waves. "I just...want this to be over. I want her to have justice, and I want it to feel right."

Kait sat on the edge of the bed, her eyes distant. "It will feel right when we know he's held accountable. That's all we can do now."

Kristin placed a hand on Chara's shoulder. "She's still here, in us. We're doing this for her. That's what counts."

Lexy, quiet for a moment, finally said, "Whatever happens today, we stood for her. We spoke for her. That's more than anyone else could have done."

Chara exhaled and let her head fall back against the chair. The sun was just rising over the horizon, casting golden streaks across the waves. For the first time in a long time, she felt a small flicker of peace amid the grief and tension.

★ ★ ★

The judge banged his gavel and announced his sentencing. "Asa Finn for the crime of negligent homicide, a class D felony, causing carbon monoxide poisoning which caused Mikaila Emery's death, you'll receive the maximum sentence of five years in prison, four years for release on good behavior and probation, and the maximum fine of $5000.00 In addition, you'll be mandated to receive behavioral modification counseling as part of your treatment plan and failure to comply will result in an extension of your sentencing, until treatment is completed. This trial is adjourned."

★ ★ ★

Outside the courtroom, the late morning sun warmed their faces. Chara let out a deep breath she hadn't realized she'd been holding. "It's finally over," she whispered, her voice trembling but steady.

Kristin squeezed her hand. "We did it. For Mikaila. She's finally at peace."

Kait rested her forehead against Chara's shoulder, her tears dampening Chara's hair. "I can't believe it. I feel…lighter. Like a huge weight has been lifted."

Lexy approached and wrapped an arm around both of them. "You three were incredible. It wasn't just your testimony. It was your courage. Mikaila would be so proud."

Chara looked out over the courthouse steps, her fingers fiddling with her beaded bracelets. "I keep thinking about how she would've reacted. She'd probably be rolling her eyes at all of us crying, telling us to stop and celebrate that justice was done."

Kait sniffled, pulling out the ring Nan had given her and holding it in her hand. "I'll keep this close to me, always. So, we never forget her."

Kristin nodded. "And we'll keep living our lives the way she would've wanted. Honoring her light, not just mourning her loss."

They stood there a moment longer, holding onto each other, letting the emotions wash through them. Chara felt a quiet kind of resolve settle in her chest.

As they walked down the courthouse steps together, their shadows stretching long across the pavement, Chara realized something important: the pain would never fully disappear, but the justice they had fought for, the truth they had spoken, had created a space for healing. Mikaila's light wasn't gone. It lived in them, and they carried it forward.

Kait reached over and took Chara's hand. "Where do we go from here?"

Chara smiled faintly, the first genuine smile in a long time.

"Forward. We go forward. Together."

And for the first time in years, they felt like maybe, just maybe, the world was a little brighter again.

45

mikaila

MAY 2006

I watched the trial play out but couldn't feel shock, dismay, or anger. The truth needed to come out.

I needed to prevent anyone else from being hurt by him. When Lexy spoke, I understood the distance she gave me. She was only trying to protect herself. Even if I had approached her about him sooner, I knew she wouldn't have said anything for fear.

When the sentence was read, I could feel my sister, my family, Asa's mom, and my friend's relief. Time for all of us to begin the healing process.

The scene shifted to the hotel room as they packed. Kristin sighed. "It was her time, but that's never a reason to lie or avoid taking accountability. I hope he learns that. 'Forgive as the Lord forgave you.'"

Chara's face tightened. "I can forgive, but I'll never forget. I have a Mikaila-sized hole in my heart."

Kait placed her hand on Chara's shoulder. "I feel the same way."

From the hallway, I waited for the dream frames to light up. When Chara's frame glowed, I stepped into her former living room in Oak Haven and plopped down beside her on the old plaid couch. The lighting from the wall lamps was just as I remembered, and I ran my fingers over the old nail polish stains on the cushion. The house smelled faintly of snickerdoodles, which reminded Chara of Nan.

Chara gasped as I materialized next to her. "Miki! It's been such a long time. I miss you so much!"

I smiled and embraced my old friend, placing a hand on her. "I told you I would always be with you. I meant that."

"Your hair still smells like your strawberry shampoo. Are you really here?"

I laughed. "I'm with you here, yes."

She grabbed my arm. "Look, you have to visit Kait."

"I will, and I'll tell her, too: I'm always with her."

Chara's eyebrows lifted. "I'm happy you're here, but how did my dreams come true? Why me?"

I held her forearms. "*Numbers 12:6. Everyone has a gift, and your gift is prophecy. It's not my place to tell you why. The reason will be revealed to you later.*"

Chara's lips trembled and tears ran down her face. "This is goodbye now, isn't it? I'm sorry for everything that happened between us."

I smiled faintly, seeing her sincerity in her eyes. "This isn't goodbye forever. It's goodbye until later. I know everything. I know you, Kristin, and Kait were looking out for me. I know you only wanted me to be happy."

Chara gulped and whispered, "You know I only tried to protect you. Life without you is incredibly hard! Every day is a struggle. And now you'll be gone forever. Forever is an awfully long time."

I placed my hand over her heart. "Be happy and live your life to the fullest, following His word. Don't waste your time being angry or sad. I'm here…in your heart, always a part of you."

She gave me one last embrace. "Love you like a sister, always."

I squeezed her back. "Love you like a sister, always."

I tapped Chara's frame and returned to the massive white room. Instead of the clothes I wore the day of my death, I wore a glowing white dress. The hallway no longer seemed endless, and a large white door appeared and opened. Beyond the door was an effervescent, bright light, no longer blinding, and a figure stepped through.

I smiled. "Hi Nan, I've missed you."

Nan smiled back, put her arm around me, and said, "Come on, dear. Let's go see Pop."

EPILOGUE

2040

Laila lay in bed, leaning against her grandmother Chara. "In my dream, you were with a lady with reddish-brown hair," she said. She was only five but spoke as if she were much older.

Chara rested her head on Laila's, smiling. "Sometimes our dreams are windows to the future, showing us what is to come. And sometimes they are windows to the past, showing us what was."

"So…I saw what's going to come?" Laila asked sweetly.

"No, dear. You were looking through the window of what used to be. A very long time ago. You saw me with my guardian angel. She used to live right here in this house," Chara explained.

"In this room?" Laila asked, eyes wide.

"Not this room, but upstairs, in your dad's old room."

"How did you get her house?" Laila asked curiously.

"One day I'll tell you the whole story," Chara said, "but for now, I'll just tell you the ending. Her sister, Kait, inherited it, rented it out, and let me buy it when I was ready. Aunt Kait moved to Ocean City and didn't need it anymore. It felt like home for me, and sometimes, it still feels like my guardian angel is here."

"What was her name?"

"Mikaila. And she would have loved you. But today, we need to get some rest so we have plenty of energy for the zoo!" Chara said with a smile.

Laila planted a kiss on Chara's cheek, rolled over, and drifted back to sleep. She looked like a mix of her father and mother, though, unfortunately, she had her father's energy and was always on the move, even in sleep. Chara gently shifted her granddaughter so her little kicks wouldn't wake Brenton.

She loved these visits. It felt like forever since she'd been able to snuggle a little one. She and Brenton had only one child, whom they had raised in the house where she grew up alongside her best friends. Laila was their only grandchild, and she was beginning to have dreams that only Chara seemed to understand. The gift of prophecy had been passed down through the female line. Her son didn't have it, but she later discovered Astrid did.

It had been a while since Chara had thought of her guardian angel, as she didn't visit her dreams as often as she used to.

She hoped that meant Mikaila was busy visiting Kaitlyn and Kristin's dreams instead. One day, she knew she would have to tell Laila the whole story so the little girl could understand how her dreams had once foretold the future, and how they were messages from Him.

For now, though, Chara was content to let Laila sleep and simply enjoy her childhood.

RESOURCES ON RECOGNIZING AND PREVENTING GROOMING

Understanding the warning signs of grooming and knowing where to turn for reliable information can make a profound difference. Below are valuable resources offering guidance, education, and support:

NATIONAL CHILDREN'S ALLIANCE – Offers in-depth guides and articles such as "The Real Red Flags of Grooming," helping parents, teachers, and the public identify concerning behaviors and know how to respond.

MHACG | CHILD ADVOCACY – Provides information on what grooming is, strategies for prevention, and advice on talking to children about boundaries and personal safety.

DARKNESS TO LIGHT – An organization dedicated to preventing child abuse, offering training for adults and resources for recognizing and reporting grooming.

STOP IT NOW! – Provides confidential helplines, educational materials, and guidance on confronting and preventing child sexual abuse, including grooming.

If you ever have concerns about a youth's safety, these organizations can provide support and assistance, ensuring that you are not alone.

ACKNOWLEDGMENTS

Firstly, thanks to my spouse and my son for their support while I wrote this book.

Thank you to my editors, Olive Press Publishing, for your insight and for breathing life into this story. Thank you to editor Brittany Yost for believing in this story, and editor Savannah Breedlove.

And to Rodney, my marketing guru, for getting this story out there!

Thank you, Mark Karis, for creating the beautiful cover and the interior formatting.

Fran, I hope you are reading this while enjoying your retirement. This wouldn't have been possible without our numerous chats. Thank you to my friends and family for providing feedback and encouragement. Thank you to my partner in crime, specifically for the endless reminders to keep my shirt on and keep my head up. Last but never least, thank you, Lord, for giving me good friends and a wonderful team. None of this would have been possible without them.

ABOUT THE AUTHOR

ASHER FREND is the debut novelist behind this compelling story. They live in the northeastern United States with their spouse and son. When not writing, Asher enjoys long walks on the beach, savoring good coffee, and getting lost in a great book. Connect with Asher on Instagram or visit their website at **www.asherfrend.com**.